HIGH PRAISE FOR J. F. FREEDMAN AND HIS EXCITING THRILLERS!

FALLEN IDOLS

"Freedman creates an intriguing plot that unravels the layers, piece by piece. Rich with clear descriptions of archeological digs and jungle wildlife. Once hooked, you will not be able to put this book down."

—IloveMysteryNewsLetter.com

"Suspenseful . . . an interesting closing twist. The story line shines . . . an entertaining thriller."

—Writerspace.com

"Compelling . . . the pacing is quick, and the resolution satisfying. This is as much a mystery as it is a psychological study of a family. Readers will find themselves compulsively turning pages to get to the bottom of things."

—RomanceReadersConnection.com

"A winding suspense filled with an interesting plot of seduction, secrets, lies, and deception that will keep the reader guessing until the end."

—FictionAddiction.net

more . . .

MORE PRAISE FOR THE NOVELS OF J. F. FREEDMAN

"Gritty, vivid . . . sexually provocative, superior suspense."

—*New York Times Book Review* on *Against the Wind*

"A high-octane blast . . . a rip-snorting, full-throttle . . . compulsively readable tale of crime and punishment. It kept me up late into the night."

—Stephen King on *Against the Wind*

"Character-driven suspense . . . steadily gripping."

—*Kirkus Reviews* on *Bird's-Eye View*

"A legal thriller of near-epic proportions."

—*Library Journal* on *Above the Law*

"Powerful stuff . . . a bruising, triumphant trip."

—*Tampa Tribune* on *The Obstacle Course*

"So good it makes the heart leap."

—*TIME* on *House of Smoke*

"Completely engrossing . . . you won't want to put this book down for a second."

—*Detroit News* and *Free Press* on *The Disappearance*

FALLEN IDOLS

ALSO BY J. F. FREEDMAN

Bird's-Eye View
Above the Law
The Disappearance
Key Witness
House of Smoke
The Obstacle Course
Against the Wind

FALLEN IDOLS

J. F. FREEDMAN

WARNER BOOKS

NEW YORK BOSTON

Cover design by Andrew Newman
Cover art by Kenneth Garrett/National Geographic

Warner Books

Time Warner Book Group
1271 Avenue of the Americas, New York, NY 10020
Visit our Web site at www.twbookmark.com

Printed in the United States of America

Originally published in hardcover by Warner Books
First Paperback Printing: September 2004

10 9 8 7 6 5 4 3 2 1

For Matthew Penfield Freedman

You may my glories and my state depose,
But not my griefs; still am I king of those.

Shakespeare, Richard II

PART ONE

CENTRAL AMERICA—JUNGLE

♦ ♦ ♦

Sitting up in the darkness, Walt Gaines, his naked body sheeny with sweat, pushed aside the mosquito netting that canopied his cot and pulled on a pair of shorts, a T-shirt, and his mud-encrusted Tevas. For a man pushing sixty, Walt, who had played varsity football and lacrosse at Middlebury back in his undergraduate days, looked tough and hardy, and he was: at six-one, two hundred pounds, he still had most of his hair, it was still mostly light brown, rather than gray, and his face, despite the lines etched across it from years of toiling in the sun, was surprisingly youthful. People who didn't know his age, upon meeting him for the first time, often took him to be five or six years younger.

In the cot next to his, Jocelyn, his wife, stirred but didn't awaken. As she breathed, steadily and slowly, her thin nostrils fluted out the faintest nasal snore, a delicate, almost musical rasp, like the buzzing of a far-off bumblebee. A woman whose mind and spirit were perpetually in harmony (unlike her husband, who was ever-restless, a man who, by comparison, would make Odysseus look like a layabout), Jocelyn could sleep through storms, hurricanes, even, her husband firmly believed, the wrath of God.

Thirty years of togetherness behind them, and Walt was still amazed by his life-mate's equanimity. It was a wonderful counterbalance to his own headstrong energy. One of the many reasons they had been a good team. Marriages don't last as long as theirs had without the important gears meshing. As Walt watched her he thought back on their thirty years of togetherness. Thirty years! Jesus. Thirty years ago, the Beatles had barely broken up. Thirty years was forever, and at the same time it was yesterday, which in some ways, it was: they still made love like they had when they'd first met, passionately and a lot. Walt was grateful to the gods of sex that he continued to be turned on by his wife; he knew too many men his age who weren't, and what that led to. Okay, so Jocelyn was wider in the hips and ass than when she was a girl, but you had to expect that, Jane Fonda's ass was bigger when she turned fifty, too. Jocelyn's body was damn good for a fifty-year-old woman who'd had three children. She was another reason—the most important one, he knew—that he'd stayed young, especially in spirit.

Their coming together had been a volcanic eruption. Walt was thirty, an assistant professor at the University of Wisconsin, when he met Jocelyn. She was twenty, a junior at the university, a student in his *Introduction to Pre-Columbian Civilization* course. They had been white-hot for each other from the first day of that long-ago spring semester when she'd entered his classroom, sat down in the front row, and, braless, leaned forward to get her notebook out of her pack. He had looked away, then back, and she was staring at him.

That afternoon they had coffee, that night they made

love. It was great, and in the morning it was even better. A week later, she moved in with him.

Partway through Jocelyn's senior year, she got pregnant. She took it more calmly than he did. To his surprise, she didn't want an abortion. More surprisingly, she didn't want to have the child outside of marriage. That was a relief to him—getting involved with a student was bad enough, knocking her up was even worse, but to have a love child? He wasn't sure if the administration would be liberal enough to let that go, even though he was one of their golden boys, a rising star.

They got married over the spring holidays—she received her diploma showing a belly as big as a watermelon. That summer, their first son, Clancy, was born. Having a child completed Jocelyn's maturation process. She quit smoking marijuana—gave up drugs altogether—and became a card-carrying grown-up. Two years later, they had another boy, who they named Tom, and a year and a half after that, Will, their third and last child, was born.

Walt loved his sons, but he would have liked a daughter. Jocelyn, though, was happy with boys. No hidden agendas, no subterfuge. She knew all about girls' perfidies—hadn't she snagged Walt, the glamorous professor who all the undergraduate girls had drooled over?

After Clancy was born Jocelyn went back to school, got her master's, and then, after having her other boys, finished her Ph.D., in sociology. The school offered an instructorship and then an assistant professorship. She didn't shine in her field like Walt did in his—few do—but she was good, she was solid. And everyone who knew her loved her; she was a genuine sweetheart.

The professors Gaines had a good marriage. It had lasted.

Stepping outside their small dwelling, Walt inhaled the night's sweet, almost cloying perfumes and looked around at the familiar surroundings, a group of small, thatch-roofed huts that were clustered in the clearing. Besides those used for sleeping—volunteer diggers were generally bunked four to a hut, although five or six could be squeezed in if there were more workers than space—there was a communications center/kitchen, an open dining pavilion, and two large buildings for storage. Solar-heated showers were located outside, back behind the main building. It was a rudimentary, simple system, but it worked.

The complex had been built over the past three years, from scratch. The small area where the buildings were situated had been hacked out of the jungle by a native crew of *chicleros*—men who roam the dense forest looking for rubber trees. One of them had discovered this site by accident, which is often how important ruins in Central America are found: he was looking for rubber trees in a remote, unexplored section of the jungle, and had stumbled upon it by accident. The site had been named La Chimenea because the tallest pyramid was shaped like a chimney.

The tight little living structures were similar to the dwellings in which the Maya had lived, on this very spot, over fifteen hundred years ago. The walls were made of thin tree trunks—trumpet trees mostly—held together with strangler vines (and baling wire), and the high-pitched roofs—tight, dense, virtually waterproof—were constructed from bay leaf palms, woven together in a tight mosaic. The few modern conveniences were rough-poured concrete floors, screened windows, and the propane and diesel tanks that powered their electric needs, their computers and other communication devices, and for kitchen essentials like ice. The student-volunteers who stayed and worked here pissed in the jungle and crapped in holes in the ground. They loved it.

Walt had been taking tours to archaeological sites throughout Central and South America for more than two decades. During semester breaks he had led field trips that typically ran for two or three weeks. These groups were comprised of about twenty people, mostly students, but also older people who were interested in archaeology and wanted an experience off the beaten track. The tours hopscotched from ruin to ruin: Mexico, Guatemala, Belize, Honduras. Two or three days at a location, then moving on to the next one. It was grueling, all that bouncing around on terrible roads in hundred-degree heat, but they covered a lot of ground.

Jocelyn had often accompanied him, especially after their sons had reached adulthood and no longer needed her attention and supervision. These field trips had been important in helping him and Jocelyn supplement their incomes. Being university professors, they were comfortably middle-class, but they liked to live nicely. The income they'd put away from these trips helped augment their modest portfolio of conservative mutual funds.

Once La Chimenea had been discovered, however, and Walt had been given the responsibility of developing it, he stopped conducting these short tours. All his time and energy became concentrated on the site. Being invited to participate alongside him was rigorous and competitive—hundreds of applications flooded Walt's office every term. From these he carefully selected a privileged handful: prime graduate students from universities all over the country, mixed in with a few of his own overachieving underclassmen.

There was one big difference between these groups

and the shorter trips he had led in the past. Nondegree applicants were rarely accepted. There were too many candidates who were deserving and needful of studying in the field under the guidance of the renowned Walt Gaines.

They had been on-site for almost three months this time around. After flying to La Chimenea and settling in, they had immediately begun working their butts off. It was hard, meticulous, back-stiffening labor, like spending eight hours a day taking a splinter out of a baby's foot—you had to be so delicate. A meter-square quadrant at a time, carefully lifting the dirt, sifting it, brushing it one fragment of a pot shard after another.

The students' attitudes had changed considerably from when they had first arrived at the site. That always happened—it was a rite of passage, especially for those who had never actively worked on a dig. At the start, when they were all bright-eyed and full of gung-ho exuberance, they would take copious notes when Walt would lecture on the day's findings. Then they would all get together for communal dinner, drink beer, and talk. It was like being in the best and most exciting summer camp in the world. They loved it, even when it hurt like hell.

By the end of the first week, though, when they'd had bellyfuls of work under their belts, the note-taking became more desultory. Days of painstaking toil under the hot, unrelenting sun made them too exhausted to make much of an effort, and their notepaper turned to mush in the heavy, oppressive vegetal moisture. Besides, being here wasn't about learning from books, observing a subject from a distance through an abstract prism. This was learning by way of your calluses, performing hard, meticulous, grinding work. The expectation was no longer a good grade and being part of history-making, as it had been when they signed up. Their desires became immediate and mundane—a cold beer at the end of the day, a change into dry clothes. Maybe sex, if you got lucky. In that regard a loose decorum was observed, which was breached easily and without fuss—those who needed privacy would disappear into the jungle for an hour at the end of the workday.

Now, their summer of work was over. Everyone except Walt was sleeping—they were exhausted. The last few days had been spent cataloguing the work they'd done here on-site, gathering the items they were allowed to remove for study, and securing their tools, photo equipment, all their various and sundry gear they were bringing back home.

Walt wasn't wearing his watch, but he could tell from the position of the moon that it was well past midnight. From out of the darkness came the cacophony of the jungle: howler monkeys screeching in the trees, cries of predatory cats like puma, calls of frogs, insects, other nocturnal animals. After decades of living in the jungle, Walt's mind, on a conscious level, had adjusted to tuning out the noise. Now, though, he wished to hear every sound as clearly and distinctly as he could. He wanted all his sensations to be acutely tuned in, this last night before departing.

Savoring the feeling, he was still for a moment. Then he switched on his flashlight and set off for the center of La Chimenea, half a mile away.

Despite the lateness of the hour it was powerfully hot out, and as humid as the inside of a Turkish bath—the normal state of affairs for this time of year. Earlier, shortly before sundown, it had rained, a hard, fast downpour. That was another of Walt's concerns—that his small convoy reach the paved road before the skies opened tomorrow. This was the rainy season; it rained almost every day. An hour or two, usually in the late afternoon. That didn't matter when they were here, on-site; but to get stuck in the middle of the jungle in a downpour could screw things up badly, even though the vans they were traveling in had four-wheel drive. There's a point where even four-wheel drive won't cut through the deep, sucking mud. That's the point where you can find yourself in serious trouble.

Walt didn't want to think about that now. He'd deal with whatever came up, when and if it happened. He always did.

He walked along the narrow path that cut through the thick growth and high trees, taking care to avoid the thorn trees that can pierce flesh worse than saguaro cactus. The thin beam of light from his flashlight was a slender knife-cut through the darkness, a darkness so deep he could almost feel it, like a cloak around his body. He was careful to stay on the path; so close was the jungle that in twenty minutes, if you didn't pay attention, you could be hopelessly lost and at the mercy of the elements. Tourists had gone lost at sites as developed as Tikal and Palenque. La Chimenea, by contrast, was almost virgin, a small clearing surrounded by dense, threatening jungle.

Walt relished these moments of being alone. He could let his mind go wherever it wanted, conjure up all kinds of magnificent visions, the stuff of dreams: what the life here was like in those long-ago times when this wouldn't have been jungle, but a bustling metropolis.

He had originally come to Central America on a whim, between his junior and senior years in college. He had been fired from his summer construction job for showing up drunk, so he had gone down to Tikal, in Guatemala, with a friend from Princeton who was studying archaeology. It was going to be a vacation, a lark; but instead, from the moment he climbed to the top of the highest temple and looked out over the endless jungle, the rest of his life had fallen into place: he had discovered his life's work. He went to graduate school at Penn, got his Ph.D., started teaching at Wisconsin, met Jocelyn, married her, became renowned in his field. And fathered three boys.

Thinking of his sons brought him back to the present. He missed them. He'd be glad to see them in a couple of days, when he and Jocelyn were back home and they'd all get together again. They were grown now, they were capable men, but they would always be his boys.

He felt the jaguar's presence before he saw it. He didn't know what it was, precisely, that he was sensing, but he knew it was something extraordinary. It was as if one of the ancient kings of this city-state had suddenly materialized here; that's how powerful the jaguar's proximity felt to him. The rest of the jungle knew it, too—the sounds had died away, almost as a homage.

Slowly, he looked up. And there it was, lying on a thick tree branch twenty feet above him, right over him, its head between its big paws, looking down at him. The great cat, the lord of the new world.

It was a male—he could tell from the size. Jaguars in this region rarely weighed much more than one hundred pounds, but this one looked like it weighed close to two hundred: a mighty specimen.

It didn't seem afraid of him, like big cats usually are of humans, especially jaguars, which are elusive, shy creatures. This one seemed to be sending out a telepathic message: *I'm the king here. You and the others are merely passing through, handfuls of dust in the wind, and long after you've gone to dirt and the jungle has once again reclaimed all of this, I will still be here. My spirit will always be here.*

Walt felt this, strongly. The jaguar was the defining animal symbol of the ancient Maya. And here, against the greatest of odds, was one in the flesh. In all the years Walt had been traveling throughout Central America, to this site and others, he had never seen a jaguar up close like this; the few times he'd spotted one the animal had been a flash, running away in the undergrowth.

He stared at the jaguar. To his astonishment, the jaguar stared back. Fleetingly, he wished he'd brought his camera with him; but then he thought, no, it's better to be here with this as it is, in the moment. To live it, but not to capture it. Because you can't—no photograph could do justice to what he was feeling.

Slowly, as Walt watched, frozen in place, the jaguar stood on the thick branch. Then it leapt from the tree and was gone, a flash of mottled fur disappearing into the jungle.

For how long Walt stood there he didn't know; maybe a minute, probably less. He didn't believe in God, not in any traditional, Western fashion, but this brief but spectacular encounter had been a truly religious experience. Maybe this was a portent that something special was going to happen. What that might be, he didn't know. But this was so unique a sighting that it had to have an incredible meaning to match its specialness.

He realized, too, that he wasn't breathing—he might not have drawn a single breath since he'd seen the jaguar. Now he sucked in air greedily. He was shaking. What a way to end this journey! And the phenomenon was his, his alone. He owned this moment, he wasn't sharing it with anyone, not even his wife, with whom he shared almost everything. *Almost* everything; a few situations, he had learned from the hard-gained wisdom of hindsight and painful revelation, are best kept secret.

Gathering himself with one more deep, cleansing breath, Walt entered the Central Plaza. Several structures were clustered around the courtyard: a large acropolis, two massive temples, each over forty meters high, that faced each other, east and west, so that the sun could be worshipped when it rose and when it set, a palace in which the nobility would have dwelled, two pyramids as big as the temples, and a ball court.

This area was the only section of the ancient kingdom that had undergone excavation. At other parts of the vast site there had been some minor digging, but most of it was still overgrown by jungle. That wasn't going to change, certainly not in Walt's lifetime. It took years to unearth one sector, and incredible amounts of money. Over the course of the past three years, since those first *chicleros* stumbled on to the site, over five thousand mounds, each covering a building of some kind beneath them, had been located. Perhaps as many as a hundred thousand people had lived here at the height of its prominence.

Walt walked until he was in the center of the plaza. He could feel the pulse of the place surging, a psychic feeling signifying the turbulent life that had existed here for almost two millennia. In some unknowable but very palpable way, the ghosts of the ancients still dwelt among these stones. This was hallowed ground, a place upon which one should tread lightly, with reverence.

He stood still, taking everything in. There was an elegant grandeur to this reaching back into the past, digging up ancient burial grounds, unearthing old secrets. As some men dream of reaching for the stars, traveling to distant planets and pushing forward into the future, others, like him, look back to ancient worlds of mystery and desire. He had thought at times, over the years, about what his life's work said about him. Why was the past more important to him than the present or the future?

He had never come up with an exact answer; he wasn't sure he wanted one. What he did know was that the discovery of a new site, a new branch of an old civilization, seemed as fresh and real to him as flying through the heavens must feel to an astronaut. When he was at an ancient site, as he was now, those who had occupied this space came alive, and were here with him.

Crossing the plaza to the far end, he went into the ball court and climbed the steep limestone steps that had been cut into one of the walls. Only a small section of this area had been reclaimed from the jungle; most of it was still under a fifteen-meter-high mound of dirt and trees. Plopping himself down on the top step, his back against the wall, he looked to the floor below.

Ball courts were Walt's favorite locations—he was an old ex-jock, he loved those areas where physical action had taken place. And this was definitely where the action had been; the ball game was the Maya's version of the seventh game of the World Series, the Kentucky Derby, the Super Bowl.

This was a particularly impressive ball court. Seventy meters long, it wasn't as large as the famous one at Chichén Itzá, but it was still impressive—grander than those at Tikal, Caracól, or Palenque. And like the great Yucatan ball court—the largest in the Maya world, measuring a hundred and forty meters, longer than a football field and a half—the acoustics were startling. A person standing at one end, talking in a normal voice, could be heard clearly all the way at the other end, almost an eighth of a mile away. This unique feature reminded Walt of the rotunda of the U.S. Capitol building, which also had this wonderful, eerie quality. Walt had visited the House and Senate numerous times as an archaeological expert witness. He was very persuasive in those committee meetings—senators and representatives ate out of his hand.

The cleared-away section of the wall that Walt was using as a backrest was adorned with elaborate hieroglyphics, which told of a fierce battle between La Chimenea and a nearby rival that had taken place during the Late Classic Period, around A.D. 800. La Chimenea, whose ruler was named Smoke-Jaguar—and a mighty ruler he was, so it was carved in stone—had crushed its rival, burned the other city to the ground, and had captured many of the losers' nobles and brought them back here. And then, in homage to the Maya gods, the losers played a ball game, a prelude to sacrificing one of them to the gods.

The ball game and its attendant rituals were highly structured, beginning with the king's preparations. On the morning of the day the game began Smoke-Jaguar would undergo a bloodletting ceremony. Hidden away in the sanctum sanctorum of the holy temple, he would pierce his penis with a sharp nettle, and, spinning like a dervish, would bring forth his own offering of blood, that he and his people might be blessed with victory, as they had been in this battle. After he was finished his bloodletting a priest would bind his wound, and he would join the other high-ranking members of the kingdom in watching the ball game, right where Walt was sitting now.

Ball games, although violent and physical, were not sporting contests. They were solemn religious events, homages to the gods. The object of the ball game was for a player to get the ball through one of the rings, which were slightly larger than the ball. The ball was solid rubber, and heavy—it weighed thirty or forty pounds. The rings, carved out of stone, were suspended from the sides of the walls that surrounded the court. The game was similar to soccer, except that players not only couldn't use their hands, they also couldn't use their feet. They had to advance the heavy ball by use of wrists, elbows, shoulders, rear ends, knees, hips, and their heads.

The game could go on for a long time—it wasn't easy knocking a thirty-pound ball into a hoop without the use of your hands or feet. If a player managed to put the ball through a hoop, the game was over. The winners were awarded the losers' clothing and jewelry, as well as clothing and jewels from some of the spectators, who would make bets on the outcome.

Then would come the sacrifice. One of the losers, generally the highest-ranking of the captured nobles, sometimes even their king, would be killed, usually by beheading. Even if no one from either team got the ball through a ring, there would still be a sacrifice.

Walt closed his eyes and entered into the past.

Perched on his royal chair, which was adorned with pieces of jade, lapis lazuli, and other semiprecious stones, jaguar pelts, and feathers from parrots of every color in the rainbow, and surrounded on all sides by his warriors and subjects, the great ruler watched as the ball game was played on the court below him. It had been going on for a long time. The participants were ragged, tired. But they had to keep playing.

The game flowed back and forth, like the sun crossing the sky on his journey throughout the day. The spectators cheered on the participants. Smoke-Jaguar watched intently. Below him, his rival, the ruler he had defeated in battle, captured alive, and brought here, was almost spent. Still a young man, strong and in his prime, he was moving more and more slowly around the court. He knew his destiny, and he had lost the will to change it.

The ruler watched all this with great satisfaction and entitlement. When this game was over, his victory, here and on the battlefield, would be written on the walls of the court for all to see, those who followed in the days and years to come. He was going to have a long dynasty, his blood was strong.

Finally, just as the sun was disappearing behind the jungle in the west, one of Smoke-Jaguar's warriors knocked the heavy ball through one of the rings. Pandemonium broke out. The crowd rose as a mob, screaming and cheering.

Smoke-Jaguar, too, stood up. He was flush with the fruits of victory. As he turned to receive the accolades of his people—

"God, it's so incredible here. I'm really going to miss this place."

Walt jerked with a start. He turned to the woman, who was standing a few feet to his right.

"You snuck up on me, Diane," he chided her. He hadn't heard her approaching; he'd been too deep into the past. "You should be sleeping. We have a long, hard day ahead of us tomorrow."

She shook her head. "I can't sleep. Not our last night here."

The tall, slender woman was wearing a simple native cotton shift she'd bought in a local market, and expensive sandals. She was without makeup; her dark blond hair was worn in a single braid that went halfway down her back. Even unadorned, however, she was very attractive, in a classy, understated way.

Diane Montrose was distinctive among this group of volunteers. She was in her early thirties, while the rest of his team were younger, some by more than a decade. And although she was a good worker, competent, helpful, and uncomplaining, there was an air of reserve about her. All the others had morphed into a big, messy family, like summer campers. She stood apart, friendly with everyone, but close to no one.

She took a couple steps toward him; they were almost touching. He could smell her. This was the jungle—bodily odors were stronger here than at home, even those of refined ladies who showered and used deodorant daily.

She smelled like sex.

"I hate it that we're leaving," she said. She seemed at ease standing close to him; as if being alone with him, late at night, in this exotic setting, was the most natural thing in the world. "It feels like we're leaving paradise. The original fall."

Her analogy was too close to the bone for comfort. "You can always come back," he replied. "The work here will be going on for decades."

"I know I can come back, but whether I will or not, who's to say?"

That was another difference between her and the rest of them: she wasn't an archaeology student, nor did she have any practical experience in the field. Under normal circumstances her application wouldn't have been considered, let alone accepted.

She'd gotten in on a fluke. Before the trip began she had sent him an e-mail, asking to be allowed to join his summer tour. He had explained via return e-mail that, unfortunately, he couldn't accommodate her—the trip was full, he was turning down worthy candidates, and he was opposed to including anyone who wasn't academically qualified.

A week before they were scheduled to depart, however, one of the accepted applicants, another woman, had e-mailed the unfortunate news that she had to drop out, which left an open space that needed to be filled—the plane fares and other bookings had already been made, and he was financially responsible for them.

He started digging through his files, scrounging for a replacement, which wasn't going to be easy—most of those he'd rejected had already made other plans. And then, while he was sitting in front of his computer, another e-mail from Diane, as if conjured by a genie, popped up on his computer screen. It was one last, eleventh-hour, impassioned plea that he reconsider her application. She wasn't an archaeologist, true, but she was an ardent student of cultures, ancient, modern, everything, she loved off-the-beaten-path experiences, she'd traveled all over, under every kind of adverse condition, she'd take on whatever lousy job no one else wanted to do. She'd scour the pots and pans every night if that was what was needed, she'd clean the latrines. Whatever it took. She really, really, *really* wanted him to let her be part of this.

Who could resist such an entreaty? Especially when you're holding the bag for more than three thousand dollars and you need a body to fill the space—a female body, for room-sharing in some of the locations.

He ran it by Jocelyn, who agreed that given the time constraints, this woman was the easiest answer to their problem. He had e-mailed back to Diane, advising her of her acceptance, along with instructions; three days later she met him at the airport with Jocelyn and the others, and off they all went.

She had worked out fine. No shirking—she pitched in as hard as anyone. She was always a lady, even when she was doing a scummy detail, but she'd never been a prima donna, or caused any trouble. And she had an adventurous spirit. He could understood that, because his was, too. It was why he'd become who he was.

Diane looked at him, her eyes steady, unblinking. "It's wonderful here, but you're the real attraction."

She raised her arms above her head and loosened the tie that held her ponytail in place. Unlike most of the other women, who'd given up caring about how they looked, her armpits were cleanly shaven. Dropping her arms, she shook her hair loose.

"Was there a game?" she asked, turning away from him and staring down to the court. "You looked like you were here, but not *here*."

He had lectured extensively on the ball games. The students knew about the games and his passion for them. Nodding in response to her question, he managed to work up some saliva.

"Yes."

"Was there a winner?"

"Yes," he answered again.

"You?"

He smiled in spite of himself.

"To the victors go the spoils," she declared. In one quick, clean motion, her dress was over her head, off. A second movement, as fast and economical as the first, and her bra was no longer on her body. It was dangling in her hand with the dress.

Her breasts were firm, the dark pink nipples puckering, rising. And while he stood there, rooted in his tracks, her cotton underpants were down her legs and off. Dress, bra, underwear—a heap at her feet.

"The spectators who lost their bets gave up their clothing to the victor, did they not?" She knew they did—he had lectured on what was known of the betting aspects of the ball game a few days earlier.

"Yes. That's true."

"And their jewels. The losers gave their jewels to the victors, didn't they, Walt?"

She took his hand and brought it to her vagina. She was sticky.

"Would you like my jewels, Walt? They're yours, if you want them."

He showered her smell off and put his clothes back on. He was having a hard time standing: his legs were rubber.

Aside from the moral implications, having sex with her out there in the open had not been a smart move. What if someone else had also been restless and come upon them? Not that anyone would come out here at this late hour, but still . . . He felt he had dodged a bullet.

Time to move on. In a few hours the group would be up and on their way. A day later, they'd be back in the States. After the hurried good-byes and the I'll-e-mail-yous at the airport, everyone would scatter to the four winds. He had to put Diane out of his mind—he had more important issues to deal with.

They had to leave at first light: that was imperative. Even then, they would be racing the clock to get out of the jungle before dark—the narrow scar of a road was terrible, in some places almost impassable. And they were going to be traveling without the military escort they'd been promised.

He had received that distressing piece of news the day

before yesterday. Citing growing disorder in the north, where they claimed their troops were more immediately needed, the government had pulled the four-man squad of army regulars that had come here three days ago to guide him and his party to safe harbor.

Walt had been blistering in expressing his anger at what he described to the bearer of this distressing information as "an extremely ill-advised, stupid, and dangerous decision." Over the scratchy wireless telephone, he had reminded the Minister of Archaeology and Culture, a man with whom he'd had a working friendship for years (who, in deference to Walt's international stature, had personally called to deliver the bad news), of the many contributions he had made to this country's archaeological discoveries, especially La Chimenea. Hadn't he slogged through the godforsaken jungles year after year, leading the efforts to unearth invaluable treasures? Wasn't he doing that right now at this magnificent site, which almost certainly, even in this early stage of excavation, was going to turn out to be the most important discovery of ancient Maya civilization since Tikal and El Mirador, potentially even more glorious than Chichén Itzá or Copán? A site, he reminded the minister forcefully, that was not only going to be important for further understanding and appreciation of Maya culture, but would also, when it was more fully developed, bring a windfall of tourist money into this impoverished country.

"Unlike El Mirador," he had reminded his caller, "which will never be opened to the world. Because the money isn't there to do it."

"I know that," the man said meekly. "We are very appreciative of everything you have done for the archaeology of this country."

Finding money to develop La Chimenea had been

Walt's most important contribution, even more than the actual reclamation from the jungle. He had raised over twenty million dollars from his benefactors. The initial funding had been spent on gouging the road through the jungle, which meant they could reach the site in a day instead of a week, and could bring in the necessary equipment to build the large infrastructure needed for an excavation of this size and scope. The road had cost millions of dollars and taken two years of intensive labor. Local workers had labored yard by yard to cut the ten-foot-wide gash through the thick jungle foliage, so that four-wheel-drive trucks and vans could get to the site.

Being able to motor there, instead of transporting everything by pack animals or human bearers, had enabled Walt and the other archaeologists working at La Chimenea to excavate and restore it on a scale much grander than that of other important sites, including the great one in Guatemala, El Mirador, which he'd brought up to the minister. Those sites were too remote to get to, and the cost to restore them was too great for the Guatemalan government. The difference at La Chimenea was that Walt had gone out and raised the money privately. The government owed him a debt they could never repay. Which made this chickenshit stunt they were pulling doubly outrageous to him.

"For the love of God," he had implored the man, "six soldiers aren't going to make a gnat's ass bit of difference in putting down some far-off disturbance." (If, in fact, one even existed. In this country there were a hundred rumors to one truth.) "But they're critical insurance right here," he argued strenuously, "to guarantee the safety of my students and me. You wouldn't want anything unfortunate to happen to any of us, would you?" Walt said bitingly. "People the world over still recoil over the massacre of the nuns. Tourism is your golden egg. You don't want to kill the bird that lays it," he added bluntly.

He could feel the man wince over the phone. That was, at least, a small piece of momentary satisfaction. But it was all he got. The minister had apologized profusely (from his air-conditioned office), but could offer no help, he had bluntly informed Walt. The decision, regrettably, was out of his hands; the military, as usual, answered to no one but themselves. They were still, as a country, learning the nuts and bolts of democracy. But not to worry: everything was peaceful where they were, everything was running smoothly. There would be no problems.

"A promise," the minister assured Walt, "from the highest authorities to you. Besides," he'd reminded Walt, trying to salvage something from this sticky situation, "the nuns were social agitators, not neutral scientists."

As if that gave their murderers license to kill—a typical bureaucratic reply.

In the end, Walt had no recourse but to accept the decision, and he knew it: despite his prominence, he was still a guest here, he had to live by their rules. But before hanging up, he'd fired one last shot.

"Let me remind you," he told the minister, "unfriendly actions like this cut both ways."

"This is not an unfriendly action," the minister had sputtered.

"What I'm trying to make you understand, my good friend, is that there has to be mutual trust. We had an agreement. You've broken it."

In fact, the soldiers had already left earlier in the day, while Walt and his people had been at the site, working their butts off under the blistering sun. Slinking away like dogs with their tails between their legs; an act done deliberately, Walt knew, to prevent him from trying to stop them. Typical behavior in this country—pass the buck, avoid confrontation whenever possible, and lie about it when you're caught.

Things had changed from the days when he was young and the government would give foreign scholars anything they wanted. Now the patron countries decided how to develop the sites. Which was the right thing to do, but hard for outsiders like him to swallow. Thank God, he thought, he was near the end of his career instead of the beginning.

"There's nothing I can do about this now," the minister had concluded. "I sincerely wish I could help you, you know that. But I cannot. Although perhaps . . ." He paused. "There might be another solution," he said slowly.

"Which is what?" Walt answered in a dubious voice. "Right now I am in no mood to be jerked around."

"I would never do that," the minister said unctuously.

"Okay, fine. So what's your solution?"

"Take the men who are guarding the site."

Hearing that, Walt groaned. "That's your solution? That's a wonderful idea."

"It would only be for a day and a half. Two days maximum." The minister didn't sound convincing, even to himself.

"We can't leave this site unguarded, not for one night," Walt answered dismissively. "Forget that. It's an insane idea. Which you damn well know."

Walt never left a dig in which he was in charge unguarded. Protection against looting and vandalism, the scourges of developing sites, superseded everything. In one night, knowledgeable *guaquereos*—tomb raiders—could swoop in and haul off precious artifacts that could be worth millions of dollars on the antiquities black market. Having your site looted was an archaeologist's worst nightmare. Which was why every night of the year, without exception, native guards armed with shotguns and semiautomatic rifles stood watch over La Chimenea, to keep predators out.

"I won't leave this site unguarded," he told his caller again.

"I'm sorry, then," the minister replied. He tried to sound convincing. "There is nothing more I can do for you."

"Not as sorry as I am," Walt shot back, his reasons diametrically opposite those of the high-ranking but ineffectual functionary sitting in his opulent office, four hundred miles away, who couldn't wait to hang up on this hard-nosed *americano* and drink a soothing daiquiri.

After Walt had rung off and taken a walkabout around the site, he'd calmed down. Jocelyn had reminded him that in all the time they'd been traveling in this country they had never been in danger, not in any serious, life-threatening way. Besides, the rebels the minister had referred to were based in the northwest, on the border, hundreds of miles from here. The rebels' struggle, Jocelyn had pointed out, was with the government, not with American archaeologists. They welcomed the opening of new sites, as a show to the world of their former glory, which stood in stark, dismal contrast to their downward descent these past five hundred years, since the Spanish had come from across the ocean and destroyed their rich culture forever.

"It's no big deal," she counseled him. "Let it go. And don't take it personally."

She was right; she was usually right about these things. But he did take it personally, he couldn't help it.

It wasn't the threat of danger that had upset him, Jocelyn was right about that: it was the lack of respect for the effort he and the others were doing here. For the next half-century this place would be in a state of excavation. Archaeologists from around the world would gather here to help dig up and reveal its myriad secrets and glories. And this ungrateful government would reap the rewards.

He moped about it for a couple hours more, then he put the slight behind him.

The four-wheel-drive diesel-powered minivans were piled high with their gear; no one had slept in, or forgot something at the last minute, or was otherwise holding things back.

But they hadn't gone anywhere.

"We went over all this yesterday, Manuel." Walt was talking in Spanish, his voice fast, harsh. "Everything was completely smooth, I thought. How many times did I ask you if everything was okay? A dozen, at least?"

He was steaming. If smoke could actually come out of human ears, his would be Mount Saint Helens.

"It was. I checked and double-checked. Triple-checked. Me and Ernesto both did. Everything was tip-top," Walt's main man on the ground said morosely, feeling Walt was blaming him for this fiasco, even though *el jefe* should know he wasn't to blame.

"We needed an early start. That's why I was so concerned with checking everything out, over and over." Walt rubbed his knuckles into his temples in angry frustration. "This is going to screw us up, big-time."

"No, no, Professor Gaines, we can fix it."

Jocelyn inserted herself into their argument. "It was an accident," she said, physically putting her body between the two men. "They do happen." She turned to Manuel. "How long will it take to fix, Manuel?" she asked. When she spoke, there was no rancor, no accusation. Her voice was soft, supportive.

Manuel had great admiration for Professor Gaines. He was the smartest man Manuel knew. Professor Gaines was responsible for all the good things that were happening here, and he treated Manuel very well, like an equal, a partner. He treated all the native workers well, he wasn't the least bit condescending, like some of the *norteamericanos* Manuel had worked with over the years. But he could be impatient when things went wrong. People who didn't know him well, as Manuel did, sometimes got the wrong impression of him.

"An hour, tops. Look, Ernesto is already working on it."

Ernesto, the do-it-all handyman of the local workers, had already pulled the broken alternator from the engine compartment and was examining it, turning the defective part over in his rough-callused hands.

"Can you figure out what happened?" Walt asked him in exasperation.

Ernesto turned the part over. "The wiring is messed up."

"Messed up? What do you mean? Burnt out?"

Ernesto shook his head. "It shouldn't have. We put it on ourselves, new. But it got messed up, somehow."

"Between yesterday, when you drove it, and this morning."

Ernesto shrugged. Manuel hung his head.

Jocelyn interceded again. "Walt, let the man fix the damn thing. Jawboning him about why or how isn't going to solve our problem. Let's get it fixed and get on the road."

"She's right, *Señor* Walt," Manuel said quickly, wanting to head off more arguing, which wasn't going to solve any problems. "Ernesto can have it ready lickety-split."

Manuel liked to throw slangy English phrases into his discussions with Walt. He felt it was another way for them to be equals, if he could speak in Walt's jargon. That he'd never heard such anachronisms come from his boss's mouth, but had learned them on old movies on television, didn't matter. He admired Professor Gaines's initiative, his get-up-and-go, his genius. This was one way to show that.

"I'm not liking this," Walt said. He took the defective part from Ernesto and hefted it in his hand. "A practically brand-new part, and it goes bad. That seems strange to me."

Jocelyn, standing next to him, rolled her eyes. "My God, you're so uptight this morning. Shit happens, my dear obstinate husband. Get over it. Let the man do his job."

She pulled him away from Manuel and Ernesto, who picked up their tools and went to work.

Walt sat under a shady tree and had a cup of coffee. He was antsy as hell, for lots of good reasons. He looked at his watch again. Eight o'clock. Damn it! They should have been on the move over an hour ago. By leaving this late it would be touch-and-go whether they would be out of the jungle, off the dangerous roads, and to a safe area—the airport—by nightfall.

The others were sitting around in small groups, talking, lounging, waiting. Walt had been keeping an eye on Diane Montrose since she'd come out of her hut and thrown her duffel bag up onto one of the vehicles. She had glanced over at him once and smiled, a Mona Lisa cryptic smile that revealed nothing. Otherwise, she hadn't come near him. She was sitting with two other women, talking quietly.

They were exchanging notes—phone numbers and addresses. It was obvious—only to him, of course—that she was avoiding any close contact. He took that to be a good sign.

"*Señor* Gaines, it's finished."

He looked up. Manuel and Ernesto were standing next to him, looking at him anxiously. Walt glanced at his watch again. Then he smiled.

"An hour on the button. Good work, guys." He got up and walked into the clearing, dumping the remains of his coffee onto the ground. "Listen up!"

Everyone stopped what they were doing and turned to him.

"A record pit stop." He pointed to Manuel and Ernesto, who were beaming, having endured Walt's earlier surliness. "Better than A. J. Foyt. So let's give these good fellows a fine round of applause."

The volunteers all clapped loudly, enthusiastically, and gratefully.

"All right, pilgrims," Walt called out in his best John Wayne imitation. "Let's saddle up and bring these doggies home!"

Manuel drove the lead minivan. Walt rode shotgun. Jocelyn sat in the corresponding seat in Ernesto's follow vehicle. This perch was a small perk of status—all the other passengers were jammed in like sardines, elbows and feet and knees and legs all tangled up. It was going to be an uncomfortable ride—eight to ten hours, with minimal breaks—but that was part of the adventure. If it was easy, Walt had preached until they all took it up as a jokey mantra, anyone could do it.

Diane Montrose was in the far backseat of Walt's van,

sandwiched in between three others. He'd assigned her to his vehicle. He didn't want her being in the same van with Jocelyn for this long trip.

She'd been cool about everything. She had climbed into the back and settled in. Half an hour later, she'd fallen asleep. Some of the others had, too. They were tired, and it was going to be a long, boring ride.

The sun was at the height of its arc. Walt checked his watch again, then looked out the bug-smeared windshield. They were making pretty good time. It was still touch-and-go, but if they could keep up this rate of speed they were going to get out of the jungle and to the safety of the airport by nightfall.

"We're doing okay," he said to Manuel. "Better than I had hoped for."

"Oh, sure, boss," Manuel chirped, down-shifting into second again to maneuver over another crater-sized pothole. The vans never got out of third gear during the tedious drive. Twenty-five miles an hour was the best time they could make. Usually it was fifteen, ten, or even five. "I knew we'd be okay, once we got going."

"I wish you'd told me that back this morning. Would've saved my belly from aching."

"I tried, but you didn't want to hear it."

"Sorry about that."

"It's okay," Manuel reassured him. "You didn't mean nothing by it."

Walt looked affectionately at the small, nut-brown man who was wrestling the steering wheel with his Popeye forearms. Manuel had been on teams with him before, at other sites, but this was the first one at which Walt had designated him to be his lead assistant. He was conscientious, thorough, a quick study, meticulous, and a good supervisor; responsibility hadn't gone to his head, the man was humble to a fault.

He was comfortable with Manuel's being in charge when he wasn't there—he knew the site would be maintained properly, that everything would be handled professionally.

"When do you think you'll be coming down again, boss?" Manuel asked him, his attention focused on the twists and turns ahead of them. "Before your Christmas break?"

Walt nodded. "I'll be down at least once before then," he answered. "I plan to take a couple of weeks off in October. And I'm going to be here a lot starting the first of next year. I'm taking a sabbatical next semester. I've got too much work to do not to be here more."

"That sounds good, boss," Manuel said enthusiastically. "But there's no rush. The work will always be here. When we are old men eating soft food with our toothless gums, the work will still be here."

Walt sat back against the hot seat. "I'm not that far off from that now," he said with a self-deprecating, albeit rueful, laugh.

Manuel laughed back. "You're as young as a fresh colt, Professor Gaines. You still kick everybody's ass."

"That's nice to hear," Walt thanked him. "But it's coming. I'm not going to fool myself. I've got to make as much hay as I can while the sun's still shining on me. I don't want to be like one of those old ballplayers who can't get around on the fastball anymore but won't face up to it."

Like most Central Americans, Manuel was a baseball nut, so he understood the analogy. "You can still hit the ball out of the park," he told Walt. "You're still the cleanup hitter."

"Today, yes. But three, five years from now?" He shook his head. "Don't think so. So while I can, I want to be here, as much as I can."

Five years. That's what he was giving himself. In five years, if he pushed hard, they could excavate and restore the Central Plaza, bringing it to the level of those at Tikal and Chichén Itzá. A Herculean task that would be his monument forever.

The road bent sharply to the right. Manuel shifted down, to gain traction. As he turned the almost-ninety-degree corner and began slowly accelerating again, they almost plowed right into the massive mahogany tree that had fallen directly across their path, blocking the road completely.

Walt stared out the windshield. Before he could begin to curse at the gods for yet another stroke of bad luck, the first drops of rain hit the windshield.

The oppressiveness of the humidity inside the vans, the steam heat that felt like they were in a sauna in which the temperature had been cranked up way too high, the body stench that was fast emerging from their sweaty underarms, groins, feet, belly-folds, the sour dry rankness of their breath, the almost caterpillar-crawl squishiness of someone's skin touching someone else's skin—all of it became intolerable almost immediately. So even though the rain was coming down in sheets most of them had gotten out of the vehicles and were huddled under the trees at the side of the road, which offered scant protection against the torrent that was beating down on them like hot liquid BB pellets, soaking everything—hair, skin, clothing. They were drenched to the bone and were becoming more and more miserable by the minute.

They had brought chainsaws with them, of course. Trees fall down in the forest, that's an immutable fact of nature. They'd had to cut through these kinds of roadblocks before, so they came prepared. The cutting went slower than usual—the tree was massive and wet, and they had to be especially careful because of the slippery conditions.

Walt had flashed a burst of ire at this insult from the elements, but he'd gotten over it fast. You can fight Mother Nature, but you won't win. He'd learned that lesson a long time ago. Survival in the field depended on rolling with the punches.

He slogged through the muck to where Manuel and Ernesto were working on the dead tree. "How much longer do you think?" He looked up to scrutinize the sky, which hung black and low with thunderheads.

"I hope not much longer," Manuel grunted, as he cut the trunk into small enough pieces to be wrestled aside.

"So in a half-hour or less we can get going again?" Walt asked optimistically. "We should make pretty good time after this, shouldn't we?"

"That will depend," Manuel said slowly, "on how bad the mud is up ahead."

"The four-wheel drive in these minivans has always worked well," Walt remarked cautiously. "In a normal rain we'd be pushing on through this."

"Yes," Manuel agreed, "but vans are not burros. And this is not a normal storm."

Jocelyn ran up to them, holding a piece of cardboard over her head in a futile attempt to keep her head dry. "What do you think?" she asked nervously. "Are we going to get through? The kids want to know."

He gave her a grim look. "It's going to be tight."

The students were still clustered in the rain. A few of the women, shoes shucked off, were performing an impromptu dance of delirious, youthful abandon.

Jocelyn watched them, almost enviously. She didn't do that kind of dancing anymore. She should go over and jump in with them. Show these kids she was as free a spirit as any of them.

In her heart, she was. But she didn't join them.

Manuel and Ernesto finished clearing the road, and at the same time, as if by divine intervention, the thunderstorm was over. The sky turned a vibrant blue, with streaks of cornstalk yellow on the horizon.

Everyone was still outside, standing. Walt and Manuel walked a short distance away from the others. Walt stirred up some mud with his boot. He looked behind him and saw Jocelyn, standing with the others, staring at him. She cocked her head: *"What?"* He turned his palms up, shrugged, shook his head, turned away.

Manuel pried a clump of the viscous gunk off of one of the lead van's tires with a stick.

"Like sticking your hand in the tar baby," Walt said, frowning at it.

Manuel looked at him in bewilderment.

"American kids story. Not worth explaining," Walt said, as they walked back to the group.

"Can we get going now?" one of the students asked impatiently. He looked like a bedraggled dog. They all did.

"Here's the deal," Walt answered. "Yes, we can start driving again. It's going to be slow-going, the road is going to be terrible, all the way to the city, practically.

We'll be hours behind schedule." He paused. "We'll be on the road long after it's dark."

That sunk in. They all knew the first rule of Third World travel: don't be on the roads after dark. They started muttering, cursing under their breath.

"You want to bellyache," he told them, "feel free. I feel as bad about these delays as anyone else. But let's review our options, okay? We continue pressing on. We'll get to the airport after dark, but our flight isn't until past midnight, so we're all right with that. Or . . ." He paused. "We go back to the site—now—so that we're there before dark, spend tonight there, get a good *early* jump in the morning, get to the airport with daylight to spare, and take tomorrow night's flight." He dropped his hand to his side. "That's it, the way I see it."

They all slumped. One of the girls spoke up. "What do *you* think we should do, Professor Gaines?"

He exhaled heavily. This was his decision to make, no one else's. "I think we have to go back to the site."

A collective moan rose up. "That sucks," one of the young guys cried out.

"Yeah, it does," Walt answered. His tolerance was growing thin—he was in no mood for dissension. "These problems happen down here, you all know that. It rains, a piece of equipment breaks down, a tree falls in the road, there's one of a thousand other snafus, and you get stuck. One more day isn't going to make any difference."

They stood there, silently acquiescing, too tired and wet to argue.

"Come on, let's get back into the vans and get going." He took a step toward his vehicle, to motivate them to move.

"One more day *will* make a difference."

He snapped around.

Diane Montrose took a step toward him, separating herself from the others. "It could make a huge difference," she said, looking directly at him. "I don't think going back to the site tonight is the smart decision."

"Why not?" Goddamnit, what the hell was she up to now?

"Our tickets are for tonight," she said, staring at him. "And what if we can't get on a plane tomorrow night? The planes are always overbooked going out of here. We could be stuck in the airport for days. We're out of clean clothes, there would be nowhere to sleep, basic stuff like that. And most of us are low on money, we budgeted for this long, but no longer."

This is what happens when you've taken that forbidden bite, he castigated himself. You can't put her in her place, which is what you should do. She owns you now, a piece of you.

Jocelyn put a supportive hand on his shoulder. "You know this country better than any of us," she told him in an almost apologetic tone of voice, "but think about the logic of what Diane's saying."

Walt looked at the others, trying to gauge their attitude. They were uncomfortable with this public disagreement; his decisions weren't supposed to be questioned. He also knew that if they got hung up in the small, cramped airport and couldn't leave the country it would go down badly, and he'd be blamed.

"You know, honey," Jocelyn continued, "there hasn't been any news of dangerous activity in this area for a long time. All the problems are up north, like the minister told you." She put a soothing hand on his forearm. "I really think it'll be okay, Walt." She glanced at Diane for a moment, then turned back to him. "Taking everything into consideration, I don't think we can turn back now. We have to keep going."

Walt cursed inwardly. Then he gave an abrupt nod of agreement. What Jocelyn and Diane had pointed out was true, but that didn't make the decision sit any better.

"Okay," he said, giving in. "Let's go. We have a long ways ahead of us yet."

The vans slogged over the wet, muddy, tire-sucking road. Walt looked at his watch. Six o'clock. In an hour it would be dark. He had put on a happy face to save face, but inside, he was seething. This was the second time in three days (the screwup over the withdrawal of the military escort was the other) that his authority had not only been put into question, but overturned.

They drove in silence for a while. Most of the others were napping. Manuel, gripping the steering wheel as if it were the reins on a bucking mustang, was keenly aware of Walt's tension and anger. He'd watched his boss lose face to his wife and the other woman. Manuel knew that Professor Gaines hated being shown up like that. He wanted to say something to make his mentor feel better, some positive comment about how letting others in on decisions showed strength, not weakness—a big man, a confident man, doesn't always have to have things his way. But he didn't know how his boss would take such a remark; it might anger him even more. So he said nothing about it. Instead, like people do when they feel they must speak but don't want to deal with the real issues, he talked about the weather.

"It's hard driving this road when it's rained so much," he complained. "These are the worst conditions I've ever driven through." As strong as Manuel was, his arms were aching from fighting the steering wheel. "Only a crazy person would attempt to drive this road tonight."

"Tell me about it. Better yet, tell my wife."

"It was not her," Manuel said carefully. He checked the rearview mirror. Diane, in the far-back seat, was zonked out. "It was the other woman," he said quietly. "Your wife was only trying to . . ."

"Head off a mutiny?" Walt looked outside for a moment, at the thick, impenetrable jungle surrounding them. "It wasn't my idea, Manuel, but she"—a cocked thumb toward the slumbering Diane—"was right about the plane schedules and the rest of it." He shook his head in annoyance. "I had two crappy choices. This one was less crappy, that's all."

He settled back in his seat, trying to find a comfortable position. Logic had been on Diane's side, he couldn't dispute that.

He needed to stay calm; more important, he needed to project an aura of calmness. He was the leader: his attitude set the tone. He knew that his jitteriness was because of anxiety over the unexpected glitches as well as by the heavy weight of the responsibilities he had taken on, but he couldn't show any fear.

All that was behind them now. In four or five hours they'd be at the airport, and with any luck—they were due some, after what they'd gone through—by tomorrow they would be home. And safe.

Darkness fell. They pressed on. You don't know how dark night can be until you're in the middle of a jungle like this, Walt thought, looking out the front window and seeing nothing past the headlights. It's like being inside the whale's belly. But he was starting to feel less stressed—they were making decent time. An hour, hour and a half tops, and they'd be out of the jungle and onto the main highway. Then the airport, only another hour after that.

It was still blistering hot out even though the sun had been down for hours. Except for Walt and Manuel, everyone had fallen asleep. Walt was forcing himself to stay alert, talking low to Manuel about nothing, anything, words to keep his aide's attention focused. He wanted to make sure Manuel didn't lose his concentration, not for one moment—a few seconds' lapse and you could drive off the road into a tree.

In the distance, lightning flashes could be seen over the foothills to the east, followed by low rolls of thunder. It's going to rain again, Walt thought with concern. Hopefully, not until we're off this road.

They rounded a bend in the road. "Jesus Christ!" Walt shouted involuntarily, as the headlights lit up a man on horseback who was riding toward them out of the darkness.

Manuel jammed on the brakes. The van lurched to a stop, sliding on the muddy passageway.

Walt stared out the dirty windshield. "What in God's name is somebody doing out here at night?" he exclaimed. This was spooky, and unsettling—they never saw anyone on this road, unless they were going to the site. There was no other reason to be on it.

The rest of the passengers had been roughly jostled out of their sleep, falling all over each other. Mumbled voices called out, "What's going on, did we hit something?"

The lone rider stopped ten yards in front of them. He seemed at ease, sitting erect on his horse. Walt, looking out the windshield, noticed with a tightening of his stomach that the man was heavily armed.

"I'd better go see what's going on," he said to Manuel,

who sat in silence, his hands gripping the steering wheel. "Find out what he's doing out here."

He reached for the door handle. And his hand froze.

Another rider emerged out of the darkness and joined the first, sitting high in the saddles on their horses. And then a third.

And then another, another, another. Out of nowhere, ten men on horseback had come out of the dark, forming a line across the road. They brandished shotguns and rifles, and some had bandoliers strung across their chests.

They had been set up!

That came clear to Walt in a flash, as he stared at the men. They had checked and rechecked the vans. Everything was working. Then a perfectly good alternator suddenly went on the fritz, for no good reason. Right there, that should've told him: it had been tampered with.

With the wisdom of hindsight, there was no other explanation. Somebody at the camp had messed it up. Whoever that person was had to be connected with the official in the government who had pulled their support troops. The corruption went from top to bottom and back up again. He had known that for years, but he thought he was impervious, because of the work he was doing.

But now, he could see clearly, he wasn't. He hadn't paid attention to the obvious, the way he should have, because he was too mad. Fixing the alternator was going to delay their departure, and that was what he had been thinking: we're going to get screwed by leaving late—not suspecting that the alternator being broken could have been deliberate. Because it was so logical—the troops that were supposed to escort them were pulled for a lame reason, which meant they were traveling without protection, then the alternator goes. Read the tea leaves, jackass, he thought, it was all right there in front of you.

His second thought, which came right on top of the conclusion about them being set up, was that some or all of his party were going to be kidnapped, either for straight ransom or for a political reason. Kidnapping had become the counterinsurgency coin of the realm all over the world, from Indonesia to Pakistan to almost every country in Central and South America.

His third thought was the most dire—some of us might be killed. Maybe all of us.

The volunteers were staring out the window. Walt could feel the panic beginning to form.

"What is this?" a girl cried out.

"Are they going to rob us?" another asked tremulously.

Walt had to hold it together. If hysteria took over, they were screwed. "Everybody stay put, and keep quiet," he told them firmly. "I'm going out there. Don't anyone else move." He turned to Manuel. "Make sure they all stay inside," he whispered.

Manuel nodded. His stare was fixed on the men outside. If they survived this he wanted to remember every detail of what these men looked like, so that he could do something in the future to balance the scales.

Walt got out of the van and approached the armed men, who looked down at him from atop their horses. Some of them were pointing their rifles at him, as if measuring him.

One pull of a trigger, and he was dead.

The man who had emerged out of the darkness spoke first to Walt, in Spanish. His voice was rough and harsh, the voice of a heavy smoker. "Turn out the truck lights."

Walt immediately turned and faced the trucks. "Kill the headlights!" he called. "Turn your lights off." He shouted loudly, so Ernesto, in the trailing van, could hear him.

With a dreadful abruptness, the lights went out. They were plunged into darkness. Walt's mind was racing, while at the same time he was trying to think rationally: How do I get us out of this? Is there any possible way I *can* get us out of this? In the darkness he could barely see them at all, but they looked Indian—the Maya were the dominant culture in this region. Maybe he could explain who he was, what he had done in the country, for the country, and maybe they'd be sympathetic. It was a wild hare of an idea but it couldn't hurt to try—he had to do something.

"We're archaeologists," he said, using the Mayan dialect that was most common in the region. "We aren't political. We're sympathetic to your culture. We're working at La Chimenea, the new archaeological site."

The man who had spoken previously, who seemed to be the leader, shook his head. "Speak in Spanish," he said curtly. He looked past Walt, to the vans. "Everybody out," he ordered. "Everybody in front, with you."

That was exactly what Walt had been afraid of. "They're only students. I'm the leader," he said, trying to sound calm and unruffled. "Whatever you need, you can tell me."

The man shook his head. "Out. Now. Everyone," he ordered. He brandished his rifle. Even in the darkness Walt could make out that it was some kind of automatic or semiautomatic rifle. He didn't know what model—he wasn't knowledgeable about weaponry—but it was big and scary-looking.

First rule of survival: don't piss them off. "Whatever you want."

He walked back to the lead van and explained what

was going on. "They want us all outside. Leave everything in here."

"Are they going to rape us?" one of the girls asked. She was on the verge of tears. Several of the others were, too.

He shook his head. "No." He had thought about that, of course. But he couldn't let these kids know it. He had to keep them calm for as long as he could. "Play it cool, you guys," he said, trying to stay calm himself. "I don't know what these men want, but getting hysterical is going to make matters worse."

They all piled out. He went to the second van and told them the same thing. They got out and followed the others.

As they were all piling out Jocelyn grabbed his arm and pulled his ear down to her mouth. "How bad is this?" she asked in a whisper.

"I don't know," he answered. "Pretty bad." He was fighting his own nerves. "But let's you and me try to stay cool. We have to be strong, we can't show fear, no matter how scared we feel, even though there's plenty of reason to. This could get out of hand really badly, really easily."

The twenty Americans, plus Manuel and Ernesto, stood in front of the men on horseback. Walt's eyes were slowly getting accustomed to the low level of light. There wasn't much to see. Their abductors were wearing dark clothes, hats that covered most of their faces, and they were sitting above them on dark horses. Black on black on black, all around. Walt knew that standing there like clay pigeons wasn't going to do them any good. Being passive was the wrong signal. He had to do something, anything.

He stepped forward. "We're all here now," he said to the leader. "What do you want from us? You want money, jewelry? Tell me what you want." Don't say hostages, he prayed.

The leader turned and engaged a couple of the others who were next to him in conversation. These guys are awfully young, Walt thought as he strained to overhear what they were saying. Some looked like they were still in their teens, younger than his students. He knew that age was relative down here. By the time you're fourteen you're working, often you have a family of your own, you're grown up, for better or worse.

He caught fragments of their discussion. It didn't sound good.

"What're they talking about?" Jocelyn whispered in his ear. His Spanish was better than hers. He had been speaking it for decades—it was almost as natural to him as English, especially when he was in a Spanish-speaking country, like here.

"I can't make out what they're saying," he whispered back to her. "I hope they're not talking about hostages."

"Oh, Jesus." She looked behind them, at the huddled, miserable group. "But how could they? There's too many of us for them to take."

That was another fear: that they'd single out a few.

The leader turned back to them and motioned to Walt to come forward. As Walt did the man's beckoning, he noticed that they'd brought extra horses with them, which shook him up even more, because they could put hostages on those horses.

He had to try to hold his ground. "Tell me what you want," he said to the leader again. He was fighting to keep his voice calm, but he was shaking inside. "We'll give you whatever you want. Whatever we have, you can have."

"Your money," the man said. "Your watches, your jewelry. Everything you have that is worth money."

Walt sagged with relief. These weren't revolutionaries or

organized kidnappers, they were highway robbers. The situation was dire, but not as bad as he had feared it would be.

He needed to find out how bold an approach he could take. "What about our passports and airplane tickets?" he asked. "We need them to get out of the country. They're of no value to you," he added, improvising on his feet, "and if you were caught with them, the government would know it was you who robbed us." He hoped he sounded rational, rather than trying to push too hard.

The leader thought about that. "All right," he answered, nodding curtly. "You can keep your documents." He looked beyond Walt. "There are other things we will take that will be of more use to us." He pointed his flashlight toward the group. "That one, that one, and that one."

Walt knew who he was pointing the light at even before he turned and looked behind him. None of the women were in any way appealing; they had been on the road for over twelve hours, they were soaked, sweaty, dirty. Nevertheless, the bandido leader had selected the three, aside from Diane Montrose, who were the most attractive.

This was the nightmare come to life. Walt's response came purely from his gut. "No," he said firmly.

The leader leaned down and stared at him, not believing what he had heard. "What did you say?" he asked in a slow, menacing voice.

Walt's mouth had acted independently of his brain. But it was a good thing it had, he knew, because there was no other way he could play this. "You don't want to take them. Take me, if you have to take anyone."

The leader looked incredulous. He pointed the barrel of his rifle straight at Walt's face. The barrel looked huge to Walt, like a cannon. Walt could feel the pulse in his neck, fluttering wildly.

"Are you crazy?" the leader asked.

"No, I'm not crazy," Walt told him. He was fighting to keep the shakes from disabling him. "I'm valuable. They aren't. You can get a large ransom for me. My foundation will pay well for my release. No one will pay anything for them, they're only students."

He didn't have a clue as to whether anyone would pay to have him released, or even if it would matter. These men could hold him until they were paid the ransom and then murder him anyway. But that didn't matter. He had to offer himself. He was in charge. The others were his responsibility. He couldn't let these men take the women. Whether or not they eventually killed them or exchanged them for money, they would certainly rape them. The women would be traumatized for life, possibly beyond repair. He couldn't live with that.

The leader stared at Walt for a moment from the height of his horse. Then he shook his head. "You are one crazy man," he said, his voice expressing both disbelief and grudging admiration. "I could shoot you, right now."

Walt braced himself. For a few seconds—he didn't know how long—everything was still, as if frozen.

The moment passed. "We will not take the women," the bandido leader said to Walt. "Because we are not animals." He sat tall in his saddle. "Regardless of what you think of us, we are men of honor."

Walt was dumbfounded. "Thank you," he replied. He started breathing easier. They were going to survive this.

"Tell your people not to hold anything back on us," the leader admonished Walt sternly. "If we think you are hiding anything from us we will search you, and if we find out you are, we will kill whoever does it. Do you understand me?"

"Yes," Walt told him. "Absolutely. No one will hold anything back. I promise that."

He walked back to his group. They were huddled tightly together, looking miserable and scared out of their minds. "It's going to be all right," he assured them. "They're only robbing us."

"Only?" one of the kids had the temerity to say. He was one of the youngest—very bright, but immature.

"Yes, only," Walt told him harshly. He wanted to kick the kid upside his head. Stupid American brat. They can travel all over the world and see the worst conditions and some of them still never get it. "Thank your lucky stars that's all they want. In Colombia last year, in a situation like this, they took twenty hostages, and after they robbed them, they murdered them."

Everybody glared at the kid like he had rabies. The poor kid was properly chastised; he hung his head like a dog.

"They're taking everything that has any financial value," Walt informed his charges. "They're letting us keep our plane tickets and passports, which is more than I expected. If the worst of this is that we have to fly home without money or watches or cameras or whatever," he said, "we can consider ourselves lucky, damn lucky. The one thing I must impress upon you is this: *do not hold out.* Nothing. Not a penny, not your grandmother's wedding ring that's been a family heirloom for a hundred years. If they think we're holding anything back they'll be on us like bears on honey, and then we'll be in much worse trouble than we are now."

Two of their abductors climbed down from their horses. They had large plastic trash bags to receive the booty. Walt led the procession, handing over his valuables—his wallet and his watch. With a sigh, he removed his wedding ring and gave it to one of the young bandits.

Jocelyn, following behind him, did the same. She held

on to her wedding ring for a moment, her eyes tearing up as she handed it over. Then she stepped back, and gripped her husband's hand.

One by one, the volunteers stepped forward and emptied their pockets and packs. They were quiet, nervously eyeballing the bandidos, who watched them carefully, making sure nothing was left behind, each volunteer stepping back after stripping off their valuables.

While the volunteers were handing over their personal belongings, Manuel and Ernesto were methodically bringing the duffel bags and large cases from atop and inside the vans and laying them on the ground. Two more of the bandidos got down from their horses and began opening the bags, rifling through them and taking out whatever their hands fell on, from toothpaste and razors to women's soiled undergarments. The young highwaymen, giggling like schoolgirls, held up a pair of bras to their chests.

Walt watched this cavorting with both dread and almost a comic sense of revulsion—it was as if they were kids playing a game, except it was a deadly game, because it was real.

The leader barked at his troops to cut the crap. They stopped messing around and went back to going through the duffel bags. Most of what they pulled out was discarded and thrown onto the muddy ground. Jewelry, money, cameras, computers, other valuable items went into the trash bags. Manuel and Ernesto kept going back and forth to the vans, bringing up more bags, as well as cases and trunks that held supplies and equipment.

Flashes of lightning lit up the sky, followed by louder and louder thunderclaps. The storm was coming closer. Walt glanced up as another bolt came down. He barely counted to four-Mississippi before he heard the thunder.

He observed that the bandido leader was also looking up with a worried expression on his face.

Jocelyn, standing behind Walt, tugged at his hand. "You can't let them open your big case," she whispered urgently into his ear.

He glanced at the pile of bags yet to be opened. About a dozen bags and cases, including his large equipment trunk, which was firmly secured with a padlock, were still back on the vans.

"I can't stop them from doing whatever they want," he whispered back, turning away so that the bandidos couldn't see them talking to each other. "You heard what he told us. We try to screw these people around, we're going to get killed."

"If they open that trunk, you'll lose all your work," she warned him.

His computer was inside the trunk. If it was taken, a year's worth of work would be lost.

"I know," he answered, keeping his voice low. "But I don't have a choice."

"And you have those pieces from La Chimenea in there," she added ominously. "What do you think is going to happen when they find them?"

Walt was taking some artifacts out of the country. Legally, aboveboard. The government had given him permission to remove them temporarily, for study purposes. He would bring them back with him the next time he returned. This procedure had become common practice since the United Nations protocol on stolen antiquities had been established in 1983, which forbade the permanent removal of antiquities from the country of origin. These guidelines allowed precious information to be studied under advanced scientific conditions, while assuring the host countries that the antiquities would be returned.

"I have the papers from the government." He patted the pocket of his pants. "Right here, with my passport."

Even as he spoke, he could see the precariousness of his situation. Jocelyn articulated his fear for him.

"Yeah, right," she hissed into his ear. "Like they're going to take the time to read some papers. That's if they can even read. They're going to think you're stealing from the site, and they're going to freak. You can't let them open that box, Walt."

He groaned to himself. She was right—he had to keep their captors from opening that case. But how in God's name was he going to stop them?

Another flash of lightning lit up the sky, followed a couple of seconds later by a loud clap of thunder. Everybody looked up in dismay. The leader cursed under his breath. "Hurry," he yelled at his men on the ground.

The bandits began cramming the loose booty into garbage bags. The leader pointed a dirt-encrusted finger at Walt. "Go help your drivers bring the rest of your things up here," he snapped.

Walt's knees almost buckled. There is a God after all, he thought, as his mind raced. This heaven-sent, albeit unconscious gift from their abductors proved it.

"Right away," he said, hoping he didn't sound too eager. "My wife will help me," he called back over his shoulder, as he hustled her away from the others, toward the vans.

Manuel and Ernesto, standing on top of the lead van, were untying the last of the bags that had been secured to the luggage rack on the roof. The ropes were wet and unwieldy. Manuel, cursing to himself, began hacking at them with his knife. Ernesto, perched next to him, was doing the same.

"We'll bring what's left back here!" Walt called up to

Manuel, as he and Jocelyn passed his two drivers on their way to the back. He pointed to the rear van.

Manuel, standing on top of the van he had been driving, nodded quickly and continued his cutting.

The large trunk that held the artifacts Walt was bringing back to the states, along with his computer and other critical materials, was in the back of the second van. He swung open the rear door. The trunk was under the few remaining duffel bags that hadn't yet been taken out. He grabbed the bags and tossed them onto the muddy ground.

The trunk was secured with a heavy padlock. It was heavy—he and Jocelyn struggled to pull it out of the van. They dropped it at their feet. Walt started to push it under the vehicle.

Jocelyn grabbed his arm. "We can't leave it here, under the truck," she exclaimed, panic rising in her voice. "It's too big to hide, they'll find it."

Walt looked around desperately. The jungle was choked with thick vegetation on either side of the road, less than ten feet from where they were standing. Cautiously, he peered around the corner of the van.

The bandidos were shouting with each other, struggling to get the bags they had filled onto the pack animals. From where he and Jocelyn were standing, they couldn't be seen.

"Take that side," he whispered, pointing to the far side of the trunk.

They grabbed the big metal box by the handles at either end. Straining under the weight of it, they carried it to the edge of the road and pushed their way about five yards into the dense foliage.

They lowered the trunk to the ground. "They won't find it here," Walt said. "It's pitch-black, you can't see anything."

"Don't you think we should go in deeper?" Jocelyn asked fearfully.

"We don't have time. It'll be okay," he told her, trying to sound reassuring.

He grabbed handfuls of wet leaves and broken tree branches and did a quick camouflage job on the trunk. Stepping back, he looked at his rush-job handiwork. From the road, it wouldn't be seen.

Another flash of lightning hit close by, followed by a loud roll of thunder. The storm was coming even closer. In a few minutes, it would be upon them.

"Come on," he said, pulling her back onto the road. "We can't hang back here, they'll send someone looking for us."

They picked up as many duffel bags as they could and carried them to the pile in front of the lead van, dropping them onto the ground. Walt, his shirt soaked with perspiration and from the wet bags he had carried, looked up at the bandit leader.

"Just a couple more," he panted. "I'll go get them."

The leader shook his head impatiently as he peered up at the increasingly threatening sky. "*Rápido, rápido,*" he yelled at Walt.

Walt raced to the back of the trail van and grabbed the few remaining bags. He brought them forward and dropped them onto the ground. Manuel and Ernesto followed him with the last of the bags from the lead van.

"That's it," Walt said in a weary voice. He looked at Manuel, who nodded in agreement. "It's all here in front of you."

The leader had a suspicious expression on his face. "That is all? You are sure?"

"Yes," Walt nodded. "There's nothing left." He hesitated—then he decided to go for broke. "Go back and look inside the vans yourself if you don't believe me."

The leader cursed under his breath. He motioned to one of the men who was sitting on his horse, a few feet behind him, to ride up and join him.

The man he beckoned, who had been watching from the background but not actively participating in the looting, rode forward. Like the others, he was wearing a wide-brimmed hat that rested low over his face, so that Walt couldn't make out his features.

The leader was obviously agitated as he spoke to the other man. The man shook his head in anger as he answered. Then he turned toward Walt and looked up, revealing his face.

Walt stared at him slack-jawed, as if staring at a ghost.

He knew this man. He had worked at the camp, and had been a troublemaker from the get-go. Walt had tried to fire him, but the man had connections with the Minister of Archaeology and Culture—the same official who had informed him that their military escort had been pulled.

Walt clearly recalled seeing the man at La Chimenea the night before; but in the morning, he remembered now, he hadn't. The man must have snuck out in the middle of the night, after everyone had gone to sleep. Maybe while he, Walt, was at the site, with Diane Montrose. The thought chilled him.

The man, hooded eyes unblinking, continued staring at Walt. Then he broke into a gap-toothed smile. It was a smile not of friendship, but of revengeful triumph.

Walt realized, with certainty now, that his instincts had been right: it had been a setup, starting with the broken alternator. His feeling of outrage toward this coward was overwhelmed by that of fear for his life and the lives of his charges.

The turncoat leaned in and said something more to the

bandit leader. The leader listened intently. Then he turned and stared at Walt.

"There is a missing box," he said, his voice harsh with anger. "Where is it?"

Walt couldn't back down now. He had to play his hand to the end. "Like I told you. This is everything."

The leader motioned to a couple of his men to dismount. "Go look back there and see if there is anything that has been left behind," he ordered them. He looked up in anxiety at the dark, lowering sky. "Do it quickly."

Walt glanced over at Manuel. His assistant gave him a quizzical look, then turned away. Don't look anywhere except in the vans, Walt prayed silently. The words were a mantra in his head. Don't look anywhere.

A shout was heard from the near distance. The two-man search party returned. They were straining as they lugged the large, heavy trunk with them. They plopped it down on the ground in front of the leader's horse.

"You withheld this?" the leader asked, as he stared at Walt in anger and disbelief. "Are you stupid, or insane? Did you not believe me when I cautioned you not to hold anything back?"

"I didn't hide that," Walt protested. "It wasn't in either of the vans. I emptied them out."

The leader turned to the men who had found the trunk. "Where was it?"

"A few meters off the road, *jefe,*" one of them replied. "Hidden in the jungle."

Walt threw up his hands. "I don't know anything about that," he vowed. "I brought up everything that was there. Everything I saw that was there," he amended.

The leader pointed his rifle at Walt. "I warned you what would happen if you held out on us." His voice was shaking, he was so enraged.

Gasps rose from the students. Jocelyn put a quivering hand on Walt's arm.

Walt stood his ground. "If you want to shoot me, that's up to you," he told the leader, trying to keep the fear tremor from his voice. "But I'm not that dumb, for Godsakes. I certainly wouldn't try to hide something that big." He hoped the lies wouldn't sound as bad to his captor's ears as they did to him.

"You were trying to cheat me," the leader spat at him, his voice thick with anger. "But you are lucky—I do not have time to kill you now, or I would." He looked up at the threatening sky. "Give me the key to this," he ordered Walt.

"I don't have it. You took it. It's in one of your bags."

The leader cursed. He signaled to one of his men who was standing on the ground. "Shoot the lock off," he ordered.

The young bandit aimed his rifle at the lock and fired. The explosion rocked the jungle, echoing up past the black trees that stood like sentries. Cries of birds and animals erupted, and flocks of birds took flight into the dark foreboding sky.

"Open it," the leader said.

The young bandido swung the top open. Handing his rifle and reins to the rider next to him, the leader climbed down off his horse and started pulling things out. Walt watched with a building sense of dread as the bandido chieftain took out his computer and other research instruments and carelessly flung them aside.

He's going to find the artifacts I'm taking out of the country, Walt thought as he watched his personal things being tossed about, and he's going to think they were stolen, just as Jocelyn had predicted. He glanced over at her. She was looking at the ground and shaking her head back and forth with a look of absolute despair on her face. He reached into his pocket for the papers that certified the legality for him to have the artifacts. Let's hope this sonofabitch can read, he prayed. And that he doesn't shoot first and ask questions afterward.

The bandit leader pulled out a package that had been securely bound up in bubble wrap and tape. Pulling the tape off, he unwound the bubble wrap and looked at the object in his hands. It was a fragment of stela on which was enscribed a drawing depicting a battle, which would assist Walt in deciphering the dynamics of the ruling situation at the height of La Chimenea's power in the Maya pantheon. He turned the piece over in his hands, staring at it intently. Then he looked at Walt.

"Why do you have this?" he asked. "Is this not from the site you are working on?"

"Yes, it is," Walt answered quickly.

"You are stealing from the site?" the leader continued, his voice rising like a volcano about to erupt. "You are stealing our culture?"

Walt shook his head vehemently. "No, no, no, I'm not. Absolutely not." He reached into his vest pocket. "I have documents explaining that it is legal for me to remove them, for scientific study. They are signed by the Minister of Archaeology and Culture." He pulled the papers out of his pocket. "Here. Look at them, please." His hand was shaking as he held the papers out. "You will see I have nothing to hide."

The leader stared at him, then at the papers in his hand. "Papers mean nothing," he said. "Anyone can forge papers. It is done all the time."

"These aren't forgeries," Walt answered. This was what Jocelyn had so presciently been frightened about.

"They have the government seal. Here, please." He extended his hand again. "Look at them."

The leader hesitated—then he walked over to the turncoat who had worked at La Chimenea with Walt, and showed him the fragment. The other looked at it quickly, then shook his head. He handed it back to the leader, and spoke to him in a low, urgent voice.

Walt strained to hear the conversation between the two. The leader listened intently.

"These papers. Let me see them," he commanded Walt.

"Absolutely." Walt took the documents out of the envelope he had placed them in. The papers shook in his hands. Holding one up, he told the leader, "Here is the document for that object you have in your hands." He turned it around so the leader could look at it in the dim light. "You see the seal of the government?" Walt asked. "And look here—see, there's a picture of it. I have documents for all the artifacts I'm taking."

The leader squinted as he looked at the document in the low light. A flash of lightning momentarily lit up the area, and he turned his look skyward in alarm. The thunder came almost on top of the flash. Any moment now, Walt knew, the rains are going to come, and they're going to come hard.

The leader looked at the papers in Walt's hand again and frowned, as if confused. Carrying the papers, he walked over to the turncoat archaeologist again. They looked at them together. The turncoat shook his head, and pointed at the trunk.

The leader crossed back to the trunk, reached in, and withdrew a second carefully wrapped package. He peeled the bubble wrap from it, and held it up.

The object in his hands was a jade statue, over a foot

high. It was trimmed in gold and other precious metals, and was exquisitely carved. He turned it over and over, staring at it.

Walt was paralyzed as he looked at the statue. *Oh shit!*, was all he could think.

"And this," the leader asked him, fracturing his thoughts. "Do you have papers for this?"

He carefully placed the statue back in the trunk, yanked out another wrapped object, pulled the plastic off. It was another jade figurine, this one of a ruler or a warrior of the elite class. Like the first one, it, too, was beautifully carved.

"And this," the leader asked. He took some menacing steps toward Walt. "Where are your papers for this?" he demanded.

Walt's mouth had turned to cotton. He swallowed some spit so he could speak. "I . . . don't have them," he managed to say.

"Because they are stolen," the leader said. He stared at Walt with a look of absolute rage.

"No," Walt protested. "I swear to God. I don't know . . ."

Before he could get any more words out, the leader turned his back on him. Carefully, he placed the jade figures back into the trunk. Slamming the lid shut, he climbed back onto his horse and took his rifle. "Lash this onto the pack animal," he commanded his men.

The bandidos on the ground struggled to get the heavy trunk onto one of the pack horses. They tied it to the animal's packsaddle with lengths of rope. It balanced precariously on the horse's back.

The leader looked down at Walt from his perch atop his own horse. "You are lucky that today is not your day to die, because you have given me ample reason to kill you. But I will not, because I am not an animal or a thief, like you." He looked at Walt's trunk on his packhorse.

"What is in here is more important to me than your miserable life."

Placing two fingers in his mouth, he whistled loudly. The others mounted up. He started to wheel his horse around, to lead his men and their bounty back into the darkness.

A flash of lightning lit up the sky, directly over their heads. It struck a huge mahogany tree, setting it ablaze in a huge fireball, lighting up the area like spotlights ringing a football field. A deafening crack of thunder as loud as a volley of cannon fire exploded on top of it.

The horses reared and bucked, whinnying in fright. Their riders fought to stay on, jerking at the reins and grabbing the pommels of their saddles.

Only two people didn't flinch from the light and sound. Walt's antagonist's eyes didn't leave Walt's face, nor did Walt's leave his.

You did this, Walt thought. You set it all up. My God.

The turncoat raised his rifle.

Another bolt of lightning came down, right on top of them. A booming clap of thunder, louder than any they had yet heard, was instantly behind it. The turncoat's horse reared up as the man fired, the bullet discharging over their heads into the dark sky.

"Get off the road!" Walt screamed. "Run!"

It was as if he had thrown a grenade into their midst. Everyone bolted, scattering into the jungle. Walt could feel Jocelyn, pressed up next to him. He pushed her away, toward the safety of the trees.

Another blast of rifle shot exploded over the roar of the rolling thunder above their heads. Before the echo had stopped reverberating, the bandits had galloped away, vanishing into the jungle.

PART TWO

MADISON, WISCONSIN

◆ ◆ ◆

Only Walt, his three sons—Clancy, the oldest, Tom, the middle brother, Will, the youngest, and Clancy's fiancée, Callie Jorgensen—were at the cremation. As Jocelyn had been an only child, and her parents, Steve and Mary Murphy, had long since passed away, no one from her side of the family was present to witness her body being returned to ash.

Getting Jocelyn's body back to the States had been a lengthy and excruciating ordeal. The government had insisted on conducting an official inquiry. Walt had spent several days in the capital answering questions from the state attorney for the National Police about the events of the night she was killed as well as those occurring on the days before they left La Chimenea.

The line of questioning was insulting and aggravating in the extreme. It was implied that he was somehow complicit in her death, a veiled allegation that he found outrageous, and which he protested in strong, angry language. He had debated over whether to tell them that the local archaeologist he had tried to fire had not only been one of the bandidos, but the very man who killed Jocelyn; but he knew that if he did, it would be like setting a match to a pool of oil. The stolen artifacts (which the police knew nothing about, thankfully), had been in his trunk, he couldn't refute that. He would have to explain where they had come from and what he had known about them, which would have put him under even more suspicion. He also knew the Minister of Archaeology and Culture would be outraged by the accusation that a man he supported had been involved in the killing, because that would have implicated him by association, which would have buried Walt's further association with La Chimenea. So he kept quiet about it.

He was there for more than a week before they let him leave with Jocelyn's remains. He departed with a sour taste in his mouth and an anguished heart.

The commemorative service was held the day after the cremation at the university chapel, which looked like an arboretum, so many wreaths had been sent. It was a lovely late-summer's morning, sunny and not too hot, but the splendor went unnoticed—everyone was in too much pain to appreciate beauty. Twice as many mourners were in attendance as the chapel could hold; the throng overflowed into the vestibule and the steps outside. Jocelyn and Walt were beloved in the university community. Jocelyn, in particular, had been adored by the younger members of the faculty, for whom she had been their den mother, their grown-up shoulder to cry on. Her killing had been a shock to their tightly knit community; even now, a week after they'd all heard the horrible news, people were walking around like zombies, expressions of stunned disbelief on their faces.

Grace Esposito, a university chaplain and one of Jocelyn's close friends, conducted the service.

"That this wonderful, exceptional woman was cut down

in the prime of her life is an unspeakable tragedy," Pastor Esposito began, standing at the altar. "But we're not going to dwell on that today, because that's not what Jocelyn Murphy Gaines was about. Jocelyn was about life, about living every single day to its fullest. She was about being a wonderful wife to Walt, a wonderful mother to her sons, a wonderful teacher to hundreds of her students. She was a wonderful woman, and a wonderful friend. That's why all of you are here today: to honor her, and to honor your friendship and love with her, and for her. To support Walt and Clancy and Tom and Will. And to remember all the good times, and all of Jocelyn's good works. And most of all, to remember all the love she brought into the world. Physical love, moral love, sensual love, emotional love. She had all of those elements of love in abundance, and she spread her love everywhere, to everyone."

Seated in the first row between his sons Walt sagged, his head dropping almost to his lap. He was drained. He looked like he had aged five years in one week.

Clancy put an arm on his father's shoulder, hugged him tight. "You gonna get through this okay, dad?"

Walt nodded. He forced himself to breathe in and out. Callie, next to Clancy, squeezed Clancy's thigh. He put his hand on hers.

The minister opened her Bible.

"Jocelyn and Walt weren't members of my church," she said. "They weren't observers in any traditional sense." She smiled. "I think the reason Jocelyn came to service once in a while was because of her friendship with me, and her support of me. But that's okay, because her reason for being here came from the heart, not from any sense of duty, or obligation."

She turned to a page she'd earmarked.

"I'm not going to read any references to death this

morning. Jocelyn would have hated that. I've chosen two short passages from the writings of Solomon, the most earthy and sensual of all the biblical authors. I think these two brief excerpts say much about Jocelyn."

She adjusted her reading glasses. "The first is from Proverbs, entitled 'The True Wealth.' *'Happy are those who find wisdom, and those who get understanding, for her income is better than silver, and her revenue better than gold. She is more precious than jewels, and nothing you desire can compare with her. Long life is her right hand; in her left hand are riches and honor. Her ways are ways of pleasantness, and all her paths are peace. She is a tree of life to those who lay hold of her; those who hold her fast are called happy.'* "

She looked up. "Long life, of course, is a relative term. When these words were written, fifty years, which was how long Jocelyn lived, was a ripe age. Today, that's not so. But if you measure longevity by how much you put into life and how much you get out of it, then Jocelyn lived a very long life indeed. For the rest of it, it's as if Solomon had Jocelyn in his mind when he wrote those beautiful words."

She thumbed through a few pages. "The second offering is from 'The Song of Songs.' It speaks so well, so perfectly, I think, about how Jocelyn and Walt felt for each other." She looked down at Walt. "I know these are such terrible times, Walt. That anything I can say right now, or that any of us can say, cannot assuage the grief you and your sons are feeling. Just know that we are there for you as much as we can be, and that you all are truly loved."

Walt looked back at her, and nodded. "Thank you," he mouthed silently.

On either side of him, his sons pressed in, holding him up.

The minister turned to her Bible again. "This section is called 'Homecoming.'

" '*Set me as a seal upon your heart, as a seal upon your arm; love is strong as death, passion fierce as the grave. Its flashes are flashes of fire, a raging flame. Many waters cannot quench love, neither can floods drown it. If one offered for love all the wealth of one's house, it would be utterly scorned.*' "

She looked out at the congregation again. "The love that Walt and Jocelyn had for each other is stronger than anything, even death. Death comes to us all, eventually. But love like theirs goes on forever, in this world, and beyond. It is an inspiration to us all, as they always were and forever will be."

People were jammed together in the house. They spilled out of the rooms into the garden out back. Jocelyn had taken great pride in her garden. It was riotous with flowers; not in neat, orderly rows, but with a wild discipline, the way she'd lived her life.

Walt stood in the middle of the living room, receiving the mourners. Each son had staked out his own area of the room, to enable the mourners to spread out and easily talk with each one.

Callie was keeping close tabs on her future father-in-law. He was holding up better than he'd done at the church; there was a calm about him, almost a transcendence. He was drinking vodka and orange juice in a tall glass filled with ice. Callie had fixed his drink—not so much alcohol that he would lose control, but enough that a bit of the edge of despondency would be taken off.

She moved about the room, acting the hostess as best

she could. For a moment she turned away from Walt to get the dean of the college a glass of wine, and when she looked back again she saw that Walt was talking to a woman, someone she didn't know, a thin, dark-blonde in her early thirties with an elusive quality about her. She looked like she would be more at home on Fifth Avenue, in New York, than in a small city in Wisconsin, even one as cultured and progressive as Madison.

The woman turned. She saw Callie looking at her, and gave her the faintest of smiles. Turning away, she said something low to Walt, who also looked at Callie, then replied to the woman in an equally low voice. She placed a comforting hand on Walt's for a moment, then moved away.

Clancy was suddenly at Callie's side. "Everything okay?" he asked.

"Everything's fine," she assured him. "Under the circumstances. Do you know that woman who was just talking to your dad?"

"The one with her hair in a French twist?"

She nodded.

He shook his head. "I don't know her. Probably a faculty wife, they come in all different shapes and packages. I don't know hardly any of the people here, they're mostly from the university, friends of mom and dad." He passed a hand over his eyes. "I can't believe she's gone. It's like any minute she'll come waltzing in and grab a canapé, you know?"

Callie nodded. "I know."

Walt came over to them. "How're you two holding up?" he asked.

"We're okay, dad," Clancy said. "What about you?"

His father gave him a dispirited nod. He handed his empty glass to Callie. "Could you get me another? It's hot in here, isn't it? I don't want to dehydrate and fall down and look stupid."

"Sure," she answered. She moved off toward the bar.

"Who's that woman?" Clancy asked.

"Which one?"

"The woman in the black silk dress you were talking to a minute ago."

Walt turned and looked around. "A friend of your mother's, I guess." He rubbed his eyes. "Everything's a blur right now."

Clancy put his arm around his father's shoulders in support. "It's okay, dad. Hang in there."

"I'm trying, son."

Callie returned with a glass of water for Walt. He took it from her and drank deeply. "Thanks," he muttered. "I'm going outside for a minute. I need some air."

"Do you want me to go with you?" Clancy asked, concerned.

Walt shook his head. "I need a minute alone."

"Sure, dad."

Walt walked across the room and out onto the patio.

"Man, is he in a world of pain," Clancy said to Callie.

She nodded. "Aren't we all."

The last of the stragglers had departed, the leftovers had been wrapped. Some of the excess food went into the refrigerator; the caterers would take the rest to a homeless shelter.

Walt and the boys and Callie sat in the living room, sprawled out on the couches and chairs. Walt was nursing a weak vodka tonic. The others were drinking beer from the bottle.

It was evening. Outside the west-facing windows the sun hung low in the sky, ready to drop.

"You should go to bed early, dad," Tom said to Walt. "It's been a long day."

"For all of us," Will added.

Walt shrugged. "Yeah, I guess." He looked off for a moment, lost in space. "It was all so stupid," he said, his voice rising in sudden anger. "So horribly unnecessary."

"Don't rile yourself up, dad," Tom said, moving over and sitting next to Walt.

"I was in charge, and I screwed up," Walt said insistently. "It was my fault, what happened down there."

"That's bullshit!" Clancy moved over and sat on the other side of his father. "You weren't at fault about anything!"

Walt shook his head stubbornly. "You weren't there. You don't know what happened." He took a hit from his drink. "I'm going to tell you."

"No, dad," Will said in alarm. "Now isn't the time."

Walt shook his head stubbornly. His face was as gray as ash. "There may not be a time later. We're all here now, together. I have to do this."

Slowly, in a halting voice, Walt told them everything that had happened, from the moment they discovered the sabotaged alternator that morning at La Chimenea until the ambush started. They sat in stunned silence, sinking lower and lower in their chairs. It was dark, but no one turned on any lights. They sat in the darkness, listening.

He got to the part where he realized one of the bandidos was going to shoot at them, that some of them might be killed. " 'Get the hell off the road!' I screamed. 'Run!' I hollered."

His sons and Callie flinched as his voice rose with the memory.

He hesitated, remembering; then he continued on, lowering his voice to a softer tone. "No one waited, not for an instant. They all scattered into the jungle. The rifle went off like a cannon, and an instant later I thought I heard the bandido leader yelling, *'Why did you shoot? I told you not to fire your rifles unless I fired first!'* He was angry and upset, I could hear it in his voice. But I didn't give a damn about their motives or what he was saying then, I was ducking for cover like everyone else.

"Our captors took off, disappearing into the jungle. Whatever they hadn't put on their packhorses was still on the ground where they had dumped it. I was lying on my stomach, covered with mud, listening to them ride away. They had the trunk with my stuff and the artifacts from La Chimenea, but at that point none of it mattered, because we had all survived.

"I waited a few minutes until it was obvious that they weren't returning, then I gathered all my people in the road again and started taking a head count, because I wanted to make sure everyone was accounted for. No one was missing, and miraculously, no one had been shot. We started gathering our stuff they hadn't taken and throwing it back into the vans. Then Manuel said to me, '*Señora* Gaines, I don't see her.'

"I wasn't worried about your mom, I knew she could take care of herself. To be honest, I thought she was right there next to me. But he was right. She wasn't there. And then we heard a low moan. Mom was lying on the ground at the edge of the jungle, a few feet off the road, just deep enough in that we hadn't seen her. She'd been shot in the stomach. I could see the blood oozing out from her, her hands were covering her belly but they were red with her blood. I remembered the second rifle shot and realized that bullet must have hit her.

"Her color was good and her pulse seemed strong. I pulled her dress up and checked where she'd been shot. It didn't look that bad, the blood wasn't gushing out, just oozing slowly. I thought, we can be at a hospital in an hour. She's going to be okay.

"We threw everything into the vans and took off and drove like crazy, I had her in the lead van with me, Manuel was driving like Mario Andretti, I was holding her, telling her she was going to be all right, she was telling me she thought it wasn't that bad. We were pushing as hard as we could."

He stopped talking for a moment and buried his head in his hands. Then he looked up again.

"Five minutes before we got to the hospital, she stopped breathing."

Walt was exhausted, both from the ordeal he'd been through, and from the remembering and recounting of it. Around him, everyone was devastated.

"Five minutes," Walt repeated. "Ten at the most. That's how close we came to saving her." His voice sounded hollow, distant, like it was coming from the bottom of a deep well.

"And how far."

PART THREE

CHICAGO

◆ ◆ ◆

Last call!" Clancy sang out in a weary voice.

The Pabst Blue Ribbon clock hanging over the backbar, a relic from whoever owned the bar before World War II, read a quarter to one. Weekdays were generally slow after midnight; only half a dozen stragglers, hard-core regulars from the neighborhood, were still hanging on. They ordered up with languid "yos" and finger taps on their glasses.

This bar, Finnegan's, on the near North Side, was Clancy's second business, the one that paid the bills. From six in the morning until five in the afternoon he was absorbed in his sports-kinesiology practice, his real vocation. That business had grown so quickly that four months ago he had formed a partnership with a couple of other physical therapists and opened a bigger place, the Evanston Sports Rehabilitation Center, a large, airy facility just over the city line. The partners had taken out a sizable loan with the bank—the equipment required to set up a facility like that ran well into six figures—but they were breaking even financially, with the prospect of making seriously good money not too long down the road, and most important, he was doing work that he loved.

He drew the last beers of the night, poured the final round of drinks. For the past half-hour he'd been methodically going through his shutdown, so that at one on the dot, as soon as he shooed everybody out and turned the neon sign in the window from OPEN to CLOSED, he'd be able to finish his cleanup in less than ten minutes, stash the cashbox in the safe, set the alarm, lock the door behind him, pull down the security grate, lock it, and go home to Callie.

They had been married for eight months now. The ceremony had taken place between Christmas and New Year's, four months after his mother's death. Her accidental murder had been a brutal blow to everyone, but Clancy and Callie had decided, after much soul-searching, to go on with their wedding, which they had already planned. Life can be shorter than you think it's going to be, that was the harsh lesson they had learned.

The most compelling reason they'd thought about postponing their wedding was Walt. He hadn't handled Jocelyn's death well at all; this was the first time in their lives that his sons had known him to not be in control. But when the question had been broached to him—very delicately—he had insisted that the wedding go forward as planned. Life is for the living, he'd told Clancy and Callie. Jocelyn would want you to push ahead, full speed.

So they tied their knot. It was a sweet wedding. Not too big, their families and close friends, fifty guests in all. After the minister performed the ceremony, which included a special prayer for Jocelyn's memory, so that her spirit was included in the ceremony, the full wedding party caravanned in limousines to Clancy's bar (which he had closed for the day), whereupon one and all pigged out on the massive buffet, danced to a rocking local blues band, and drank.

The next day, after sobering up, everyone scattered. Walt drove himself back to Madison, Tom and Will went to their respective homes in Ann Arbor and Minneapolis, Callie's parents flew back to South Dakota. Clancy and Callie honeymooned in Paris and Florence for two weeks. Then they came home and settled back into their everyday lives.

Callie Jorgensen was Nordic-blond, blue-eyed, a shade over six feet, a few years out of college when she and Clancy met. She had been a volleyball player, an All-American at UCLA, then two years on the pro circuit.

It had been a great life—how many twenty-four-year-olds are making six figures a year to hang out on beautiful beaches in California, Florida, and Hawaii, wear great-looking two-piece swimsuits, slug a volleyball over a net, and smile at the camera for the Gatorade and Nike commercials? Not to mention hanging out with Derek Jeter, Pete Sampras, and Vince Carter. The answer is, damned few.

When she blew out the anterior cruciate ligament in her right knee it was like the end of the world. Women's volleyball wasn't that big a sport that she could survive the operations and recovery time she'd need to get back to her peak and be a force again, not only as a player, which was questionable, given the severity of her injury, but more important, as a commercial entity. If you can't jump, you can't play. If you can't play, you have no market value.

Callie Jorgensen was twenty-four years old and she

had already been through, and completed, an entire career. She was miserable, dejected, and lost.

And then along came Clancy Gaines.

Clancy was Callie's physical therapist. He was completing his master's degree in physical therapy and anatomy at the University of South Dakota, and was working at a local rehab clinic to make money and get practical, hands-on training. He had never worked with a professional athlete before. Having that opportunity was exciting to him—you don't normally find a professional athlete rehabilitating a serious injury in Vermillion, South Dakota. Callie was there because her parents lived nearby, in Sioux Falls, and she had gone home to lick her wounds and have a stable support system, far from the glitz of the world she'd been living in.

Callie was the hardest-working client Clancy had ever worked on. Regardless of when he'd show up for their morning appointment, six o'clock or whatever ungodly hour they'd scheduled, she would be there, waiting impatiently. He would put her through her routine, really punish her, and she would finish it and want to do more. No matter how bone-tired she was, no matter how much her leg hurt, she wanted to keep pushing. She wanted to get better faster, and she wanted her leg to be as strong as it had been before her accident.

After months of grueling exercise, pain, and mental effort, the knee recovered nicely, but not like it had been. There had been too much damage. Callie could do anything on the reconstructed joint she had done before—ski, play volleyball, basketball, run, ride a bike—but she couldn't perform at the rarefied level that's required of a pro athlete. Her operation and rehabilitation, by any regular standards, was a success. But in this case, the patient—her career—unfortunately died.

When Callie finally accepted that she could never again compete professionally, she went through a period of heavy denial. She had never been drunk in her life, but there were occasions those first few months when she woke up puke-stained from having gotten shit-faced the night before. Drugs, too—when she was rehabbing she was taking cortisone and other muscle enhancers, under her doctor's supervision; after she was finished, she kept taking them, under the table. She felt like she was making up for the time she'd lost when she had denied herself the forbidden pleasures that her nonathletic friends had taken for granted while at college.

She was lost, and she was angry.

But she was lucky. Early on, her relationship with Clancy had gone beyond one of therapist and patient to deep friendship. But not romantic, because if her rehab was successful enough for her to return to the high-powered world of pro volleyball there would be no place for him, unless he was willing to be a passive supporter, accompanying her from tournament to tournament, hanging in the background, giving up a life of his own. Which he wasn't going to do—he had a life, he liked it, it was productive.

If Callie had been able to go back to her sport, that would have been the end of them. But she wasn't, and he was there for her. Steady, supportive, caring. Gradually, she came to honor and appreciate that, and as she accepted the changes in her life the bitterness faded away; and as it did, they stopped denying the obvious—they had fallen in love.

About the time Callie was coming out of her funk, they took a weekend trip to Chicago. Clancy had gone to Northwestern as an undergrad, and had close friends living in the area. One Saturday night, after a hearty Italian meal, they repaired to Finnegan's Bar on the Chicago-Evanston divide, a bustling place that was popular with the college crowd—Loyola, Northwestern, DePaul. Clancy and his friends had been regulars there, and he had fond memories of it.

"This is a cool place," Callie observed, as the group worked on their second pitcher of Pete's Wicked Ale.

"No kidding." Clancy looked around the bar, which was jammed beyond legal capacity. "I used to want to own a bar, like this one. Not a restaurant—they're a hassle. Just a nice, simple bar with a cash register that goes ka-ching, ka-ching, all night long. No one loses money owning a bar, not in Chicago, anyway."

"I guess everybody's had that fantasy," she'd said.

"My father's generation's was a nymphomaniac who owned a liquor store."

"Nymphomaniac? God, that dates him. Anyway, I don't think your father ever had to worry about getting women."

"I doubt it, yeah. His wild-oat days were behind him by the time I came along, though."

"With a woman like your mother, I would think so."

Callie liked Clancy's mom and dad. They were the neatest parents she knew. There was nothing old about them, except chronologically—they were younger in spirit than the parents of her other friends. Much younger that way than her own parents.

Jimmy Finnegan, the owner, a retired Chicago fireman who had been a fixture in the neighborhood for years, came over and joined their table.

"Hey, big guy, where you been hiding?" he joshed Clancy, punching him hard in the biceps.

Clancy punched him back, and explained that he didn't live around here anymore. He ran down his recent history for Jimmy, and introduced Callie. Jimmy was pushing seventy, but he still had an eye for the ladies.

"You're a keeper," he complimented her in a jovial, heavy-handed manner.

"You're so subtle," she answered in kind.

"She's a keeper," Jimmy told Clancy.

They all laughed. Jimmy ordered them another pitcher, on the house.

The friends drifted off, but Clancy and Callie stayed until last call. Not drinking a lot, just grooving on the place. Only a few diehards were left, which was fine—it was nice sitting at the dark oak table, with the light low and the Coors and Budweiser fluorescents glimmering blue and pink over the backbar. A Domino's kid came in with a couple of boxes, courtesy of Jimmy, and they all grabbed a slice. Jimmy closed up the cash register and joined them again.

"You doing good?" he asked Clancy, glancing at Callie. There were no rings on her fingers, he didn't know the lay of the land.

"Doing great." Clancy grabbed another slice of pepperoni. "Thanks for the pizza, too."

"Gotta keep your strength up."

"You know, Jimmy," Clancy said, washing the pie down with some beer, "this isn't a bad life here, what you've got. As long as the colleges stay open, you're always going to have a captive clientele." He looked at Callie, and winked. "I wouldn't mind owning a business like this, someday."

Jimmy sat back, put his stein on the table. "You think?"

Clancy laughed. "Hell, yes. Who wouldn't? You've got to be the richest ex-fireman in Chicago by now, man.

Not to mention all the cute little girlies who traipse through here. Keeps a man young, I'll bet."

Callie gave him a kick under the table.

Jimmy smiled and nodded. "Young as a fresh stallion."

"The miracle of Viagra," Callie threw in, to razz him.

"Whatever it takes," Jimmy told her unselfconsciously. "I've always been a results-oriented guy. How a fireman's mind works—results." He looked at Clancy again, the smile off his face now. "You serious about what you were saying? Owning a joint?"

The three of them had breakfast the next morning. Jimmy was ready to sell the place and retire, move to Florida. He would always root for the Cubbies, but the harsh Chicago winters had worn him down. If Clancy was earnest about buying the place, Jimmy would make him a sweet deal.

Clancy and Callie took a walk along Lake Michigan and talked it over. They walked slowly—Callie was still wearing her bulky knee brace.

"This is so far out of left field, I don't know how to respond," Clancy said. "I'm not a businessman, I'm a physical therapist. I mean, it's a cool dream and all, but I'm not there."

She turned to him. "*I?* Or we?"

"You want to own a bar in Chicago?" he asked, surprised.

"I like Chicago. I'm not going to live in South Dakota, and neither are you—you like it here, most of your friends are here. They need more therapists in Chicago, it's a boomtown for them, all the sports teams. You could still have your career, we wouldn't have to work the place full-time. That's what you hire people to do. This is a chance to own our piece of the rock, Clancy. People our age usually don't get an opportunity like this."

They relocated to Chicago and bought Jimmy out. They had to put in long hours, longer than they'd realized—you don't absentee-manage a bar, even if you have decent help that doesn't rob you blind. Callie began substitute-teaching junior high school phys. ed. part time in the Evanston public school system. When the school day was over she would go down to the bar, around three. She would look over the receipts from the night before, check on supplies and place orders, go to the bank down the street; the various and sundry details of running a daily business that dealt mostly in cash.

Clancy would join her after he had put in a full day at the clinic. They worked together until the happy-hour rush was over at seven and the students and older regulars hadn't yet come in, then they would go have dinner at one of the local restaurants. There were dozens of good, decently priced places to choose from, and it was their only quiet time together.

While they were on their dinner break, their bartenders would run things. They had three part-time bartenders—two male graduate students from nearby DePaul, and Pete, a middle-aged bachelor who was one of Jimmy's old crew and had stayed on. Pete wasn't the brightest bulb in the chandelier, but he was honest. Having Pete backstopping him allowed Clancy the luxury of not having to be there seven nights a week; he customarily took Sunday and Monday nights off (except during football season, when the games were televised and all hands were needed on deck).

After dinner Callie would hang around for an hour or so, then she'd go home. She couldn't stay up as late as Clancy could—she needed her sleep. How her husband got by on four or five hours of sleep a night was a mystery to her.

* * *

The drive home took less than twenty minutes. At this time of night, there wasn't much traffic. They had a nice apartment in an old building near the Northwestern campus, a block from the lake.

Clancy parked under the building, rode the elevator up to the third floor, unlocked the front door to their apartment and let himself in, moving as quietly as possible so he wouldn't wake Callie. Tiptoeing through the dimly lit living room, he went into the kitchen and looked in the refrigerator to see if there were any leftovers.

"Clancy?" Her voice didn't sound like she had just awakened.

"Yeah, honey." He grabbed a carton of milk, a jar of spicy mustard, and a hunk of salami. "How come you're up?" he called to her.

"Couldn't sleep." She came in the kitchen doorway in her robe and slippers, her eyes slits, adjusting to the light. "Didn't you eat?"

"I got busy and forgot to." He grabbed a loaf of bread from the breadbox on the kitchen counter, started hacking at the salami. He smeared two slices of bread with mustard, laid the salami on top. After biting off a chunk, he held the sandwich out to her. She leaned over and ate a mouthful out of his hand, wiping the mustard off her lips with a dish towel.

"Tom and Will called," she informed him. "They're both getting into Madison around noon. They'll share a cab from the airport and meet us at the cemetery." She pressed a hand to her lower back. "That's why I couldn't sleep, thinking about it."

Clancy nodded somberly. "I know. It was slow tonight in the bar, plenty of time to let your mind wander. I thought about her most of the evening."

Today was the first-year anniversary of Jocelyn's

death. Clancy, his brothers, and Callie were going to Madison to visit her gravesite.

"Is your father coming?" she asked. She tried to keep the anxiety from her voice. Walt's behavior was a touchy subject in the family these days. "Have you heard from him?"

"We exchanged e-mails last week, but we haven't talked on the phone in a pretty long time. He never picks up, and he doesn't return messages. It's the same with Will and Tom, he doesn't talk to any of us. He only stays in touch via e-mail, so he doesn't have to deal with us directly." Clancy shook his head in frustration. "He isn't coming. He would've said so if he was."

"Aren't you worried about him?" she asked, not for the first time.

"Of course I'm worried," he answered. "You know that." They'd had this discussion too many times already. He was sick of it. "We all are. We'd be crazy not to be. But we're not going to tell him what to do, or how to feel. We can't. He's the father, we're the sons."

"He needs his family, now more than ever," Callie said stoutly.

"I know that." Clancy washed down a mouthful of sandwich with a swallow of milk. "But he's decided to keep his distance from us, and that's how it's going to be until he changes his mind. Nobody tells Walt Gaines what to do or how to act," he said, both in irritation and sorrow. "No one ever has, and no one ever will. So let's drop it, okay? Talking about it isn't going to solve anything."

She ran a placating hand along his forearm. "Okay."

Clancy thought about what his father had gone through over the past year. He knew that Walt's life had been turned upside-down since his wife had been killed.

No, not just turned upside-down. His entire world had been ripped apart.

The troubles started with the filing of a complaint against the university. The parents of one of the students who had been on the ill-fated trip (the same spoiled, immature kid who had whined about being robbed, when his and everyone else's life was on the line) brought charges of negligence against the university for allowing their son to be put into a situation where he could have been killed. That their son and everyone else had signed releases specifically waiving any such claims, due to the potential for danger in the region, didn't matter to them. They held the university responsible, not only for educating their child, but for baby-sitting him, too.

The fear of being sued, and the bad publicity that would accompany it, put the school between a rock and a hard place. The trip hadn't been university-sanctioned—both Walt and the school had been clear about that in the prospectus. The onus was on Walt, not the university, so legally, they were blameless. But he was one of the most important members of their faculty, a figure of worldwide renown. And he had just lost his wife.

With some reluctance, the university hung tough. They stood behind Walt, and after a brief period of blustering and posturing, the family backed down. Their son hadn't suffered any real harm, after all, except to his fragile psyche. He wouldn't go on with a career in archaeology, but better to learn that was the wrong profession now than later on, after he'd spent years of his life and thousands of his parents' dollars chasing the wrong vocation.

Walt was teaching his fall semester courses while all this hullabaloo was going on, but his heart wasn't in it.

He could feel a vague undercurrent of hostility toward him from certain elements of the faculty, the conservative members who had always resented his high-profile flamboyance, celebrity, and independence from the rules which those who had less prominence had to follow. He was no longer the golden boy—there was a cloud over him now. It was almost as if what had happened down there was his fault, even his own wife's killing.

No one spoke to Walt about this directly, but he could feel it. There were fewer invitations to school functions, fewer dinner invitations. A man who had been at the center of university life, he was now being frozen out of the social vortex. Even some members of his own department were keeping their distance.

Those snubs hurt, but they were peripheral; the people who were turning their backs on him were cowards, second-raters showing their true colors after years of kissing his rear end. He didn't give a damn about them, they were beneath his concern.

The primal change in his life—the death of his partner—was what he couldn't transcend. Without Jocelyn as his rudder, he felt lost.

In November, Walt went to the dean of the college and requested that he be permitted to take the next semester off. He wasn't going to return to La Chimenea, which had been his intention—too many bad memories. He needed a change of scenery, to live someplace where he wouldn't see daily reminders of Jocelyn. He had decided to go to Los Angeles. He planned to collaborate with some members of the UCLA archaeological department he had worked with over the years.

His request was expeditiously approved. He would go on sabbatical (with full pay and benefits) for eight months, after the fall term exams were over. Then he'd come back to Madison the following autumn, reinvigorated and ready to go again.

Unfortunately, those plans didn't pan out. Walt couldn't hook up with his UCLA colleagues; there was no way they could fit him into their schedules, he hadn't given them enough lead time to prepare—even a scholar of his stature doesn't just waltz into a department, find an empty office, and get working. There are protocols that have to be adhered to.

Walt was disappointed at this turn of events, but he understood the situation. Undeterred by this setback, and unwilling to return to the place that held too many bad memories, he decided to stay out west. He rented a bungalow in Santa Monica and began working on a book about his life's work. His publishers, of course, were interested. Once he submitted an outline, they'd pay him a nice advance.

He kept his sons apprised of what he was doing, and seemed to be fine with it. When they talked to him on the phone, he sounded upbeat. Somewhat distant, but getting along okay.

Then in March, two and a half months after he'd left Madison, Walt flew back and met with the president of the university. The meeting was a tightly kept secret—only the two of them and the dean of the college were present.

A day later, Professor Walter Gaines, chairman of the Archaeology Department at the University of Wisconsin, holder of the endowed Allenby Chair of Archaeology, one of the most celebrated archaeologists in the world, formally submitted his resignation from the university at which he had taught for over thirty years. He was retiring, with full benefits.

A stipulation of the agreement between the two parties

was that neither side would announce Walt's leaving until the end of the spring semester. It was to everyone's advantage to keep this under wraps. Walt didn't want the hassle of having to explain why he was leaving, and the university didn't want the bad publicity they were certain would come up—it would be assumed they had forced Walt's resignation, because of the fallout from the deadly field trip. By the time the announcement was made, in May, the story would be old news.

The university wished him well, and that quickly, his career was over.

Once he severed that connection, Walt moved fast. He cleaned his office out that same night, discreetly put his house up for sale in a private listing, and in a week he'd sold it. He was packed and gone less than a week after that; what he didn't ship west, he sold or put in storage. It was as if he had never lived in Madison, never taught there, never raised a family there.

No one knew he had done any of this, including his sons.

At the end of May, a few days before the moratorium keeping Walt's retirement a secret was over, Walt sent each of the boys an identical letter.

> Dear Clancy (Will, Tom),
>
> What you are about to read may initially come as a surprise, but once you think about it, you'll understand the logic of what I've done, and why.
>
> I've resigned from the university. It happened a couple of months ago, but I kept quiet about it for political reasons, which I'm sure you can appreciate, having grown up in an academic family. Now I can tell you.
>
> Thirty-two years is a good run for anyone, and I've

come to the end of mine with them. I would be less than candid if I sloughed off the unpleasantness surrounding this decision—you know what I'm talking about, the petty little minds and their two-bit jealousies and suspicions. There was a cloud hanging over my head, and no matter what I did, I couldn't shake it. This despite the fact that I am the only one in that sad affair to have suffered a loss. Academic life can be wonderful, but it can also be mean and myopic and even vindictive. There are other reasons as well, mostly having to do with knowing when it's time to say good-bye, which is to do it while you're still at the top of your game. So I'm out of there, and I'm better off for it.

I have sold the house in Wisconsin. Since I won't be living there, and none of you do, there was no reason to keep it. It was our house, your mother's and mine (and yours, until you grew up and moved out), and without her, it felt wrong to stay. I am in the process of buying a house not far from UCLA, where some of my friends teach. I should be settled in within the month. I'm using the profits from the old house as a down payment (don't worry, I haven't raided your inheritances). I'll send you my new address and phone number, once I have them. In the meantime, you can reach me through my cell phone or via e-mail.

For now I'm doing a bit of writing and consulting and sorting things out, my life primarily. At some point I may go back to teaching—I have offers from many universities in the area. Other than that, I'm taking it one day at a time.

The only thing I'm requesting of you is that you not visit me here, not yet. I need more time to decompress. Your mother's death was a mighty blow, and I'm still recovering as I'm sure you are.

I'll keep in close touch.

Love, Dad

The boys were surprised and upset upon getting this letter. They knew their dad was going through a miserable period, with their mother's death and the behind-the-back stabs at him stemming from the Central American fiasco; but to leave the university, which had been his home, his anchor, for over thirty years, was inconceivable to them. That he'd made this decision unilaterally, without even having a conversation with them about it, only worsened how they felt about it.

But although Walt had promised to keep in close touch with his sons, he didn't. More than a month passed before he sent out his new address and phone number, and only then because Clancy forced them out of him. He didn't call, he didn't write, he answered their phone calls reluctantly. By the time July came around he wasn't picking up the phone at all. His e-mails, the few he sent, were short and curt.

He still needed more time—that's what he told them. He'd let them know when that was. Not yet.

The boys were frustrated and hurt, but they respected their father's wishes. Today, though, his not being with them was going to be particularly distressing.

Madison

♦ ♦ ♦

The meeting at the gravesite was scheduled for one o'clock, so by nine-thirty in the morning Clancy and Callie were on the road. They drove west a dozen miles, then picked up I-90, a straight shot all the way to Madison. Not the scenic route, but they weren't in a feel-good frame of mind today. This was to be a day of remembrance, and family. A family without parents: mother dead, father missing.

Tom and Will were already at the cemetery by the time Clancy and Callie arrived. Both were dressed casually, in khakis and short-sleeved shirts. It was hot out, and unlike the situation at Jocelyn's funeral the year before, with its hordes of guests, there was no one to dress up for and impress with the seriousness of their grieving. It was just going to be the four of them and the little marker commemorating their mother. Grace Esposito, the minister who had officiated at Jocelyn's funeral, had offered to come and conduct a short service, but they had declined. They didn't want that; being with Jocelyn's spirit was all that mattered.

Tom and Will saw Clancy and Callie pull up and park, and waved. Callie took Clancy's hand as they walked toward his brothers. Clancy was carrying a bouquet of flowers to lay on her marker.

Two peas in a pod and a ringer—a radish or a chili pepper, something fiery, Callie thought, not for the first time, as she looked from her husband to his siblings. No one would ever mistake Clancy and Will as anything but brothers. They were both tall, blond, with light eyes—Clancy's blue, Will's green. Good-looking, rangy men. Like their father. They were built like swimmers or wide receivers.

Tom was the redheaded stepchild, in a manner of speaking. He was shorter—five-ten to Clancy's six-three and Will's six-one, wiry like a long-distance runner, and he was dark. Dark brown hair, brown eyes. Neither of their parents were dark, although Jocelyn had that gene from her father, who Tom vaguely resembled. The difference between Tom and the other two extended to personality, as well. Where Clancy and Will were generally easygoing, taking life on its own terms and making the best of it, Tom was restless and impatient. He was always the first to come to a decision, which often meant a rush to judgment. His rashness had gotten him into trouble in life, and he knew it, but sometimes he couldn't help himself—it was like an inner demon would take him over. But he was generous of spirit, and loving. They all were. They had gotten that gene from their mother, too.

The brothers and Callie hugged. A big group hug.

Will and Tom were crazy about their sister-in-law. Clancy had hit a home run, hooking up with her. Neither of them had found a soul mate; if they could come up with a woman like Callie they'd consider themselves damned fortunate. Callie, likewise, knew she was lucky she had married into this family. They were good people. Jocelyn had been a second mother to her, which was one of the reasons she was so upset over Walt's recent conduct. It was as if her own father had gone off the deep end.

She knelt down in front of the stone. As Jocelyn had been cremated, her actual gravesite was small, only a couple of feet square. She read the inscription: *Jocelyn Murphy Gaines. 1951–2001. Beloved wife, special mother, wonderful friend.*

"We miss you, Jocelyn," Callie whispered in a choked voice. She placed her hands on the stone, as if in benediction.

"Yes, mom," Clancy said, standing over her. "We all miss you."

Will knelt next to Callie. Putting a hand on his mother's stone, next to Callie's, he said, "Mom, wherever you are, we're thinking of you." He paused. "Dad couldn't be here today, but he misses you, too."

Tom, watching this, turned away for a moment. Then he looked at the stone. "We *think* he misses you, mom." There was anger in his voice. "But we don't know for sure, because—"

Clancy put a hand on his brother's shoulder. "Back off, man. He misses her. You know damn well he does."

"I want to think that," Tom answered. "But he isn't here, and I'm not clairvoyant."

Callie pushed herself up to her feet, dusted off her hands. "Your father's in pain," she said to Tom. "So let's none of us judge him, okay? We're here to celebrate her life, not put down the man she loved."

Tom nodded. "You're right." He smiled, hunkered down. "Mom," he called, putting his mouth next to the stone. "Can you hear me, wherever you are? We're here, mom, and we love you, and we're okay." He started crying. "We're okay, but we miss the hell out of you."

Clancy squatted down on his haunches. He put the flowers on the stone. "We do miss you," he said. He looked at the others. "Anyone want to say anything more?"

"We love you, mom," Will said.

"Yeah, mom," Tom added. "We're always thinking of you."

They stood for a moment, in silence. Will squinted as he looked up, shielding his face against the bright sun. "It's boiling out here," he said. "Let's go cool down and decompress."

The boys had spent many happy occasions at Ludwig's Beer Garden near the campus when they were young and their parents would take them there for Sunday dinner, shared with other faculty members and students at one of the big, long tables in the center of the room. Now they and Callie sat in a booth in the back, drinking tall steins of dark German beer. They were also yeomanly working their way through a mountain of French fries and a large platter of spicy Buffalo chicken wings.

"Am I the only one who thinks that dad is being too weird about this?" Tom wiped his greasy fingers on a paper napkin.

"Dad's dad," Will said, dipping a handful of fries in the ketchup puddle in the middle of the plate. "He's like Frank Sinatra. He does it his way."

"What the hell's that supposed to mean?" Tom asked. The beer was freeing up feelings he'd been holding in for months. "Cutting his family out of his life isn't his way. Dad's far from perfect, we all know that, but family's always been the most important thing in the world to him. Mom's dead, but we aren't." He drank some beer, wiped his mouth with the back of his hand. "Hey, I'm sorry, but I'm pissed at him."

"So are we all," Clancy said in agreement.

"It's been a year," Tom went on. "We don't have a clue about what he's doing out there. For all we know, he's sitting in a room staring at the four walls all day."

"I doubt that," Will said. "He's probably working like crazy on a bunch of projects. He's not a brooder, he's the most active person any of us know."

"He *was*," Tom corrected him. "We don't know what he is now. Because we never see him or hear from him." He turned to Clancy, the oldest. "Don't you think this estrangement has gone on way too long?"

As Tom had always been the son who most easily got on the wrong side of their father, Clancy was the most easygoing about Walt's personality. From birth he'd had a special grace attached to him by virtue of being the oldest son, the fulfillment of his father's dreams of passing on his special torch.

He nodded. "I agree with you," he said, keeping his emotions tamped, "and I'm worried about him, too. But short of shanghaiing him and chaining him to a post outside one of our houses, I don't know what we can do about it. The man has a right to be left alone, whether we like it or not."

"Well, that may be true, but I share how you feel about him, too," Will joined in. As the youngest son, Will was essentially above the fray. He hadn't been under the microscope like his older brothers, so his feelings about his father were less intense, both positively and negatively. He was more objective and clinical. "He could be going through clinical depression. We're his sons—we have an obligation to check up and see that he's all right, don't we?"

"Yes, you do," came the answer to his question.

They all turned to Callie, who had been listening silently.

"There's something going on with him that's unhealthy, or at least that we all think is unhealthy, yes?" she asked them.

"For sure," Tom said.

"None of us are psychologists," Callie continued, "but it feels to me like he's carrying a ton of guilt. He blames himself for your mother's death. You do know that, don't you?"

"But he wasn't," Will said, doggedly. "She was the one who wanted to press on, not him."

"Factually, that's true," she agreed. "But this is about feelings, not facts. It doesn't matter whether it was her that wanted to keep on going. He was the leader, the weight fell on him. The impact of it has knocked him to his knees, and he hasn't figured out how to get up."

"You're right, honey," Clancy said. "But that doesn't matter. He's the one who has to do it, not us."

"But what if he really is clinically depressed," Will argued. "He'd need help from the outside, and who else is there to do it for him except us?"

Clancy leaned back. "It is a problem, for sure," he said slowly. "But I don't have an answer. Do either of you?"

Will and Tom shook their heads no.

"Do you?" he asked, turning to his wife.

"Maybe. I've been thinking about it."

"What?"

"That bodywork symposium you're going to in a couple of weeks, in San Diego. You could drive up to L.A. and see him afterward. I'm sure he'd love to see you."

"I'm not at all sure," Clancy answered dubiously.

"It's worth a try, isn't it?" Will said, picking up on Callie's idea. "If you're going to be out there anyway. What's he going to do, refuse to answer the door?"

Clancy sat up straight. "You mean surprise him?" he exclaimed.

"Damn straight," Tom said. "Give him a chance to say no, he's going to take it. That's what he's been doing for a year now."

"I think it's a good idea for me to try to see dad, I agree with you about that. But to barge in on him unannounced . . ." Clancy shook his head. "That could piss him off really badly. We don't want to push him further away than he already is."

"Dad's already as far away from us as he can get, short of leaving the country," Tom said, his face flushed from annoyance and drink. "I agree with Will. Surprising him is the right way to go about it. The only way," he added pessimistically.

"I'll think about it," Clancy said. "The best way to do it."

"However you do it, you have to see him," Tom pressed. "This is nuts, what's going on."

Clancy felt cornered. Being confronted like this was uncomfortable. He agreed with them that something had to be done, but he didn't want to be the one who had to do it.

"Okay," he agreed. "But I'm not going to blindside him. I'll let him know in advance I'm going to be out there, and that I'm coming to see him."

"And that you're not taking no for an answer," Will said.

"Yes, okay, already. I hear you," Clancy said defensively. "I won't let dad turn me away. I'll call him before I leave Chicago."

Los Angeles

♦ ♦ ♦

Fudging his promise to his brothers, Clancy chickened out about phoning his father before he left for the coast. He waited until he was in San Diego, two days before his conference ended, to call the new number Walt had recently sent them.

To his surprise, Walt answered the telephone. Clancy had been prepared to leave a message. Now that he actually had his father on the line, he was flustered.

"Dad. It's me. Clancy."

"Hey, big fella," Walt answered heartily. He seemed jovial, in better spirits than Clancy had heard in his voice for months. "How're you doing? You caught me in the nick of time. I was heading out the door to go to dinner."

"Fine, dad, I'm doing fine. How's your new house?"

"It's okay," Walt answered casually. "Livable."

"Listen, dad . . ." Clancy began. He wanted to announce his visit before they got sidetracked in trivia.

Walt was too quick for him. "And Callie. Healthy and happy, I hope."

"She's fine, dad. She sends her love."

"And mine back. Listen, Clancy," Walt continued. "About last month. The get-together at your mother's grave, you and your brothers. I apologize for not being with you. At the time, I didn't think I'd be able to get through it, but later, when I thought more deeply about it, I realized I should have been there. To see all of you, and pay my respects." There was another short silence. "Not a day goes by that I don't think of her. I can't tell you how much I still miss her."

This wasn't going to be so difficult, after all. Walt was opening the door, without prompting or pressure. "We miss you, too. Tom, Will, me, Callie. We all do, dad."

"I know, son. It's been too long. So—what gives?"

"I'm in San Diego."

"San Diego?" Walt repeated. He sounded off-balance.

"I had a conference down here."

A hesitation. Then: "Oh? For how long?"

"Four days."

"I see."

"I want to come up and see you, dad." No, wrong. Not *want*. Don't give him an out. "I'm *going* to drive up."

"When?"

"The conference is over the morning after tomorrow, so I'd drive up after that. I'd be in L.A. by mid-afternoon."

"The day after tomorrow?" Walt asked.

"Right."

"I can't do that."

This conversation was turning in the wrong direction. Clancy had to straighten it out. "Dad. I haven't seen you in months. None of us have. I'm coming up. It's no big deal." Despite himself, almost plaintively: "Don't you want to see me, dad?"

"Of course I do, of course I do," Walt almost yelled.

"Of course I want to see you, I want to see all of you. But I can't, not the day after tomorrow."

"Why not?"

"'Cause I won't be here."

Clancy felt like he'd been keelhauled. "Where will you be?"

"Seattle. I'm flying up to meet with some people from the University of Washington. They have a project they want to involve me in. We won't be here."

"We?" Clancy asked, dumbly.

"Did I say *we*? Figure of speech. Sometimes . . . your mother . . ." Walt left whatever else he was going to say unsaid.

Clancy knew what his father had been unable to articulate. That Jocelyn was no longer alive was at times, for all of them, still unfathomable.

"Damn," Walt exclaimed. He sounded genuinely unhappy about the circumstances. "Why didn't you call me earlier, if you knew you were coming out to the coast? I could have changed the meeting. It's too late to do that now, people are flying in from all over the country."

Sonofabitch! Clancy thought. "I'll bag tomorrow's stuff," he told Walt. "It's not that big a deal, I've gotten what I needed out of this. I can be in L.A. by noon."

"Noon," Walt parroted.

"It's what, two hours from here to there? I'll rent a car, drive up, we can hang out until you have to leave. I'll change my ticket so I fly home out of the Los Angeles airport instead of the one down here."

"Well . . ." Another pause. "The thing is, I won't be here then."

"But you said . . ."

"I'm leaving tomorrow. My plane's at seven in the morning."

Clancy, sitting on his bed in his hotel room, sagged. He felt like kicking himself. "I should have let you know earlier, dad. That I was coming out here. Jesus, I feel like an ass."

"Don't be ridiculous. You didn't know."

Screw it. He was only two hours away. "I'll come up now."

"What do you mean?"

"I'll drive up now. They have a Hertz counter here at the hotel. I can jump in a car and be there by"—he looked at the clock on the nightstand—"ten-thirty."

"No, that wouldn't work," Walt answered with alacrity. "I've got this dinner meeting I'm going to now, I'm already late, I don't know how long it's going to go, then I have to pack when I come home and get a few hours of sleep, because I've got to be up at four to catch that seven o'clock plane. It won't work, son. I'm sorry."

Clancy could hear the avoidance in his father's voice. "Dad. We have to see you. All of us do." He was begging. He didn't care. "This is unhealthy, the way it's been."

"I know, Clancy. It's been way too long. I'm going to change things."

"When?"

"Soon. Very soon. I promise."

Clancy had blown it. He had to salvage something. "Let's make a plan. Now."

"E-mail me, we'll set it up. I've got to run. Give my love to everyone."

The phone went dead in Clancy's hand. He resisted the temptation to hurl the receiver against the wall.

"He's screwing us over again."

"You don't know that for sure."

"C'mon, Clancy, this is how it's been all year long," Tom complained. "There's always some excuse."

After his father hung up on him, Clancy had called his brothers. It was late—they lived two time zones ahead of the West Coast, but they would want to know how he'd botched meeting up with their father.

Will had been out; Clancy left a message on his service. Will was often out, until all hours of the night. He was a young colt. He liked the ladies, and they liked him. He had been semiseriously involved with a woman for a year while in college, but it didn't stick. He wasn't ready to settle down yet. Basically, Will liked everybody—it came with being the youngest, he'd learned from the cradle how to make friends.

Will had received his MBA at the University of Minnesota the year before last and was making serious money working in the bond department at Merrill Lynch in Minneapolis, a way station to the home office in New York, where he'd be transferred in a couple of years if he kept on doing as well as he was now. Clancy had no doubt that his younger brother would make it. He was good with money. Once Clancy got his head above water and had some disposable income, he'd give it to Will to invest for him.

Tom, unlike his social-animal kid brother, was at home, in Ann Arbor. Clancy could picture him, sitting in his small apartment near the University of Michigan campus, watching a game on television, a beer in his hand and a scowl on his face. Tom was the most volatile of the brothers, the quickest to anger. Although he didn't like to hear it, particularly from his family, he was also considered the brightest. They were all smart—they came from smart stock—but Tom was a true brain.

He was also the least focused. His stated ambition was to solve a key mystery of the universe, earning him worldwide acclaim and the Nobel Prize, but he wasn't anywhere near doing that, because he was still in school. He had been dicking around on his Ph.D. dissertation on mathematics for three years now, and he wasn't close to completing it. Sometimes he despaired that he ever would; that after years of being a perennial graduate student the university would weary of his dallying, he'd be kicked out of his program, and would have to get a humdrum job in the real world. He envied his brothers, both of whom had found their vocations and gone for them with purpose.

Like Will, Tom wasn't involved with anyone, either, but for a different reason: he was too demanding. He expected perfection, and was disappointed when whatever particular woman he'd gone for turned out to be mortal, with flaws. His mother had been the model he'd held other women up to, and none had ever approached that standard. His social life, consequently, was considerably more limited than his brothers'. One of the reasons he was taking their father's alienation from them the most personally.

"It's pretty damned coincidental that on the very day you want to go see dad, he has to go out of town," Tom said. "That he's in such a hurry he has to leave as soon as he gets off the phone with you."

"I guess," Clancy admitted. He knew that what Tom was saying was true; he'd been trying to suppress that same feeling, to give their father the benefit of the doubt. But there was doubt.

"He probably isn't going anywhere. He flat-out doesn't want to see any of us. It's freaky. It's like he had a personality transplant after mom died."

Clancy felt a heaviness in his soul—this was a lot of weight to carry, for all of them. "He did say he wished he'd come out to the gravesite with us for the commemoration, and that he wanted to get together soon."

"When pigs fly," Tom snorted.

"I'm going to take him at his word, one more time," Clancy said. He didn't want to defend his father this go-around; he was as put off by Walt's erratic behavior as Tom was. But squabbling about it among themselves wasn't the answer. That just got all of them even more upset.

"Well," Tom said grudgingly, "you gave it a shot."

"I should have called him earlier."

"Or gone up there and sabotaged him. That's what I would've done."

"And driven him away even more? No thanks. Sooner or later, he has to become involved with us again," Clancy argued. "He can't stay apart from his family for the rest of his life."

"I sure hope you're right," his brother said gloomily. "But the way he's been acting, it feels like that's exactly what he wants to do."

Callie was more sympathetic about Clancy's striking out than his brother had been. "He isn't ready to come back to the fold yet. When he is, he'll let us know. Don't beat yourself up over this," she counseled her husband gently. "Whatever's making him act this way will change. It's going to take time. You can't force time, Clancy. You work with injured athletes, you know that."

"But it's so damned frustrating."

"Leave it alone."

"Since I have no choice, I have to. I wanted to see him, Callie," Clancy lamented. "I need to know that he's okay. He's never lived alone, he never had to deal with the day-to-day, routine stuff. Grocery shopping, laundry, bills. Mom always handled all that for him. He could be living like a bag lady, for all we know," he said, forcing a laugh.

"I sincerely doubt that," she replied. "Your dad can take care of himself. He's a capable man. Give him credit."

"I guess." Clancy didn't sound convinced. "He always had mom at his side. Being on his own is foreign to his nature. He could never stand a void."

"He'll be fine," she said again. Clancy's fretting was becoming exasperating. "You're the one I'm worried about. Let's not talk about this anymore now, okay? It's making you get agitated. I'll pick you up at the airport the day after tomorrow, we'll go home and talk about it. Without stress."

"Yeah, that'll be good. Incidentally, I'm flying home out of L.A. instead of San Diego."

There was a brief pause. "Why are you going to be in Los Angeles?" she asked.

"One of the guys I met here at the conference has a clinic in L.A. that's similar to mine but with newer equipment, stuff I haven't seen yet. I'm going up there with him to check it out. I'm out here already, so why not?"

"If you want to," she said, sounding dubious. "This has nothing to do with Walt, does it?"

"How could it?" he answered quickly. "He won't be there."

"Okay, then," she said. "I miss you, honey. I want you home."

"I miss you, too."

Clancy hadn't been serious when he had told Callie he was worried his father could be living like a bum; that was nonsense, and they both knew it. But voicing the possibility of deterioration, out loud, had made real the true concern they had about Walt—that he wasn't in control of his life. Not his outward life; Clancy knew his father wouldn't fall apart physically, he had too much vanity about how he looked. But it was obvious to all of them that Walt's emotional life, the life of his mind and heart, was increasingly becoming a cause for alarm. A passionate professor doesn't quit his prized, lifelong post without fighting back, and a loving father doesn't turn away from his children unless there are deeply felt issues left unresolved. Losing the one absolute in your life, as had happened to him with Jocelyn's sudden and violent death, could have thrown everything out of whack for Walt, who was a colossus, not only in the world, but more important, in his own mind. A man who couldn't be bothered with life's petty aggravations, who pretty much didn't even know they existed because of how his wife had sheltered him from them, could be thrown for a loop when he unavoidably had to confront them, now that he was alone.

Clancy couldn't literally be with his father now, since Walt was conveniently not going to be in L.A. (a spur-of-the-moment invention, Clancy thought, but motive was irrelevant; Walt wasn't going to be there), but at least he could see the physical circumstances of his father's current situation. That would be better than nothing. He was only a hundred miles away. Besides being concerned, he was curious. They had lived in the same house in Madison since Clancy was six years old. It had been the family's shelter from the storms of life, a big, rambling place, full of happy memories. Walt had often vowed, half-jokingly, that they'd never get him out of there until he was dead.

Now, instead, his mother was dead and a large part of

his father, Clancy knew, was with her. So the house had to go. Clancy could understand that. It was better not to live among those memories if the person you had created them with wasn't there to share them.

What would this new house be like, Clancy thought? Similar to the old one, or a deliberate departure?

It would be dumb not to take advantage of the proximity to find out.

Changing his schedule cost Clancy an additional seventy-five dollars. He paid with his mileage-plus Visa card and put the Dodge Neon Hertz rental car on the same card. At least he'd get some frequent-flyer miles out of the transaction. The counter attendant gave him directions to Walt's address in Los Angeles.

He checked out of the hotel at nine-thirty in the morning; there was no reason to rush. He'd arrive at his father's new house around noon, satisfy his curiosity, be at the L.A. airport in plenty of time for his evening flight home. Throwing his duffel onto the backseat of the little rental car, he hit the road.

The journey to Los Angeles was uneventful and boring. The I-5 took him up into Orange County, where it melded into the I-405. An ugly drive. Mile after mile of billboards, chain hotels, high-rise office buildings, each one a weak carbon copy of the other, their unifying feature being floor-to-ceiling windows tinted dark against the sun, dozens of floors of them. Anonymous, benignly foreboding. As he entered Los Angeles County he passed by massive oil refineries that were lit up even in the brightness of day, their natural gas waste fires flickering against the cataract sky.

Following the instructions on his map, he got off the

freeway at Sunset Boulevard and drove east for a brief spell, then took a right on Beverly Glen, heading south. To his left, a short distance away, he could see the red-brick towers of the UCLA campus.

He reached Walt's street. It was brisk inside the car from the air-conditioning, but he felt clammy. Nerves. His dad wouldn't be home, but he was jittery anyway. He was intruding into a situation he had been firmly requested (ordered, to be precise) to keep his ass out of.

He'd take a quick look around. If there weren't any nosy neighbors lurking about he'd try to get a glimpse inside through a window. As he got closer, checking the house numbers against the address on the slip of paper in his hand, a slow burn started inside his gut, a reaction to his angst about intruding.

Screw this defensive-attitude feeling, he thought. There was no reason for him to be guilty about what he was doing. Walt was his father. He had every right to be here. He had to know that his father was okay.

Three quarters of the way down the block he saw his father's new house. It was one-story, Southwestern-style. Classic-looking, like pictures Clancy had seen of movie stars' homes: whitewashed walls, turquoise wood window frames, Mexican tile roof. It was set back about twenty yards from the street, fronted by a well-manicured lawn. A large fig tree threw shade onto part of the lawn and house. The yard was bordered with tastefully arranged desert succulents, small cactus, and iceplant. On the left, a driveway led from the street to a detached garage behind the house. The garage door was closed. The wooden blinds on the house windows facing the street were three-quarters drawn.

Clancy sat in his rental car, staring at the house from

across the street. Now that he was actually here, he didn't know what to do. Okay, so he'd seen the house.

Now what? It was a very nice house, nicer than he'd expected, but that's all it was—a house. What he wanted to see was his father, and his father didn't want to see him. Or his brothers. His father had hastily improvised a trip to take him a thousand miles out of town, to avoid seeing his son.

Nothing I could do about that, Clancy thought, looking at the house. If he doesn't want to see me, I can't force it.

He got out of his small, cramped car and leaned against the door, stretching his back and legs. There was no foot traffic on the block. The people who lived on this street were either inside minding their own business, or at work.

A silver BMW Z3 convertible, the top down, turned onto the street and headed in his direction. As it approached, Clancy ducked around to the opposite side of his rental car, using it as a shield. Whoever was driving the Beemer wouldn't know him, but he didn't want to be seen—an instinctive, gut reaction.

The Z3 turned into Walt's driveway, stopping when it was parallel to the front of the house. The driver, a woman wearing sunglasses and a Nike baseball hat over her light blond ponytail, got out. She was dressed in shorts and a tank top. The shades and hat obscured her face, but she looked good. Nice figure, stellar legs. Bare, tan, long. Opening the trunk of the little car, the woman took out a couple of shopping bags—Fred Segal and Gelson's, Clancy could read the logos from where he was watching—closed the trunk, walked along the stone pathway that led from the driveway to the front door, unlocked the door, and went inside. The door closed behind her.

What the hell?

Could he be at the wrong house? Or even on the wrong street?

He looked at the address he'd written down. No, he was in the right place. Right address, right street. That was his father's new house.

Who was this woman? She had her own house key, she was carrying groceries. Walt hadn't mentioned anything about a woman. But he had been tight-lipped about his new life in general.

His mother had been dead for a year now. Clancy knew one thing about his father—Walt wouldn't remain celibate. He was a robust, attractive man who had always liked women, and had been liked by them, too.

He didn't know how to handle this. He could go over, knock on the door, introduce himself. Assuming the woman was involved with his father, she would know who he was, certainly. But then what? Go inside, look around? Clancy didn't care what was in the house. Old furniture and pictures belonging to his parents? He knew that stuff, he'd lived with it all his life. Seeing their old furnishings in new, unfamiliar surroundings would make him feel melancholy, another sad reminder of the special woman who was no longer with them.

This had been a bad idea, coming up here. He should have respected his father's wish to rejoin the family on his terms, when he was ready. Not before, and not forced.

He turned away from the house and started to get into his car. A sleek new-looking black Mercedes sedan, gleaming in the midday sun, came in sight around the corner. As it drove closer Clancy pulled his door shut and scrunched down in his seat. The Mercedes turned into his father's driveway and parked next to the BMW.

Walt Gaines got out.

He looks good, was Clancy's first, from-the-gut reaction. *You're not breathing* was the thought that followed immediately after the first. He forced himself to take a deep breath: in through the nose, out through the mouth. He worked with athletes, he knew that deep, steady breathing was the best way to keep yourself from freaking out.

His father stood in the driveway for a moment, like a stag in the forest who is sniffing the air, checking for signs of danger. Clancy was frozen, crouched down in the too-small car seat. He knew that his father couldn't see him, hidden there in the protective cocoon of the rental car.

Stay where you are, he cautioned himself. Wait until he goes inside, then drive away, go to the airport, get on your plane, and go home.

He took another deep, cleansing breath. Then he opened the door and got out of the car.

It was like throwing a pebble into a cosmic stream—Walt sensed the ripple. He turned in Clancy's direction and looked at him, squinting against the sun in his eyes. For a moment, who he was seeing didn't register; then his mouth opened wide, an involuntary jaw drop.

The two men, father and son, stared at each other, as if taking the other's measure. Then Clancy walked across the street, into his father's driveway. He stopped fifteen feet away from Walt.

"Hey, dad," he said.

Walt peered hard at Clancy, as if not believing what he was seeing; or not wanting to. Then he nodded, a gesture of recognition, Clancy thought, rather than of invitation.

"What're you doing here?" Walt asked. His tone was not accusatory, exactly. The words were neither angry nor inquisitive. It was more a statement than a question.

Clancy took in his dad. Walt was dressed casually—shorts, a short-sleeved shirt, sandals. Like he always dressed in the summer. Except the shorts were Ralph Lauren, not Dockers, the old Hanes pocket T-shirt was now a Tommy Bahama silk, and the sandals were Italian leather.

The older man raised a hand over his eyes to shade them from the high, hot light. "Do I get an answer?"

"I could ask you the same question," Clancy answered.

Walt twitched. "I live here."

Clancy walked a step closer. "You were going to Seattle. Some last-minute conference or something." His father hadn't said "last-minute," but Clancy knew that it was. If there had been a conference at all.

Walt didn't bite at the implied accusation. "Oh, yeah, I forgot about that," he said casually, as if the question was a fly he was brushing off his leg. "One of the participants got sick at the last minute. They canceled it." He gave his son a wary smile. "So you. What's your excuse?" His smile widened, a joker's smile. The boys and Jocelyn had nicknamed this look Walt's *I'm the boss motherfucker in town* smile. It could be intimidating. It was now. "You spying on the old man?"

Clancy almost winced visibly. This was his father, he knew his son from the inside out.

"I had to come to L.A. anyway," he lied. "There's a clinic up here a friend runs. I wanted to check out his new equipment." It was important to tell Walt the same lie he'd told Callie. Someday, hopefully a better day, this might come up, in casual conversation. He needed to keep his lies straight. It was getting harder. "I had a few hours to kill before going to the airport, so I decided to drive by the old man's new digs, check 'em out. Wanted to make sure you weren't living in a double-wide," he said, forcing what he hoped sounded like an easy laugh.

Walt grinned. "Nope, no trailer park life for me. Not yet, anyway." He paused. "You don't have to sneak around," he said. He sounded hurt. "What's mine is yours, Clancy. You and the others. You've always known that. Haven't you?"

"Yes, dad. That's how it's always been."

Always *had* been.

They eyeballed each other for another moment. Then they came together, their arms around each other's bodies, bear-hugging tightly.

"Goddamnit!" Walt cried out, when they broke and looked at each other from close range. "I've missed you, son."

It was hard for Clancy to speak. "We've all missed you, dad."

"You have some time? Before you have to go?"

"I have as much time as you want to give me."

Except for a few artifacts his father had collected from his expeditions over the years, Clancy didn't recognize anything inside the new house. In their old place the furnishings had been a hodgepodge of couches and chests and armoires, the rooms overflowing with too many pieces, heavy wooden things given them by Jocelyn's parents, or items they'd bought piecemeal at department stores. Mix and match, or unmatch, as his mother used to joke. It was homey furniture, unpretentious. Theirs was the kind of house that had coffee tables overflowing with academic journals piled next to MAD comics cheek by jowl with books, books, more books. Half-made beds, pots and pans in the sink.

A decorator had furnished this house. That was obvious. Stickley furniture, beautiful dark wood, hand-rubbed, covered with rich leather. Native American rugs were scattered over the hardwood floors. The art was a mixture of California plein air realistic landscapes, some of Walt's Central American pieces, African masks, a few abstract sculptures. It was all first-rate.

Walt led his son on a quick tour. Living room, dining room, newly redone kitchen, big master bedroom and bath, nice study, the works. It was impressive. A house for people with taste and culture. And the money to spend making it so.

Clancy didn't see the woman he had spotted earlier. She was making herself scarce deliberately, he was sure.

The backyard was spacious. More lush grass, recently mowed and edge-trimmed. A fieldstone deck, furnished with Adirondack chairs and lounges and a wrought iron dining set, abutted the rear of the house. Deeper into the property there was a barbeque area with a built-in range, a lap pool with an accompanying Jacuzzi, and at the far reaches of the property, a good-sized greenhouse.

"Very impressive," Clancy said admiringly. "Who's the gardener?" he asked, pointing at the greenhouse. He grinned. "Have you finally developed a green thumb?"

Walt was notorious for never seeing a garden through a full crop. He had started half a dozen vegetable gardens over the years, but had always let them go fallow—he liked to plant, but then he lost interest. The zucchini and melons and tomato plants, so lovingly placed in the freshly turned soil, would turn to weeds.

"Not much," Walt answered. "That was already here.

Gives the place a Midwest touch, don't you think? Out here, you don't need it, the weather's good year 'round. One of the earlier owners raised orchids," he explained. "That's one of the few plants you need a hothouse for. Not my style, orchids."

They were bantering easily enough, but Clancy sensed an uneasiness coming from Walt, a reticence to open up about anything under the surface. That was understandable; they hadn't seen each other for almost a year, you don't jump-start deep feelings in an hour.

It was good to see his dad, nonetheless. Clancy hadn't realized how much he missed him, and how hurt he was about Walt's turning his back on them.

"Let's go inside," Walt said, throwing an arm around Clancy's shoulder. "I'll buy you a beer."

They sat in Walt's spacious study, drinking Mexican beer from the bottle. Walt's desk was snugged up against one wall; adjacent to that was a block of poster boards covered with pictures of La Chimenea and other sites Walt had worked on. Archaeological volumes overflowed the bookshelves. It was the only room in the house that had any feeling like old times, Clancy thought; except there was nothing of the family. No pictures of his mother, or him and his brothers. It was as if Walt was forging ahead into a future that had no relationship to his past.

Walt eyeballed Clancy over the top of his beer bottle. "You're pretty uptight about this," he commented.

"About what?"

"Me. What I've been up to." Walt tilted his bottle back and took a drink. "That's why you came up here. To scope out the mystery. Whatever happened to Walt Gaines."

"I didn't expect you to be here," Clancy said cautiously. "But of course I want to know what's going on with you, dad. It's like you're not there anymore. Not for us."

Walt shifted in his chair. "I kind of feel, in some ways, like I'm not there for me, either."

"What's that supposed to mean?" Clancy's tone of voice was harsher, more judgmental than he'd intended.

"Hey." Walt pointed a finger at Clancy. "Back off with the attitude. I'm your father. Don't forget that."

"Sorry," Clancy apologized. "I don't mean to be . . . it's been weird, dad. You've been avoiding us, and we don't know why. I know you're going through a lot of grief, with mom dying and the school screwing you over, but we're your family. We're the ones who you can count on to stick by you."

"I know that," Walt said. "That's not the problem for me."

"What is the problem?" Clancy pressed. "That is, if you're willing to talk to me about it."

He was uncomfortable about setting out into these uncharted waters. Walt had never confided in his children about things that bothered him, even after they had reached adulthood. He always had to be on top of everything—his self-image and need to be in control was too powerful for him to ever show any signs of weakness, especially emotional. But things were different now, Clancy felt. He had lost his wife and his career, the two most important pieces of his life.

Walt nodded, as if thinking about what Clancy had said. "The problem. Yeah. I'm not going to lie to you, say there isn't one. It's complicated. It's not one thing, it's a bunch of things."

"Mom."

"Of course. That the most."

"And the university. Leaving."

"That, too. Although I don't miss it nearly as much as I thought I would. I thought I needed it as a security blanket. I've found out that I don't. In some ways, that part of what's happened to mc is liberating."

"I'm glad to hear that," Clancy said.

"Not that I don't miss some of it. The perks. It's not as easy to do what I do without the institution being behind me. I still have the Smithsonian and the other grants, but it's harder. The money people get nervous without some official imprimatur to blame if the shit hits the fan, like it did." He paused. "I haven't been back to La Chimenea since . . ." He waved his hand in the air, as if brushing away a cobweb.

Clancy didn't know that—this was the first he'd heard of it. La Chimenea had been the focus of Walt's work for the past several years. It was going to be the crown jewel in his career.

"That's a bitch," he said. "What's going on down there? Who's running the show?"

"I don't know."

"When are you going down again?"

Walt looked away. "I don't know that, either." He turned back to Clancy. "I don't want to talk about that now. Later, okay?"

"Sure. Whatever you want, dad." He wanted to ask his father about the woman he'd seen entering the house, but he didn't think the time was right for that yet. "So what have you been doing? Besides buying a house," he said instead, trying to make a joke of it.

Walt shrugged. "I have plenty to do." He pointed at the computer on his desk. "I'm writing a big overview-style book on Maya culture, something I've wanted to do for years, but never had the time. A definitive book," he proclaimed. "Who better than me to write it, right?"

"Absolutely," Clancy agreed. He believed it, but he also knew his father wanted to hear it. "You're the man, dad."

"And I'm lecturing," Walt went on. "UCLA, USC, I've been up to Berkeley and Stanford as well. I'm dickering with UCLA on something longer-term, it would be a cherry position, full professorship pay and benefits and I wouldn't have to teach too much, mostly do my research and have a few graduate lectures a quarter. They have a strong department, but I'd bring a lot of prestige."

"That sounds great," Clancy said, making sure he sounded enthusiastic. "Would you begin this fall? They must be starting the fall quarter soon."

"Yes, they are, but no, I wouldn't start now. Next quarter, maybe. I have to decide whether it's what I want to do." He finished off his beer, tossed the empty into a nearby trash can. "I've been teaching my entire life, until the last few months. It's nice to not have to read a bunch of crappy papers and prepare for classes every week. So I'm pondering on it. I'll be associated with them, one way or the other," he said airily. "Exactly how is yet to be decided."

There was a light knock at the study door.

"Come on in," Walt called out.

The door opened. A woman took a step into the room. Clancy recognized her as the same woman he'd seen getting out of the BMW earlier. She had changed into a sundress and her hair was damp, as if she'd just showered and toweled it dry. Now that he could see her up close, he realized she was young—his age, maybe a few years older.

"I'm going to the market," she said to Walt, glancing over at Clancy. "Do you need anything?"

"No, I'm set," Walt answered. He extended his arm. "This is my oldest son, Clancy. Clancy, this is my friend, Emma Rawlings."

Clancy stood. "It's nice to meet you."

"Thank you," the woman said. She smiled.

This was disconcerting. Clancy glanced over at his father. Walt gave him a nod, as if to say, "I'll explain about her later."

"I'll be back soon," Emma said. "Are you staying for dinner?" she asked Clancy.

Before he could answer, Walt did it for him.

"Yes. My son is staying for dinner."

"Where are you?" Callie asked.

"At my dad's."

"Where?"

Clancy was on his cell phone. He had gone out into the backyard to have privacy; he didn't want Walt inadvertently overhearing him. His father was in his study, banging away on his computer—urgent mail he had to get out before the end of the day, so he claimed. Before Clancy went home he would answer all his questions: a promise from father to son.

"What are you doing there?" she asked. He could hear the concern in her voice. "Is he there?"

"Absolutely, he's here. I mean, he's not standing next to me. He's in his study, working, and I'm outside. But yeah, he's here."

"How is he?"

"He seems fine. Healthy." He paused. "Sane."

"That's good to hear." She took a moment. "How did

you connect with him? I thought he wasn't going to be there."

"It's complicated. I'll tell you later."

"When are you getting into Chicago? What plane are you on?"

"That's another thing. I'm staying over. I won't be home until tomorrow."

There was a moment's silence.

"You're staying over? There? With him?"

"Yes. He insisted, and of course, I wasn't going to say no, not after wanting to get together with him for all this time. We're going to have dinner together, and then we're going to have a good talk. His choice of words."

She whistled through her teeth. "What's going on out there, Clancy?"

"All kinds of interesting shit. I'll fill you in on everything when I see you."

"What kind of interesting shit?" she persisted. "You can't leave me hanging like this."

Clancy glanced toward the house. "I don't have time now." He didn't want his father catching him on the phone. "I'll give you one tidbit that'll blow your little mind. There's a new woman in his life. I think she's living with him."

He could hear her sharp intake of breath.

"She's young," he continued. "My age, a little older, maybe."

There was a silence on Callie's end. Then she asked, "How does this feel to you, a new woman in Walt's life? Who's so much younger."

"Very strange. Like an episode out of Alice in Wonderland."

"Well, don't go falling down any rabbit holes, okay?"

"I'll watch my step."

"And call me if you learn anything else important," she said, her voice rising in excitement. "This bothers me, Clancy. Not that he has a new girlfriend—that's good . . . I hope . . . but that we hadn't heard anything about her. I know he's been uncommunicative, but this is going pretty far in the secrets department. And her being that much younger than him kind of bothers me, too."

"It's bizarre all around, I agree. But that's what he's been doing, keeping his life secret from us. On the plus side, though, he seems to be in great shape. He's active, he's working, he appears to be coping better than we've been imagining."

"That is good," she conceded. "But this still sounds off-kilter to me."

"We shall see. I'll have a better feeling before I leave." He glanced back at the house again as he heard a car pulling into the driveway. "Somebody's coming. I'd better get off."

"Okay." She made a kissing sound over the line. "I love you. Be careful."

"Me, too. I will." He started to say good-bye; then he added, "Don't mention anything about this to my brothers, in case you speak to them before I get home. I don't want them calling while I'm here. It's going fine, but I'm walking on eggshells."

"Mum's the word. I'll see you tomorrow, honey. Give Walt my love."

Emma Rawlings carried the bags of groceries into the house, went into the kitchen, and began putting the food into the refrigerator.

"Need any help?"

"Oh!" She jumped, then turned. "I didn't hear you." She smiled at Clancy. "You snuck up on me."

"Didn't mean to. Sorry."

"Don't be silly. I wasn't expecting you, that's all."

He smiled back. "There's a double entendre there, I think."

She nodded. "Yes, that's true. And no, I don't need help with this. Is Walt in his office?"

"Uh huh."

"He's a workaholic," she said. "Has he always been?"

"Yes."

Clancy pondered whether or not he wanted to talk about his father with this woman, who was a stranger to him. She's here, he decided quickly. No getting around that.

"He always wanted to stay ahead of the competition," he told her. "He used to tell us the academic world is filled with piranhas who will tear you to shreds if you let down your guard. So he didn't."

"But they ate him alive anyway," she commented, in a soft, supportive voice.

Her frankness threw him. "He lost his balance," he said.

She looked at him as if making a calculation. "You don't know me," she said, voicing what he had been thinking. "We shouldn't be talking about your father this way. Until we get to know each other better, which I hope we will."

Now it was he who was off-balance. Who was this Emma Rawlings person, what was her story? She was very cool, very much in control of herself, particularly considering that he had barged in, unexpected and uninvited.

"Yes," he agreed. "Let's not discuss him."

She started putting the rest of the groceries away. Over her shoulder, she asked, "You aren't allergic to shellfish, I hope?"

"Nope, no food allergies. What're you making?"

"Cioppino. The same as bouillabaisse, except it's Italian instead of French. More San Francisco than Italy, the way I make it."

"Sounds great." Here was an opening. "Are you from San Francisco?"

"No. This is going to take a while," she added.

As is getting an answer from you, he thought. He was going to have to be more adroit in his prying. "In that case, I think I'll take a walk around the neighborhood."

She nodded in approval. "There's a park a couple of blocks down, with a pretty flower garden."

"I'll head there then."

"Do you want to take a beer with you?"

"Won't I get busted? I've read stories about the LAPD."

She laughed. "You don't have to worry, you have the right skin color. But if it'll make you feel less threatened, I'll put the bottle in a paper bag."

Clancy dropped his spoon in his bowl. He was stuffed. His platter was littered with empty shells from the fish stew—clams, oysters, mussels, crab, Pacific lobster.

"Awesome," he told Emma.

"Thank you, kind sir. The chef accepts the compliment." Emma mock-curtsied as she got up and started cleaning the table.

"Let me do that," Clancy offered, starting to get up.

She put her hands on his shoulders and pushed him back

down. "You're our guest. Guests eat, they don't bus dishes."

"She can cook, can't she," Walt praised Emma, patting her on the behind as she leaned over the table. She batted at his hand playfully.

"And then some," Clancy agreed. It was disconcerting, seeing his father being openly familiar with a woman other than his wife. Of course, Jocelyn was dead now, so Walt could carry on with anyone he wanted; still, this behavior was unsettling. He felt like a voyeur.

Wanting to redirect the focus, he picked up the bottle of wine they'd had with the meal and read from the label. "Brewer-Clifton Chardonnay, Sanford & Benedict vineyard. This is good."

"It's from Santa Barbara County," Walt informed him. "Great Burgundy grape region," he said, with the assurance of a connoisseur. "Emma and I have started going up there on the weekends. I'm putting a decent wine cellar together, under the house. I'll show you later."

A wine cellar? His father had always been a shot-and-a-beer Midwesterner, a self-styled regular guy when it came to "lifted-pinkie crap" (his scornful term) like being a wine snob. How many ways was his father changing? he thought.

"Do you want dessert?" Emma asked. "I have fresh raspberries. I could whip up some cream with a little Kahlúa or brandy," she offered.

"Thanks, but no." Clancy patted his stomach. "I'm full. Couldn't stop eating. It was too good."

"We'll get out of your hair," Walt told Emma, getting to his feet. "Come on," he said to Clancy. "We have some serious catching up to do."

* * *

They were in Walt's study again. This time, with cognacs in hand—Rémy Martin XO, which Clancy, a saloon owner, knew retailed for close to a hundred dollars a bottle. Not a cognac that a self-styled shot-and-a-beer kind of guy buys, he thought.

Clancy was comfortably settled in a deep-cushioned love seat that was draped with a worn Navajo rug. Walt sat across from him in a Herman Miller Eames lounge chair, his feet propped up on the matching ottoman. One lamp, a Tiffany (a real one; Clancy had checked it out earlier), burned on Walt's desk; otherwise, the room was unlit, giving the space a pleasant shadowy glow.

Clancy looked around the room more carefully than he had the first time they'd sat here, when he'd been flummoxed merely by being with his father. The Maya artifacts and pictures of the various digs Walt had supervised he remembered from the past, of course; they were, in large part, the physical evidence of his father's life, the work side of it. But there were other items on display that were new, that didn't jibe with what he knew about his father.

I don't know a lot of things about him, he thought as he sipped the cognac, which went down like liquid gold. It was a disconcerting thought—the dominant one he and the others had had for months: *Who is dad? We always thought we knew, but did we?*

"So you want to know what's been going on in my life."

"Damn straight I want to know," Clancy answered more testily than he wished, in response to what felt like a disingenuous question. "Doesn't that go without saying?"

"Of course it does. And I'm glad you care enough to

get pissed off at me for how I've been toward you and the others."

"You're our dad. Our only remaining parent. What else could we feel?"

Walt nodded. "Yes." He drank some cognac. "It's nice here, isn't it?"

"Yes, it is," Clancy agreed. "It's real nice." His father was taking his sweet time getting to it, and he didn't want to push any more than he already had. "Did you pick out the furnishings?" he asked, thinking of something to say that was neutral, nonthreatening. "Doesn't feel like your style, dad."

"You mean the organized chaos school of decorating?" Walt asked, his mouth widening into a big grin.

"More *disorganized,* but yeah. This is like . . . very neat. Nothing out of place."

"One person doesn't make much of a mess," Walt offered by way of explanation. "You're thinking of how things were with three active boys in the house. Back when."

Clancy nodded. His father was right—he had been recalling the family as an idyllic memory, a frozen group of moments from their past. Not a good way to think now. Dangerous. He needed to be here, in the less-comfortable present.

"What're those?" he asked, pointing to a shelf behind Walt's desk.

Walt swiveled around in his chair. "Kachina dolls. Hopi. They represent deified ancestral spirits. I suppose I should research them, to find out what each one means. They could have negative mojo that I ought to know about."

"Yeah, you don't want to bring bad mojo into your life," Clancy agreed.

As soon as the words had left his mouth he realized that what he'd said could be taken several ways, most of which were accusatory. "They're only dolls," he added, covering.

If his father felt stung by the unwitting remark, he didn't show it. "This is true. And since we aren't Hopi, we probably don't have to worry." He swirled the contents of his glass and took another sip, holding it in his mouth for a moment before swallowing, then leaned forward.

"We go through life blind," he stated. "Even those of us who are clever, not the ones who think they're clever, but those chosen few who everybody knows are truly brilliant, have blinders on. We don't know this, of course. *Especially* if we're smart, we think we're open to experience, to every new day's freshness."

Clancy sat up and put his brandy snifter down on the side table next to the couch. This was not a bunch of superficial junk his father was saying to appease him and avoid dealing with truthfulness. This was real. He needed to pay attention.

"I led a charmed life," Walt continued. "But I didn't know it, because there were plenty of things to bitch about—you know how cutthroat the university life can be. I'm not saying I was a complainer," he added quickly. "I was a positive person, most of the time. You know me—I'm a full-bore extrovert, rehashing old slights has never been high up on my list."

He paused for a moment to finish the dregs in his glass. Reaching for the Rémy, he poured himself another three fingers, held the bottle up. "Refill?"

Clancy shook his head. "I'm fine."

Walt put the bottle down. "Help yourself when you want to. There's more."

He keeps more than one bottle of hundred-dollar brandy in the house, Clancy thought. That's a rich man's indulgence.

"So here I was," Walt went on. "Living. I had a great career, I had—still have, thank God—three wonderful sons, and most importantly, I had your mother. My wife. She was the ideal woman for me, and I knew it, right from the start. You know, Clancy," he said, leaning forward to emphasize his point, "before I met your mom, I was doing okay. But after we took up, things changed. I grew—you know what I mean? As a man, as a conscious human being. Something about your mother's being my mate let me grow into a larger stature than I would have otherwise. I became the best I could be, and it was because of her. Because of her faith in me, and because of who *she* was. Her spirit."

He paused for a moment to wet his whistle. Clancy was sitting up straight. All his antennae were quivering. He had never heard his father speak this way, so deeply and movingly personal, especially about his mother and what she had meant to him.

"I became a star in my constellation because of your mother," Walt said. "She was the bedrock beneath my feet, and because of that, because I *knew* that, I could reach for the heights without fearing that if I fell I'd be shattered. Because she was always there to catch me."

He looked down into his glass for a moment, as if looking at something in it besides cognac. His wife, Clancy thought, some sense memory of her.

"The way we were, that strength of hers, was so ingrained in us that I took it for granted. She was always going to be there until the day we both died, which wasn't going to be for a long time. Decades. Two old geezers in their rocking chairs on the front porch, their grandchildren sleeping in their laps. Norman Rockwell stuff."

He stopped and drank.

"Except she died. And I got hit with a dose of reality that knocked me so sideways it almost blew me away."

Without realizing it, Clancy had picked up and finished the contents of his glass. Pushing up from the deep cushions, he reached over for the bottle and poured himself another shot.

"In that one awful moment," Walt continued, "everything changed, and I couldn't pretend that it hadn't. Which is why I'm not teaching at Wisconsin anymore, and why I'm living here instead of there, and why I've been acting like I've been."

He reached over and touched Clancy on the forearm with his fingertips; a delicate gesture. "I didn't want to abandon you and your brothers," Walt said. "But I had to go off and be alone." He shook his head, like a lion shaking off a swarm of mosquitoes. "No, that's not it, that's a shuck. I had to *not* be with you guys. Can you understand that? I had to figure out how to keep on going, and being around you and your brothers wouldn't have let me, because I would be constantly seeing her, in you." He paused. "Like I do now."

He took a deep breath. "I had to learn how to live a new life. I couldn't survive if I didn't. And I had to do it myself. Which is why I've been the way I have. Do you understand?" he asked, almost beseechingly.

Clancy could feel tears welling at the corners of his eyes. He blinked, fighting to hold them in. He didn't want to break down in front of his father. It had taken a lot of courage for Walt to open up like this. He had confided in Clancy both as a father to a son and as a man to another man, equals. Tears would bring a maudlin sentimentality to Walt's honest outpouring, diminishing it.

"Yes, dad." The tears stayed behind his eyeballs. "I do."

They didn't go down to the wine cellar. They stayed in the low-lit room, slowly polishing off the bottle of expensive cognac. Clancy thought he heard, a few times, rustling sounds in another part of the house. That would be Emma, he assumed. Was she living here? She seemed to be, but he wasn't sure, and he didn't want to ask Walt about that, not now. He wasn't sure of anything at this moment, not after that extraordinary cathartic release of emotion from his father. All he knew was that he felt a hell of a lot better about him than he had for a year. Better, and overwhelmingly relieved. Walt hadn't fallen off the face of the earth, as they had feared.

"Walt?"

Clancy turned with a start. He hadn't heard Emma enter the room. She moves like a cat, he thought. On silent feet.

"What is it?" Walt asked. He was slouched down low in his chair, his legs spread out on the ottoman.

"Can we talk for a minute?" She glanced at Clancy, gave him a quick smile. "I'm not disturbing you, I hope."

"Of course not." Walt smiled at Clancy as he shambled to his feet. "We're all caught up here."

Clancy watched her, watched her look at his father, watched Walt look back at her. There was an undeniable intimacy between them.

It took him a moment before he placed what was out of the ordinary about this woman, besides her obvious physical attractiveness. It was her scent, her female aroma. He hadn't noticed it earlier—all his senses had been channeled into his feelings about seeing and being with his father. But now, having gotten past that initial surge of emotion, he was more tuned in to the rest of his surroundings, particularly her.

She smelled feral, like an animal in heat. Even standing ten feet away, he could detect her essence drifting off her, permeating the room with erotic perfume. Emma Rawlings threw off an unmistakable smell of sex. It was subtle, but it was unmistakable.

"I'll be back in a minute," Walt said.

He and Emma left the room. Clancy heard them walking through the house, their heels clicking on the tile floor. He crossed behind Walt's desk and picked up one of the kachina dolls from the shelf where it was lined up with the others.

"What kind of mojo do you bring?" he asked the doll, turning it in his hands as he examined it. "Good, or bad?"

The doll didn't answer.

Clancy stood in the backyard, which was a good vantage point to see the driveway. Emma's car was gone, so he assumed she had left. He hadn't heard a car driving away, but maybe from inside you couldn't.

He knocked back a big swallow of the cognac he'd brought outside with him. He was uncomfortable about standing here with this glass of spirits in his hand; a full glass, he'd poured it almost to the rim. Part of the discomfort was that he didn't want to get more of a buzz on. There was something in the air that could bend him in the wrong direction if he wasn't vigilant. He didn't subscribe to the notion of vibes anymore, but there was a presence hovering over all this. Like a fine mist you can feel on your skin.

The other part of his uneasiness, the big part, had to do with Emma. He had a queasy feeling about her. About her and his dad. This was his father's house (and maybe hers, he didn't know), but she felt like an intruder to him. Not a legitimate feeling for him to have, he knew, but there it was, anyway.

Maybe she doesn't live with him, he thought. It would be a relief if she didn't. Of course Walt was a free agent, and what he did with his life was nobody's business but his own; nonetheless, Clancy had a strong proprietary feeling toward his father, and an even stronger one for his mother—how could he not? He and his brothers were the keepers of his mother's flame, and he wasn't ready to pass that torch on to another woman. He didn't expect his father to be in mourning forever—he didn't want him to be a life-widower, he wanted Walt to get out into the sunshine and find happiness again. But this relationship seemed to have ripened awfully fast. It was obvious, from the way Emma moved about the house and how she flitted around his dad, that they had been together for some time now; familiarity and ease like the two of them were openly showing takes time to grow. How much time, he thought? How long before his mother had been buried had his father taken up with this new woman?

He didn't want to think about stuff like this now. That would be real bad mojo. He and Walt were together again, father and son. For the moment, that was enough.

"One good thing about out here, we don't have to worry about getting eaten up by mosquitoes at night, like we did at home. One of the many blessings of the vaunted California life-style."

Clancy turned. His father was standing on the back

patio. How long has he been out here, Clancy thought, watching him? Shake it off, he scolded himself—that was his own stuff talking, his personal unease at being here. His father had come out to join him. There aren't always hidden agendas.

Walt waved; Clancy waved back and walked across the lawn, to where his father was waiting.

"I'm going to bed pretty soon," Walt told him. "You need anything?"

Clancy shook his head. "I'm fine."

"Emma laid out fresh towels for you in your bathroom. Toothpaste and whatever in the medicine cabinet. She put a pitcher of water on your bedside table before she left."

So she wasn't here. "That was nice of her."

"She's thoughtful that way."

Clancy hesitated—he hadn't wanted to get into this now, but his father had opened a door. It might not be open again while he was here.

"She doesn't live here?" he asked, trying to sound nonchalant.

Walt gave him a raised-eyebrow look. "Why would you think that?"

"No particular reason," Clancy answered. Damn it. He shouldn't have opened his mouth about this. "The shopping, the cooking. Fixing up my bedroom. Lady-of-the-house kind of stuff."

Walt shook his head. "She has her own place, close by. She does spend nights sometimes, but with you being here, she didn't feel right about staying over. She's old-fashioned that way."

Emma Rawlings didn't feel old-fashioned in any way to Clancy, but he wasn't about to say so. Instead, he said, "This is a lot of house for one person."

His father squinted at him, his eyes blinking against the light from the Chinese lantern that hung from a beam at the edge of the deck behind Clancy's head. "That's true," he said, "but once I saw it, I couldn't resist it. I was about to buy a condo in Venice on one of the canals down there, but then this came available, and I went for it."

Clancy gave a noncommittal nod/shrug. Where his father was living and the size of his house wasn't his business.

"The thing is," Walt went on, "I got such a good deal it would've been criminal of me *not* to buy it."

"Oh?" His father seemed to need to explain about the place, which was fine with him—he was curious, but he didn't want Walt to know that. This was his father's night for baring his soul. If he stayed patient, what he wanted to know would be revealed. Or so he hoped.

He was right, about the house, anyway. "It was Emma's doing," Walt said.

"Emma's?"

Walt nodded. "She found it for me. She knows her way around, real estate agents, bankers. She heard about it." With a sheepish smile, he added, "It was an inside deal, to be honest. Emma knows people in high places."

That Emma knew her way around didn't surprise Clancy; that his father told him so was a surprise. He would have thought his father wouldn't want to talk about his mother's replacement, given the choice.

"The bank owned it. The previous owner had died unexpectedly," Walt explained. "He'd bought it fifteen years ago, before prices skyrocketed. He was a gay man with no family, no heirs, so the title reverted to the bank. I got it cheap." He laughed. "Well, not cheap. Nothing in this area of L.A. is cheap. But considering how much it would have gone for if it had been put on the open market, I made out. Emma finagled it so the bank let me take over the existing loan. I had to make a down payment, of course, but it was within my price range."

He said this smugly, as if he had pulled the wool over someone's eyes. Is he trying to do that to me, too? Clancy wondered.

"I made out darn well on our old house," Walt continued. "We'd been living there since you were born, practically. It only cost us thirty-five grand back then. And I had my savings, plus my university pension. I retired on almost full pay—one of the perks of toiling in the university gulag for as long as I did. So . . ." He waved an arm expansively, taking in his new property. "Here I am."

"Well, you did good, dad."

"Thank you. After all the misery I've been through I think I deserved a few breaks, don't you?"

"For sure."

They went inside. Walt picked up the bottle of Rémy, held it to the light to see how much was left. "We did a number on this puppy, didn't we," he said with the grin of a kid who's pulled one over on his parents.

"It wasn't full when we started, was it?" Clancy couldn't believe the two of them had drunk almost the entire bottle.

"Almost." Walt snatched Clancy's glass out of his hand, poured some more cognac into it. Filling up his own glass emptied the bottle. "Hey, we're celebrating. You don't hold back when you're celebrating."

"That's what my steadies at the bar tell me," Clancy said.

Walt clinked his snifter against his son's. "To our lives, Clancy. To happiness."

* * *

Clancy came out of the guest bathroom after brushing his teeth, washing up, and pissing a mighty stream from the wine, cognac, and the other libations they had consumed. He was ready to hit the bed. He didn't know how much sleep he'd get—his mind was awhirl with the events of the day.

"You have everything you need?"

Walt was in his boxers, bare-chested. His glass of cognac dangled from his fingers. He's still a specimen, Clancy thought, looking at his father as Walt stood in the hallway. He'll rage against the dying of the light until the day he dies, and in the after-life, too, if there is one.

"I'm fine. Thanks, dad. It's been a great day."

"It has." Walt hesitated. "About Emma . . ."

He stopped. Clancy waited for his father to continue. He was going to let this come to him, rather than force anything.

"I'm sure you must have mixed feelings about her, doubts, whatever," Walt went on. "But I have to tell you, son—she's been a lifesaver for me."

"That's good, dad. I'm glad."

He was tired, emotionally as well as physically. He didn't want to talk anymore tonight. They could pick this conversation up in the morning, when his head would be clear.

"She's a bright woman. More importantly, she's a good woman."

"I . . ." What could he say to that? That he knew that? He didn't.

"She's almost finished her Ph.D.," Walt said, as if having an advanced degree made her a weightier person.

"That's good," Clancy said. He knew that was what his father wanted to hear.

"I ran into her at a get-together one of my friends in

the department was throwing. She knew who I was, of course, being involved in archaeology like she is. She'd even read some of my writing, which is more than I can say for most of my actual students over the years. We wound up leaving together and going for coffee, and it was instant rapport. I could talk to her. I hadn't talked to a woman like that since . . ." He trailed off.

He's snockered, Clancy realized. Not drunk, but his tongue is damn well lubricated. Maybe he needed that crutch, to open up the way he has.

"It was logical that we started seeing each other. I didn't know that many people, not any women. She'd been unhappy in a relationship she'd recently gotten out of, so we were both lonely. And then, over the course of a few months, we came to understand how much we cared for each other. It's not the perfect match—I had that, with your mother. Emma's much younger than me, for one thing. But somehow . . ." He trailed off.

"The heart knows what it knows," Clancy said. He felt a sudden twang of compassion for his father. Who was he to judge this man?

Walt smiled. "That's good. Who said that?"

"Woody Allen, I think."

"One of our great philosophers," Walt commented wryly. He brought his glass to his mouth again, but it was empty now; he let his arm drop. "Emma doesn't need me. She has plenty of guys sniffing around her like dogs—you can see she's an extremely attractive woman. And she has her own money, she's not a gold digger," he said, almost as if daring Clancy to argue the point.

"Of course not," Clancy said; but he couldn't help thinking, Methinks the gentleman doth protest too much.

"And she has a great eye. She did the decorating. You

know me, I'm not a style maven. But I like what she's done here, don't you?"

"It's a great-looking place, dad," Clancy agreed. He threw an arm over his father's shoulder. "I'm happy for you dad, all around. But I'm wiped. We'll talk more in the morning, okay?"

Walt blinked, as if he'd been in a dark room and the light had suddenly been turned on. "Sure. It's been a long day for both of us."

He started to go. At the doorway, he turned back to face his son. "Don't judge Emma by her looks, or her age, or how she's different from your mom. Your mom was irreplaceable. We all know that. But you can try to accept Emma for who she is, can't you?"

The words stuck in Clancy's throat. He nodded instead.

"Someday I hope you'll understand," Walt said, as he closed thc door behind him.

Sleep came hard, tossing and turning, throwing off covers. Sometime in the middle of the night Clancy thought he heard a car pull up outside, but then he fell back asleep and didn't remember.

The early-morning sun slanting through the wooden blinds woke Clancy up. For a moment he was confused, until he remembered where he was: in his father's house. His new house, not the one Clancy was used to, the one that held all the memories.

He looked at his watch, which he'd left on the bedside table. Six-forty-five. Early. He drank a glass of water from the pitcher that had been set out for him. Like the rest of the house, this room was nicely put together.

Egyptian cotton sheets and an old chenille bedspread covered a wooden-post queen-sized bed. The chest of drawers in the corner was stressed pine, the rug on the dark hardwood floor a fine sisal. And this was the guest room. The other rooms were even more nicely furnished.

There was money in this house. And taste that money can't buy. Walt Gaines had never had either, not on this level.

He showered, shaved, brushed his teeth, packed his small bag. His flight left at noon—he had time to kill before he left for the airport. More time to spend with his father. He drank another glass of water, trying to clear the cotton out of his mouth. It helped, but not completely.

Emma was already bustling about in the kitchen when he came in. She was dressed, showered, set up for her day. Clancy wasn't surprised that she was there—he would have been surprised if she hadn't been. He remembered, vaguely, hearing a car in the middle of the night. Was that her, returning after he had gone to bed? He didn't know, and anyway, what did it matter? She and his father were together. Get over it.

"Good morning," she sang out. "Sleep well?"

"Like a brick," he lied easily.

"Coffee?" she asked, smiling at him.

"Please."

She poured him a cup of coffee. "There's milk on the table. Help yourself."

The table in the breakfast nook was set with three places. Knives, forks, and spoons were laid out neatly on linen napkins, there was butter in a china butter dish, jam in a small bowl, cream and sugar in matching pewter servers. A large bowl of fresh peaches and nectarines resided in the middle of the table. Martha Stewart couldn't set a better table, Clancy thought bemusedly.

"Walt should show his face soon," Emma said. "He's an early riser." She smiled at him again. "I guess it runs in your family. I'm going to make waffles, but would you like anything else in the meantime? There's juice, bagels, cereal."

"This is fine. Thank you." He sat down and poured some milk into his cup, stirred it.

Something about this domestic tableau was annoying—it was too damn neat, almost antiseptic, a photo shoot out of Architectural Digest. Not Walt Gaines's style. His father was a very different man now from the one Clancy had known his entire life. How much has he changed? Clancy wondered. What other changes am I going to discover that I don't know about yet? And how many others won't I like?

Emma took off after breakfast. She and Clancy said their good-byes; she was glad he'd come to visit them, the first of many visits, she hoped, the usual palaver people say when they don't know each other well enough to say anything meaningful. He said the same things back to her.

After she left, Clancy filled Walt in on what was going on with him and his brothers. It all sounded good to Walt, he and Jocelyn had done their job—they'd taught the fledglings how to fly without crashing.

For his part, Walt expanded on what he was doing: research on his book, guest-lecturing at various colleges in the area, consulting with museums and foundations. He didn't miss Wisconsin at all.

"What's going on with La Chimenea?" Clancy asked, after his father had touched the other bases. It had been over a year since Walt had been there. "When are you going back down again?"

Walt's face clouded. "That's up in the air." He hesitated. "I can't handle being there."

That his father was reticent to return to the site was understandable, but it still came as a shock to Clancy. The development of La Chimenea was going to be his father's monument. Now he was thinking of abandoning it? Clancy understood that being there would be traumatic, because of the memory of his mother being killed. But it hadn't happened there, and time had passed.

"La Chimenea didn't kill mom."

Walt looked at him sharply.

"She loved it down there." Clancy could see that his father didn't want to get into this, but he felt he had to. Ghosts have to be buried, or they'll haunt you forever. "Mom would've wanted you to."

"You don't know that," Walt said darkly.

"I know that she loved that you loved your work," Clancy replied. "She wouldn't want you making this kind of sacrifice for her."

Right thing to say, but the wrong time. Clancy knew that before he said it, but he couldn't help himself. He didn't want to rile his dad up, especially now that they'd reestablished their relationship, but it had to be said.

"She's the one who sacrificed," Walt said. He was glowering. "She put my wishes and needs before hers, her entire life. And look what it got her."

"It got her you, and us, and a life she loved."

"It got her killed."

"It was an accident, dad." Damn it, why had he ever started up on this? He put up his hands in a defensive posture. "Let's not talk about it anymore, okay? It's not my place to tell you what to do or not to do. You'll do what's right for you, dad, I know you will."

Walt looked away for a moment. When he looked

back, he was forcing a smile. "I'm gonna try. Hey, we've had a good time, haven't we?"

"We've had a great time, dad."

Walt walked Clancy to his car. They hugged.

"It's going to be different between us from now on," Walt promised Clancy. "For all of us."

"That's super, dad. That's what we all want."

"Give my love to Callie. And your brothers." He grinned. It was the first honest smile Clancy had seen that harked back to the old Walt Gaines. "Tell them that from now on, when they call me, I'll answer the phone."

He saw Walt waving in the rearview mirror until he turned the corner and couldn't see him anymore. Man, was he glad he had come up here. Granted, Walt wasn't supposed to have been home, but maybe the reconciliation was destined to come about the way it did. It had happened, that was the important thing.

He drove a few blocks past houses that were similar in size and feel to his father's—this was a high-class neighborhood, for sure. Looking out the front windshield, he noticed a FOR SALE sign planted in a front lawn. The house was California Spanish in design, like his father's. Walt's house was slightly smaller, and this house was on a larger lot, but they were roughly similar.

I wonder what these places cost? he thought. If you paid the going price, which his father, luckily, hadn't had to do.

He pulled over to the curb and jotted down the address, and the name and phone number of the listing agent's office.

* * *

"I'd like to speak to Louise Bernstein, please."

Clancy stood at a pay phone in the United Airlines terminal. His plane would begin boarding in five minutes. He'd called Callie and told her it was, miraculously, on schedule. Since he had a few minutes to kill, he'd made this call.

"This is Louise Bernstein." The voice of the woman who came on the line was crisp, businesslike.

"I'm from out of town," Clancy told her over the phone. "I'm considering relocating my business out here, and I saw a house you represent in a neighborhood I've been touted on." He read off the address.

"Well, you picked one of the best areas in Los Angeles, Mr. . . ."

A name. He glanced at the boarding pass in his hand.

"O'Hare."

"Mr. O'Hare. What business are you in, if I may ask."

"Fitness centers." Not much of a stretch.

"Oh, that's good." He could hear her voice brightening—she was talking to a man with money, not some waste-my-time looky-loo. "That's a great business to be in, especially out here. I belong to two clubs myself."

"I'm sure you're fit, then," he bantered.

"I try. It's a never-ending battle." She paused a moment—he imagined she was picking up pen and paper. "Would you like to see the house?" she asked. "I could arrange a tour, although not until tomorrow."

"I'm returning to Chicago today. But I'll be back in a couple of weeks. We could do it then."

"I could probably get you in today," she replied quickly. "A house of that quality in that neighborhood isn't going to be on the market for long. I've only just listed it. I'd hate for you to miss out without having a chance to see it."

"Umm . . ." He waited a moment, as if pondering the thought. "I have people waiting for me on the other end, that's the problem. But maybe I could rearrange my schedule. What's the asking price?"

He listened for a moment; then he almost dropped the phone, along with his jaw. *How fucking much?* got to the tip of his tongue before he managed to choke it down.

"Mr. O'Hare," the broker was saying to dead air. "Are you there? Have we been cut off? Mr. O'Hare?"

He replaced the phone on its cradle.

CHICAGO

◆ ◆ ◆

The brothers were hanging together at Clancy's bar early on a Sunday morning. Today was the first time the three of them had been able to get together since Clancy's return from the coast. They had talked on the phone and exchanged e-mails, but Tom and Will wanted a face-to-face lowdown on their father's situation.

From Labor Day until Christmas, Sunday was Clancy's biggest moneymaking day, courtesy of the NFL and satellite TV. (Monday, because of Monday Night Football, was the second busiest). The pregame shows came on at eleven, which was when he unlocked the doors. By the time the first of the five televised games of the day started—the twelve o'clock and three o'clock on FOX, the same on CBS, and the seven-thirty on ESPN—the place would be rocking, patrons four deep at the bar, bumping up against each other, hefting their glasses and yelling at the TV screens, particularly if the Bears were on against one of their archrivals, like the Lions or Vikings.

Now, though, at nine o'clock, the place was empty except for the three of them. The bartenders and waitresses would start drifting in around ten-thirty. Callie had stayed home—she avoided the Sunday mosh pit.

Tom and Will had flown into Midway early in the morning, coordinating their flights to arrive close together. Clancy had picked them up, having already stopped at a deli on the way to the airport to load up on lox, bagels, and Danish.

He put a pot of coffee on. The bar didn't serve food, but he had a microwave and a toaster oven for heating up carry-in, so they could toast the bagels. There was milk in the refrigerator for the coffee, and orange juice as well. They sat at one of the dark oak tables, upon which decades of students had carved initials into the wood, their breakfast goodies laid out before them.

"Dig in," Clancy exhorted his brothers, loading up a plate for himself.

"Okay," Tom said, smearing cream cheese on his bagel. "What's up with the old dad? Spare no details."

"Well, for openers, he's involved."

"With a woman?" Will asked through a mouthful of cherry Danish.

"No, dipshit, a rhinoceros. Of course a woman."

Will looked puzzled, and upset. "Who is she? How did this come about? When you say 'involved,' what do you mean? Dating her, sleeping with her, what?"

"This is pretty unsettling," Tom added. "Mom's barely—you know, we just buried her."

"It's been over a year," Clancy reminded them. "But I know what you mean, I was taken aback when I saw her with him."

"At his house?" Tom asked. "You saw her with him where he's living?"

Clancy nodded.

"So is she living with him?" Tom again.

"Technically, no, according to dad," Clancy answered. "She has her own place, near his. But she was there when I woke up, so I'm sure she's spending nights, at the least."

"Shit, man." Tom was getting agitated.

"What does she look like?" Will asked. He was taking this news more calmly than Tom, who was always the quickest to assume the worst.

"About five-eight, blond, nice figure, on the willowy side. A very attractive woman."

"Yeah, like dad's going to go for a skank," Tom said. "Does she remind you of mom?"

Clancy shook his head. "The only similarity is that she seems devoted to dad, like mom was."

"Well, that's one thing in her favor," Will offered up.

"It is. As he is to her," Clancy added.

"Damn," Tom muttered under his breath. "What other grenades are you going to lob at us?"

"She's thirty-two."

Tom, who had bitten into his bagel, almost involuntarily spat it out.

"Thirty-three, thirty-four tops," Clancy said. "A couple years older than me," he added as a frame of reference; not that they needed one.

Will whistled through his teeth. "Dad's involved with a woman half his age?" he said. His tone was one of half-disbelief, half-admiration. "That old hound dog."

Tom scowled. "Okay, so he's got a new sweetie who's the same age as his kids. He's not the first man who's done that. What else?"

Clancy topped up his coffee cup. "He's living very well. He's driving a new Mercedes."

Will laughed. "No more Mr. Volvo? What the hell—

out there even the maids drive Mercedes. A Mercedes seems kind of stodgy, though. You'd think a BMW, at least a Lexus."

"She drives a Beemer," Clancy informed him. "The little sports car model."

"Okay, so he's got that covered. Anything else?"

Clancy put his coffee cup down. "His house is worth millions."

"That *has* to be bullshit," Will said with incredulity. "I know it's expensive living out there, but dad can't afford a million-dollar house."

"Millions," Clancy corrected him. "Plural, not singular."

"How do you know?" Tom questioned. "Did you ask him?"

"No, and he wouldn't have told me." He walked behind the bar, reached into a drawer under the cash register, took out a sheet of paper, brought it back to the table, and set it down. "It's a real estate listing."

Will looked at it. "Westwood, California? Pretty fancy." Bending closer, he read, "*Two point two million dollars?* Are you shitting me?" He looked up at Clancy. "You're not telling us this is dad's house . . . are you?"

"Man, this is insane," Tom added, equally stunned.

"No, it isn't his house," Clancy said quickly.

Will exhaled. "You had me going there for a second, Clancy."

"But dad's is pretty much like this one. Same neighborhood, same style."

"Where the hell would he get that kind of money?" Tom asked. "Where did you get this?"

"Don't get your bowels in an uproar. Yes, he's living in a very expensive house, but no, he didn't spend millions on it. And I got that offer sheet from the listing agent for this house. She faxed it to me when I got back here. I conned her into thinking I'm a prospective buyer."

"That'll be the day," Tom said.

The front door swung open. A young woman dressed in jeans and a T-shirt with the Finnegan's logo stenciled on the front breezed in. "Hey, Clancy," she sang out.

"Hey, Rhonda," he called back.

"Bears–Tampa Bay, first game out of the box on FOX," the woman called out merrily. She stood behind the bar, tapping the kegs to see how full each was. "Could be blood on the floor. You order extra kegs?"

"We're covered," Clancy assured her.

She headed for the walk-in refrigerator at the back.

"Eat up, guys," Clancy admonished his brothers. "I've got to start getting this show on the road."

"The house," Tom persisted. "How's a retired college professor afford a house like this? He bought it, right? He isn't renting it."

"He bought it, yes. The woman—Emma—snuck him in the side door."

As they ate he explained about the previous owner's sudden death, and how Emma helped Walt take over the existing loan and mortgage without having to refinance.

"He lucked out," Clancy said. "After the crummy hands he's been dealt lately, he deserved some good luck." He recalled that Walt had said the same thing to him when he'd questioned him, as his brothers were doing now.

Will shook his head. "This sounds fishy, Clancy. Getting a two-million-plus house for under a million? Why would a bank blow off that kind of money? They're in the business to make money, not piss it away."

"That's what I thought," Clancy said. "But the way dad explained it to me, they're in the bank business, not the real estate business. And he got a sweet deal for the house in Madison, so he was able to swing it." He ticked the salient points off on his fingers. "He has no expenses anymore to speak of. We're all off the payroll, he has his university pension, he's going to start teaching at another university out there, he still has his grants. More power to him," he added.

"And mom's insurance," Tom added. He seemed to be the most unhappy of the three of them about the direction his father's life was taking.

"There wouldn't have been much insurance on her," Will rebutted. He was in the money business, he knew about this stuff. "It would've been a waste of money. They had those strong pensions coming, and they always lived pretty modestly. If there was a policy on her, I doubt it was more than a couple hundred thousand dollars."

"Enough to swing a down payment on a discounted house," Clancy pointed out. His brothers' suspicious attitudes were upsetting, because he'd had similar feelings when he had been out there.

Will nodded. "That's true," he allowed reluctantly.

The other bartenders and waitstaff were arriving, exchanging greetings with Clancy. They started setting up for the day's business.

"We're going to have to wrap it up," Clancy said. He was glad they weren't going any further with this now, it was giving him a headache. "We'll continue at dinner tonight." He hadn't gotten around to mentioning the wine cellar or the kachina dolls and the other expensive furnishings in their father's new digs. "You guys gonna stick around and watch the games?"

They both shook their heads no. "I'm going to meet some friends from school downtown," Tom said.

"And I'm going to check out the art museum," Will

added. "There's a Matisse show I've been wanting to see."

The two younger brothers walked out together. Clancy finished his cup of coffee. "Hey, Sadie," he called out to one of the barmaids. He pointed to the barely eaten spread. "Lay this out on the counter. We'll be an old-fashioned saloon today. First customers in get a free lunch."

It was after midnight. Clancy returned to his apartment from driving Tom and Will to the airport. Callie was in the bedroom, asleep.

His mind was racing. He sat in darkness at the kitchen table, drinking a beer. At dinner and afterward the brothers had gone around and around on their father.

Okay, so he's changed in ways we don't like. Okay, he's with a woman we don't know and don't approve of. Okay, he's recklessly spending a lot of money we didn't know he had. Okay, despite all his brave talk, he seems adrift.

And so on and so forth, for hours.

They had come to an unhappy but realistic conclusion: their father had changed in some very fundamental ways from the man they had known all their lives, a man whose *rhythms* and *personality* and *essence* they had known all their lives, depended on all their lives, to someone different. Someone else. The shell was the same, but not what was inside. And what they had come to, over much expressed anguish and breast-beating, was: GET OVER IT. Their father had no obligation to be what they wanted him to be, which was the wax museum Walt Gaines, the daddy of their (mostly) sunny and happy youth. He was, they had to grant, doing what you are supposed to be doing throughout the course of your life—changing. Maybe growing, too (although they expressed their doubts about that), but definitely changing. Not in a direction they wanted him to, which would have been predictable and safe, especially for them, but still, he was peeling off an old skin to reveal a new one underneath. With a young, desirable, mysterious woman who was nothing like their mother.

It was his life. He had to live it. He was *going* to live it, with or without their approval. He knew, being their father, that their approval would be lukewarm at best. Which was why he had distanced himself from them.

The decision was up to them. If they wanted their father in their lives they would have to bend, because he wouldn't.

"When are you coming to bed, Clancy?"

Callie's tired eyes were slitted from being awakened from a troubled sleep. She leaned against the kitchen door threshold. "It's almost one."

"Pretty soon. I'm decompressing."

"Not a fun evening," she commented. She slumped into a chair alongside him. "I have to say something." She had listened to their carping and critiquing all evening, but had kept out of it. "I need you to know how I'm feeling about this."

He stared at her balefully, but didn't say anything in reply.

"You guys are talking yourselves into troubles you don't need, and certainly shouldn't want."

"I know."

"And what's the point?"

He looked at her in surprise. "Of talking about what's going on with him? He's our father, how can we not?"

"No." She shook her head. "Of worrying about it. I don't mean worrying, you can't stop yourselves from doing that, I wish you could, but doing something, which is what I was reading between the lines."

He started to protest, but she cut him off.

"Don't bullshit me, Clancy. More importantly, don't bullshit yourself. What is going to come of beating this thing up, chewing it to death. What do you guys want?"

He sighed. "For things to be the way they used to be, of course. To set the clock back a year and a half."

"Which you can't do."

"Which we can't do," he agreed. He tilted his head back and drank some beer. It had gone warm. He put the bottle down. "It's human nature to want to fix things that got messed up."

She leaned forward on her elbows. "The expression, 'get a life'?"

"Yeah?"

"You have one. A good one."

"I know. Believe me, I know."

"You *think* you know, but I want you to get serious about this. You're running two businesses, either of which is enough to stress out anyone. And the bottom line is, there's not a thing you can do about Walt, Clancy."

Her voice rose, both in volume and pitch. "Look, we've gone around and around on this, but can we stop now? We have a life of our own, Clancy. It's a great life. It's going to get greater. But not if you get stressed and distracted worrying about things you have no control over." She grabbed his hand. "Let it go. And I mean, completely. You . . . *we* . . . have our life. Let's not get sidetracked over stuff we can't control."

She squeezed his hand. "When kids grow up, parents have to let them go. They teach them as best they can and then they kick them out of the nest and hope they can fly on their own. Well, the same thing's true in reverse."

He leaned over and kissed her. "Okay."

"Okay, what?"

"Okay, I'll leave it alone. You're right. I have as much as I can handle without taking on being responsible for someone who doesn't want me to."

"Is this a promise?" she pressed.

"Yes," he answered. "It is."

In contrast with Sunday and Monday, Tuesday nights at Finnegan's were quiet. Only the hard-core regulars ventured in on Tuesdays. Some nights, business was so slow that Clancy closed early. That he hadn't done so yet was only out of pity for the few remaining poor bastards who nursed their 7&7's and draft beers at the bar, hanging around to forestall the inevitable acrimonious encounters with the neglected spouses who awaited them at home; or who had no one waiting at all.

In a few minutes, he'd go to his own home. Pete would close up. Pete could handle a small crowd—it was the multitudes, the young college kids, who unnerved him. Particularly the girls, with their pierced belly buttons and their tits bulging out of their halter tops, teasing him with their casual sexual bantering, playfully offering him a peek at their tattoos, the ones on their tight buns and other hidden spots.

Pete should have been a country priest instead of a bartender, Jimmy Finnegan had told Clancy when he handed over the reins. Or a farmer. The American equivalent of those Irish bachelors who live with their unmarried brothers and spinster sisters and make a yearly pilgrimage to the city to get laid. The city for Pete was

Las Vegas, which he visited for three days every year, the week after Easter. By going then, he could finesse confession for months before having to come clean. He had been patronizing the same hooker for over ten years in a row, and was madly in love with her. He fantasized that she felt the same way about him, and would be happy to leave Sin City for a life of domestic bliss, but he was too shy to broach the subject, and too poor to afford a wife, anyway. Plus he knew, deep in his soul, that fantasy and reality, particularly when it came to hookers and matrimony, were trains whose tracks would never converge.

Pete was washing glasses in the sink at the far end of the bar. "I'm taking off in a minute, Pete," Clancy called down. "Close up whenever you feel like it."

"That's a positive ten-four," Pete answered. Clancy smiled. The man was a die-hard fan of cop shows on television, particularly the old, square ones that Jack Webb used to produce.

He drew a short draft for himself and carried it to an empty booth in the back. Sliding onto the wooden bench, he unfolded the slip of paper he'd been carrying around in his wallet, on which he had printed the name and phone number of the real estate broker in Madison who had sold his parents' house. His stomach tightened as he looked at it—he had promised Callie he'd let this alone.

His rationale for breaking his vow was that this was no big deal. He had already obtained this information before he had made his pledge. This was nothing more than tying up a loose end. Better to tie them all in a neat bundle than to leave one dangling. That's how you hurt yourself, you trip and fall on a dangling loose end, like an untied shoelace. He would make this one call, and that would be it.

He took his cell phone out of his pocket and dialed.

Okay, he thought, making a spur-of-the-moment, minor-league Faustian bargain with himself: If a service picks up, I won't leave a message, and I'll walk away from this. If a live person picks up, I'll follow through. He was hoping the service would pick up.

"Hello?"

Not the service—a live voice. "Brooks Martinson, please," he read from his note.

"Speaking." The voice on the other end of the line was deep and resonant. A voice that had been self-trained to make deals.

He'd made a pact with himself—now he had to follow through. "Mr. Martinson, my name is Clancy Gaines. I'm Walt Gaines's son. Professor Gaines, from the university."

"Of course," Martinson boomed out. "How are you, Mr. Gaines?"

"Fine, thanks. I hope I'm not calling too late." He glanced at the clock on the wall. Nine-forty-five.

"Not at all, not at all," come the reassuring answer. "I do much of my business in the evening, after people have gotten home and had their dinner. How can I help you?"

"You were the real estate broker who handed the sale of my father's house last year, weren't you?" Clancy asked.

"Yes, I was. Fine man, your father," Martinson added, with a salesman's ass-kissing slickness. "The community was sorry to see him leave."

"I'm sure." A harmless lie. "But sometimes you have to move on, whether you want to or not."

Now the voice was sympathetic. "I understand." Alluding to the unspoken—Jocelyn's death. "So . . ."

The point of this call. "I'm helping dad with his estate

planning, and I need some figures. I'd get them from him, but he's out of the country, on work."

"Yes, of course," Martinson said. "His archaeology work."

"That's right." Walt's extensive travels, common knowledge in Madison, were a good cover for this skulking around. "What I need to know is, what did the house sell for? Actually," he continued, "I need to know what he netted, after commissions and other expenses." He paused. "Shoot, I just realized. You're at home, and your files would be at your office."

"I am at home," Martinson answered, "but I have the information here. If you'll give me a moment, I'll dig it up for you. Or would you prefer I call you back?"

"That's okay. I'll hold."

"It won't take but a few seconds."

Clancy patted his pockets for something to write with. Having pen but no paper, he grabbed a napkin from the holder.

In less than a minute, Martinson was back on the line. "All my transactions are on my computer, so it was a cinch to bring up the information," he explained, his tone insinuating that not all his competitors were so professional. "Are you ready?"

"Yes."

"The house was listed at four hundred and forty-five thousand dollars, and we sold it for four-fifteen."

Clancy scribbled the numbers on the napkin.

"We could've done better if we had held firm on our asking price," Martinson continued, somewhat defensively, "but your father wanted to sell as quickly as possible, so he took the first bid that was in the ballpark. Four-fifteen is still a good price," he added hastily, "considering the age of the house and the neighborhood.

Nowadays, people spending over four hundred are looking for a newer house. But that was a fine house," he added quickly. "Solid construction. I personally prefer the older neighborhoods. I understand your father is living in the Los Angeles area now?"

"Yes."

"Big difference between real estate prices here and out there," the broker said. "You get a lot more bang for your buck here," he added in defense of his home turf.

"True," Clancy agreed. "Do you know what they bought the house for, back in '77?"

He had been five, going on six, when they had moved to the big old Victorian with the acre of backyard and the big trees they'd hung swings from. He was going to miss going back there for holidays with his own children.

"I have it right here. Your parents paid thirty-five thousand dollars for it. Seven thousand down, with a twenty-eight-thousand mortgage." He chuckled. "Things have changed since then, haven't they?"

"No kidding. And that was what, a thirty-year mortgage, twenty-five?"

"It was a twenty-five-year mortgage, that's correct."

Which meant his father had owned the house free and clear. After paying Martinson his six percent commission, that would come to—he quickly ran the figures in his head—three hundred and ninety grand. A good grubstake.

"So he cleared close to four hundred thousand dollars," he said, to verify his calculation. He wrote *$390K* on the napkin.

"Well, no."

"No?"

"That *would* have been the amount, if your parents had

maintained their original mortgage," Martinson explained. "But with the refinancing, that wasn't the case."

Clancy sat back. His parents had refinanced their house? He hadn't known that; not that it was any of his business. Still, it seemed odd. They were frugal in their life-style.

He put the thought aside. "The refinancing, right. I'd forgotten. How much was that again?"

"The most recent one?"

There was more than one? "Yes."

"That would have been two and a half years ago, and it was for two hundred and seventy-five thousand dollars," Martinson said, clicking off the figures.

Clancy felt numb as he wrote the numbers down on the napkin. "Two seventy-five."

"That's correct," came the voice from the other end of the line.

"So then the profit would have been . . ."

"One hundred and forty thousand, before commissions and other fees," Martinson said crisply, sparing him the calculation. "It came to a net profit of about a hundred and ten thousand dollars."

Clancy tried to recall what his father had told him about how much he'd made on the sale. That he had done well? Something like that. Pulling a hundred grand out of a more than four-hundred-thousand-dollar house isn't doing well, any way you cut it.

"Mr. Gaines?"

"Yes, I'm still here. I was writing the amounts down. You were saying the most recent refinancing was for the two-seventy-five. Were there others?"

"Yes." There was a short pause. "Your parents refinanced their house three times. Not a bad financial strategy," he added, "given how the value climbed, particularly over the past decade."

Clancy wrote the number *3*, underlined it. "Could you give me the years they did that? Besides the most recent one, which was in 1999, would it have been?"

"Nineteen ninety-nine, that's correct. The other two times were in '94 and '97. Taking advantage of low interest rates and a rising stock market, one would assume. Quite a few of my clients did that. Many of them got burned when the market crashed, of course, but the lucky ones took their profits and put them into conservative, safe investments. I'm sure your father was one of the prescient ones. He's a very smart man, it was a pleasure to do business with him."

"Yes, he's smart," Clancy agreed. But not with money, money was never a big deal with his parents. Theirs was the life of ideas, and adventure. He wanted to consult with Will about this, because of his younger brother's expertise, but he couldn't imagine his parents as big plungers. He'd certainly never seen any indication of their having wealth, until he had been inside his father's new house.

"Is there anything else I can assist you with tonight, Mr. Gaines?" Martinson asked.

"No," Clancy answered. "You've given me everything I need."

"Well, glad to be of help," the broker responded cheerfully. "Please give your father my best regards."

"I'll do that," Clancy said woodenly. "Good-bye."

He turned his phone off. Smart play, asshole. You think you're going to tie up one loose end, and you wind up unraveling the whole damn ball of yarn.

* * *

"How was business?" Callie asked, when Clancy came in the door and flopped on the couch, turning on the television to ESPN to catch the scores. He needed to keep up—if a client had an injury it was important to know about it before he got the call from the team's doctor, or more commonly, the athlete's agent.

"The usual for Tuesday. Barely enough to pay the help."

"You should start taking Tuesdays off. Pete can open as well as close."

"I should, yeah." He watched some footage from the Bears practice. They had squeaked by Tampa Bay in their season opener, but this coming week they had the Rams. Talk about out of the frying pan into the fire. The spread in Nevada would be close to ten points, but there would be plenty of fools from Chicago taking it.

The stuff on TV was boring, and he was distracted. He channel-surfed, catching some Headline News, other sports channels. The Cubs, who had tantalized their fans during June and July by playing smart, winning baseball, were well into their usual September swoon. And now that Michael and Scottie were gone, the Bulls were going to be garbage for a decade. A great town, Chicago, Clancy thought of his adopted city, but if you follow sports you'll go nuts.

"Did you eat?" Callie asked. "I could heat up last night's chicken."

"I'm not hungry, hon. Thanks anyway." He turned the set off with the remote. "I did something stupid tonight."

She stared at him, hands on hip. "Don't tell me it's about your father."

He nodded. "Yes," he said balefully, like a kid anticipating a scolding from a teacher.

"You promised, Clancy."

He could hear the irritation in her voice. "What did you do?" she demanded.

He recounted his conversation with Martinson, the real estate agent. "Dad didn't make squat on his house," he said, after he had given her the details.

"I don't think a hundred thousand dollars is squat," she rebutted. "I wish we had a hundred thousand in the bank."

"It's squat when you should've pulled four hundred out. But that's the tip of the iceberg. Why were they refinancing the place?"

"I'm sure there's a logical explanation." Callie paused. "You aren't going to dig deeper into this, are you?"

He gave her a sad-sack half-shrug.

"So a promise to me means nothing."

"Come on, it's not like that."

"It isn't? How is it, then? What are the rules for justifying breaking a promise, Clancy? Like, when's it okay to?" She was steaming. "Does this go both ways? Boy, great marriage we're having here tonight."

"Look, honey, I don't want to fight about this." He had messed up, and he didn't like that she was busting him for it, although she was well within her rights to do so.

"Then you shouldn't have done it."

He didn't answer her.

"So now what?" she demanded. "When's the other shoe going to drop? How many shoes?"

"I—"

"Screw it," she snapped, cutting him off. "You want to go off on some cockamamie wild-goose chase, be my guest. Just don't tell me you're doing it. When ignorance is bliss . . . I want to be ignorant, of everything. Leave me out of the loop." She paused. "What about Will and Tom? Did you tell them?"

He shook his head.

"You going to?"

"Probably."

She shook her head, more in sadness than in anger. "You guys are cruising for a bruising," she warned him. "You'd better be damned careful about asking questions you might not want answers to."

"Curiouser and curiouser," Tom said. "Which doesn't surprise me, although it does make me more nervous and pissed-off about dad than I already was."

He was on the phone with Clancy; his older brother had called him. "You talk to Will about this yet?" he asked.

"No, I called you first."

It was nine o'clock, the following morning. A warm, balmy day, almost tropical in feeling, the beginning of Indian summer, Clancy's favorite time of the year. He was in his office at the fitness center, on a short break between appointments. Between the disconcerting news from the real estate agent and Callie's bitching at him, he had hardly gotten any sleep.

He looked outside the glass partition of his office to the large therapy room. The place was abuzz with activity. You're up to your neck running two businesses, he thought, and now this? What he was finding out about his parents was giving him an ulcerous pain in his stomach. He figured Tom and Will had the same nauseated feelings in their guts, too.

This latest development was going to make things even worse.

"What do you think this draining of funds from the family treasury is about?" Tom asked.

"How should I know?" Clancy responded. "We've already discussed how it's none of our business what they did with their money. I don't give a damn about that." His trying to understand and then explain his parents' erratic behavior was becoming more difficult and aggravating.

"Bullshit."

Busted. "You're right. I do care. But it's not my affair."

"Or mine," Tom replied testily.

"Mine, ours, it's the same deal." Jesus, it was so easy to hurt Tom's feelings. "The thing that bothers me is that it's so out of character. This is becoming like a wooden Russian doll. You keep opening one up and finding more inside."

Tom was silent for a moment. Then he asked, "Even if it is none of our business, don't you want to know where the money was going? What they were using it for? I never noticed any big changes in their life-style."

"Who knows? The real estate broker speculated they were putting it into investments."

"Walt and Jocelyn Gaines?" Tom's voice was laden with skepticism. "I can't picture that. They were wild and crazy kids in their life-style, but where money was involved they were buttoned-down reactionaries. I never told anybody this, but a few years ago I hit them up for a loan. Not much, a couple grand. I didn't know if my fellowship was going to be renewed, and I thought I might have to go out into the cruel world and get an actual job."

He laughed; to Clancy it sounded like he was mocking himself. That would be vintage Tom.

"They sympathized with me—you know how mom was, the greatest shoulder in the world to cry on—but they flat turned me down. Said they couldn't afford it, all their money was going into their retirement fund, which they implied was ultraconservative. Going out on a limb in the stock market would not be how they would have invested."

"The more I learn about them, the less I know," Clancy sighed. "Knew," he corrected himself.

"There's an easy way to find out."

"How?"

"Ask dad."

Clancy moaned. "That's a *great* idea. Why didn't I think of that? Hey, dad, I found out that great sucking sound we've been hearing was you and mom pulling money out of your house. What were you using it for, your drug habit?"

"A bit on the direct side, I think," his brother replied. "There are subtler ways. You could tell him you're thinking of investing and ask his advice. Or ask him who his broker is. See how he reacts."

"I can tell you his reaction: A, I'm nuts, and B, I'm prying. He's not stupid, he'd see right through that."

"Fine, then," Tom snapped. "So what do you want to do? You called me."

"I don't know what I want to do," Clancy confessed.

"We're going around in circles."

"Like a whirlpool."

Tom was silent.

"What do *you* think?" Clancy asked.

"I'm glad you asked that question, Clancy, because I've been thinking about it myself," Tom answered. "For openers, we'd better know what really is going on with dad before we start jumping to negative conclusions, which is what we've been doing—me the worst, I've been the quickest to jump on him. The point I'm making is, people do all kinds of crazy, irrational stuff, whether it's bailing out of a secure job, moving to Disneyland, taking up with a young tomato, whatever. Maybe it's time for us to stop reading sinister motives into everything dad's done and is doing."

"Well said," Clancy agreed. "Speaking of young tomatoes, wait'll you meet this new one. The proof, as they say, is in the pudding. And she is one tasty pudding."

"So you've said. Sounds like she worked her wiles on you, married man," Tom teased.

Clancy remembered the almost animalistic sexuality Emma Rawlings had emitted. "Callie's all the woman I'm ever going to want." Which was true. "But this one is pretty hot and tasty."

"I oughta go to L.A. and check her out myself," Tom suggested. "If she's that hot she might burn poor old dad to a cinder. I might need to help him put out the fire."

Tom was joking, but the banter, particularly the sexual undertone, had a hard edge to it. The competitiveness between them, not only among the brothers but also between father and sons, was intense. Walt had always pushed his boys to do better, achieve more, to try to come up to his exacting standards. School, Little League, the quality of the girls they were dating, anything. When they succeeded, he was generous with his praise. When they didn't, which by his high standards was a lot of the time, he let them know it, in no uncertain terms. He was loving, but he was formidable. Even now, as grown men, there was a spark of fear of Walt that still smoldered in all of them.

Tom had taken more than his share of their father's disapprobation. He had always been the son who tried the hardest and disappointed the most. One of the main reasons, Clancy was sure, why Tom had stayed cocooned in his graduate studies without producing his thesis or making any real progress toward finishing his doctorate. As long as there was nothing to criticize, he was safe.

Clancy knew that Tom's choosing to go into academic life, albeit in a different discipline from Walt's, had been worrisome to their mother, who zealously defended her offspring. She knew that Tom's choice of vocation was a two-sided coin: heads you please and win approval, tails you self-immolate. He had his father's sharp mind but not his tough hide.

Clancy agreed with his mother, but he would never tell Tom how he felt. It wouldn't be taken in the spirit in which it was given. Clancy was the older brother. He was always going to be the older brother.

"At some point you'll meet her," he said, referring to Tom's statement about checking Emma out. "It's inevitable."

"I'm not counting on being offered an invitation," Tom answered. "Look, Clancy. I'm sorry to hear this about the mortgage thing. It's one more piece of a puzzle I have no clue how to solve, and neither do you. If you think we should check up on what mom and dad were up to with that money, I'd go along with it. Grudgingly. But I'm into wanting him back as dad, the hell with his money and what he and mom were doing with it. We lost one of our parents, Clancy. My desire is to not lose both."

Sound advice, Clancy thought, after they said their goodbyes. It was going to be hard to take, but he knew he should. Callie wanted him to, and now Tom, the most aggressively upset about the changes in their father, was voicing the same sentiment.

For the remainder of the morning he worked nonstop, one client after the other. An assistant brought him a turkey sub for lunch, which he wolfed down at his desk. He put in a fast call to Callie, and they made plans to go out to dinner at a French country-style bistro she'd read a good review about. Maybe a movie after, if they had the energy. He was going to relax, let Pete handle business, and let the cares of the world go by, at least for tonight.

His telephone buzzed. He picked it up.

"Your brother, line six," the receptionist informed him.

"Thanks."

So Tom couldn't sit on this after all. He wiped mayonnaise off his mouth and punched up the blinking line. "Hey, Tom, what's up now?"

"It's Will, Clancy."

"Oh. Hi. How's it going?"

"Not good. We have another dad problem."

Bad news travels at mach speed, Clancy thought morosely. "You talked to Tom?"

"Tom?" Will asked, confused. "Not for a couple of days. Why?"

He hadn't? Then what was this?

"Tom and I had a conversation about stuff having to do with dad," Clancy explained. "I assumed he'd called you to fill you in. I was going to, but I've been overwhelmed here."

"What about?"

"You tell me your news first, then I'll tell you mine."

"Okay. How dad bought his new house? Taking over the bank payments?"

"Yeah?"

"He didn't."

Clancy sucked air.

"Clancy? You still there?"

"Yes, I'm here." He looked out the glass partition to the therapy room, where his next client, a woman with frozen shoulder syndrome, was taking off her sweats. He caught her eye and gave her an "in a minute" signal. She nodded and started doing stretches.

"How do you know that?" he asked.

"I got to thinking about what you'd told us last Sunday, how dad had been able to take over the payments on the existing mortgage," Will said. "An inside deal? That sounded strange to me, a bank *not* wanting to make money. That's why they're in business. Our firm doesn't do that stuff directly, but we're tied in to most of the major lending institutions around the country, so I called up a guy who knows the mortgage business in California. He said that what dad told you doesn't work that way. It can't, it's against the law."

"Are you sure?" Clancy didn't want to believe this, not on top of what he'd found out last night. "If dad's friend Emma had an in, couldn't they have finagled a deal?"

"No," Will answered unambiguously. "Transfer of title is public record. A transaction like that would be a red flag to the state and L.A. County government, because they make money when houses are bought and sold. The property taxes go up, there are expensive fees. It can be a significant amount if it's a substantial sale. Which this was."

"How significant?"

"I'll tell you in a minute. You're gonna shit. Let me first clarify how it works in a foreclosure sale when there are no heirs to the property, which was the situation here," Will began explaining. "A broker is assigned by the court overseeing the foreclosure. The broker is obligated to sell the property to the highest bidder. That's how it happens, through a bidding process. Usually there's a floor to the bids, so it can't go way below fair market value. When that happens they take it off the market and put it back on later. You with me so far?"

"Yes."

"The broker assigned to that house determined a fair asking price was two point two million. At that price, there were no bids. Which was okay, they start ten, fifteen percent high, in case they find a buyer who has to have it and is willing to pay for it. This one sat on the market for five months. So then they dropped the price to one-nine, with a floor of one-seven. At that point, it became a decent deal. They got three bids. All below asking, but close enough. The bids were a million seven on the nose, a million seven-fifty, and a million eight."

"You know all this for a fact?" Clancy asked. His head was spinning.

"Got the numbers right here in front of me. It's all in the public records, anybody can check them out. You just have to know where to find them."

Which I didn't, Clancy thought, annoyed at Walt for lying, annoyed at himself for having bought his story at face value, when he should have known better. That's why he was here, working with disabled people, and Will was on his way to becoming a millionaire.

He could at least figure the rest of it out. "Dad offered the million eight."

"Give the man a giant panda. Yes, Walt Gaines was the high bidder. That's in dollars, not pesos or lira. Cash, no contingencies. Which meant he had to check the property out first, satisfy himself it was structurally okay and that there weren't any hidden liens or other legal action against it, and then he had to have his financing in place. It's like going to a car auction, if you're not ready to write the check, it goes to the next highest bidder and you are shit out of luck."

Another shoe hit the deck with a crash. "Dad had almost two million dollars in hand," he said, almost numbly.

"He had to. Those were the conditions."

Neither spoke for a moment. Finally, Clancy broke the silence. "This is incredible. Inconceivable."

"Mind-boggling, to use one of dad's ancient phrases."

"When did you find out about this?"

"Just now. I called you as soon as I had the pieces put together. I've been checking into it since Monday, when I got back here. It's only been a couple days since we talked about this."

"I know."

"What I've been trying to figure out is, where in the world would he get that kind of money? I've got to tell you, Clancy, I really freaked out when I got this information."

"I'm sure," Clancy said. At least he wasn't in on this alone now.

"What you and Tom talked about," Will pressed. "Is it connected to this?"

Clancy's muscles were knotted from tension. He stood up and stretched.

"Yes, it is, but I don't want to talk about it over the phone. We're going to have to get together again. This whole situation with dad is becoming too heavy a load to ignore."

Clancy didn't tell Callie that he and his brothers were going to meet up again to discuss the dad problem. For one thing, they hadn't decided when they could. They were all busy, especially him and Will, they couldn't drop everything on a moment's notice. Sometime in the next couple of weeks, in Chicago again, they had mutually decided, as it was the most convenient location.

That Clancy was going to keep the meeting a secret from Callie was wrong. He knew that, but he had to. She would hit the roof if she knew what they were planning, and Clancy didn't want her pissed off at him more than she already was.

Tonight, she was in a good mood. She had splurged on a girlie day—she'd bought a new dress, got her hair cut, had a manicure and a pedicure. The restaurant she'd selected was a tiny patch of the Loire Valley plunked down in Wicker Park. It felt authentic, because it was so squarely old-fashioned—the young waitresses wore heels and real stockings and spoke in heavy French accents, and the hostess, a Simone Signoret look-alike, could have stepped out of a 50s black and white movie on AMC.

Callie squished her bread in the garlicky escargot butter. "This is so decadent!" she gushed as she bit into it. Clancy, eating his onion soup, nodded in agreement. His wife was happy, and that was all he needed tonight.

"Listen, honey," she said. "About last night."

"Forget it," he came back quickly. "I was out of line. I made you a promise, and I broke it."

And I'm going to break it again, he thought dolefully. He had decided—sadly, because she was his wife and his closest confidant—to take Callie at her word: to *not* tell her anything else about what he and his brothers were doing or thinking regarding Walt. He hated lying to his wife, but that was less painful than any other choice he could think of.

"No," she said. "Listen."

"I was," he insisted, "wrong."

"I know, but listen." She reached across the table and

took his hand. "I can't tell you not to be worried about your father. He's your father. That's selfish of me, and how could you not worry anyway, if you think there's cause to?"

"Thank you." What a woman, he thought. How lucky a guy you are, which you sometimes forget to remember.

"I just wanted you to know that."

"Thanks."

The waitress cleared their appetizers and set down their entrées, salmon Wellington for her, coq au vin for him. She poured their wine, the house red.

Callie tasted it. "This isn't bad. So about your father . . . what are you guys going to do?"

"I don't know. Hopefully, nothing."

"Me, too. For your peace of mind, if nothing else. But if you have to, I don't want to hold you back."

He felt a huge weight lifting off his shoulders. "Thanks, Callie. I really appreciate your doing this for me."

"I'm doing it for us. We're partners, for better or worse, isn't that what we said? It's my family, too."

"Yes. We're partners."

But until he and his brothers decided what they were going to do he wasn't going to involve her. He couldn't. She was family, but this was blood.

"I'm curious about her," Callie said, digging into her meal. "I'd like to see her with my own eyes."

"Who?"

"The girlfriend. She must be pretty special, to have snagged your dad."

"Oh." She'd caught him off-guard. "Sooner or later, you will, if they're still together."

She chewed slowly. "I miss your mother. She was such

an old soul. I hope your dad's happy with this new woman, I really do, but your mom is irreplaceable."

By a lucky coincidence, Callie let Clancy off the hook from having to lie to her about the reason for getting together again with his brothers. She was overdue for paying her parents a visit. She would stay a week, long enough to give her parents a good dose of her, but not so long as to get antsy.

Clancy drove her to O'Hare. Her plane was leaving at one. He was taking the rest of the day off—the other therapists would cover for him. He'd also alerted Pete that he might come in late to the bar, or not come in at all. Pete had taken the news with his usual grumbly equanimity. The bar ran itself as long as there were enough hands to fill the glasses.

They said their good-byes at the security gate. "I'll call you later, at the bar," she told him.

"Don't call there," he said. If she did and he wasn't there, she might be uneasy. "It's too noisy. Call me at home later, or tomorrow. It isn't urgent." She had given him freedom to pursue his inquiry into his father's erratic and disturbing behavior, but he didn't want her to know he was doing so; not yet. If anything came of it, then he would. Until then, why stir up a hornet's nest? "Don't worry," he said, smiling at her, "it's only a week."

"I miss you already." She squeezed his hand.

"Me, too. You'll be fine. Give my love to your parents."

"Be a good boy. Don't get into trouble."

"Trouble is my middle name," he quipped lamely.

"I know. That's why I'm warning you not to."

"I'm the last thing on earth you have to worry about," he assured her.

"I do, anyway."

He had an hour to kill. As before, his brothers had scheduled their planes to arrive close to the same time. The three of them would spend the afternoon, evening, and the next morning hashing over what they knew, what they thought, and then decide what further action, if any, they were going to take. They had less than twenty-four hours—Will had to be back in Minneapolis the following night for a company dinner, and Tom was going back-packing in northern Michigan with a friend, leaving early Sunday morning.

Tom was arriving first. Clancy looked at his watch. Checking the ARRIVALS screen, he headed down the concourse.

Pretty soon, by Thanksgiving at the latest, the weather would turn and there wouldn't be nice days like this until April. They drove into the city and walked through Lincoln Park, stopping at an outside café where they could get a beer, sit under a shady umbrella, and talk.

Nearby, three pretty young college girls, their bicycles propped up against a bench, were lying on the grass in workout shorts and bikini tops, intent on getting one final tan of the summer. Occasionally one would glance over at the brothers, then turn back to her friends and say something. They'd all have a quick look, turn away, and pretend they hadn't.

"I ought to move here," Tom said, as he checked out the girls. "I'm getting bored with Ann Arbor. The women there know all my lines. I need to go where they don't know my stale jokes." He looked at the girls again. "You think they'd like to hear a good joke?"

"Everyone likes a good joke," Clancy said. The girls didn't register on his radar screen—he saw dozens exactly like them every Friday night at the bar.

"What about your thesis?" Will asked. The women didn't interest him, either, except as physical specimens. He had all the action he could handle back in Minneapolis.

"I don't have to live there to write it, I can write anywhere," Tom answered. "If I ever do."

"Jesus, not that old song again. You're going to finish," Clancy said in exasperation.

"Sometimes I think I ought to chuck the whole deal and get a real job. Something tangible."

"You want to tend bar, I can give you a shift."

"I might take you up on that one of these days."

"We only hire Ph.D.'s."

"And 36Cs," Will kicked in.

"For that you only need an equivalency diploma," Clancy said, laughing.

They had gone around on this for a long time, almost from when Tom started his graduate studies. By now, Clancy didn't put any stock in his brother's bellyaching. It was Tom's way of getting attention. His mother had always fallen into that trap, flattering and encouraging Tom, but his father had gotten wise to it years ago and would call Tom on it, daring him to quit, to get off the dole and go out into the cold, cruel world; the implication, of course, being that he couldn't make it in the so-called real world, which Tom had always thought was duplicitous, coming from a man who'd spent his life in the sheltered halls of academe. Of course, he never took his father up on the dare. In his heart he was afraid Walt was right, that he couldn't cut it. It was a stupid, unfounded, self-pitying fear, but there were times—the present was one—when the feeling hung heavy on him.

Tom looked over at the three pretty sunbathers. Two were lying on their stomachs with their eyes closed. The third was giving herself a pedicure, carefully applying blood-red nail polish. The girl felt his stare and looked back at him, almost challengingly, over her shoulder. He turned away, chagrined at being caught.

"I've been wondering . . ." he began. He stopped.

"What?" Will asked.

"What if he's really sick?"

"Like what, cancer or some incurable disease?" Will shook his head.

"I don't know. It's possible, isn't it? It would explain why he's acting so out of character. If he does have an illness that could be terminal, why not chuck all the old baggage overboard and spend what time you have left living your life to the hilt?"

"It sounds like a TV movie," Will said dubiously.

"This is speculation," Clancy said. This was so like Tom, going off on a crazy tangent. "But sure, let's check it out. I'll call his doctor in Madison. Maybe he'll talk to me."

"Let's go on the assumption that he isn't sick," Will said. "I don't agree with you, Clancy, I think that's the one thing he *would* tell us about. If he was really dying he'd want his family to know. Go ahead and check it out, I think we should, but I don't think that's what's going on."

Clancy nodded. "You're right. Let me throw something else out that's more feasible. What do you think about the stock market? Refinancing the house to play the market."

"Where did you come up with that?" Will asked, clearly dubious of the notion.

"His real estate broker in Madison mentioned it. Apparently, a lot of people like mom and dad were doing that in the mid-to-late 1990s, to get in on the action. If they made out in the market, that would explain where he'd gotten the money to pay for his new house."

"Then why wouldn't he say so?" Tom asked. "Why lie about where he'd gotten the money? That's what's bugging me about all this, the lies. How much he cleared on the old house, his story about taking over an existing mortgage when he didn't. You don't lie if you're not hiding something. What's he hiding?"

"That's the million-dollar question," Will agreed. "Multimillion, in dad's case." In response to Clancy's question, he said, "I can't buy this stock market idea. That's my business, they would've consulted with me if they were going to invest."

"Unless they were into investments they knew you'd disapprove of," Clancy responded.

"Like what?" Will shook his head. "People like mom and dad, with good jobs, great pension plans, owning their home, they don't take on financial burdens they don't have to. What would be the point?"

"I don't know. That's why we're here, to brainstorm this. Okay, here's another idea: insurance. Dad could've used mom's life insurance money to pay for the house."

Again, a negative shake of the head from Will. "People like mom and dad don't carry life insurance. Or if they do have policies, they're small."

"Why don't they?" Tom asked.

"Because it's a waste of money. Their pensions are their life insurance," Will explained. "A man in dad's position, factoring in the amount of money he made and the number of years he had tenure as a full professor, gets almost his entire yearly salary when he retires. Mom's would've kicked out plenty, too."

"Another reason for you to finish your doctorate," Clancy chided Tom.

"Except there's no jobs for math professors," Tom answered, pissed off at his older brother's pushiness. "We're a glut on the market. Leave me out of this, okay? We're here to pick on dad, not me."

"Sorry, you're right," Clancy said, properly chastened. "I was joking. Lighten up."

"Nobody's picking on anybody," Will said. As the youngest brother, he had grown up playing the mediator between his two older siblings.

"What else?" Clancy asked. "How far do we go with this?"

They stared at each other.

"You mean, how much prying into dad's life do we want to do?" Tom asked, laying it on the table. "And how involved do we want to get in this?"

"Yes," Clancy answered. Will nodded yes also.

"What if we find out stuff we don't like?" Tom pressed. "I mean more than we already have. What then?"

Clancy shook his head. "I don't know."

"None of us do," Tom said, driving home his point. "That's the bitch of it. What if we uncover some really ugly shit?"

"I hope to God we don't," Will said.

"But what if we do?"

The prospect was sobering to them; frightening.

"Here's what I think," Clancy said. "We'll check up on what we've been talking about today. Hopefully, nothing terrible will pop up. In which case, we let go of it."

"That sounds good," Will said quickly.

"But what if something does?" Tom persisted.

"Like what?" Clancy countered. "Some hypothetical smoking gun?"

"There isn't one," Will said doggedly.

"Of course not."

"But what if there is?" Tom was playing the devil's advocate—someone had to.

"There isn't," Clancy said with finality.

"But if there was," Tom persisted, "then we'd pursue it."

"Yes," Clancy sighed. "If there is, then we will. But there isn't," he added firmly.

Tom stood up. "I'm going out there."

His brothers looked at him with startled expressions on their faces.

"You guys're doing all the checking up," Tom said. "You've got it all covered. There's nothing for me to do."

"That's not true," Will answered reflexively.

"It is. I'm the fifth wheel. You two have the expertise, I'm just the asshole who can't finish his dissertation and grow up."

"Tom, give it a break, okay?" Clancy came back at him.

"*You* give it a break. You two have it made. You've got your great career, great wife, you own two businesses. Will here's the hot young financial whiz on the fast track to a million-dollar-a-year salary. I have nothing to do until school starts back at the end of the month."

Like many doctoral candidates, Tom was an undergraduate teaching assistant. It covered part of his fellowship stipend. To make extra money, he also tutored privately. Neither job paid very much, but he lived in student housing and was tight with his expenses. He was used to it, he had been living that way for years, but more and more, his spartan existence was getting him down. His car was an old

Saab he'd bought secondhand, he never ate out at an expensive restaurant unless someone was treating him, never took a regular vacation. He envied his brothers their extravagant (from his perspective) life-styles, but he felt trapped, no way out.

"I want to see the situation for myself. I want to see dad's new house, I want to see his new lady friend. With my own eyes, not through anyone else's filter." He stared at Clancy. "Maybe I'll find something out you didn't. Is that a problem?"

Clancy swallowed his ire. This had been Tom's MO since he was a little kid—to feel sorry for himself, and then to lash out. He was too old to play this game with Tom anymore. "Not at all," he said conciliatorily.

"Look, I didn't mean to get testy with you, Clance, I just—"

"It's okay," Clancy said, stopping this before it got heavier than it already was. "I think you should go see dad." He turned to Will. "I think you should, too, when you can."

They finished their beers and got up to leave. They'd go to Clancy's bar, watch the games, Clancy would act like a civilian and let the help wait on them, then they'd go out for a good steak (Clancy's treat, they'd paid to come here). They'd had enough of gnawing the bone about this for one day.

As they were walking away, Tom looked across the expanse of lawn, to where the girls were sunbathing. While he had been haranguing his brothers the girls, unnoticed by him, had been joined by a couple of young guys. The girl who had eye-flirted with Tom smiled coquettishly at him, as if to say, "You had your chance. Too late now."

He stared at her for a moment longer, then took off after his brothers.

Los Angeles

♦ ♦ ♦

Walt, citing a heavy schedule, tried to talk Tom out of coming to see him, but in the end, he reluctantly relented. He had opened his door to Clancy; he couldn't deny the same invitation to another son. He didn't know how much time he'd be able to spend with Tom, he cautioned, but he'd try to rearrange his affairs as best he could. He also advised Tom to rent a car, reminding him that without one you're hopeless in Los Angeles, it's not like a Midwestern city where everything is bunched up and there's decent public transportation.

Yet another change, Tom reflected, after he hung up the phone. When he used to visit his parents in Madison (if he hadn't driven there himself), his mother would lend him her car. It was also a not-so-subtle dig on his father's part that he wasn't going to be responsible for his under-achieving son's expenses.

Browsing the Internet, Tom booked the cheapest flight he could find, and reserved a subcompact car through the same site. The fees went on his current credit card—he could dodge the charges for a couple of months, until his teaching pittance started trickling in again, and then pay them off in drawn-out installments. He had gotten into the clever habit of taking out a new credit card every six months. He would use it as long as the low introductory interest rate was in effect, then he'd drop it and switch to another. That way he could afford the monthly payments and not get overwhelmed financially. It was either that or live even shittier than he was doing.

Thus far, he had resisted the temptation to go into the lines of credit that the cards offered—that was a sure path to perdition. He had friends in similar circumstances to his who were into their credit card companies for tens of thousands of dollars, and had no intention of paying off their debts. Their rationale was that the companies ripped off their customers with high usury rates, and it was not only legal but ethical to turn the tables on them. If they got in too far over their heads they could declare bankruptcy, walk away from their unpaid bills, and start over.

Tom had never gone that far. If he declared bankruptcy due to credit card abuse the university would kick him out, and all those years of work would go to waste. Although he was fed up and tired of what he was doing, he had no other financial options on the table.

This was going to be the make-or-break year. By the end of this year he would either finish writing his thesis, defend it, get his coveted doctorate and find a real job, or he'd chuck the whole mess and do something completely different. A friend of his, in similar circumstances, had quit on his thesis when he had almost reached the finish line and had gone to work as a journalist. That was two years ago, and the man was already assistant city editor for the *Dayton Daily News*. Tom could see himself as a modern-day Woodward or Bernstein, rubbing elbows with the rich and famous and covering cool stories around the globe. It would be a great way to meet interesting women, too.

Maybe next year. He wasn't ready to take that radical a step yet.

Clearing security, he walked out of the terminal at the Los Angeles airport and boarded the bus to the rental car lot. He noticed, immediately, the lack of moisture in the air. It had been hot in Detroit when he'd gotten on the plane at six in the morning (it was now mid-afternoon, L.A. time; he'd been on airplanes and in terminals—Chicago, then Denver—for almost twelve hours), but more than the heat, the humidity all throughout the Midwest was brutal, in the nineties. Here, even though it was hot, it didn't feel hot, because of the dryness. No snow in the winter, either—as kids they would watch the Rose Parade on television and beg their parents to move to Los Angeles.

Now his father had. Maybe he and his brothers had overlooked the simplest of reasons: Walt Gaines had gotten tired of shoveling snow. Wouldn't that be a kick in the ass, after all the angst they'd been putting themselves through.

But that was wishful thinking. Not with the lies about the houses.

Tom drove into Westwood, following the directions his father had given him over the phone. Clancy was right, he thought, as he watched the scenery go by—this is the high-rent district. Nothing in his hometown compared to these houses. This was as upscale, in a California way, as was Grosse Point, Michigan, the town near Ann Arbor where the GM and Ford millionaires and billionaires lived.

Seeing this display of riches firsthand was a real eye-opener; that his father, the jungle explorer, discoverer of ancient civilizations, university professor, a man who was almost disdainful of the trappings of wealth, was living in it, was astounding. Walt Gaines was living the life of a millionaire.

Where had he gotten the money? Tom wondered, yet again.

He turned a corner, drove halfway down his father's street, and there it was: his father's house. From Clancy's description he had formed a picture of what it would look like, but this was much more impressive than he had imagined.

There was no one outside the house that he could see, no cars in the driveway. He parked in front, got out of his cheap rental, and stared at it. For a moment he felt like a tourist who had bought a map of the stars' homes and was checking them out—this one belongs to Michelle Pfeiffer, this one to Bruce Willis, this one to Warren Beatty. And this one, ladies and gentlemen, that you are presently looking at (and drooling over), belongs to Walter Gaines, the renowned archaeologist.

Carrying his small bag, Tom crossed the street, walked to the front door, and rang the bell. There was no response. He reached up to push the button again, but before he could, the door opened.

A woman stood in the archway, her hand shielding her face against the late-afternoon sun. "You must be Tom," she said, giving him a welcoming smile.

"Yes," he responded. So this was her, he thought, as he stared at her.

"I'm Emma." She dropped her hand from above her eyes, extended it.

He took her hand. It was soft, but her grip was firm. The grip of a woman who works with shears in the garden, plays a lot of tennis and golf but always wears gloves.

"Hello," he said back. His lips were dry. He licked them, reflexively.

"Is that all you have?" she asked, referring to the small bag slung over his shoulder.

"I have another one, in the car." He pointed his thumb back over his shoulder.

"Why don't you get it, and come on in?"

He turned and walked back down the long front walkway to his car. As he opened the trunk to retrieve his large bag he looked up, to the house. She was standing there, watching him. Seeing him looking at her, she waved. He grabbed the bag, slammed the trunk shut, and walked back to where she was standing.

It was cool inside the house. The air-conditioning hummed quietly. As he followed Emma through the front hallway into the living room, he glanced about admiringly. She had been the decorator; he remembered Clancy had mentioned that to him and Will. She had a good eye—the style suited a rugged man like his father.

Standing in the middle of the living room, she turned to him. "Would you like something to drink? A soda, water? Beer?"

"A beer would be good, thanks."

"I'll be right back."

She walked to the kitchen, a bit of which he could see around the corner.

Where was his father? Why wasn't Walt here to greet him? He knew when Tom was getting in. What was going on?

The woman came back with a dark beer in a frosty mug. "Dos Equis," she said, handing it to him. She smiled at him, a more open smile this time than the one she'd given him at the door.

He smiled back, took a long swallow. It went down

cold. He took a look around. "This is really nice. You've done a nice job of decorating."

"It's your father's house, not mine. I helped him, but he made the selections."

Tom knew that wasn't the truth. This house was beautifully done, but it wasn't his father's doing. Walt wouldn't know how, and wouldn't take the time. Then he caught himself up. Maybe he would. He has the time now. But still, it didn't feel like his father. It felt like a woman trying to make it right for a certain kind of man, a man like his dad. Or like she thought his dad was.

He was gratified that he had insisted on coming out and seeing his father's life-style firsthand. Clancy hadn't prepared him for this. Maybe Clancy hadn't been paying that much attention to the physical surroundings—breaking the ice with their father was what he had been mostly concerned about.

He turned back to the woman. She was standing still, looking at him, as if expecting something from him. She's really attractive, he thought, taking her in. Like Catherine Zeta-Jones, the kind of easy, sophisticated woman he had always felt awkward around. Leave it to Walt Gaines—even now, at sixty, when most men are dandling their grandchildren on their knees and bitching about their prostates, the old man was with a winner. His father cast a mighty shadow—it was hard to get out from under it.

"So where is he?" he asked.

"He isn't here."

What?

"He was called out of town unexpectedly," she explained, acknowledging the surprise and disappointment on his face. She seemed embarrassed. "Berkeley. A last-minute thing, some lecture series they want him to do.

He'll be back by eight—his plane gets in at seven-fifteen. So . . ." She spread her arms wide, a gesture both welcoming and apologetic. "Why don't I get you settled into your room, and then you can decide what you want to do."

Tom unpacked and put his personal items away and sat on the edge of the guest room bed. He was pissed—this was so much like Walt. If it had been Clancy or Will his father wouldn't have been absent when they arrived. He would have gone to the airport to pick them up. But Tom had to fend for himself, and if something else came up—anything else—too damned bad. He could wait.

Tom had built a construct in his mind of his family being similar to the Kennedys—in miniature, as there were only three children as opposed to the eight or nine or however many Kennedys there had been. Walt was old Joe Kennedy, the patriarch, the builder. Clancy was JFK, the handsome prince with the beautiful wife. Clancy was charismatic, athletic. People gravitated to him. Will was Teddy, the youngest. Also a charmer, who could always squirm his way out of a jam. And like those two Kennedys, the women went crazy over his brothers.

He was Bobby. The runt of the litter, the brother who always had to push harder to get attention, the one who would always live in the shadow of his older brother. Because of his status, Tom was a momma's boy, Jocelyn's favorite—so the others thought. She had always doted on him, praising his achievements and forgiving his failures, explaining them away.

They all missed her, but he missed her the most.

The Kennedys were a romantic fantasy. There was another family that Tom sometimes compared his to, although it wasn't as flattering a comparison. The Corleones, with him as Fredo, the vain, shallow middle brother, played by John Cazale in the films. The hapless one, the one you couldn't trust to get the job done.

If there was a job to be done about his father, he wouldn't be hapless. If anything, he'd be the one among the brothers who would find out what was really going on, and do it.

Whatever that meant. As of now, he didn't have a clue.

She was in the house somewhere, but he didn't want to intrude on her space—being alone with her like this, without his father around, made him nervous. He walked out to the backyard and looked around. The sun was hitting the pool at a low oblique angle, so that the water, from where he was standing, appeared to be moving, like small waves in a much larger body, a lake or an ocean. He was used to the Great Lakes, particularly Michigan and Erie, but he hadn't spent much time on either coast.

That was one thing he wanted to do before he went home—swim in the Pacific. He had the rest of the afternoon to kill. No time like the present.

Emma suggested that he drive down the Pacific Coast Highway to one of the beaches past Malibu—Zuma or Carillo State Beach. It would take about forty-five minutes, but they were better beaches for swimming than those in Santa Monica. And, she said with what he thought was a teasing smile, the girls were cuter. She wrote down instructions on how to get there.

He changed into his trunks, grabbed a towel, and headed out the door.

"Don't forget this," she called from the kitchen. She tossed him a tube of Bullfrog. "You're a Midwest pale-face. You'll burn up otherwise. And this, too." A bottle of water came sailing his way.

"Thanks," he told her, pleased by her thoughtfulness. He stuck the lotion and water bottle in his pack.

"Have to watch out for you while you're here," she told him cheerily.

Her friendliness was disconcerting. She looked aloof, but acted like she had known him for a long time. "I'll be back by seven," he promised.

"Don't rush. Like I said, Walt won't be here until eight. Enjoy yourself."

The drive to the beach was easy—a straight shot down Sunset to the coast highway, then north fifteen miles. He drove through Malibu, savoring the sights and smells of the ocean to his left. Malibu! The very name was exotic, evoking images of movie stars. Mel Gibson lived in Malibu—he'd read that in People, while waiting for his appointment at the dentist's. Kate Hudson, he thought. Winona Ryder. It would be cool to run across a famous actor (better a famous actress) at the beach. Something to tell tales about back in Michigan later in the year, when the snow was a foot on the ground. *Yeah, I was catching some rays, taking it easy, this woman comes walking by wearing a bikini the size of two cocktail napkins, looks kind of familiar, I smile at her, she smiles back, I say, "Aren't you Ashley Judd," she says, "Yeah, I am," I introduce myself, we talk for a while, grab a cool one. Really nice, not standoffish at all. Nothing happened, I had to get back to have dinner with my father, but who knows otherwise? She was as friendly as any other woman, a regular person.*

In your dreams, he thought, as he turned into the Zuma Beach parking lot.

There weren't any movie stars on the beach, none he

recognized, anyway. There was hardly anyone at all. Summer was over, the local schools were back in session, and it was a weekday. Mostly it was kid surfers, out on the water. The beach was almost a mile long and a quarter-mile wide, and he had a big piece of it to himself.

He rubbed some lotion on and lay down on his back on his towel, hoping to get the beginning of a tan. But it was hot and he was restless, so he took a walk along the beach at the water's edge, looking out at the surfers who waited patiently on their boards for waves to ride. It was low tide and the ocean was calm, not much wave action that he could see. When one did come, rising up with its foam cape, all the surfers would begin paddling in unison, getting up on their boards as the wave crested, trying to ride under the curl. A few did. Mostly, they wiped out.

If he lived here one of the first things he'd do would be to learn to surf. If you were going to live in California, that was one of the prerequisites. He wondered if his father had tried it. He could see the old lion, standing up on a board, hair all tangled with saltwater and sand, gnarled toes gripping the edge. His father would try anything. This move out here was a radical example; yet as Tom walked along the sand, feeling the water at his feet, looking out to the horizon, he thought that maybe the move wasn't so strange after all. His father had spent his life trying to find lost civilizations. How different was that from trying to find a new life? Yes, Walt had lied about things, like the mortgage. But he might have legitimate reasons for not telling the truth. Maybe he and his brothers really had rushed to judgment. Standing here at the water's edge, feeling the sun on his face and the surf lapping at his feet, Tom decided he was going to give his dad the benefit of the doubt, at least until Walt showed him otherwise.

He took a long, easy swim out to the buoys, then down

three, then back, then in. He was a good swimmer, he exercised in one of the university's pools. He had been a swimmer in college, middle-distance freestyle. Nothing great, but good enough to win letters in his junior and senior years.

The sun, melting like an overheated yellow lollipop, was descending in the hazy sky. Tom checked his watch. It was almost seven. He walked across the cooling sand to his car. He didn't want to be late.

He dried off from his shower and put on a clean shirt and khakis. He hadn't seen his father for over a year. He wanted to look good.

Emma was in the kitchen, on the phone. As she heard Tom approach, she turned to him. She looked angry, and chagrined. She handed him the phone.

"It's your father."

"Hey, dad."

"I won't be making it home tonight," Walt said brusquely, over the line. No "hello, how are you son," no "I'm sorry."

The instrument flared hot in Tom's hand. He felt like he should be holding it with an oven mitt. His stomach tightened. "Why not?"

"Got hung up here. Need to meet with them tomorrow morning. I won't be back until tomorrow afternoon."

"Jesus, dad . . ."

"I told you I couldn't make any promises. I have commitments, Tom. I can't drop everything because you decide to come out and pay me a visit."

I'm your son, you asshole! Tom wanted to shout. *I haven't seen you for over a year! Change the schedule. What's the big deal?*

"That's a bitch," he said flatly. He looked over at Emma. She shook her head in sympathy.

"I know." Walt's voice and attitude softened. "You're here for a couple more days, right?"

"Yeah."

"So we'll have tomorrow and the next day. That's plenty of time for us to be together. I tried to get out of this, but I couldn't. I really am sorry. Can you forgive me, this one time?"

What could he do? Throw a tantrum? "Yeah, dad, sure."

"Great. You know how these things are, you're in the academic world, the same as me. When they say 'jump,' you ask 'how high.' Am I right?"

Walt Gaines had never jumped for anyone—not through a hoop, not off a cliff. Now he had to? Maybe trying to start over at a new school wasn't that easy, even for a man of Walt's renown. He had vowed to give his father the benefit of the doubt. This was a test for doing that.

"I guess. I'm not in that rarefied atmosphere yet. I'm happy just to get noticed and tossed a bone."

"That's all going to change as soon as you finish your thesis," his father said heartily. "You'll see. They'll be pounding on your door. And you know I'll be helping you, any way I can. I still have friends in high places," he said boastfully.

"First I have to finish it."

"You will, you will. So we're cool with each other about this?"

Tom sighed. "Yes, dad. We're cool with each other."

"Good. Put Emma on the phone."

He held the phone out to Emma, who took it and half-turned away from him with an embarrassed look on her face. Grabbing a beer from the refrigerator, he headed toward the backyard. As he was opening the French doors that led to the outside, he heard Emma angrily say, "That's no excuse, Walt. You could have tried harder."

Tom stood at the edge of the deck, drinking his beer in long swallows. Emma came outside. She walked toward him. "We could go out to eat," she offered. "On me."

He shook his head. "You don't have to bother yourself on my behalf. I'll find something to do."

"I could make you an omelet."

"Thanks anyway. I'll go out on my own." He needed to get away from here. From his father's house, his father's woman.

She handed him a key. "The kitchen door. I'll probably be asleep by the time you get back, so I'll say good night now, and see you in the morning."

"Okay," he said. "Thanks."

She bit her lip. "I want to apologize for your father's behavior. It was rude and inconsiderate."

"You don't have anything to apologize for. It wasn't you."

"Still . . . he shouldn't have done that."

"He has to do what he has to do," Tom told her. Thinking, when hasn't he?

Tom walked along Main Street in Santa Monica, checking out the shops and bars. It was a bustling scene, mostly younger people who were intent on having a good time. He wished he felt like they did. Goddamn his father! He was pulling another one of his power plays: I come first, kid. If there's anything left over, you can have that. But you're not at the top of my priorities.

He had a couple of beers in a couple of bars, then

ducked into a hole-in-the-wall sushi restaurant, where he sat at the counter and watched the chefs wield their knives like samurai. After that he walked over to the Third Street Mall and took in a movie, slumping low in his seat as he watched an Albert Brooks comedy that flew out of his head as soon as he left the theater. Then he worked his way down the mall, stopping in each bar he came to, having one beer and moving on.

It was late when he got back to the house. He had a buzz on, but nothing serious. No lights were on, although shards of moonlight filtered through the windows. He stood in the hallway outside his room until his eyes became accustomed to the darkness, then he fumbled his way, taking care not to bang into a piece of furniture or some other large object, toward the kitchen. Finding a clean glass in the dish-drainer, he crossed to the built-in Sub-Zero refrigerator and held the glass under the cold-water tap in the door.

As he navigated his way back toward his bedroom at the far end of the house, he sensed something from the outside; a presence, or more accurately, a premonition? He didn't know what it was, or why he was drawn to it. Backtracking across the living room, he opened the French doors that led to the outside patio, and stepped out onto the deck.

The moon was full, so he could see his surroundings more clearly than he had been able to from inside the house. There was definitely something out there. For a moment, he didn't know what it was. Then his senses coalesced, and he identified what it was. He was hearing the sound of moving water.

Venturing a few steps farther from the shelter of the house but taking care to remain hidden in the shadows, he looked across the lawn and saw Emma, swimming laps in the pool.

She was naked. Her stroke was strong, purposeful, arms reaching out, pulling, turning her head for air, the moonlight glimmering off her sleek hair that was combed back like a seal's coat, a soft diffusion as if filtered through sheer silk, lighting her bare torso, her ass, the backs of her thighs, calves, the soles of her feet.

She swam back and forth several times before stopping. Then, reaching the far end of the pool, she stood in the thigh-high water, pushing her hair back from her face.

Tom took an involuntary step backward, deeper into the shadows. He could see her clearly, her breasts, the dark triangle between her legs. Drops of water glistened on her body like silver fish. She leaned back against the pool's edge, her elbows on the deck, resting.

He stood stock-still, mesmerized, afraid to move, afraid any movement, even breathing, would reveal him.

The way she stood there in the shallow end, leaning back, it was almost as if she knew she wasn't alone. But she couldn't see him. He knew that. He was under the eaves of the overhang, where the moonlight couldn't reach.

She dipped her knees and pushed off and started swimming again and he stood there, watching her. He didn't know for how long: five minutes, ten. Time had stopped.

Then she was finished. She climbed out of the pool, grabbed a towel she had thrown on a nearby chaise, and started drying off vigorously, her hair, then her arms, body, legs, ass, snatch. Picking up a dark terry cloth robe, she put it on and knotted the cinch around her waist. She slung the towel over her shoulder and started walking up the lawn toward the house, to where Tom was standing, watching her. Spying on her.

It was as if he had been frozen in a block of ice that was suddenly broken apart. He turned quickly, silently, reentering the house, closing the door behind him. Before she reached the patio he had made his way back to his bedroom and closed the door.

He sat on the edge of his bed, shaking. His breathing was fast and shallow, like a dog's pant. He drank the glass of water that was still in his hand, listening to see if she was approaching, if she would throw open his door and bust him.

He remained where he was, his tailbone aching from tension, for several minutes, but she didn't come. She hadn't seen him.

There wasn't any hand cream in the medicine cabinet. He fumbled in his pack and found the sunblock she had given him. Standing over the toilet, SP30 lotion smeared on his cock, he masturbated, coming so violently that when it was over he went light-headed, almost fainting from the blood-rush. His knees buckled and he slid down onto the cool tiles of the floor, hugging the white porcelain bowl for support.

"How did you sleep?" Emma inquired, when he staggered into the kitchen in the morning. She was in a casual summer dress, looking fresh as a daisy.

Tom waggled his hand *comme ci comme ça*. "It takes me a few days to get over the time change."

"Coffee?" she offered.

"Yes, please."

"With or without?"

"I'd better have it black this morning."

She drew him a cup, handed it to him. It was hot. He blew on the rim.

"Do you have plans for today?" she asked. "Until Walt gets back?"

"I thought I'd be spending all my time with him, so no."

"I understand," she answered sympathetically. "I'd escort you around, but I'm busy."

"It's not your problem. I'll find something to do."

"Okay. Your dad called earlier, he will definitely be back at four. We'll have a nice dinner, and you two can catch up with everything then. Stay around here as long as you like, take a swim in the pool. The pool's nice for swimming laps."

He nodded. He had already seen how nice it was.

A swim was the ticket. It cleared the mush from his brain, lubricated his constricted joints. After he had finished, shaved, showered, and put on clean clothes, he felt better.

Casting about for something to do, he remembered that one of his dad's former students, Perry Bascombe, was at UCLA, in the graduate archaeology program. Perry and he were the same age, in the same undergraduate class. He had become friendly when Perry was still in Madison.

He had lost touch with Perry, but maybe he was still here. If so, he'd be a teaching assistant, in which case he might be on campus, preparing for the fall term. Tom had never been on the UCLA campus. He decided to drive over and check it out.

Once he got off the city streets and inside the body of the campus, he felt at ease in the thick red-and-yellow-brick buildings, the wide walkways, curving bike paths, kiosks with events plastered on top of each other; all the familiar and sheltering details of the cocoon of university life. School wasn't officially in session yet, but there was plenty of activity. This would be a nice place to teach, if he ever got his head out of his ass and finished up, so he could apply for a job. The big *if.* Sometimes it loomed as an insurmountable wall in front of him, reaching so high he couldn't see the top.

He had to finish. What other choices did he have?

Locating the building that housed the Archaeology section of the Anthropology Department, he looked up Perry's name on the rosterboard. It wasn't there, but that didn't mean anything. Graduate assistants usually weren't listed, there were too many of them and they didn't have their own offices. Scanning the board again, he found the name and office number of the department chair, a man whose name he didn't know. If Perry was still here, the chairman's secretary would know how to locate him.

"North Carolina," she informed Tom briskly. "Chapel Hill. The minute he finished his degree here last year UNC gobbled him up. He was one of our prizes. North Carolina got themselves a winner in Perry." She peered at Tom over her bifocals. "Are you a friend?"

"From a long time ago," he said, feeling deflated; not only that Perry wasn't here, but that he had finished up and moved on. Another reminder of his own torpor. "We'd lost track of each other."

"I can give you his e-mail address," she said briskly. "Hold on a minute."

He was about to say "don't bother," but he held his tongue. Somewhere down the line it would be nice to get back in touch with Perry. Too bad it wasn't going to be today.

She handed him an index card with the information written on it, and turned back to her computer. He stuck the card in his back pocket and went out. As he was walking down the steps, he heard someone call his name.

"Is that Tom Gaines?"

He turned. A small, wiry, middle-aged man, balding

red hair sticking up from his birdlike skull like he had stuck his finger in an electric socket, came bounding down toward him.

"You are Tom Gaines, aren't you?" the man asked. He was dressed in standard university mufti, khaki pants, loose sports coat, tennis shoes.

"Yes, I am."

"I thought that was you." The man's face broke out into a smile. "It's been a long time, but you haven't changed that much." He stuck out his hand. "Steve Janowitz. Your dad and I spent a summer together at a dig, eight years ago. You were there helping out, with your brothers and your mother." His face dropped. "I'm sorry. That was so awful. She was a great woman."

"Thank you," Tom said. "Of course I remember you." Steven Janowitz was one of the most prominent archaeologists in the country, among the few accorded a position in the same pantheon in the field as his father.

"How's your dad?" Janowitz asked anxiously.

"He's doing okay, all things considered," Tom said, thinking, haven't you and dad seen each other if he's been lecturing here, been having discussions about coming here to teach?

"Do you have a few minutes?" he asked Janowitz. He'd like to find out what was going on with this, if he could.

"Sure," the older man replied with a smile. "I'll buy you a cup of coffee."

The faculty dining room was almost empty. They carried their coffees to a corner table. Janowitz emptied three packets of sugar into his mug. A true archaeologist, Tom thought with an inner smile. You live in the field long enough, you pick up the natives' habits. Indians love their coffee sweet.

"What're you up to these days?" Janowitz began.

"I'm finishing up my Ph.D. in mathematics at Michigan."

"Theoretical?"

Tom nodded.

Janowitz whistled in appreciation. "Are you teaching, doing research?"

"Some, to pay the bills. Mostly I'm finishing my thesis. I'll be done by next spring. After that, I haven't decided. I could join the faculty, they'd like me to stay on, but I'm thinking maybe something in business, where I can apply what I know on a practical basis, like at one of the tech companies. The money's better," he said candidly. "I'll be paying off my student loans for years. I have several irons in the fire," he added.

"Sounds great." Janowitz blew on his coffee, took a tentative sip. "That was a disgrace, the way they treated your dad, after all he'd done for them."

Tom assumed he was talking about the situation in Madison. "It definitely was," he agreed.

"Pure stupidity," Janowitz said. "Walt raises millions of dollars to develop La Chimenea, the most important excavation they've ever had in that pissant country, it's going to be a huge boost to their economy, not to mention their historical perspective, and they thank him by tossing him out."

"La Chimenea," Tom said, concealing his surprise.

Janowitz's head bobbed vigorously. "Look, I'm not naïve. We're old hands, your dad and I. I know there were rumors of stolen artifacts down there. That happens at the beginning of every dig that contains valuable artifacts. You can post guards with machine guns around the clock and you aren't going to stop thievery, it happens everywhere, most of the time by the government themselves. But you don't pull the plug on a man of Walt Gaines's stature." He was building up a good head of steam. "They think they can do it themselves, without outside help. They're going to have a big comeuppance." He sighed. "It's terrible for your dad, though. They needed a scapegoat to explain away the problem, and he was the most visible target. He had nothing to do with any of the theft that went on down there, I know he didn't. I've known him too well and too long to ever believe he'd do what they accused him of. He has too much integrity."

What in the world is this about? Tom thought. This was more than a new paragraph in the ongoing saga of the metamorphosis of Walt Gaines. This was an entirely new chapter.

He couldn't let on to this man that he didn't know anything about this. But he damn sure was going to try to find out.

"I should give him a call," Janowitz said. "We haven't talked since right after that terrible time." Wistfully, he added, "I haven't been a very good friend in that regard."

"He travels a lot," Tom vamped. "Hard to pin down."

"That's good. A man his age needs to stay active."

"And he's thinking about teaching again," Tom said, baiting a line.

Janowitz didn't bite. "He'd be an asset to any department. I'd love to bring him in here." He frowned. "But between the problems with Madison and the difficulties at La Chimenea, it would be a hard sell. Plus there's his age. Our department's already overstaffed. All the universities are. Now that mandatory retirement has been banned, the pipeline's clogged with brilliant young professors who are stuck because there's no room for them to advance. I'd be very surprised if your father's ever going to be offered a position of the status he had again, certainly not one commensurate with his worth."

"So there's no chance he could ever join the faculty here."

Janowitz shook his head. "It would take an act of God. And I doubt God's paying close attention to the details at UCLA these days." He looked at Tom sadly. "I'll be frank, Tom. I'm afraid your father's teaching days are over. He should have swallowed his pride and hung on at Wisconsin. They were giving him flak, I know, but he could have forced them to keep him."

"What about a lecture series?" Tom was fighting a panic attack, but he needed to nail this down.

"If he wanted to come out here, we'd certainly be open to his giving a talk. He'd draw a nice audience, I'm sure. He'd have to pay his own way, of course," he added quickly, in case Tom was acting as Walt's courier. He gulped down the rest of his coffee. "I have to run. It was good seeing you."

"You, too."

As they stood and cleared their table, Janowitz asked, "By the way, I forgot to ask. What brings you out here, Tom?"

"I came out to see an old friend." He paused. "An old, close friend."

"Well, you and your friend enjoy yourself. And give my best to your father."

Walt was bounding out the front door by the time Tom had pulled up to the curb and gotten out of his car. His face wreathed in a leathery smile, he grabbed his son in a bear hug, almost lifting him off the ground.

"Where the hell have you been?" he boomed. "I caught an earlier flight, so I could be with you more."

"Around," Tom murmured, after they'd broken free from each other. You're twenty-four hours late, he thought to himself, so don't start guilt-tripping me. "You told me you weren't going to be here, so I went off on my own."

"Where'd you go?" Walt asked, as he flung an arm around Tom's shoulder and guided him to the house.

"Westwood." He didn't want to bring up UCLA. "Then I cruised up into the hills, Mulholland Drive."

"That's a beautiful area," Walt exclaimed. "One of the locations I looked at before I decided on this place. At my age, being in the flats made more sense. You'd love living up there, though. Next year, when you've completed school and you start job hunting, you might want to consider moving out here."

"It's a possibility," Tom said vaguely. *Maybe I can get a job at UCLA, like you.*

Emma was in the kitchen, up to her elbows in cooking. She smiled brightly when she saw the two men come in. "I was afraid you might have gotten lost and couldn't find your way back," she said to Tom, sounding genuinely relieved. "L.A.'s so huge, it's like a Chinese puzzle out there if you don't know where you're going."

"I lost track of time," Tom explained.

She ladled some liquid out of a large, steaming pot, sampled it, began adding seasonings. "I hope you're hungry."

"Smells delicious," he said. "What is it?"

"Cioppino. Like bouillabaisse, but Italian. It's a specialty of mine."

Walt started laughing, a big belly guffaw. "She serves it whenever a son of mine comes to visit," he told Tom.

"It's like prime rib for Christmas, reserved for special events or special guests."

"Clancy had it?" Would he always be condemned to playing second fiddle to his older brother?

"The only two times she's made it since I've known her," Walt said, giving Emma a frisky rib tickle.

She jumped and swatted his hand away. "Stop that." She was flush, as much from Walt's insouciant sexual ease in front of his son, who she barely knew, as from the steam coming out of the pot. "I don't cook fancy when it's only the two of us, it's too time-consuming," she explained. "And I have to watch your dad's cholesterol, because he won't," she added proprietarily.

"She does take care of me, even though she's busy here, busy there, busy everywhere," Walt sing-sung, like a demented canary. "Work, school, always on the go."

This is awfully manic behavior for the old man, Tom thought, as he watched his father cavort about the room. It's as if he's turned back the hands of time. A beautiful young woman can do that for an older man. And she was certainly beautiful. He almost ached, thinking of Emma in the pool last night.

"You're in school?" he asked her. Had Clancy mentioned that? He didn't remember. "What in?"

"I've dropped out temporarily."

"You'll go back," Walt said. "You're too smart not to. Don't let her looks fool you," he said to Tom. "This woman has it . . ." He tapped his forehead. "Up here."

"Walt, stop. You're embarrassing me." She was trying not to smile.

Tom, watching this playful, almost intimate bantering between lovers, was the embarrassed party. His father was showing off for him—see my new lady, isn't she grand, isn't everything so peachy-wonderful? His father and Emma seemed to be much more serious about each other than Clancy had prepared him for. It was a sobering understanding. His father's woman was his mother. Emma seemed, from the brief time he had observed her, to be a good person and devoted to his dad; but it hurt, seeing them like this.

"Why don't you two let me work in peace?" Emma prodded, in mock vexation. "I'll come get you when dinner's ready."

As he had with Clancy, Walt took Tom on a tour of the grounds. Showing off, Tom thought, a taste of sour anger rising in his mouth at the petty materialism his father had embraced so enthusiastically. The lord of the manor. Walt Gaines had replaced the glories and excitement of a new, important excavation in the Central American jungle for a rich man's house in the middle of make-believe land. This was a stellar house, no question, but he didn't feel his father had gotten his money's worth in the exchange.

He had come here to see for himself, firsthand, what was going on with his dad. Now that he had, he halfway wished he hadn't. He nodded mechanically as Walt explained the solar system that heated the pool, how he had replaced the old, sagging wooden back deck with stone, the pleasures of a gas-ignition Genesis barbeque over a dirty, time-consuming charcoal-burning Weber, like the ones they'd used summers back in Wisconsin, whenever he was home from one of his exotic locales.

"It's very nice, dad," Tom rotely commented, as they stood at the edge of the pool, watching the automatic cleaner glide along the edges, its rubber tentacles, like those of a giant jellyfish, sweeping the bottom clean. "Hell of a house."

"Thanks." Walt's eyes were gleaming with pride of ownership.

"Pretty highfalutin," Tom added, unable to hold his tongue.

His father looked at him with a sideways squint. He brought his hand up to shield his eyes against the twilight sun that was shining in his face. "What's that supposed to mean?"

"Nothing. It's just different from what . . . from how you and mom lived."

"That's what this is about, isn't it?"

Tom played innocent. "What what's about?"

"Don't shit me, Tommy. It wasn't that long ago I was wiping your ass."

Tom flinched. He hated it when his father used the diminutive of his name. It made him feel like he was six years old.

"I know you, son, I know all my boys like I know my own heartbeat. Your coming out here to pay a visit to poor old dad who you miss so much, that's what. Your brother got on his high horse about the changes in my life and wham, you've got to see it for yourself, too." He shook his head, a gesture encompassing in equal measures hurt, sadness, anger. "I don't mean the heartache changes. The material ones. My new place . . ." He turned and cocked his head behind him, toward the house. "Emma."

"I came out to see you, dad, that's all." He wasn't going to let his father bait him into a fight he couldn't win. "It's been a long time. Is that a bad thing, me wanting to see you?"

Walt faced him squarely. "If it's from love, no."

"That's all it is, dad."

His father scrutinized him carefully. Tom felt like he

was being X-rayed. Then a smile broke through Walt's dark facial clouds.

"Okay. If that's what it is, then great. 'Cause I've missed you, too. All of you. More than you can imagine." He looked away for a moment. "Your mother is dead, Tom. No one has grieved for her more than me. But we can't live in our grief forever, or it'll pull us under. I'm making a new life for myself, the best I can. I would hope you'd be pulling for me. Like I always have for you, and Will, and Clancy, in your own lives."

Shit. What do you say to that?

"Of course I am, dad. If you're happy, that's all that matters."

"I'm trying," his father said, his eyes suddenly glistening. "That's all any of us can do."

Besides whipping up a gourmet meal Emma had found the time to shower, freshen her makeup, and put on a party dress, a silk Chinese-style sheath with the skirt slit partway up her thigh. She really is lovely, Tom thought, watching her as he sat down at the beautifully laid dining table. If he had half his father's magnetism for women, he'd be in clover.

Flowers had been arranged in a cut-glass vase on the table, and two tall candles in silver candlesticks sent up small twisting flames. The dishes, the cutlery, the wineglasses, all spoke of elegance, and money. Emma had already brought the salad and bread to the table; now she emerged from the kitchen bearing a large, steaming tureen containing the cioppino, which she carefully placed in the center of the table.

"My compliments to the chef," Tom told her.

"You should try it before you give away your compliments," she said with a pleased smile. She began ladling the soup into large bowls, passed them to Tom and Walt, dished out a third for herself and sat down.

"I don't have to taste it. I can smell it's perfect."

Walt poured the wine, a California Rhone he'd brought up from his cellar, and raised his glass in toast. " 'Get the fatted calf and kill it, and let us eat and celebrate,' " he proclaimed. "We're having scallops and halibut instead of a side of beef but you get the idea."

"The prodigal son was a wastrel," Tom reminded him. "Is that how you see me, dad?"

Emma, her wineglass poised to drink, stopped and looked from son to father.

"Hardly," Walt replied, with a trace of annoyance in his voice. "I'm using the quotation in a familial sense. We've been separated, now we're back together, and we're having a feast to celebrate."

"I'll drink to that, although I can think of another verse that might be more appropriate. 'Take your father and your households and come to me, that you may enjoy the fat of the land.' " He smiled at Emma. "I'm paraphrasing, but you get the idea."

Emma was amused and impressed. "What is this, dueling biblical scholars? This family is so erudite, it's humbling."

"Anyone who uses 'erudite' in normal conversation shouldn't feel humble." Tom drank some wine, swirled the rest in his glass and regarded it. "Very excellent, dad. You're a connoisseur now, I take it, since you have your own wine cellar."

"I'm a connoisseur of many things," Walt said loftily. "The difference between the way I used to be and now is that I'm not denying myself pleasure anymore."

"You've always enjoyed yourself," Tom said, quarreling with his father's self-assessment. "Your work, your family. You have twice as much zest as anyone I know."

"I'm referring to material pleasures," Walt responded. "The mind and the heart are vital, but so are the more brutish senses, because while we may be at the top of the evolutionary chain, we're still animals." More seriously, he added, "Life is finite, Tom, I know that all too well, as do you. What's that saying, if you've got it, flaunt it? I'm not the flaunting type, but happiness can be found as much in this"—he held up his glass—"as in a loved one's caress."

"Very poetic, dad." You're so full of crap, he thought, but what the hell, tonight was for good times, and reconciliation—he hoped. Later, when he got home and told his brothers what he had found out, there would be plenty of time to deal with the real issues.

They dug into the tangy salad, the crisp bread, the steaming broth. And she can cook, Tom thought in jealous wonderment. The old man's found the complete package—another one. They broke the mold when they made his mother, that was a given, but this new lady wasn't shabby. Again, he saw her in his mind's eye, swimming naked by the light of the moon. Are you going to do that again tonight, he wondered? Hoped.

"So what about it?" Tom heard his father's voice.

He looked up from his soup bowl. "Did you say something, dad? I was somewhere else." He dipped his spoon into the bowl. "In here, with the fish," he joked.

"I said," Walt repeated slowly, for emphasis, "how is your thesis work going? You must be in the final lap."

"It's going." Tom didn't want to talk about this now.

"What's your timetable?" Walt pressed. "You are going to be finished by the spring, aren't you?"

"That's the plan. Great meal, Emma."

"Thank you." She cast a "drop this" look at Walt, which he disregarded.

"Aren't you?" Walt repeated.

Tom put his spoon down. "I hope so, dad. I don't have a crystal ball. But that is my intention, yes."

Walt used his spoon as a lecturer's baton, pointing it at his son. "Intentions are like snowflakes, Tom. They're beautiful, but they melt on contact. You have to have a concrete plan, and stick to it. By the time I was your age I was already an associate professor." He thumped a fist into a palm for emphasis. "You gotta get your ass in gear. You can't dick around, because there's a phalanx of hungry kids coming up behind you who will steamroller you flat if you're not moving forward. I've seen it happen, time and time again."

Tom could feel the heat rising in his cheeks and ears. "I'm handling it, dad," he said tightly. "Don't sweat it."

"If I don't," Walt rejoined heatedly, "who will? Certainly not you."

The table fell silent for a moment; then Walt broke it. "You have the finest mind in our family. You have a better brain than me, or your mother, or your brothers."

Tom had put his spoon down and was staring fixedly into his bowl.

"Can we drop this?" Emma implored. "Please."

"In a minute. You're brilliant, Tom, you're great at what you do. I can't tell you the number of times I've bragged on you to people: I've got a son who's a genius."

"I'm far from a genius," Tom said, keeping his head down.

"You are, and you should be proud of it. But you are also—and this is what hurts so much—the least motivated person in our family. You had how many majors in college, a dozen, before you finally stuck to math? It was the only one you hadn't dumped, as I recall."

"Three," Tom muttered. "Lots of people change their majors, that's what college is for, to let you explore before you settle into one."

"I don't dispute that." Walt was trying to be reasonable, he felt he was being reasonable, but his voice was rising. "That's not a put-down, I was the same—"

"It sure as hell sounds like it."

"—when I was in school," Walt rolled right through, "until I found my métier. But once I did—and here's the point I'm trying to make—I focused on it. I buckled down and moved forward. Which is what you have to do. *You have to!* You cannot allow yourself to waste this precious gift of a fine mind." He took a deep breath. "I will not let you."

Tom looked up. "It's not up to you, dad. You're not wiping my ass anymore."

"Stop this," Emma pleaded. "For Godsakes, Walt, please."

Walt sat back, shaking his head, either in disgust or resignation, Tom couldn't tell. It didn't matter, he was sick to his stomach now.

"You were your mother's favorite. She babied you and coddled you . . ." Another mournful head shake. "She worried about you, Tom. You were the one she worried about." He rubbed his eyes with the heels of his hands. "But she isn't here to worry about you anymore, son. And what I just said, about holding your feet to the fire? I'm not going to. Because you're right—it isn't up to me. It's up to you. I just hope you don't—"

He stopped. He had gone too far, and he knew it.

"Blow it?" Tom finished for him.

"Ah, Jesus!" Walt cried out. "I'm sorry," he said contritely. "Jesus, I can be such a tyrant sometimes. I don't mean to harm you, Tom, you have to believe me. I just care so damn much. You came all the way out to see me and I show my appreciation by haranguing you." He raised his glass again, but it was a halfhearted gesture. "I wish I had another appropriate biblical quotation, but I can't think of one, so I'll make one up. To my brilliant and loving son." He looked at Tom.

Tom didn't reply. I have one for you, he thought: *Let he who is without sin cast the first stone.*

He kept his mouth shut and took another spoonful of the fish stew. What had been delicious a few minutes ago had no taste now.

They sat in stony silence until Emma began clearing the table, at which point Walt abruptly excused himself and disappeared into his study. Tom gathered up his dishes and carried them into the kitchen. Emma was loading the dishwasher. He handed his dishes to her.

"Thanks," she said, rinsing them. She turned to Tom with a look close to bereavement on her face. "That was uncalled for. I apologize."

It seemed to him that she was always apologizing for his father's behavior. "You have nothing to apologize for," he said. "You're not the one who assholed out."

She poured more wine into her glass, and without asking, poured more into his, too. "He needs to see a therapist."

"Buy him a punching bag. It's cheaper."

"I'm serious. I think . . ." She faltered. "He wakes up at night sometimes in tears. We've become close, he and I, you can see that, it's obvious. But he misses your mother terribly." She finished stacking the dishes, turned the machine on. "Sometimes I think I shouldn't have gotten involved with him, given him more time to mourn. But he wanted to, he was the one who pushed it. You can't stop living—he told me that on one of our first dates. He said if it had been the opposite, he would have wanted her to find someone new as soon as she could." She drank some wine. "He was incredibly lonely, and needy. I didn't know him before, of course, but I'll bet he had never been needy in his life."

Tom nodded. What an emotional clusterfuck this was turning out to be. "No, he never was. He was as oblivious to need as any man I've ever known."

"Which was probably why the fall was so hard," she said perceptively. "If you've never known pain, when it finally comes you have no mechanism to cope with it."

"I suppose so." What he was about to ask her was delicate, but it had to be voiced. "Is he having a breakdown? Could he be?"

She shook her head. "I don't think so. That's not why I think he needs help. What he needs is to process his grief."

Tom shook his head. "He won't do that. He'd think it was an admission of defeat."

"I know," she replied. "He's so stubborn, and his ego is so strong. Too strong, sometimes. Like now." She took one of Tom's hands in both of hers. "In so many ways, he's wonderful. And he very much loves you and your brothers. People go through amazing changes when a tragedy like that happens to them. I know you don't want to now, you're outraged at him and you have every reason to be, but you're going to have to forgive and forget. At least forgive."

"That's not going to be easy," he said with brutal candor. "And why the hell should I?"

"Because he's your father. And because you have no other choice."

* * *

Tom needed relief—the atmosphere in his father's house was toxic. Grabbing his keys, he headed out.

"Where are you going?" Emma asked in alarm.

"Don't worry, I'm not leaving town. I need some time away from here. Clear my head."

"It's been a miserable trip for you," she sympathized. "You go all this time without seeing each other, and then he acts like a jerk. It's tragic, for both of you."

Tom nodded tightly. "What he said about my being my mother's favorite? That was true. But not because she loved me more than Clancy or Will. It was because I needed the most protection from him."

He had never told anyone that before, not even, in a drunken moment, his brothers. This woman, his father's lover, was an unlikely, perhaps even dangerous candidate to be confessing to. But he felt better for having done it.

He went looking for action. Some mindless physical activity that would distance him, for a few hours, from the rage he was feeling toward his father.

The club, which he'd read about in LA Weekly, was tucked away in an industrial area at the south end of Venice. Several people, most of them younger than he, were standing outside, smoking. After being ID'd by the bouncer, he pushed his way in and found a place at the end of the bar, where there was enough room to stand and not feel like a Tokyo commuter. He ordered a shot of premium tequila and a draft beer from the scantily dressed female bartender, gave her his Visa card to run a tab, and leaned back against the bar to check out the scene.

He was immediately struck by the absence of cigarette smoke; then he remembered that smoking was banned indoors in California, even in clubs, which explained all the kids clumped outside. He didn't smoke—as a fitness freak he detested cigarettes—but a bar without a low blue cloud of cigarette smoke didn't feel authentic.

The band, a couple of guitars, bass, keyboard, and percussion, sporting a punk look: dyed, spiked hair, torn jeans, multiple earrings, the usual mélange, came back from their break and straightaway started rocking the joint. The bassist and one of the guitar players were women, and they kicked righteous ass. Both guitar players, male and female, sang, the woman's voice a low, throaty, seductive alto, the guy's a cigarette-roughened baritone. The group was reminiscent to Tom's ear of Bob Seger, the Detroit icon he had seen in concert back in Motown. Several couples jumped up and squeezed onto the matchbox-sized dance floor.

The tequila went down smooth and he tapped on his glass for another, which the bartender poured with an experienced wrist. This feels *gooood*, he thought, sipping his drink as his body relaxed into a slouch. He looked around. There were some decent-enough-looking women who didn't seem attached to guys—they were hanging out in girl packs of three or four. He thought about how it would be nice to hook up with one, although he didn't expect to. He was throwing off the wrong vibe, still coming down from the bad feelings he'd brought with him.

It had been a long time since he had picked up a woman in a bar. He wasn't sure of the protocol. Back home, you asked to buy a woman a drink, and if she accepted, that was the signal that it was okay to make a move. You'd dance a few dances, then you might get her phone number. If you were really lucky you could detach her from her friends and take her to her place, which would be a cool bacheloress pad well stocked with massage oil, French ticklers, and other exotic toys.

That's a good fantasy, he thought, almost as good as the one about Ashley Judd at the beach. With about as much chance of probability, or even less.

The couple next to him paid their tab and left, and the space was immediately taken by two women who had been wedged in against the far wall. The one closer to him, a petite, stacked bottle blonde, gave him a quick smile as she glanced at him, then turned away and started talking to her friend above the din.

The band started another number, and the girl rotated back to him. "Want to dance?" she asked.

He nodded and tossed down the rest of his shot. They pushed their way onto the floor and shoehorned a space for themselves. Her high breasts under her light sleeveless blouse banged a drum roll against his chest. They danced—standing in place, weaving and grinding—until the song was finished. Then they made their way back to the bar.

"Buy you a drink?" he asked.

"Sure."

He ordered another double tequila and beer chaser for himself, while she requested a Cosmo on the rocks.

"It must be a hundred degrees in here," the woman complained, pulling her blouse away from her body and fanning herself.

He held up his shot glass. "To . . ."

"Whatever." She took a deep swallow. "I sure needed that."

"Agreed." He knocked back half his double, swallowed some beer.

"I haven't seen you in here before," she said.

"I'm new in town."

"I figured. You're an improvement over most of the numbnuts who hang out here."

He grinned. "I guess that's a compliment. I'm Tom."

"Renee. This is Rachel," she said, nodding at the other woman, who was sulking.

"Hi." He leaned across Renee to look at her friend.

The woman named Rachel nodded tightly. "This place sucks," she complained.

"Lighten up, girl," Renee chided her friend airily. She knocked back the rest of her drink. "Down here," she called out. "Both of us."

"Hold the beer," Tom said. If he drank much more beer, his kidneys would wash away.

The barmaid put their drinks down in front of them. Renee picked up her glass. "Where do you live, Tom?"

With my father. That would go over like a pregnant high-jumper. "I'm staying with friends in Westwood, until I get my own place."

"Westwood's cool. I live in Redondo Beach. What do you do?"

"What is this," he joked, "*Who Wants to Be a Millionaire?*"

"Time is short," she answered, "and so am I." She laughed.

He laughed with her. This was easy, at least so far. "I'm a broker." In case this went somewhere, his brother Will's life seemed more interesting than his own. Certainly more enticing.

"Neat. I'm a paralegal, O'Melveny and Myers. They're the biggest firm in L.A. I'll be starting law school next year. Nights, I can't give up my day gig."

She's not an airhead, he thought. Normally that would be a bonus, but tonight, given the amount of time he would be in Los Angeles and the direction he hoped this might be going, intelligence could be a detriment.

"I want to go," Rachel announced from behind them.

"Oh, come on," Renee moaned. "Don't be a party-pooper."

"This place sucks," Rachel complained. "And I have to be at the office early tomorrow. You do, too, Renee," she added. She picked up her purse. "Come on."

Renee sighed. "Next time, I'm bringing my own car." She smiled at Tom. "Do you want to exchange numbers?" she asked, digging into her purse.

The offer was out of his mouth before he had time to think. "I could take you home."

She stopped. "Oh. Well . . ."

"Renee," the other woman said darkly. "You don't want—"

"Oh, hush up," Renee said, cutting her off. She put her hand on Tom's arm. "You sure? It's the opposite direction from where you're staying."

"It's fine."

She beamed. "See you in the morning," she told Rachel in dismissal.

"You're being stupid. You don't even know this guy."

"I do, too. His name is Tom." She smiled at Tom. "You're not some weirdo, are you?"

He shook his head. "I'm probably the most sane guy you'll ever meet."

"Not completely sane, I hope."

The other woman gave one last head shake of disapprobation and pushed her way out of the bar.

"Party-pooper," Renee said to her back. She smiled at Tom again. "She's pissed because I got to you before she could."

"That's . . . flattering."

She put her hand on his. "Do you want to go someplace less noisy, where we can actually talk without shouting in each other's ear? There's a coffeehouse not far from here."

This was going faster and better than he had dared to hope for. "Sure."

He air-wrote for the bartender, who rang up his tab and brought it to him, along with his credit card. Ouch, he thought, looking at it. What the hell—he was on vacation, he was having fun, and with any luck at all, he was going to get some action. If nothing else, being with this woman had buoyed his spirits.

The cool night air almost knocked him over. Oh, man, he thought, I've had too much to drink. He swayed in place for a moment, until he got his sea legs under him.

"You okay?" Renee asked with concern.

"I'm fine." He took a deep breath. That was better.

She took his arm. They turned the corner and walked down the deserted street toward where he had parked his car. Might as well go for it, he thought. "Why don't we go to your place now?" he suggested.

She stopped and looked at him for a moment. "Okay. But no promises."

"Not to worry. There's my car, up there," he pointed. Hastily, he added, "it's a rental."

"It's cute. Like a toy car."

"Renee!" A man's voice behind them, calling.

She froze. "Damn," she said quietly.

"What?" Tom asked. It was dark out. The nearest streetlight was at the far end of the block. He turned in the direction of the voice.

"You stood me up again," came the unseen voice. "It's the third time in a row."

"What's going on?" Tom asked, feeling his chest tighten. He didn't like the sound of this.

From out of the darkness the man emerged, walking

toward them. He was dressed as if he had come from work—expensive-looking suit, white shirt, tie. He was a few years older than Tom, about Tom's size. His hairline was receding, but he looked like he was in good shape.

"Go away, Rudy!" Renee called to the man. She grabbed Tom's arm more tightly.

"I'd like an explanation," the man called. From the tone of his voice he seemed more hurt than angry.

"Who is he?" Tom asked. This was getting uncomfortable.

She sighed. "A lawyer from the firm. I dated him a couple of times. Nothing serious, but he keeps bugging me, making dates I tell him I'm not accepting. He must've been lurking outside, stalking me. Poor bastard."

She stood in the middle of the sidewalk, hands on hips, glaring at the man, who was coming closer. "Rudy, please go away. You're embarrassing yourself. We can talk about this tomorrow, at the office."

The man kept coming, until he was only a few feet away from them. "Who's he?" he asked Renee, staring at Tom.

"My date." She regripped Tom's arm.

"*We* had a date," the man said doggedly. He looked miserable.

Renee shook her head. "No, we didn't. I never accepted. I don't feel comfortable going out with anyone from the office, Rudy. It only leads to trouble. You know that as well as I do."

"You stood me up," the man said again. He was like a dog who wouldn't let go of a bone.

"Why don't you work this out tomorrow, like the lady suggested?" Tom said, stepping between the two combatants. "She's with me tonight."

The man called Rudy glared at him. "Who the hell are you?"

Tom glared back. The guy had pushed too hard. "That's none of your business. Now take a hike."

The man was breathing heavily. He looked away for a moment.

The sucker punch caught Tom square in his left eye. He went down in a heap.

"Rudy, you bastard!" Renee screamed at their assailant. She started pounding on his chest with her fists.

Tom staggered to his feet. He lunged at his assailant, but the man dodged him and rabbit-punched him across the back of the neck, at the same time putting a knee into his gut. Tom fell again, into the gutter.

Renee was screaming. "Rudy! Stop it! You'll hurt him."

"He started it," the man shouted back at her. "All I wanted was to talk to you."

"Go away," she yelled. "Get out of here!"

"Not without you," the man told her.

Tom was on all fours in the street. He put his hand to his face. It came away bloody. As he started to push himself up again, he felt a discarded bottle, lodged against the curb.

He staggered to his feet. "Hey!" he called out.

His assailant turned toward him. "You want more?" he asked.

Tom swung the bottle like a haymaker. It caught the man flush across his nose, shattering in Tom's hand. Immediately, the man's face was full of blood. He fell to his knees, clutching his face with both hands.

"Jesus! You've blinded me!"

From a couple of blocks away came the wail of a police siren.

"Someone from the club must've heard us and called in an alarm," Renee yelled. She pushed Tom toward his car. "Get out of here!" she screamed.

"What about you?"

"I'll be all right. But you could get into trouble. Go!" she said, pushing him.

He ran to his car, unlocked it, found the ignition with the key. As he was driving away he could see the police lights in his rearview mirror. For a panicked moment he thought they were coming after him, but they stopped where Renee was standing over the recumbent Rudy. She was kicking him in his bloody head as hard as she could.

By the time he got back to the house it was after midnight. With luck, his father would have gone to bed and he wouldn't have to deal with him until morning—he'd had enough grief for one night. Walking down the driveway, he looked in the windows. All the lights were out. Very quietly, he let himself in through the kitchen door with the key Emma had given him, and made his way to his room.

His face was a mess. His left eye was swollen half-shut, beginning to turn dark. His right cheekbone was lacerated and bloody from where he'd fallen in the street. His lip, too, was bleeding, and his jaw hurt like hell. The entire left side of his face would be black-and-blue tomorrow.

He washed his face off with cold water. There were no ointments in his bathroom medicine cabinet, no alcohol or hydrogen peroxide. Holding a towel to his face, he quietly made his way through the dark house into the kitchen. He opened the freezer and took out a handful of ice, wrapped it in a dish towel, and pressed it to his aching cheek. Then he went back to his room, took his clothes off, dropping them in a heap on the floor, put on the running shorts he was using as pajamas, and lay on the bed.

His head was throbbing. He wouldn't be able to fall asleep. Coming out here had been a disaster, from start to finish.

He heard the sound of water, lapping rhythmically. He got up and went outside onto the dark, sheltering deck, where he could hide and watch.

The moon was a diffused spotlight on Emma as she swam. Once again, Tom stood in the shadows, breathing with her, stroke, stroke, breathe, stroke, stroke, breathe.

He didn't know how long he stood there watching—five minutes, ten. Maybe longer. He didn't care. He didn't want this to end. He forgot the fight, the pain in his head. He was transfixed by the vision of her.

She finished swimming and got out, her hands wiping the excess water from her body, slicking back her hair. She toweled the rest off, rubbing vigorously, her legs, her ass, her back, the silky triangle. Then she put on her robe and walked across the lawn toward the house in her bare feet.

He didn't run away this time; he couldn't, he was frozen. Instead, he moved deeper into the shadows, hugging the far wall. Emma came up on the deck, hesitated for a moment as if she had forgotten something, then opened the French doors and started to go into the house.

And then she turned, came back onto the deck, and walked toward him.

"How long have you been here?" she asked. Her voice wasn't angry or accusatory; it was almost playful. She had an enigmatic smile on her face, as if they were playing hide-and-seek.

Then she saw him, saw his battered face. "My God!" she exclaimed breathlessly. "What happened to you?"

"Got in a fight," he muttered. He turned to go back into the house.

"Wait." She grabbed his arm and turned him around to face her. Carefully, she put a hand to his cheek. "Is anything broken?" she asked.

"I don't think so. No."

"You should have this looked at." Her fingers lightly probed his face. He forced himself not to wince. "I'll drive you to the emergency room at UCLA."

"No," he said quickly. "It'll be all right. It looks worse than it is."

She turned his face so that the moonlight caught it. He could see the concern in her eyes. "This needs to be taken care of," she said. "Go back to your room. I'll be there in a minute."

He sat on the edge of his bed. She knelt in front of him as she dabbed at the cuts and abrasions with an alcohol-soaked cotton swab.

"Ow!" He jerked.

"Try not to move. You don't want it to get infected."

Very gently, she began rubbing aloe vera on the bruises. "How does this feel?" she asked.

"Better." His face hurt like hell and he knew it would feel worse tomorrow, but her touch more than made up for the pain. She was very close to him, inches away. He could smell her breath, the aroma of mouthwash. His own breathing was slow and deep.

She finished attending to his bruises and stood up. The robe slid off her body to the floor. Her hands pulled his shorts down, pushed him down onto the bed on his back.

She turned the light off and got on top of him, her lips moving down the length of his body, her breasts caressing his chest, thighs, his aching cock. As she took him in her mouth she swung her body around so her knees were draped over his shoulders. He grabbed her ass and buried his face in her vagina.

She knelt above him and put him into her. Leaning down onto her elbows, she took his battered face in her hands and they kissed, her hands moving on his shoulders, his hands on her behind, her back, the backs of her thighs. When she could feel that he was about to come she held his penis at the root until he was able to hold back, then they fucked some more.

Her orgasm came in a silent scream and he erupted inside her.

She got up and went into his bathroom. He could hear the shower running. When she came out, she was wearing her robe. He was sitting on the side of the bed. She sat next to him.

"This didn't happen, Tom."

He nodded. He knew she was going to say that.

"I can't explain why I did it. I mean, I'm not going to. I have my reasons, but I can't tell you what they are. So please don't ask me."

He nodded.

She smiled as she touched his face. "You're going to look like hell in the morning."

"I don't care. I feel great now, that's all that counts."

Her fingers lingered on the battered cheek. "You're a beautiful man. I can see that, so clearly." She stood up and gathered the robe around her. "It's so sad that your father can't." She paused. "Or won't."

* * *

Emma brought a plate of scones and a pitcher of orange juice into the breakfast nook. With her face clean, hair pulled back in a ponytail, she looked younger than he did. If anyone who didn't know walked in on the three of us, Tom thought with a wistful longing, they'd think she and I were the couple entertaining my menopausal father, rather than the other way around.

"Did you sleep well?" she asked Tom with a bland pleasantness. She poured coffee into his cup, then looked him full in the face. Her eyes were guileless, betraying nothing. "You don't look very good, but it could have been worse."

"Thanks to you." He stared back at her, forcing himself to hold her gaze.

She smiled. "You're leaving shortly?"

Tom picked up his mug. "Right after this."

"I'm sorry your trip didn't work out."

There was a delicate vein running down the side of her throat. Tom watched it pulsating. He could feel an electric curtain of tension between them. "It wasn't a complete bust, as you know," he told her. "I learned some things I needed to know."

Their conversation came to an abrupt halt as Walt came into the kitchen. "How's everybody this morning—" He stopped as he saw Tom's swollen face. "My God! What happened to you?"

"Ran into a buzzsaw."

"Are you all right?" Walt asked with concern. "Did you see a doctor?"

Tom shook his head. He glanced quickly at Emma. "I had it taken care of. It looks worse than it is."

"Jesus," Walt exclaimed. "That's awful."

"It doesn't feel that bad," Tom assured him. "Really."

"Good," Walt answered. He sat down and poured himself a cup of coffee. Then he looked at Tom again. "Emma gave me a hell of a tongue-lashing after you left last night."

A stinging retort popped into Tom's head, but he kept his mouth shut.

"Walt . . ." Emma stood with her back against the stove.

"Which I deserved. I don't know what got into me, Tom. I just . . ." He shook his head. "I want so much for you, for all of you. But I'm so inept at expressing it. I really apologize, Tom." He blew on his coffee. "We have to bury the hatchet. You can't go home with things as they are."

Tom was exhausted, both physically and emotionally. Bracing himself, he walked over and sat down opposite Walt.

"I'll see you before you leave," Emma said to Tom.

"Okay," Tom said. "Thanks for everything."

"It was my pleasure."

She left the room. He watched her go.

"What time's your flight?" Walt asked, oblivious to the electric storm raging above his head.

"Ten-thirty."

"You'll have to leave soon, then. Security at LAX is a bear. My last flight, it took over two hours to clear." Walt shifted in his seat. "Listen, Tom . . ."

Here it comes, Tom thought. The opening of the vein.

"I don't care what you do," Walt said earnestly. "Drive a dump truck, play in a rock band, win the Nobel Prize, it doesn't matter to me, it really doesn't. I only want one thing, and I mean this straight from the heart. I want you to be happy. I want you to find love."

You sure have a piss-poor way of expressing it, Tom thought. "That's what parents are supposed to want for their children, isn't it?"

His father's eyes flickered a moment. "Yes. But too often, as I did earlier, you forget that. It's so simple and basic you take it for granted. You get hung up in careers and goals and all the crap that in the long run doesn't mean a damn thing." He paused for a moment. "Like I did."

"You were happy. You found love."

Walt nodded. "Yes, I did. I was amazingly lucky. They go together, happiness and love, because when you have love, you are happy. The rest, as the old rabbis are supposed to have said, is commentary. The trick, and this is the hard part, is to remember it, to not forget, to not take it for granted."

He slumped back. "Too often I took your mother for granted. Everyone takes things for granted, but that's no excuse." He pounded his open fist on the table. "You have to keep remembering it, remembering it, remembering it."

The vehemence of Walt's expression and feeling knocked Tom off-stride. "Mom loved you, dad." The words sounded trite in his ear, but he couldn't think of anything better to say.

"I know," Walt said, almost in irritation, as if he needed to get this sentiment out as fast as he could, without interruption, or it would vanish. "That's not the point. The same thing applies to you, how I feel toward you. Getting your doctorate will be a great accomplishment, but that's a thing, a credential, a compilation of knowledge. All admirable, yes. But that's not love."

He helped himself to some more coffee. "You and your brothers are all I have left. Emma, too, now, thank God, but it's not the same. You're my blood, and I have to pour as much of my love into you as I humanly can." He sagged back. "Or I'll never be happy, and neither will a big part of you."

Walt got up and came over to Tom, as Tom was afraid he would. It was a sloppy hug, and the kiss on the cheek was even sloppier.

"I love you, son."

Tom was supposed to reply "I love you, too, dad," but he didn't have it in him.

After Walt went into his study Emma came back into the kitchen. She closed the door behind her. "How did it go?" she asked.

"It could have been worse," Tom answered flatly.

"Are you going to come back?" she asked nervously, as if fearful of the answer. Not about her, about Walt.

"I don't know."

She reached over and lightly touched the back of his hand. "I hope you do."

Her touch fluttered like a bird's heartbeat—his entire body ached with desire. What was she doing to him, he wondered? Had it been a mercy fuck, a show of defiance or anger toward his father? Or even—he was afraid to allow himself to consider this possibility—that it was simple attraction, that she was the kind of free woman who went after whatever she wanted, regardless of consequences?

He wanted to take her in his arms, right here, right now. But he couldn't. She had made that clear, last night.

"I'd want to know beforehand that he isn't spoiling for a fight," he told her. "Of course, his actions could belie his words. Saying and doing . . . very different."

She nodded in understanding. "I honestly believe he can't help himself, because I know he was looking forward to seeing you. If it makes you feel any better, he was like this with Clancy, too. Although not as vicious," she admitted. "For some reason you brothers bring out a dark side in him. It's tragic."

He lashes out at us from guilt, Tom wanted to tell her. About being with you. "So everything's fine until we show up. Super."

"I didn't mean it like that. My God, this turned out so badly!"

"It's okay," he told her. "I'm leaving."

And as he said this a sense of calmness came over him that he hadn't possessed since he'd gotten on the airplane to come here. He *was* leaving, returning to his own world. Messed up it might be, but it was his, and he owned it.

"This is not about you, Emma." He looked over at the closed kitchen door. "But I'm coming around to believing his instincts were right about not wanting to be with us. If he wants to be left alone, we should honor that. We're his sons, but we're not his keepers."

"Except he doesn't," she said passionately. "When you're not here, he talks about you ceaselessly. He has a real hunger for his family."

"Until he bites in, and then he gets indigestion."

She smiled. "A biteful of you wouldn't make anyone sick."

Care to find out again? he thought. But even as he did, he knew he had to give that up, unless she decided otherwise. And he knew, with yet another ache, that she wouldn't.

"Will you stay in touch?" she asked him.

"He knows how to reach me." He paused. "So do you."

Walt and Tom stood at the curb by Tom's rental.

"I hope you'll give me another chance," Walt said.

"It's up to you, dad," Tom replied bluntly. He felt good.

Better than good—liberated. He wasn't in thrall to the great god anymore. If they ever did reconcile, it would be a balanced relationship.

"I swear to God I'll make it up to you."

"That would be great, dad." *But I'm not holding my breath.*

Walt wrapped his arms around Tom, who stood and took it.

Tom got into his car and began driving away. Looking in the mirror, he could see Walt waving him good-bye, opposite of the way it used to be when he was a little kid and his father would drive off to work in the morning. And farther behind, in the half-shadow of the front door arch, there was Emma, watching.

Just before he reached the corner she turned and went back inside.

CHICAGO

◆ ◆ ◆

Will moved to Chicago the weekend after Tom returned from his trip to Los Angeles. Merrill Lynch transferred him there, at his request. It wasn't New York, but it was a big step up. He'd be running his own section with more autonomy, and they were giving him a large raise.

The firm had rented a beautiful apartment for him in a six-story pre-war brownstone in Lincoln Park. The new digs were on the top floor of the building. The front door opened onto a small foyer, which spread out into a thirty-foot-long living/dining room, with built-in Art Deco cabinets, that ran the length of the building, front to back. There was a full-size, well-equipped kitchen, two large bedrooms, each with its own private bath, an additional guest half-bath off the foyer, twelve-foot-high ceilings with elaborately carved crown moldings, and sweeping bay windows that looked down onto the street, which was shaded by a high arching canopy of birches, aspens, and elms.

"The baby mogul's moved up to the high-rent district," Callie quipped, as she walked from room to room, checking it out. She dodged the deliverymen who were bringing in some of the new furniture Will had ordered. "There's going to be a conga line out the door once the babe hot line gets the word out that Will Gaines has moved to town."

"I wish," he said with a grin.

Callie ran her finger along the burnished cherrywood wainscoting in the dining room. "What're you going to do with all this space?"

Will, his arms laden with hanging clothes he'd carried up from the U-Haul he had driven from Minneapolis, grinned good-naturedly. "Throw wild, debauched parties, of course."

It was a fabulous apartment, but he could well afford it. His company was paying part of the rent, they had paid for his moving expenses, and had given him a furniture allowance. What he hadn't told his brother and sister-in-law, because he didn't like to blow his own horn, was that one of the big New York bond firms had tried to steal him away and he had used their offer as a bargaining chip. He also didn't tell Clancy that he'd insisted on being sent to the Chicago office, which was bigger than the Minneapolis one—their second-largest. He could have gone to the home office in New York, which would have accelerated his climb up the ranks, but he specifically wanted Chicago. The enormity and intensity of New York was off-putting to him—he wasn't ready for that radical a change yet. He was young, he had time. Unless he completely screwed up he'd still be a partner by the time he was thirty-five. New York could wait a few years.

The main reason he had wanted to come here, though, rather than remain in Minneapolis or move to New York, was family. He would be living in the same city as his oldest brother and sister-in-law, and Tom was a three-and-a-half hour drive away, less than an hour on the

Detroit–Chicago shuttle. It was important now for the brothers to be close, not only emotionally, but in actual physical proximity.

He and Clancy had talked to Tom, after Tom had returned from Los Angeles. The old man's behavior had been ugly and selfish, but it was in character with the way he'd been acting for the past year, so that information, although it pissed them off, wasn't a surprise. What had really scared them was Tom's discovery regarding Walt's nonstatus at UCLA, and the phantom job offers. Either their father had gone round-the-bend delusional, or he was weaving a dense web of lies about his life.

And it had gotten worse. During the past few days, Will and Clancy had contacted the archaeology programs at every major college and university in California that had one. The information they had uncovered was uniformly bleak. None of the name schools—Stanford, Berkeley, USC, the other UC schools that had archaeology departments, the Claremont Colleges—had tendered faculty positions to Walt. Most of the departments they'd gotten in touch with had not been in contact with him at all. No lectures, no symposiums, nothing. They knew Walt had left Wisconsin but none of them had any knowledge of his whereabouts, particularly that he was living right under their noses. There were a few allusions to the circumstances that had driven Walt from Madison, and one cryptic comment about La Chimenea, but otherwise, it was a blank slate.

The brothers hadn't wanted to dig deeper into the life of Walt Gaines. Now, with these new and stunning revelations added to the information Tom had discovered, they felt they had no choice.

* * *

Through the bay windows, the sun could be seen going down over the darkening treetops. The guys opened folding chairs around Will's new dining table while Callie spread out paper plates, plastic utensils, and cups—the regular stuff was somewhere in the stacks of unopened packing boxes that were strewn about the floor in the midst of the rest of the furniture, which hadn't been arranged yet.

Tomorrow, Will would start putting things in order. He had time to shape the place up, he was taking a week off before starting in at the new office. Tonight was for kicking back. And after dinner, serious talk.

But first, a toast. Callie poured from the bottle of Taittinger she had brought to memorialize the occasion and held her own glass aloft.

"To Jocelyn Murphy Gaines," she said in a clarion voice. "We will never forget you."

The brothers nodded gravely and drank. Then Clancy stood and raised his glass. "And to Walt Gaines. We'll never forget you, either, dad, no matter how hard you try to make us."

The Chinese food they'd ordered in was good but the meal wasn't festive, not the carefree celebration they had planned for when Will had told them he was moving to town. There was unfinished business hanging over their heads now, a cloud that was following them wherever they went. While they ate, they talked about everything except Walt. How it had gone at Finnegan's today, what kind of crowd to expect tomorrow—a larger-than-usual one, since the Bears were on the road for a critical game against the Redskins. Clancy had ordered four extra kegs, and he'd need them. They talked about today's game, a cliffhanger that Northwestern had won at the final gun on a blocked field goal attempt from point-blank range. They talked about Will's new neighborhood, where the good restaurants were, the good bookstores, clothing stores, coffeehouses.

Callie unearthed a pot in the jumble of packed boxes and made cowboy coffee. They drank it laced with bourbon Clancy had brought from the bar and smoked a joint, which Callie rolled with an expert's panache, the three of them sitting back in their fold-up chairs as the dry pungent smoke drifted up to the high ceiling.

There was no way of putting off the inevitable any longer. "So what're we going to do about dad?" Clancy asked. "We need a plan."

"Follow the money," Will answered crisply. A pad of paper and a ballpoint rested on his lap. "That's the cardinal rule. Whenever there's a situation like this, the money trail will lead you to the source, or close. The firm hires investigators who do nothing but that."

Clancy shook his head. "We're not bringing detectives into this," he said in a sharp tone of voice. "This is family, strictly."

"I'm merely telling you how it's done professionally."

"You may have to, at some point," Callie prodded her husband. "There might be information you need to get to that you don't know how."

"Later—if we absolutely must—we'll deal with professionals," Clancy said forcefully. "We're nowhere near there yet."

Neither Will nor Callie responded. They didn't need to verbalize what they all knew, including Clancy: that they were.

Clancy was half-asleep on his feet—his perpetual shortchanging himself of rest, on top of the anxiety this mess was causing, was draining. "You're right. Money is the logical place for us to start, because of the discrepancies over it."

"You mean lies," Callie corrected him. "Deceits."

Clancy shot her a dark look. "Yeah. Lies and deceits."

"You guys are the ones who said that, not me," she pointed out. "But if you're going to dig up your dad's buried bodies . . ." She caught herself. "That's a terrible metaphor. I'm sorry."

"It's okay."

"If you're going to chase after whatever you can find about Walt's secrets, financial or otherwise, no matter how unsavory," she rephrased, "you can't be sentimental about it. You're doing detective work, you need to be as objective as you can. Sentiment clouds your vision." She looked at him. "Are you mad at me for butting in? Should I excuse myself?" She started to get up.

Clancy grabbed her arm and pulled her back down. "I'm not mad at you. I'm mad at dad. I don't mean to take out my hostility on you."

"This is a bitch," she commiserated.

"I know. But we're there now, so let's keep going and hope nothing more terrible turns up."

Will's expression was dubious. "Let's don't pretend nothing else will. We have to be prepared for more bad news." He picked up his pad and pen. "Let's make a list and stop conjuring up bogeymen."

"Right on," Clancy said. He raised a forefinger. "Insurance. What kind they had, how much, how it was dispersed."

Will wrote on the pad. "And dad's retirement package from the university, and mom's," he said. "That should be the most important, that's where they'd have the most money. They were going to live on it." He paused, looking up into space. "I still can't believe she's dead."

Clancy nodded. "I know. I'm always expecting her to walk in the door. Okay, what else?"

"Investments. Stocks, bonds, IRAs, mutual funds. Maybe they had money salted away in places we wouldn't have expected them to." Will scribbled another note. "I'll do that. There's a database program at the office that should give me access to whatever we need."

"Is that legal?" Callie asked dubiously.

"No," Will told her candidly. "But it's done all the time. Privacy in this country is as extinct as the dinosaur. Every kid on the Internet knows that."

"We can debate civil liberties some other time," Clancy said impatiently. "Let's stay on focus. I'll look into their retirement packages from the university and their insurance policies."

"It's going to take me a week or two to ramp up," Will said. "First I've got to dig out of this mess"—his hand swept the room that was a jumble of unpacked boxes and crates—"and get set up in my new office."

"There's no rush," Clancy said. "These questions aren't going away."

Will tossed the notepad aside. "This is not going to be pleasant."

"Tell me about it," Clancy answered dolefully. "Dad's financial situation is only part of what we need to get into. We know he's been lying about going back to teaching. What about the rest of it? The big book he claims his publisher is breathing down his neck for, for instance. Is that real or is that bullshit, too?"

Will nodded. "And don't forget La Chimenea. Tom told me that when Professor Janowitz at UCLA told him dad wasn't teaching there, and wasn't going to be, he also threw out a cryptic remark about thefts at the site that were somehow associated with dad."

Clancy nodded. "Tom mentioned that to me, too."

"That could be a land mine, if there's problems down

there like that dad isn't copping to," Will said. "La Chimenea was going to be the pinnacle of his career. Now he doesn't even want to talk about it." He grimaced. "We're going to have to find out about that, too, I'm afraid, sooner or later."

"What a mess," Clancy groaned.

Callie had been listening as they formed their plan. Now she spoke up. "Aren't you forgetting something?" she asked.

"What?" Clancy said.

"The woman Walt's living with. What's her name again?"

"Emma," Clancy told her. "Emma Rawlings."

"Who is she?" Callie questioned. She paused, then asked, "Could she be connected to any of these issues you guys are wrestling with?"

Clancy sat back. "I haven't thought about that." This was spinning out of control. "Why would she be?"

She ticked the obvious reasons off on her fingers. "Because when a young, beautiful, intelligent, financially secure woman—she's all these, right? . . ."

He nodded. "Yes, she's all that."

". . . when a woman like that gets together with an older man, there's usually an agenda." She smiled. "Which is usually money—his. But if she has her own, then it's different."

"Dad said she does," Clancy answered morosely. "But now you've got to wonder about whether anything he's telling us is the truth."

Callie nodded. "Maybe there isn't any connection," she continued. "But here she is, all of a sudden, with your dad. An attractive woman is with a man twice her age, who's going through a terrible ordeal. Granted, Walt can run rings around plenty of men who are younger than him, but still, doesn't this relationship feel peculiar somehow? Don't you want to know about her background, since every other aspect of Walt's life is now under suspicion? I know I do." She rocked on the heels of her shoes. "I'm remembering something you told me about him and her that's making the hairs on the back of my neck stand up."

"What?" Clancy asked, almost fearfully.

"You told me Walt met her at a party, at UCLA. She's a graduate student there, right?"

"Yes, that's what he told me," he answered slowly. He could see where this was going.

She said it before he could. "Except this Professor Janowitz told Tom that Walt hasn't had any connection to UCLA. They don't even know he's living in L.A. So how could he have met her there if he's never been there?"

"This is getting to be as complicated as Rubik's Cube," Clancy lamented.

"Hold up," Will said, interjecting. "We need to find out more about Emma Rawlings, I agree. But she's secondary. We can't juggle a dozen balls in the air. Let's take this a few steps at a time. If we're still dissatisfied after we find out about dad's financial affairs, we'll look into her."

"Agreed," Clancy said with alacrity. "This is much more complicated than we thought it would get." He put his arm around Callie's shoulder. "We'd better get going. Busy day tomorrow. You coming down to the bar?" he asked Will. "It'll be a zoo, but it'll be fun."

"Maybe," Will said. "Depends on how much of a dent I make on this place."

"I'll come help you," Callie volunteered. "This apartment definitely needs a woman's touch. There's one more thing we need to talk about," she added, picking her coat up and slipping her arms into the sleeves.

"What else?" Clancy asked. He was weary of all this, he wanted to go home, make love, and fall asleep. Hopefully he wouldn't fall asleep first.

"Tom."

Clancy shrugged on his jacket. "What about Tom?"

"Shouldn't he be included in this?"

The brothers exchanged a look. "He's in this as much as we are," Clancy answered. "More, emotionally. He's been the most upset and suspicious from the beginning."

Callie shook her head. "You know what I mean: proximity. You and Will and me are here. Tom isn't. He's going to be upset if he finds out we're doing things about your father he isn't involved in."

"He can be involved as much as he wants," Clancy replied with a rare show of pique. "He can handle the whole mess, as far as I'm concerned. I've got a job. Two. So does Will. Tom's the one with the free time." He groaned. "I'm sounding more and more like dad. He's been beating up on Tom forever about not being focused."

"So don't you," she admonished him. "That's another thing that worries me. The three of you at each other's throats."

"We won't be," Clancy avowed.

"You were just ragging on Tom. I had to remind you not to."

Will went into the kitchen to get himself a glass of water. He came back and sat down Indian-style. "Tom ought to move here," he said.

Clancy turned to him in surprise. "How can he do that? His work is in Ann Arbor."

"What work?" Will asked, almost pityingly. "Teaching freshman calculus for twelve bucks an hour? He meets with his doctoral advisor once every couple months, the rest of the time he could be living in Tahiti, for all they'd know or care."

"That's not a bad idea," Callie chimed in enthusiastically. "He could work a shift at the bar. Nights. It would take the pressure off you, honey. And he'd be here. That's important now."

"I don't know," Clancy answered slowly. "He might . . ." He trailed off.

"Might what?" she pressed.

"Think it's a handout. That I'm throwing him a bone."

"It wouldn't have to be like that," she said. "You could present it like you're asking him to do you a favor. And that you'd all be close by, so you could coordinate your strategy."

Clancy thought of Tom's defensive fragility, always lurking just below the surface, waiting to erupt at the first slight. "I don't know . . ."

"He could live here, with me," Will volunteered. "I could house half the Notre Dame football team in here and still have room left over."

"What is this, *Friends*?" Clancy joked feebly. "Maybe Callie and I should move in, too."

"Over you know what," Callie replied.

"Tom's my brother," Will said somberly. "And yours."

Callie became serious again. "It can't hurt to ask him," she pushed Clancy.

Clancy gave in. "Okay. If you guys think it's the right thing to do, fine by me. You're the one who's got to live with him, Will, not me. I'll call him tomorrow, tell him what we're thinking." He laughed weakly. "The worst that can happen is he'll tell me to go fuck myself."

Ann Arbor

♦ ♦ ♦

Tom secured the ball joint of the U-Haul onto the bumper hitch the machine shop had welded to the frame of his car. He rigged the electrical wires to make sure the trailer lights would go on when he hit the brakes, tightened down the chains that secured the trailer to the car, and pulled on them to make sure they were taut. Satisfied that nothing would fall off, he went back into his apartment.

He had finished packing. Everything he was taking with him to Chicago was crammed into the small trailer: his bed frame, box spring and mattress, a few other pieces of furniture for his bedroom at Will's, his clothes, books, CDs, tapes, his old Sony TV, and his Bose bookshelf music system. His computer and the pieces of tech gear he used for work, computer games, and downloads were piled in the backseat of the car. The rest of his stuff—furniture, dishes, cooking utensils, other odds and ends—had been donated to Goodwill. There wasn't much of it. It was cheap and crappy, stuff you find in shabby secondhand stores. Not worth trying to sell.

Yesterday, he had gone to the bank and closed his account, taking the money in a cashier's check. One thousand, six hundred, and forty-three dollars: the sum total of his wealth. When he got to Chicago he'd hand the check over to Will and ask him to invest it. He was twenty-eight years old, and he owned almost nothing.

"Chicago's a great town," his faculty advisor exclaimed jealously, when Tom informed him he was moving there to live with his brother. "Everything New York has, but more accessible." He'd flipped open his Week-at-a-Glance. "Keep me abreast, we can do that via e-mail, and every couple of months you'll come back here and we'll spend a few hours, right?"

Tom had nodded, and kept his silence.

"You're doing well with your final draft," the professor said, brandishing the section of Tom's thesis he'd recently edited. "There's no reason you shouldn't be presenting this by spring."

Tom nodded again. No reason at all, he thought, except I'm not going to finish it. And after today you'll never see me again, unless it's by accident.

The calls from Clancy and Will had initially stunned him; but then, after he'd had time to reflect on the possibilities they offered, it was as if he had been thrown into a freezing shower. Not that the two of them had made the decision to dig further into their father's life; he'd expected that. If they hadn't, he would have done something about it himself. He hadn't figured out what that action would be, or how he would go about it, given his limited resources. But now he wasn't going to have to Lone Ranger it—the three of them were going to work together.

Once he had decided to take Clancy's job offer at the bar, and Will's invitation to share his apartment (rent-free,

Will had stressed), Tom moved fast. He withdrew from his teaching position and tidied up his other university affairs. He gave his landlord the required thirty days' notice, and got (after some verbal sparring and threats) his four-hundred-dollar deposit back, part of the sixteen hundred dollars tucked away in his wallet.

His academic life, as of today, was officially over. The university didn't know that, but he did. He hadn't realized how much he had wanted to make that decision, until it was thrust upon him by his brothers' generosity. Naturally, he was concerned about life outside the gilded birdcage, beyond the temporary bartender's job in his brother's saloon; but that problem would take care of itself down the line. What was important, overwhelming, exhilarating, was that he was *free*! He felt as if a tremendous weight had been lifted from his shoulders, a blindfold removed from over his eyes.

The revelation, although it had come after years of indecision, had been simple: he didn't want to be an academic. He had come to understand, finally, that the world of the university had been his father's life, and that he couldn't follow that act. Walt Gaines cast too wide a shadow. Even now, with the pall that had fallen over him, he was still formidable. Too formidable for any of his sons to follow in his footsteps.

Clancy and Will had always known that. They had never considered emulating Walt. Tom, though, was the stubborn brother, the one who couldn't stop banging his head against the wall. He was going to prove he could compete on the same level.

But he hadn't, and he wasn't going to. At best, he'd be a run-of-the-mill professor at some run-of-the-mill college. It was time to get out of the shadows, literally and figuratively.

His first reaction to his brothers' phone calls, though, had been confusion mixed with irritation: a free room in his kid brother's ritzy apartment and a job working nights at his older brother's bar? His knee-jerk reaction had been to tell them thanks but no thanks: he was happy where he was, he was finally finishing his dissertation, he was looking forward to his fall teaching assignments. He even told them he'd recently met a woman he was seeing regularly. He appreciated the sentiment, he'd said, but he was staying put.

All of which was a total crock. He was overwhelmed with self-loathing and self-anger almost as soon as he hung up after their calls. He was stuck on his thesis. He knew it, and he suspected his advisor did, too, and had been uttering mealy-mouthed pieties about presenting it in the spring to avoid an unpleasant confrontation. Although he had once truly loved teaching he had now come to loathe it, particularly at the level at which he was doing it. It was remedial pabulum, basic stuff any respectable math major should have learned as a high school sophomore or junior.

The story about the new woman he'd met was the lowest deceit. He hadn't had a date since his return from L.A. The only women he had met in months had been Renee from the Venice bar, an encounter that had resulted in his being seriously beaten up, and Emma Rawlings.

Emma. He thought about her constantly, incessantly. Often he could think of nothing else but her. Several times he had picked up the phone to call his father, not to speak to him, but because she might pick up the phone. But he never made the call. She didn't pick up Walt's phone, and even if she had, what good would have come of it? Any contact with her, even her voice over a line from two thousand miles away, would only tear him up inside even more. There were times, when seeing them making love in his mind's eye, he would become enraged with his father—not because of the betrayal of his mother's memory, but because his father had already had his special, perfect woman. Why did he have to be a hog and suction away another? Why couldn't Emma have been his woman instead?

Because she wasn't. And if her relationship with his father ended tomorrow, she never would be, either. He still had no comprehension, intellectually or emotionally, of why she had selected him to be her lover for that one night—the mercy fuck theme, getting back at Walt for being an asshole, the other possibilities, he knew none of them held any water. It was something basic in her, that he would never begin to know or understand.

It would have been better if having sex with her had never happened. He wouldn't be a slave to the memory, as he was now.

He hadn't told his brothers about that night. He wanted to—he wanted to tell someone, partly for bragging rights and also because he was bursting from holding the awesome secret in, but he didn't know how, and more important, if he should. It would complicate an already tangled situation, and he didn't feel that it had any direct relationship to the rest of the problem they were facing.

Maybe, down the line, facts would emerge that would change his mind. For now, he was going to have to keep what had happened to himself.

He drove I-94 west across Michigan, passing through Battle Creek, Kalamazoo, reaching the eastern shore of Lake Michigan at Benton Harbor, continuing south into Indiana, a mercifully short drive through the squalor of Gary and Hammond, and then he was over the Illinois line and into Chicago. Piloting his car and the balky trailer through heavy city traffic, he maneuvered onto Lake Shore Drive, made his way through the center of town, then to Will's neighborhood.

He parked illegally in front of a fire hydrant, the only way he could fit his caravan into a space, got out of his car, and stared up at Will's building. So this is how someone Will's age—my kid brother—lives when he's making money, he thought. And that thought was followed by another—there's more to life than material pleasures, but man, have I been missing out.

MADISON

◆ ◆ ◆

Clancy found a space in the visitors' parking lot without having to circle it a dozen times. A lucky omen, he hoped—parking spaces were almost always impossible to find. After getting out of the car and stretching to work the road kinks out of his back, he walked across the campus to the administration building, where the office of the university's retirement benefit program was located.

Because he wasn't in a hurry, and wanted to see the changing of the season, he had peeled off the I-90 at Rockford and motored up old U.S. 20 to Freeport, from which point he had headed north into Wisconsin on even smaller, less-traveled state and county roads that were cut through thick stands of forest. The fall season, which had been late in arriving, had finally exploded over the northern Midwest. The leaves of the elm, oak, beech, ash, walnut, and chestnut trees were changing colors so rapidly they almost appeared to be transforming before his eyes as he watched. When he was a kid, one of the traditional chores he and his brothers had been assigned was to rake the leaves from the front and back lawns of their parents' house. The boys would form monster-sized piles, taller than they were, and then would jump into the mounds as if they were wild dogs, scattering them all over the yard. Then they would rake them up again, and repeat the process. After they were done messing around, Walt would light the ceremonial fires and they'd watch the dry, burnt leaves curl up in smoke into the graying late-afternoon sky.

Yesterday, he and Callie had gone around the neighborhood collecting trash bags of fallen leaves, which she was going to use to create festive decorations for Halloween and Thanksgiving. Making wreaths and other ornamental pieces from the leavings of nature was going to be one of Callie's contributions to the building of their own traditions. *If* their mother were still alive, and *if* their father hadn't gone off into his new and frightening life, it would be perfect.

But those were two insurmountable *ifs* too many.

"I went ahead and pulled your parents' records," the administrator told Clancy, as he settled into a university-logo-emblazoned captain's chair in front of her desk. Her name plaque identified her as Rebecca Duckworth. She was an open-faced, cheerful-looking woman. Tortoiseshell bifocals hung from a chain around her neck. Although she had the heat turned up, she was wearing a forest green turtleneck sweater under her dun-colored J. Crew jumper. Clancy had spoken on the phone with her yesterday, when he'd called and told her what he was looking for.

"This is confidential information"—she tapped a short, unpolished fingernail on one of the files on the desk in front of her—"but since you are their son and are helping administer your late mother's affairs for your dad, I can bend the rules." She smiled, as if to let him know she wanted to be helpful. "What a sad business that was," she added sympathetically.

She opened the thicker of the two files. "It was untimely that your father resigned when he did," she said. She paused for a moment to put on her glasses and wet a finger to turn a page. "From a financial point of view," she added, looking up at him. With her thick glasses on, her weak, pale gray eyes were magnified.

"Because of . . . ?" Clancy ventured.

"His age. His length of tenure, also."

"Right." Clancy wasn't sure what she meant, but he didn't want her to know that he knew less than she presumed he did.

"He was too young," she amplified, glancing down at the document in front of her. "Ordinarily, fully tenured professors don't retire at age sixty. The ones who do, generally, do so because of health problems. Your father, from what I understand, was not in ill health."

Clancy nodded. "His health is fine." His physical health, he thought. Mentally, that was different. None of her business.

"That's good to hear." She frowned. "His decision was costly to him, though." She scanned the page in front of her. "If he had stayed on for another year and a half, the academic year he cut short, plus one more, he would have had thirty years as a full professor. His retirement package at that point would have been considerably more substantial." She looked up at Clancy and smiled. "It's like being in the military or the civil service," she explained. "When you reach certain milestones, your benefits are better. I suppose he felt he had no choice," she added, seemingly embarrassed.

"He was in an uncomfortable position," Clancy reminded her, since she had already alluded to the situation.

"Yes, I know. Many of us were dismayed. It was a hotly discussed topic." She hesitated. "I'm talking out of school here," she said softly, as if the walls had ears, "but he didn't have to go."

Clancy gave her a guarded shrug.

"The university would have kept him on if he had fought for his job," she continued. "They would have had to, he was one of the most popular professors here. And getting rid of a tenured professor is not easy," she continued, her face grimacing. "The faculty senate was prepared to stand by him." She paused for a moment. "The impression we all got was that he didn't want to stay any longer and used the fallout from that trip as an excuse."

"It was his decision," Clancy said firmly. The woman was trying to be kind, but this was an uncomfortable discussion.

"Of course." She turned some pages. "You're aware of the changes your parents made in their distribution, aren't you?"

"I knew they had . . ." He backtracked, because he didn't know. "Run that by me, would you? The details."

"Here, take a look." She came from behind her desk, stood over his shoulder, and turned the file toward him, so he could read it. She smelled faintly of camphor. "Until a few years ago—about a year before your mother . . ." She hesitated.

"Died," he said firmly.

"Yes." She ran her finger along the page. "Up until then, they had been enrolled in the standard defined benefit plan, with full survivor benefits." She lifted her eyes from the page so she could look at him. "That's done for the financial protection of the surviving partner, particularly if that partner has a smaller pension, which was the case with your parents. Your dad's pension, given his status and length of tenure, was substantially greater than your mother's. In other words, if your father had passed away before your mother did, instead of what actually happened, she would have gotten more money from his pension plan. The downside, of course, is that under that plan, the beneficiary, who would have been your father under those circumstances, would have gotten less per month, because more was being saved for your mother."

"So what was the change?" Clancy asked guardedly.

She glanced at the page again, then looked back to him. "It was redone so that when she retired, all of her benefits would come to her. Had she passed away first, which from an actuarial perspective was unlikely, given that she was younger and a woman, he wouldn't get anything from her plan."

"I see," he said slowly. He didn't, not yet.

"His plan, on the other hand," she continued, "remained as it had been."

"So if she died first," Clancy said, thinking this through, "he wouldn't get any of hers, but if he died, she'd get some of his."

She nodded. "That is correct. And that's not uncommon," she pointed out. "His package was substantially larger than hers, so that if they both retired, they could still live comfortably on his partial benefits and her full ones; but the opposite wouldn't be true, because her benefits were much smaller, so if he had taken his plan in full, as she'd done with hers, she would have gotten less if she had survived him. Much less," she added.

This is a surprise, Clancy thought reflexively—both the alteration of his mother's plan, and his father's unselfish magnanimity in maintaining his own. His father wanted to make sure his wife was properly taken care of in case he died first.

Clancy felt a surge of good feeling toward his father. It was the first feeling like this he'd had for months. "Yes," he said, now understanding. "He didn't need any of her money. He had enough of his own." To live as he had then, not as he was now. That was still a major obstacle. "And he has his book deals, lectures. He has years of quality service still ahead of him."

It sounded strange to his ears, proclaiming this defense of his father. He realized that he hadn't done that for months; just the opposite.

Rebecca Duckworth nodded vigorously. "Of course he could. He *should.* He's a valuable resource. Men like your father shouldn't be discarded because of a tragedy that was not of their making."

The insurance agent, Milt Longoria, had known Walt and Jocelyn Gaines for almost thirty years, from shortly after Clancy was born and the young couple bought their first life insurance policy. He and Clancy squeezed into a small booth in a restaurant a block from the state capital, near where his office was located. It was lunchtime—the café was crowded with politicians and their staffs. Snippets of conversation floated in the air: affirmative action policies at the university, funding for this or that bill, deals to be cut, the dumbness of Washington politics that they had to deal with on the state level; the usual swapping and embellishing of stories. Brett Favre and the Packers were prime topics of discussion—they had a real shot at winning the Super Bowl this year. Just like in my own joint, Clancy thought as he listened to the boisterous caterwauling.

Sports and politics, the dual American secular obsessions.

"So how's your dad doing out there in La-La Land?" Longoria asked as he peered over Clancy's shoulder to see the specials listed on the chalkboard.

"He's doing fine," Clancy answered flatly.

Longoria nodded. "He's a survivor. It takes a strong man to overcome what he's gone through."

The waitress set glasses of iced tea in front of them. Longoria dumped two packets of sugar into his, stirred it with his spoon. "Why do you want to know about your parents' insurance policies?"

Clancy was prepared for this. Prying into someone else's finances, even if that person is your parent or another blood relative, carried the possibility of raising a red flag where there hadn't been one.

"Dad isn't teaching right now," he explained. "He might in the future, but he isn't presently. He has his pension from the university, and there's a book deal pending, but he isn't bringing in as much income as he had been. And living in southern California is more expensive than here. My brothers and I want to be at ease that he's on solid ground financially, in case he doesn't go back to teaching."

"Tell me about the cost of living in California," Longoria replied. "It's through the roof. None of my clients are retiring there anymore. Now it's all Florida and the Carolinas, which aren't that cheap, either, but nothing like California." He paused for a moment as the waitress put their sandwich plates on the table. "Anyway, he is living there, so he must be able to afford it." He took a bite out of his club sandwich.

Clancy speared a French fry, dipped it in the ketchup he'd shaken out onto his plate, popped it into his mouth.

"I guess mom's life insurance policy came in handy with that."

Longoria shook his head. "Not that much. It wasn't a big policy. Neither of them carried much insurance, it wasn't cost-effective." He swigged down some tea. "Their retirement packages from the university were their safety nets. I steer clients like them away from buying expensive life policies, it's a waste of money. Costs me on commissions, but my obligation is to see that my clients have the proper amount of coverage, not the most."

"So they didn't have large insurance policies."

"No, they didn't."

"May I ask how much?"

"Why don't you ask your dad this?" Before Clancy could answer, Longoria grinned. "Because he wouldn't tell you, he's too stubborn. He's a super guy, I admire him greatly, all he's done, but he can be intimidating. I wouldn't want to ask him, either." He took another bite out of his sandwich. "Two hundred and fifty thousand."

"Each?"

Longoria nodded. "Yes."

"That's all?"

Longoria's mouth was full; he nodded.

"How long did they have their policies?" Clancy asked.

The broker put up a hand—he was still chewing. After swallowing, he said, "Twenty years."

"And they didn't add on to them later on? Amend them?"

Longoria, in mid-bite, nodded. "There was one amendment, a few years ago."

Clancy's antennae went up. "What was that?"

The broker swallowed. "Originally, half went to the

surviving partner, the other half to the children. They changed the policies so that each was the sole beneficiary of the other."

"So my brothers and I were going to get half of it?" Clancy asked.

Longoria put up a hand like a traffic cop. "Don't get upset," he said with alacrity. "It's common practice."

"It is?"

"Jesus, I should've kept my mouth shut," Longoria said, chagrined. "Yes, it is. On a policy of that size. One third of one hundred twenty-five thousand? That's forty thousand bucks, it's not significant. But a hundred twenty-five to one beneficiary, that would be."

Tell that to my brother Tom, Clancy thought. Forty thousand dollars would be over the moon for him.

"In the end, you guys'll get it all," Longoria went on. "And now you don't have to worry about your dad. Not that this was his golden parachute," he reiterated. "His pension was his nest egg."

Clancy rearranged the fries on his plate. "Whose idea was it, to change the beneficiaries?" he asked. This was important. "Mom's or dad's?"

Longoria smiled. "Neither. It was mine. Your parents told me how well you and your brothers were doing—you with your rehab practice, one brother a bond trader, the other finishing his Ph.D.—you young fellows didn't need the money. An older person, such as your father or mother, would." He paused. "It's their money. They earned it," he gently reminded Clancy.

Clancy sat back, a feeling of relief washing over him. If his father had initiated the change in the insurance policies, he would have been even more distressed than he already was. Now, for this piece of the puzzle at least, he didn't have to be.

CHICAGO

◆ ◆ ◆

It was a slow evening at Finnegan's. The after-work crowd had come and gone, and it was still early for the after-dinner regulars. Tom, manning the bar by himself, polished a wineglass, squinted to make sure there were no water spots on it, and slid it into a notch in the hanging rack above his head. Two weeks on the job and he had the mannerisms of a veteran bartender down cold.

He was enjoying working here. His brain was on holiday; remembering how to mix drinks was the most taxing part of the job, and that wasn't difficult, compared to the kind of work he had been doing. Pete had been happy to cut back on his hours. After decades of being on his feet eight hours a day, his legs were going. He had been wearing support hose the past few years, but the varicose veins still throbbed.

The older man had spent two days giving Tom a basic tutorial, more about organizing his space than fixing cocktails. There had been more than enough training for what was needed—most of the hard-liquor drinkers who imbibed here went for the basics—martinis, sours, whiskey with mixers, like 7&7's and rum-and-Cokes. The dog-eared Mr. Boston bar guide in the cash drawer bailed him out when he was stumped.

Earlier, Will had stopped in for a drink after he'd finished up at the office. The brothers sat around and shot the breeze for a short while. They were getting along well. It was easy for Tom, living with his younger brother. Will didn't make him feel like he was an interloper. The few nights Tom had been off since he'd started they had hung out together, once double-dating—Will had introduced Tom to a woman who consulted with his firm. The evening had been pleasant, but nothing more. Which was okay with him, he wasn't ready to get involved. Sorting his life out was as much personal work as he could handle. And he still had Emma on his mind, although as the days went by he was handling that better. He didn't think about her as much now. He didn't know if that was a good thing or a bad thing.

Will was gone now—he had a date to see a play, with a woman who lived on his block. She was too much of an urban princess for him to want to date with any regularity, Will had told him, but she had season tickets to the Goodman, and he liked her dog.

Rhonda, the young waitress who worked a couple evenings a week and Sundays, ordered up a pitcher of draft Heineken and half a dozen shots of Crown Royal for a group of college guys who wanted to drink depth charges. Tom drew the pitcher and poured the shots. Pretty early in the week to get plastered, he thought. But when you're young, like these guys, barely old enough to drink legally (Clancy was a stickler for checking IDs), you're dumb. And invincible.

As he looked over at them, laughing and carrying on, he saw himself seven or eight years ago. Where does the time go, he thought? He wasn't even thirty yet, but he was feeling the weight of his years; the years he had wasted, the way he saw it now. He had gone into something he thought he loved, and it turned out he didn't, and he had wasted five years finding that out. Now he had to make up the time he had lost. Except you never do, it's gone forever.

And yet. If his mother hadn't been killed, his father would still be teaching at the university, still carrying on with his research. (The problematic situation at La Chimenea needed to be ferreted out, but he was certain that was connected to his mother's killing, too.) And if his parents' lives hadn't been ripped apart, his own life wouldn't have changed, either. He would still be unhappy, but he would have swallowed it. The death of his mother had been an earthquake with far-reaching fault lines.

Despite these fundamental changes in his life, though, Tom was feeling good about himself. He liked living in Chicago, with the art galleries and jazz bars and funky restaurants and people from all over the world. He liked being close, for the first time since Clancy had gone away to college, to his brothers. He even liked bartending. It was a people occupation, constant interaction. So different from his old, cloistered life.

Last night he, Will, and Clancy had gathered at Clancy's apartment to mull over the information Clancy had gleaned from his trip to Madison. That their father had left a lot of money on the table by bailing out early could be construed as rash, even irresponsible, but it wasn't venal or criminal. Walt hadn't been thinking rationally then, he was running on emotion. There were too many memories in Madison, and with the cloud over his head, he had lost his zest for his work. Under the same circumstances, each of them might have made the same decision. There are times when the heart prevails over the brain, and this had been one of those times.

The rest of what Clancy had learned was confusing, because it was heartening, and they hadn't been heartened by their father's behavior this past year and a half. He had sacrificed money for his old age so that his wife would be properly taken care of. That was a bighearted thing. It spoke of his love for Jocelyn, and his feelings of protectiveness toward her.

Two steps forward, a step back. That's how they were feeling about this investigation. They couldn't let go of their suspicions and fears, there were far too many unanswered questions that seemed to be leading down dark corridors. But they wanted to think well of their father. They wanted, badly, to continue loving him the way they always had. He could be too large, too domineering, too selfish, too critical; but he always had been. He could also be generous and supportive. Even his criticism, like his flailing at Tom for not finishing his doctorate, came from his intense feeling that his sons were special, that they had been put on the planet to do special things, that they weren't *supposed to*—no, not *supposed to*, they were not *allowed* to be ordinary. They were his sons—perforce, they couldn't be ordinary.

"Because that would make him ordinary, by proxy," Tom had pointed out. Being ordinary was the worst epithet Walt Gaines could imagine being applied to him. He would rather be known as an assassin or a lunatic than to be thought ordinary.

"Another pitcher and another round of shots," Rhonda called out from the serving station.

"How many rounds is this?" Tom asked as he grabbed a pitcher from the cold storage bin behind the bar.

"Three."

"Last one, then. They can drink more beer, but no more hard stuff."

"I'll tell them. They'll be glad to hear it," she said sarcastically. She hefted the tray with the pitcher and the fresh drinks and weaved her way across the floor.

Tom watched her hips sway as she walked, balancing the heavy tray. She was sweet. A couple years out of college, moonlighting here while pursuing her master's in primary education and getting her teaching certificate. If he didn't work here, he would ask her out. But he did, so she was off-limits. That was a rule of Clancy's, and it was a good one: don't date the help. It comes to hurt feelings in the end, which is followed by the aggrieved party giving notice. Clancy didn't want to lose valuable staff over hurt feelings.

If—when—he moved on to something more substantial, he could ask her out. That was a question looming on the horizon, but not yet imminent. What was he going to do now? Law school was a possibility. He had checked the application forms over the Internet for Northwestern and the University of Chicago. He had also bought an LSAT prep book. Getting into law school would be a piece of cake for him, with his background and smarts. The big question was, should he? He had already taken one wrong turn. He didn't want to do that again.

He had time. He could take the boards next month and send in his applications. He wouldn't have to make a decision until spring, five months away. In five months he would have a better feeling for what he wanted to do.

The dog had left a calling card on the living room floor. Not on the Persian carpet, luckily, Tom saw as he squatted down to examine it, but on the wood floor, up against the stand that held the thirty-six-inch high definition television, the VCR, and the DVD player. All new, purchased when Will moved in. His brother also had an excellent music system. Along with a few cases of premium California Cabernet, Will possessed the necessary accoutrements for a young man about town.

The dog, an excitable young beagle hound, jumped up and down on his hind legs, darting from the floor to the couch, then back down again, trying to get Tom to play with him. He yipped, rather than barked, a high sound like a bird call. His leash was on the entry hall table, next to a woman's small beaded evening purse and her stylish lambswool jacket.

From Will's bedroom down the hall came the low, lush sounds of a couple in some phase of coitus, Tom couldn't tell which, before, during, or after. Moans and squeals, bursts of female laughter.

"What's your name, boy?" he asked quietly, hunkering down and rubbing the dog behind the ears. He looked at the dog's tag. "*Rachmaninoff?* You poor little mutt. No wonder you crapped on the floor."

He scooped up the small dry dog droppings with paper towels and deposited them in a Ziploc bag, which he dumped into the garbage can under the kitchen sink. He went back into the living room and sprayed Lysol on the floor where the dog had crapped. Going into the kitchen again, he washed his hands and poured himself a short snifter of Hennessy. Then he opened the sliding doors that led to the small balcony and stepped out. The dog followed, sniffing the cement floor as if tracking an animal.

He sat on one of the two wicker porch chairs and took a pack of American Spirit cigarettes out of his pants pocket. Popping a wooden match with his thumb, he put his feet up on the rail and inhaled, then slowly let the smoke drift out of his mouth. Since he'd moved to Chicago he had started smoking again, limiting himself to three a day, none before dinner. Working in a bar and living in a downtown apartment was conducive to having a smoke now and then. He didn't even feel guilty about it. He went to the gym a couple of times a week, ran almost every day, and rode his trail bike along the waterfront. In a few months, he'd quit. He wasn't an addictive personality. He was in a state of flux, he was allowing himself small pleasures. He took another drag and sipped his cognac.

The dog jumped into his lap. He scratched the pooch behind his silky, floppy ears. "Who asked you up here?" he asked. The dog rubbed up against him. A low rumble came from his chest, almost like a cat's purr. Tom smoked and drank and looked out at the city lights and rubbed the dog's ears. Law school might not be that bad, he thought. Lawyers make money. It would be nice to have money, a good apartment, a devoted pet like this mutt. An urban princess to have sex with on the side.

"Rachi, where are you?" a woman's voice called from inside.

Tom snuffed his cigarette, flicked the butt over the edge, and stood up, lowering the dog to the floor. He started back inside. The dog followed, as if he'd been trained to heel at Tom's feet.

"Out here," Tom called.

The dog's owner was wearing a short black cocktail dress, half-zipped up the back. Her legs were bare, her shoes were off, her hair was mussed. She jumped, hearing Tom.

"I didn't know there was anyone else here," she said as he came inside. She sounded put-off.

Tom extended his hand. "I'm Tom Gaines, Will's brother. I camp out here. I just got off work."

The woman bent down to the dog, who was barking and jumping up and down in excitement. "Were you a good boy?" she asked in an irritating, high-pitched baby-voice. She looked around the floor, worried that he had pissed or dumped. "Sometimes he gets a nervous bladder when he's in strange surroundings," she said defensively.

"He was fine," Tom assured her. "Not a drop."

"Good," she said, relieved.

"Hey." Will came into the living room, tucking his shirt into his pants. He, too, was shoeless. "You're home early, aren't you?"

"It was a slow night. I closed up early," Tom explained.

Will nodded. If he was put out by Tom's coming in while he was having a romantic interlude, he didn't show it. "This is Lindsay Weiss," he said, putting a casual proprietary arm around the woman's waist. "We went to see *Mother Courage* at the Goodman. It was a good production. You ought to go."

Tom nodded. He felt like an intruder. "Maybe I will. I'm going to have a shower," he said, by way of taking his leave.

"I'm going to walk Lindsay home. I'll be back in a little bit." Will held the woman's coat out to her, as if saying "it's time to go now."

"I have to get my shoes," she said, holding up a freshly pedicured bare foot. Looking peevish, she darted down the hall and into Will's bedroom.

"Sorry about busting in on you," Tom apologized.

Will waved a dismissive hand. "No big deal. I forgot to tell her I had a roommate."

The woman returned from the bedroom. She had pulled on a pair of sheer dark pantyhose and was wearing high-heeled pumps. "I'm ready," she announced curtly to Will, as she snapped the dog's leash to his collar.

Will slipped on his old high school letter jacket that was hanging on the hall coat tree. "I won't be long," he said to Tom, winking behind his date's back.

"Adiós, dog," Tom called. "See you around the neighborhood."

They were sprawled out on the living room couches, listening to Bob Dylan: *Blood on the Tracks.* The vegetal, perfumy aroma from the joint they were passing back and forth wafted in the air.

"You working tomorrow?" Will asked Tom.

"No, I'm off. You got something you want to do?"

Will shook his head no. "I wish, but I'm buried in work. I need to find some time to start looking into mom's and dad's finances, see if they had any money stuck away we don't know about." He frowned. "I've got to figure out how to, if I can. I wish I had some kind of lead, somebody who was involved with them we don't know about." He toked on the joint Tom passed him, handed it back. "The money they were pulling out of their house, and mom's insurance policy. What did they do with it?" he asked rhetorically.

"In dad's new house?"

"Why would he have gone through that song-and-dance about the refinance, then?" Will came back. "That's the fishiest part of this whole deal to me. Where is that money? What did they do with it?"

"Isn't there some database you can access?" Tom asked. He was a babe in the woods when it came to high, or even low, finance. "You're on the inside."

Will smiled ruefully. "Hell, no. Money's the most liquid commodity in the world. Dad could have it squirreled away in a savings account, or buried under his mattress." He took one last hit from the joint. "You want any more of this?"

"No, I'm high enough."

Will wet his thumb and forefinger and snuffed the joint. "I'm bushed. See you *mañana.*"

Will was long gone by the time Tom woke up. He went for a run along the lake, showered, dressed, made a pot of coffee, read the paper. His normal morning routine.

He was feeling restless. He had an entire day off and nothing to do with it. He had been going to movies in the afternoon, cut-price matinees. There wasn't anything showing this week that he already hadn't seen, except for the crap he wouldn't waste his money on.

He was out of the loop—that was what was really bugging him. Clancy had hooked into Walt's retirement package and their parents' insurance policies. Will was going to try to use his insider knowledge of the financial markets to find out where the rest of the money had gone. So where did that leave him? Nowhere. Once again, he was the odd man out. He had more free time than his brothers, but he wasn't involved.

He needed to be included in the hunt, for his own peace of mind as well as for whatever factual information he might uncover, particularly since he didn't know, specifically, what he was looking for. Earlier this morning, while out on his daily run, he had reflected on what

Will had said last night—that he didn't know where to look for the missing money, because there was no one he knew who could help them.

Through the glass wall that separated the reception area from the main therapy room, Tom could see his brother. Clancy was with a client, a middle-aged woman whose left leg, from hip to ankle, was in a soft cast. She was lying on the floor, on her back. Clancy was bending her other leg back and forth. The woman was in discomfort—Tom could see the unhappy expression on her face. Clancy leaned toward her and said something. The woman nodded, gritted her teeth, and pushed against him with her good leg.

Clancy, having helped his client to her feet, caught his brother's eye and smiled. He waved Tom in. Tom walked into the workout room as Clancy assisted the woman to the door.

"Hey," Clancy said, low-fiving Tom, "what brings you down here? You want to work out? You can use one of the treadmills upstairs. The weight room's not full right now, either."

"I ran this morning, thanks."

Clancy gave his brother a love-tap on his shoulders. "You're getting to be a real stud, man. But you need to do weight training, too. Any time you want to come down here, just do it. Keep a set of workout clothes in a locker. I don't have to be here."

"Thanks, I will." Tom looked around. "You're doing great here."

"We're doing okay," Clancy acknowledged modestly. "One thing you can count on in this world—people are always going to get hurt. So . . . what's up?"

"I was thinking of driving up to Madison today."

"Oh, yeah? What for?"

"Dad put his and mom's stuff in storage, didn't he? All their furniture, mementos? And our stuff, our old things, baseball mitts, class albums. Didn't he store it all somewhere?"

Clancy nodded. "He rented a unit in one of those commercial places out by the airport. Was there something specific you're looking for?"

"Nothing special, just some of my old things," Tom said. "You forget about that stuff, it gets lost forever."

"I know. Callie and I have been meaning to go up there and go through it ourselves, make a rough catalogue. There's things of mom's she'd like, and there are dozens of photo albums. Dad didn't take much with him. I guess you noticed that when you were out in L.A."

"He wanted to leave it all behind," Tom said. "He did a good job," he added caustically.

"Let's not go there today."

"No, I don't want to, either. Is there somebody up there who can let me in?"

"There's a guard there to let you in the gate, but they don't have keys to the individual units. Only the owner of the facility and the renter have keys to the units, to protect against theft."

Tom was disheartened, and angry. "I hate thinking about asking dad for the key."

"I know how you feel," Clancy sympathized. "I'd hate to ask him, too. But you don't have to, 'cause I have one."

"How'd you do that?" Tom asked.

Clancy grinned. "I faked dad out into giving me a duplicate. I told him in case it had to be gotten into fast, like a fire or some other calamity. He went for it. It's right here in my office. Hold on, I'll get it for you."

MADISON

◆ ◆ ◆

It was like an oven inside the fifteen-by-twenty-five-foot cinder block storage unit. A thin layer of dust like the residue of a sandstorm hovered in the stagnant air. Tom stood outside for a few minutes until some of the hot air had drifted out the open doorway, then he went in and started looking around.

The space was piled high with furniture and taped-up Bekins storage boxes. The contents had been hastily thrown in, without organization—boxes were perched precariously on top of old pieces of furniture, large, heavy pieces lay askew on lighter, smaller ones. Framed pictures and large mirrors had been stacked against the side walls, without any protective covering.

This could take days, Tom thought pessimistically, as he surveyed the mess. To compound his problem, none of the boxes were labeled as to their contents. Taking a deep breath, he cleared a space on the hard concrete floor, wrestled a large box down from on top of the pile, and pried the packing tape off.

Three hours later, he had gone through less than half the boxes. He was sweating buckets, and his clothes were filthy with greasy dust and dirt. Although he hadn't found anything having to do with his parents' finances, he had come across several items that had stopped him cold when he saw them; almost brought him, in some instances, to tears.

His parents' wedding pictures. Photos of Clancy's birth, his own, Will's. (They had all been home births, the boys delivered by Walt with assistance from a midwife.) The baseball glove Clancy had passed down to him when he was six and signed up for his first T-ball team, which he, in turn, had handed on to Will. Pictures taken of his parents' twenty-fifth-anniversary party, seven years ago. Jocelyn had recently turned forty-five. The first tendrils of gray were showing in his mother's blond hair. She was still a beautiful woman, but she was no longer the young woman he remembered from his childhood.

Why am I doing this, he thought? This hurts. What also hurt was that his father had left all these treasures in this dump, discarded. It was as if the family's past was meaningless. All these things, the pictures, the elementary and high school diplomas, the sheet music from their childhood recitals, Clancy on trumpet, him on cello, Will on alto sax, the swimming and tennis medals, hundreds of pieces of priceless memorabilia—consigned not to the junk heap of history, but worse, to a storage vault that might not be visited for decades, as long as Walt (or his estate) paid the annual storage fee. Over time, the pictures would fade until the likenesses were barely distinguishable, the medals and trophies would turn green with tarnish. His mother's dresses, including her wedding dress, wrapped in tissue, were already coming apart at the seams.

Why didn't his father want any of this? Especially his mother's things, her rings, her necklaces, other pieces of jewelry. Her special coffee cup, that Clancy had made her in sixth-grade ceramics class. Was Walt afraid that Emma, his new young lover, would be angry at him for keeping them?

Emma. She came into his consciousness more than he wanted her to, but he couldn't help thinking about her. Not a good thing to covet your father's woman. There was something heavily Oedipal there, even if she wasn't his wife and was your age rather than his.

He didn't need to go into that, not now. He had a ton of work to do. He methodically dug into the boxes again.

Tom looked at his watch. It was almost five. He'd been here all afternoon. The facility closed at six; he could stay less than an hour. Whatever he was looking for, he hadn't found it. He was going to have to stop searching soon, because he wanted to take a few boxes with him, his mother's personal stuff, items belonging to him and his brothers. They shouldn't be relegated to a concrete box in a dingy commercial mall, he thought, as he put them aside.

A battered couch had been buried under piles of loose junk. He wrestled it to the side and discovered a couple of legal-sized accordion folders that had been hidden under it. Sitting on the couch, he opened the first one.

His mother's passport was on top of the pile. It had been issued in 1992, when she was in her early forties. She was laughing into the camera, as if something offstage had amused her.

A feeling of sorrow engulfed him. Ah, mom, he thought. I really miss you. He put the passport in his pocket. That was coming home with him.

There were a few manila envelopes inside the folder. He opened one up and took out a sheaf of papers. The top page bore the letterhead of a stock brokerage firm in Milwaukee. The letter was addressed to his mother, regarding information she had inquired about. Leafing through the pages, he saw what appeared to be an assortment of stock transactions, some of them for five figures. Much of it was high-tech stuff—Cisco Systems, Intel, Qualcomm, among others. He put everything back into the folder, picked up the second one, opened it.

The documents in this folder had been jammed in hastily, a rush job. He dug one out. It was a manifest from his parents' final trip to La Chimenea, including a list of the student volunteers who had been there, along with their addresses and phone numbers. He glanced over the names. None of them rang a bell.

Putting that aside, he fished out a thick, legal-sized envelope that was also from a Milwaukee firm. Inside, he found a set of policies from an insurance company. He scanned them quickly.

"Jesus Christ," he whispered to himself. "What in God's name is this?"

It was getting dark. The facility was closing in ten minutes. He carried a few boxes of memorabilia out to his car—the precious things he didn't want to leave behind—along with the two accordion files. Then he turned off the lights, locked the unit, and hightailed it back to Chicago.

CHICAGO

◆ ◆ ◆

A hard rain had been falling since before dawn. Will awakened in darkness as it pelted down on his windows and the small balcony outside his living room. Although he normally had his morning coffee and whatever else for breakfast at his office—fruit, a container of yogurt, once in a while a croissant or scone—this morning, because it was still too early to go in, he brewed up a pot of coffee and drank it sitting by the windows, watching the rain as it came down in sideways sheets, washing the remaining leaves off the trees, forming small rivers in the gutters along the sides of the street. No one was outside braving the elements. Even though Tom was in the other bedroom, sleeping, he felt alone.

He had been up late last night, looking over the documents Tom had brought back from the storage unit. Clancy had joined them. It had been a somber time. By the time Clancy went home, after midnight, they were more upset than they had been before, which was saying a lot. On the face of things, the documents, particularly those relating to stocks, were very upsetting. More than upsetting—they were potentially terrifying. He'd find out more this morning, when he got to the office and started checking them out.

The gist of what he'd read was that his parents had been heavily involved in buying and selling stocks for several years, starting in the mid-1990s. It looked to him, going through these papers, that they might have even been day-trading on their own. The broker they had used would know. That would be his first call this morning. He was swamped with his own work, but he was going to get into this right away.

This was why they had been refinancing their house; that was obvious to him. He knew people who had done that, mortgaged everything to get in on the stock boom. Friends of his in college had done it, their parents had done it. It was like those commercials for Ameritrade that had run a few years ago with the punk-looking kid who squawked like a chicken, egging on his girlfriend's square father to get in on the gold rush.

Some of the people he knew who had jumped on the bandwagon had made fortunes. Others—most of them—had risen with the tide, and then had crashed on the rocks when the tech boom collapsed. You didn't see commercials like those Ameritrade ones anymore, or read about all the instant dot.com millionaires, most of whom were broke now. Will didn't know if his parents had had the foresight to cash in their chips and leave the table, or if, like most people who had never owned stocks until the urge to make easy money became irresistible, they had kept on gambling long after their luck had turned.

Maybe they had gotten out okay. His father had recently bought a very expensive house, and from what Tom and Clancy had told him, was living large in other ways as well. Maybe the money his parents had made went into that. He hoped so. But if that had been the case, why hadn't his father said so, instead of lying about getting a special deal on the mortgage? He would have thought Walt would be crowing about making out in the market, when so many others had fallen on their asses.

If their broker was cooperative, he'd know in a few hours. He didn't know the man, but someone in his office would, or would know someone who did. Assuming he was able to talk to the broker, he could have the information he was looking for by lunchtime.

Even with milk and sugar, the coffee was rancid in his mouth. He dumped what was left in his cup down the drain and went to shower and get ready for the day. He wasn't looking forward to it.

It wasn't yet seven-thirty, but every broker was at his desk, almost all of them on the telephone. They did it all day long. You got in early and you went home late. That's why it was a young person's game. At twenty-six, Will had the stamina to do it. He didn't know if he would at thirty-six, or older. By then he'd be a partner, and wouldn't have to.

He sat at his desk, his parents' information spread out in front of him. He had on his telephone headset, which he put on when he came in and kept on until he left for lunch, or when his day was finished. He had been lucky—one of his co-workers knew the Milwaukee stockbroker. That had saved some time. Looking at the phone number in front of him, he dialed.

"Jesse Warsaw," came a man's crisp voice into his ear.

"Hey, Jesse, this is Will Gaines, from Merrill Lynch in Chicago. You got a minute?"

"Sure, Will," the voice said with instant ease. One broker to another. More enjoyable talking to a fellow broker than a panicking client, which too often was the case these days.

"I need some information on an account you were handling a few years ago."

"One of my accounts?" came the guarded reply.

"My parents," Will interjected quickly. "Walter and Jocelyn Gaines."

"Oh, uh huh." The voice relaxed. "So you're their son?"

"One of them. I have two other brothers. Listen, Jesse. I'm cleaning some stuff up here." He paused. "You heard about my mom?"

"Yeah, I did." The voice came over heavy. "That was awful. I'm really sorry. She was a damn nice woman."

"Thank you. She was. So you did know her. Not just over the phone."

"Oh, sure. She was a spitfire." The conviviality came back into Warsaw's voice again. "I always enjoyed her visits."

"She saw you at your office? In Milwaukee?"

"Yep."

Will shuffled through the documents. "Those accounts. They're not open anymore, are they?"

"Do you have the account numbers handy?" Warsaw asked.

Will read them off.

"Give me a minute."

Will waited while his counterpart brought the accounts up on his computer. All over the large room, an entire floor of the building, brokers were working, making calls, buying and selling stocks and bonds, setting up meetings. It was a perpetual motion machine that never broke down, regardless of whether the markets were going through the ceiling or the floor. Rust never sleeps, Will often thought, and neither does commerce.

Warsaw came back on the line. "All those accounts are closed," he confirmed.

Will had expected that answer. The next one was the key. "For how long?"

There was no hesitation. "It's been a couple of years now."

A couple of years. From before his mother's death.

"So how can I help you, Will?" Warsaw asked pleasantly.

MILWAUKEE

◆ ◆ ◆

Clancy hastily arranged for his partners to cover his afternoon appointments; those that couldn't be fitted in, he postponed. Shortly after noon he swung by Will's apartment and picked up Tom, and the two drove I-94 north to Milwaukee. The rain had abated slightly, but it was still a slow, gnarly drive. Eighteen-wheelers fantailed sheets of dirty water across the windshield of their car, making it hard to see much beyond the car ahead. To compound the misery, the highway was under construction from Route 137 to the Wisconsin border. For several miles, traffic crawled along in one lane at fifteen stop-and-go miles a hour.

Before he left his clinic, Clancy had talked to Will. The news about their parents' heretofore unknown stock transactions was brutal. Will hadn't gotten into details over the phone, it was too complicated. This evening, after Clancy and Tom met with the insurance broker whose name Tom had found in the buried documents, the three of them would talk everything out.

The insurance agent they were braving the elements to

see didn't know they were coming; rather, he knew he had an appointment, but he didn't know it was with the sons of Walt and Jocelyn Gaines. Clancy had called his office that morning and set up a meeting for three-thirty, using a pseudonym. He wanted to sandbag the man, catch him by surprise. Most crucially, he didn't want the agent calling their father before the meeting, to inform Walt that his sons were investigating his insurance policies.

Clancy hated acting covertly, but they had no choice. What Tom had uncovered was too incendiary to be prematurely exposed to their father. Walt would have the mother of all shitfits and would order the agent to have nothing to do with his sons, a demand which the agent, of course, would honor. They had to blindside the man and worry about the consequences later.

What was normally an easy two-hour drive took an extra hour, but they had left early enough, so they weren't late. The insurance agency was located in a downtown high-rise commercial building. After parking in the underground lot, the brothers rode the elevator up to the agency offices, where Clancy gave the phony name (Clancy as surname, rather than first) to the female receptionist. She dialed her interoffice phone, and a moment later a middle-aged, ruddy-faced man in a nice-looking double-breasted charcoal gray suit appeared in the lobby from behind closed double doors to greet them.

"Mr. Clancy?" the man asked expectantly, looking from one of the two athletic-looking young men standing in front of him to the other.

"That's me," Clancy answered. "This is my brother. He came along for the ride. My wife's busy, and I didn't want to make the drive alone," Clancy explained. "You're Phillip Holbrook?"

The man nodded. "Yes. Where are you from?" he asked blandly. "How did you get my name?"

"Down south," Clancy answered, deliberately vague, to the first question. "From a satisfied client of yours," he responded to the second.

"I see," Holbrook said, in the tone of someone who doesn't but assumes he'll get an explanation. "Come on back."

They followed him through the double doors, which led into a maze of offices of various sizes. Holbrook's space was one of the nicer ones, with a view of the city below and Lake Michigan, barely visible in the rain, in the distance. Settling in behind his desk, he motioned for the two to sit opposite him.

"Can I offer you something to drink?" he asked hospitably. "Coffee, soft drink?"

"No, thanks," Clancy answered for both.

"This weather's terrible," Holbrook commented blandly, looking out the window behind him. "Did you have any problems getting here from—"

"No," Clancy answered, cutting him off. "No problems at all."

Shrugging off Clancy's rebuff, Holbrook picked up a legal pad and a Mont Blanc fountain pen. "Well, then. How can I help you today, Mr. Clancy? What sort of insurance were you looking for? Life insurance, you mentioned over the phone." He glanced from one brother to the other. Tom looked back at him, his face inscrutable.

Clancy nodded. "I want to discuss life insurance, that's correct."

"Are you familiar with the various types of policies available?" the agent asked, ready to go into his spiel. "Term, whole life, so forth? Do you own any insurance at present? Are you married, do you have children?" He poised pen over paper, ready to write. "What is your occupation, Mr. Clancy?"

"We're interested in these policies, specifically," Clancy replied. He took the certificates Tom had found in the storage unit from his inside jacket pocket, leaned across Holbrook's uncluttered desk, and laid them in front of the agent.

Holbrook picked them up, looked at them, and recoiled as if he'd put his hand into a box and touched a snake. "Where did you get these?" he asked. He dropped the papers onto his desk.

"You issued these?" Clancy answered in turn.

Holbrook leaned away from his desk, to put some distance between himself and the two determined men facing him. "These policies are confidential. I can't discuss them without getting permission from the policyholder or beneficiary. In writing," he added emphatically.

"Walt Gaines being the beneficiary," Clancy said. "Since the policyholder is deceased."

Holbrook licked his hips involuntarily. "Yes." He picked up the policies again. "Did Mr. Gaines give these to you?" he asked, now not only suspicious but alarmed.

"Indirectly," Clancy answered. He smiled thinly at the man, as if trying to disarm him, or at least to not intimidate him, as he clearly was. "Walt Gaines is our father. I'm Clancy Gaines, and this is my brother Tom." He stood and pulled his wallet from out of his back pocket, took out his driver's license, and showed it to Holbrook.

The insurance agent blanched as he looked at the license Clancy was holding under his nose. "I see," he said tremulously. He looked from Clancy to Tom, who was staring at him as if measuring him for something unpleasant.

Clancy put the license back in his wallet. "I'm sorry

I deceived you over the phone, Mr. Holbrook," he said. "But I didn't think you would see us if I told you who I was, and I didn't want you talking to our father about my calling you."

"You're right on both counts," Holbrook answered angrily. He put a finger on the papers, as if testing them for heat. "I'm afraid I'm going to have to ask you to leave."

Clancy shook his head deliberately. "And I'm afraid we're not going to, until you explain these to us." He leaned forward and tapped the documents.

"I couldn't if I wanted to, which I don't," the man responded. "There are confidentiality laws I'm obligated to uphold."

Clancy leaned across the desk. "This is our mother and father we're talking about here, not some fucking legal abstraction, Jack." His voice, although low in volume, was suddenly fierce with threat. "I want you to explain these policies to us, in detail, now. Or . . ." He hesitated.

"Or what?" the agent croaked.

"Or I'm going to the state attorney general and ask him to investigate what's going on here," Clancy replied. He stared at the man. "This is a hell of a big insurance policy for a couple of middle-class university professors. I touched base with some other agents before I called you," he continued. "They told me these figures were wildly out of line." He paused again. "One of them told me there must have been some kind of a kickback involved here."

"A kickback?" Holbrook's voice rose an octave. "Are you crazy?"

"Look," Clancy said, his voice dropping in intensity. "I'm sure you're an honest man. But my mother was killed under mysterious circumstances, and over a year later we find this policy. We want you . . . we need you to explain this to us. Because I can tell you right now, sir, we're going to find out about this, one way or the other."

Holbrook's Adam's apple bobbed up and down. "I could get into trouble, talking about this to you," he said.

"Not if nobody knows you did."

The agent's head swiveled to Tom. Those had been the first words out of Tom's mouth since he'd walked in the door.

"There's nothing illegal about these policies," Holbrook said nervously. "Or even improper."

"No one's saying there is," Clancy said. "But you have to admit that our mom getting killed in the jungle down in Central America, and this insurance policy, is pretty damned coincidental. Don't you think?"

The man sighed. "It is coincidental, I agree. We checked into it, thoroughly. But there was nothing out of line, that we could find." He looked from Clancy to Tom. "Were we wrong?" he asked, his eyes widening fearfully.

Clancy shook his head no. "Her killing was an accident, there were twenty witnesses to that. But we still need to know about this policy. For our own peace of mind."

"Come on, man," Tom kicked in, "you can tell us. Nobody's going to know we talked to you. That's a promise."

Holbrook took a deep breath. "All right. But on one condition. Your father is not to know about this."

Clancy and Tom looked at each other. "Don't worry," Clancy assured the nervous agent. "He's lived in hell the past year. The last thing we want to do is cause him any more grief by bringing up old wounds."

Holbrook spread the documents out on his desk. Clancy and Tom came around to the agent's side and looked over his shoulders.

"Your mother came to see me a few years ago," the agent began. "Shortly after your father had started on a new and important project."

"La Chimenea," Tom informed him. "It was a newly discovered Maya site that our father was in charge of excavating," he explained. "One of the biggest and most important that's been found in the past half-century," he added. There was filial pride in the way he'd said that, he realized. He hadn't felt pride in his father for years now. It was a confusing emotion.

"That's what she said," Holbrook replied. "It was going to be the capstone of your father's career."

Clancy and Tom exchanged a look over the man's head. "It was," Clancy said without further elaboration.

"She told me they traveled all over Central and South America, several times a year," Holbrook continued. "Countries like Guatemala, Colombia, Peru, where there is rampant civil unrest. She felt that they needed to augment their existing life insurance policies. Given those circumstances, I agreed with her."

Clancy looked thoughtful. "Did she or my father explain why they didn't use their regular insurance agent, in Madison?"

"No," Holbrook answered, "and I didn't ask her." He hesitated a moment. "My supposition was that she was afraid he would try to talk her out of it. That's common, with smaller agencies. Insurance is a cautious profession, but sometimes we can be overly cautious, to the detriment of our clients' protection."

"But you didn't. Try to talk her out of it," Clancy asked.

"No," Holbrook answered. "I thought it made good sense, given the dangers they might be encountering. The risks were small, I'll grant you that, but they were legitimate concerns. Why do people buy insurance policies at the airport when they're about to fly on a plane, which statistically is the safest way in the world to travel? Same thing here." He tapped a finger on the documents in front of them.

"But the amounts!" Tom blurted out, still blown away after having known about this for over a day now.

"Two million dollars is not so much these days," Holbrook replied blandly, as if he wrote such policies every day. "It's not that expensive, when you pencil it out. I'm sure your father was happy they took out these policies in the amounts they—" He stopped. "I'm sorry. I didn't mean it to sound the way it did."

"That's okay," Clancy told him. "You were doing what they asked you to do."

"That's right," the agent agreed vigorously. "I was giving my clients what they wanted."

"And he got all the money?" Tom asked.

Holbrook nodded. "Each named the other as sole beneficiary. That's common practice. I'm sure your father has amended his policy now and named you as beneficiaries."

Clancy thought of Emma Rawlings, the new love of his father's life. He thought about saying "I'm not sure about that," but he didn't.

Tom put his finger on a line in his mother's policy. "Explain this to us, would you? This is what threw me the most."

Holbrook sat back. "Yes, I can understand that," he said, his voice measured. "Accidental death and dismemberment. What's known as an ADandD kicker in the industry." He looked up at them. "In a nutshell, if the policyholder has this rider, which has to be purchased separately, the policy doubles in value, under certain circumstances."

"Such as the circumstances our mother died under," Tom said.

The agent nodded. "Yes. If either she or your father were accidentally killed, the other would receive four million dollars in benefits." He paused. "Which your father did."

That explains where he got the money for the house, Clancy thought gloomily. But it raises a lot of other questions, none of them good. He and Tom exchanged another glance. Tom shook his head, as if he couldn't believe what they had just been told.

"That's a lot of money to pay out," Clancy remarked. "How did your company feel about that?"

Holbrook grimaced. "Not good. It was a considerable amount of money, but those are the risks we take. We hope never to have to pay on those policies, and we usually don't—only one half of one percent of these policies pay a claim." He cleared his throat. "I'm sure your father didn't care about that, he wanted his wife to be alive. Although he took the money, of course."

"You did investigate it, though," Clancy said.

"Absolutely," Holbrook answered vigorously. "We sent a representative down, interviewed dozens of people, including several of the people who were there when it happened."

Clancy hesitated before he asked his next question. "Did you interview our father?"

Holbrook looked away for a moment. "Yes, we did. It was an extremely upsetting position for us to be in, as I'm sure you can understand."

"So there was never any thought on the part of your agency or the insurance company to challenge the claim," Tom interjected.

Holbrook shook his head. "We couldn't."

Tom looked perplexed. "Why not? I'd think that given

what happened and where it happened someone would think about it, at least."

"I'm sure someone did," Holbrook said. "But our hands were tied. Not that we did think anything was shady," he added quickly.

Outside, a sudden bolt of lightning, followed almost immediately by a loud crash of thunder, diverted everyone's attention. The sky, already dark with rain, was now also losing the feeble ambient sunlight that had tried to break through.

Tom turned away from the window and addressed Holbrook. "You said your hands were tied. How?"

Holbrook picked the policy up and flipped through a few pages. He put his finger on a paragraph. "There's a two-year incontestability clause after a policy like this is issued, during which time the insurance company can challenge a claim. After that, the payment is automatic, unless there has been a criminal act by anyone who could benefit by it, in this case, your father. Since there was none, we paid him. It's cut-and-dried."

"So the policy was bought more than two years before she was killed," Clancy asked in confirmation.

Holbrook's head slowly bobbed up and down. "Two years and two months." He handed the policy to Clancy, along with the second one, the one that had insured Walt under the same conditions. "The dates are in here."

Slipped in right under the wire, Clancy thought. This inquiry had turned out to be the worst possible scenario they could have imagined. He put the policies back in his pocket.

"One last question," Tom said.

"Yes?" Holbrook asked.

"When did our father actually get the money? How long after she died?"

Holbrook thought for a moment. "My recollection is

about six months after. I could look it up, if you want the exact date."

Tom shook his head. "That won't be necessary." He looked over to Clancy. "Right when he quit the university and left Madison."

Clancy nodded. "What an amazing coincidence," he said with bitter sarcasm. He turned back to Holbrook. "Thanks for talking to us." He offered his hand. "I can understand why you didn't want to."

"I'm glad I did, now," the agent replied, shaking Clancy's hand. He shook Tom's as well. "It's good that you know." He hesitated a moment. "Your parents never discussed this with you? Before . . . or after?"

"No," Clancy said. "They lived in their own world."

More than we knew, he thought sadly. So much more.

Holbrook walked them to the elevator. "Be careful driving out there," he cautioned. He forced a smile. "You have insurance, don't you?"

Clancy smiled back. "We have insurance."

"Well, if you ever want to talk more about life insurance—for yourselves—give me a call. I'll do good by you."

"Thanks," Clancy said. "I'll talk to my wife about it."

Holbrook edged close to them, looking over his shoulder to make sure no one was in earshot. "What we talked about in my office stayed there, right?" he whispered.

"Most definitely," Clancy answered. "He's never going to know."

Chicago

♦ ♦ ♦

The drive back was a misery. To avoid the construction on the Interstate they took U.S. 41 back, a longer and more winding route. The rain, which if anything was coming down harder than it had been earlier, pounded them all the way, and the wind coming off the lake as they got closer to home was blowing almost gale force.

The climate was worse inside the car. Everything they knew about their father until now had been dispiriting, even scary; but this went beyond anything they had learned. He had been paid four million dollars because their mother was killed, and he had never said a word to them about it.

Will was waiting for them when they got back to Clancy's apartment. Callie had roasted a chicken and made a Caesar salad, but no one was hungry. They drank, though. Not to excess, they needed to have their wits about them, but a couple of healthy belts of Scotch all around went down fast.

Clancy and Tom told the other two about the insurance policies, and the accidental death clause that had made their father a wealthy man. That explained where he'd gotten the money to buy his fancy new house in Los Angeles, they agreed, and why he had been willing, even eager, to leave Madison as soon as there was any whiff of controversy.

"If that student's parents hadn't filed against him, he would have come up with some other excuse," Tom commented. "He was lucky the kid gave him such a convenient exit."

That was low thinking, but none of the others contradicted Tom. They all felt the same way, not only that Walt had deceived them, but that he had acted ugly and underhandedly. And maybe worse.

"The view from where I stand isn't good, either," Will announced, as he began recounting his telephone conversation of earlier in the day. He read from a sheaf of papers on which he'd scribbled his notes. "They started investing in 1994, about the time the tech boom was gathering steam and the economy was coming out of recession."

"That was the first time they refinanced their house," Clancy recalled.

Will nodded. "Yep. It's obvious now that they refinanced to come up with the seed money. And they did very well, for a number of years. They refinanced the house again in '97, as you know, and then again in '99."

"Mortgaging their future," Tom commented. "That house was the biggest investment they owned."

"*Was* is the operative word," Will agreed. "Because they made serious money up until the middle of 2000."

"How serious?" Tom asked.

"Over a million. In net gains, profit. They were making out like bandits. You didn't have to be a genius then, it was like throwing darts at a board blindfolded.

Whatever you hit was a winner, especially in the big tech issues. They were into Intel, Cisco, all those glamour stocks. Even dicier ones that were going up in multiples of thousands. Real high-wire stuff. I know people who parlayed ten thousand dollars into ten million."

"Except most of them didn't keep their ten million," Tom commented. He could see where this was going. They all could. He felt like he was standing at the side of a road watching a train wreck about to happen in slow motion and was powerless to do anything to stop it.

"Most didn't," Will agreed. "Including mom and dad."

"How much did they lose?" Clancy asked. He got up from the couch where he was sitting with Callie, went into the kitchen, and came back with the bottle of Laphroaig. He poured himself a few fingers. "Anyone else?"

Both his brothers held up their glasses. He tipped a bit into each. Callie wasn't drinking. She sat next to him, not saying anything, taking it all in.

"They lost everything," Will told them. "Almost everything."

"They had the house, still," Tom said.

"Yes, but it was burdened by a big new mortgage. They were getting older, they would have owned it free and clear. Now they were looking at a mortgage that would outlive them."

"Stupid," Tom commented bitingly. "Jesus, what were they thinking?"

"It gets worse." Will stuck his finger into his drink, sucked it.

Tom and Clancy both looked up. "How?" Tom asked.

"They were borrowing against their pension plan."

"Ah, no," Clancy groaned. "You've got to be shitting us."

"I wish," his brother answered. "They dipped into it pretty heavily. Dad isn't taking nearly as much out of it every month as he should have been. Most of it's going to pay down loans he took out against it to play the market."

"Like he really needs it," Tom spat out. He was white-hot with anger. "Four million in the bank, who gives a damn about some sorry-ass pension plan?"

They sat in silence for a moment, until Callie broke in. "We need to take a break. This is an awful lot to digest in one bite. Speaking of which, you guys have been drinking on empty stomachs. I made this nice dinner, I want you to eat it." She got up, pulled Clancy to his feet. "Come on."

They sat at the dining table, with the bottle of Scotch as the centerpiece. Callie dished up the portions. They pushed the food around their plates, but no one had an appetite.

"It's good, hon," Clancy said, forcing down a mouthful.

"Real good," Tom echoed. "Thanks."

Will pushed his plate away from the table. "Someone has to say it."

They looked at him. The youngest, the baby of the family, all grown up now, their king of finance.

"They were living over their heads for years, taking stupid chances on things they didn't know squat about, they mortgaged their future, and then they got waxed. And then mom gets killed, and dad's a rich man suddenly. He benefitted from her dying, financially. That scares the hell out of me, to think of where that could lead." He rubbed his eyes, then looked up. "We've been ostriches, burying our heads in the sand, but we have to get real now."

They stared at each other. No one wanted to say it.

"Screw it," Tom said finally. "I'll break the ice. Was

dad involved in mom's death? That's what we're looking at, isn't it? Was mom's killing something other than a random, tragic accident?"

The atmosphere in the apartment was that of a funeral home. Outside, the rain was still falling.

"It's still all circumstantial," Clancy said. "There's no smoking gun, no gun at all. All those people were there. They all saw and said the same thing. It was how you just described it, Tom. A random, tragic accident. Everything we've learned is terrible, ugly, scary. But it does not mean dad had anything to do with mom's killing." He pushed away from the table; if he'd had any appetite at all, it was gone now. "If we're going to accuse him—"

"We *are* accusing him," Tom butted in. "That's what all this has been about. Let's stop lying to ourselves, for Christ's sake!"

"You guys aren't seeing the forest for the trees."

They turned to Callie.

"Cherchez la femme," she said.

"Meaning?" her husband asked.

"The mystery lady in his life. What do you know about her?"

They looked at each other, but no one spoke.

"My point exactly: nothing. I brought this up before, and you tabled it. I think it's time to look at her again."

Tom shook his head. "I don't buy that at all," he said with force.

"Why not?" Callie asked. "Shouldn't everything Walt's been involved in over the past few years be under suspicion, or at least checked out?"

"He didn't even know her then," Tom pointed out stubbornly. "He met her after he moved to California."

"At a party at UCLA, isn't that what you told me?" Callie asked Clancy, who nodded. "But UCLA doesn't know diddly about Walt, so he couldn't have met her that way," she exclaimed strongly. "So what we have to find out is, how did he really meet her?"

"Okay, so he lied about that," Tom conceded. "What difference does it make?"

"It could make a world of difference if he had met her earlier," Callie answered.

"If," Tom said grudgingly. He was living with a romantic and erotic image of Emma in his head, an image that carried with it a yearning that was painful to think about. He didn't want to have it taken away from him.

"I'm going to lay a piece of information on you guys that's going to blow your minds," Callie said. "It isn't pretty, but it's cut from the same cloth as all these other ugly revelations." She paused. "Emma Rawlings does not exist."

"Babe," Clancy said. "You're pushing it."

"I don't mean there isn't a body there. You and Tom have seen her, spent time with her. But she's a spook, she has no record."

Tom almost leaped out of his chair. "Why in hell would you say that?" he asked her harshly.

Callie's answer was emphatic. "Because I checked on her."

All three brothers gaped at her.

"She's never fit in the picture for me," Callie said. "You guys wanted to check on all these other areas, which was what you had to do, so I did it—looked into her background." She got up, went into the living room, and came back with a looseleaf notebook, which she flipped open. "There is no Emma Rawlings enrolled in any school, undergraduate or graduate, at UCLA, which gives the lie to Walt claiming she was close to getting her graduate degree there. She isn't at USC, either. Those are the only two universities in the L.A. area that have graduate archaeology departments."

She sat back.

"Sonofabitch," Tom spat out. His head was reeling. "How many more lies are there going to be? Is this ever going to end?"

"We're going to have to deal with this now, too," Will said. "Good work, Callie."

"Thanks. Sorry to be the bearer of more bad tidings."

"So now what?" Clancy said. "Anybody have a bright idea what to do next?"

Callie raised her hand. "I do."

"What?"

"I want to see this woman. Up close and personal."

"What difference is that going to make?" Will asked, curious.

"Women's intuition. We see things in other women that men are blind to."

Tell me about it, Tom thought. He wanted to tear handfuls of hair from his head, he felt so angry at himself. So self-deceived, yet again.

Tom and Will left. Everyone was exhausted—their emotional tanks were empty. Tomorrow, Clancy would call Walt and invite himself and Callie out. He'd make up some excuse—business for him, a chance for Callie to see old friends from her volleyball days. It would take a few weeks to set up, because he was booked solid at the clinic, and he knew his father wouldn't be available immediately, either. Teaching a clinic at Stanford, a lecture series in Arizona. Some excuse, which, up until a short time ago, would have been perfectly plausible. Now it was lies, all lies. He felt like his world was caving in on him.

"Are you all right?" Callie's hand reached for his.

They were in bed, under the covers. They'd been too tired to make love. She snuggled up against him.

"No," he answered truthfully. "I feel horrible."

"Me, too. Why is this all happening?"

"I don't know," he answered. "I don't know if I want to know."

She propped herself up on one elbow. "I have something else to tell you. I didn't want to earlier, with the other guys around." She smiled. "It's good news, for a change."

She leaned over and kissed him on the mouth. "I'm pregnant."

LOS ANGELES

◆ ◆ ◆

Walt was overjoyed with the news that he was going to be a grandfather. "It's about time," he had crowed over the phone, when Clancy called him. Of course he wanted them to come out for a visit, as soon as possible. He was tied up for the next couple of weeks, unfortunately, but he would make himself available right afterward. "If only your mother was still alive," he lamented. "She would have been so happy."

They made a firm date, and Clancy bought the airplane tickets.

Two weeks later to the day, Clancy and Callie arrived at Walt's house, shortly after six in the evening. The sun was almost down, a few fingers from dropping below the horizon. The full-leafed trees, in contrast to the sad bare skeletons they had left behind in Chicago, cast long shadows on the street.

Callie got out of the car, stretched, and looked around.

Her lower back was sore. Now that she was pregnant she needed to drink more water, to keep her kidneys flushed.

It was balmy out. That was the thing she loved the most about southern California, it never got cold.

"Which one?" she asked. They all looked impressive to her.

Clancy, taking their bags out of the trunk, pointed across the street. "That one."

She shaded her eyes against the sun, which was full in their faces. "Pretty impressive."

"Yes, it is." He stared at it. Walt's Mercedes and Emma's BMW sports car were both in the driveway. "You can buy a hell of a lot of house with four million dollars in the bank."

They walked across the street and rang the doorbell. Almost immediately the door swung open and there was Walt, grinning from ear to ear. He grabbed Callie in a bear hug.

"Oh, man!" he cried out. "This is absolutely incredible." He stepped back and looked her up and down. "You aren't showing yet."

"It's only six weeks, Walt." She hadn't seen him for over a year. He looked good, she thought, but he definitely looked older.

"Oh, man," he cried out again. "I haven't felt like this since . . . Will was born, I guess. Jesus. If only your mother . . ." He trailed off, shaking his head. Smiling again, he grabbed her hand in both of his. "Come on in. Come on."

They followed him into the house. "You know where the guest room is, Clancy," he told his son. "Go ahead and drop your stuff. I'll show my future grandchild's mother around." He took Callie's hand again. "Come on."

He led her through the house, pointing out this particular rug, how old it was, where it had come from, where he'd bought this painting, that old vase. His voice was prideful with ownership of these fine things. She told him how nice everything was, how tasteful.

"That's Emma's doing. She has a great eye." He looked toward the bedrooms. "She'll be out in a minute." He leaned toward her like a conspirator. "She's nervous about meeting you. Another woman, my son's wife, family." He was exuding energy. "You're going to like her. She's your kind of people."

"I'm sure," Callie answered.

They walked around the spacious backyard, the light now a deep purple-green in the dying throes of the day. It was quiet back here, no traffic noises, no radios or televisions, no human voices. The crickets were starting to sing, and somewhere in the distance she heard a bullfrog's croaking. This is some life, Callie thought. But at what a cost. She looked at her father-in-law, in his shorts and faded tennis shirt and worn boat shoes on his tanned legs, his skin like dark burnished leather from his years of being out in the tropical sun, and she felt, despite what she knew about him and his deceptions, a surge of warmth, almost compassion. He was the father of her husband, the man she loved. The grandfather of her unborn child. The same blood ran through all their veins, even hers, now that she was pregnant by his offspring.

Please let there be an acceptable answer to all this, she thought silently to herself.

Clancy hadn't joined them. Deliberately, she knew. He was giving her private time with his father, on the chance there was some vibe from Walt she might pick up that would be disturbed by the presence of a third party.

She didn't feel any vibe; not yet, anyway. If there was

one, it would transmit not from Walt, but from Emma. Whoever she was.

"Hello."

They turned. A woman was standing on the back patio, framed by the open French doors. Her face was in darkness. She hesitated a moment, as if waiting to make her entrance, then walked across the yard toward them.

"I'm Emma."

"Callie."

"It's nice to meet you, at last."

Callie looked at her closely, as if trying to see past Emma's eyes to what lay behind. "Thank you," she said. "You don't know how much I've been wanting to."

They sat in the living room, Callie and Clancy on one sofa, Walt and Emma on the other, holding hands like lovebirds, the two happy couples looking at each other across the coffee table, which was an old steamer trunk. From the original Queen Elizabeth, Walt told them. Emma had found it. Emma had wonderful taste, and a great nose for hidden treasures.

They had changed to go out to dinner. Walt was taking them to "the best restaurant in L.A.," his personal favorite. Cost be damned tonight! he'd sung out like a Venetian gondolier.

Before dinner, a glass of celebratory champagne. Walt raised his flute. "To family," he toasted, his voice firm and bold. "To all the Gaineses, past, present, and future. Especially future." He beamed, looking at Callie.

As Clancy drank he thought of the Gaines who wasn't here. She wouldn't have fit in. He and Callie didn't, either. Not even his father, not really. It was a man's house, decorated with a strong masculine feel, but it wasn't his dad's. It was her taste, the woman sitting next to his father. What she felt should be Walt's surroundings.

They walked outside to Walt's Mercedes to drive to the restaurant. It was dark; the street was quiet. Callie and Emma lagged behind father and son, who were talking to each other about Tom: his decision to take a leave of absence from grad school (Tom's explanation to his father). Walt was upset, and Clancy was trying to assure him the hiatus was temporary. Callie looked at Emma's profile. What was it about this woman that was so upsetting to her, she pondered, aside from the damaging information they had learned so far? This feeling she had right now was something else, something she was getting from direct physical proximity. That woman's intuition she had talked about in Chicago was churning inside her.

Time to go fishing. "Do I know you from somewhere?" she asked Emma.

Emma turned to her in surprise. "I don't think so. Where would you know me from?"

"I don't know, that's why I'm asking." Callie thought for a moment. "I lived in California on and off a few years ago, when I was a professional volleyballer. Were you ever involved in women's sports?"

Emma laughed. "I'm a C tennis player, that's the closest I've come to being a sports person. I've never even seen a volleyball game in person." She paused. "I haven't lived in L.A. that long."

"Guess I was wrong. You must remind me of somebody else."

"I've been told that before," Emma said with an easy smile. "It's not uncommon, I don't think."

"I suppose not." Callie shrugged. "I must have been mistaken."

* * *

Dinner was at Valentino's. Clancy had eaten at Charlie Trotter's in Chicago, and had thought it the best meal he'd ever had in his life. This one matched it. Walt had ordered in advance, matching special wines with each course. He talked easily to the waiters and sommelier and even the owner, who bustled from table to table but had time to stop and converse at length with them. Clancy, taking it all in, thought of Fitzgerald. The rich definitely are different from the rest of us, he thought, as he made his way through course after incredible course. They not only have more money, Hemingway had noted, they know what to spend it on. Themselves.

Walt was a charming if overly energetic host. His mission, both Clancy and Callie figured out early on, was to get them to like Emma, and more important, to accept her. How smart she was, what a great cook she was, what a gift she had for everything artistic, literature, theater, music. They had season tickets to the L.A. Philharmonic. They went to the Catalina Bar and Grill to listen to Sonny Rollins and Chick Corea. They were on the invitation list to every hip art gallery opening in town. On and on.

"Walt, please stop," Emma said, when he had particularly extolled one of her outstanding attributes. "He can get going a bit much," she said with a tone of embarrassment. "Tell me about you," she said to Callie. "Do you have a preference as to what sex you want your baby to be?"

Callie shook her head. "As long as it's healthy, I don't care."

"Are you going to do a . . . what do you call it, when they can determine the sex?"

"Amnio." Callie shook her head. "No. I want to do everything naturally."

Emma looked at her. "I envy you."

Callie put her fork down. Here was an opportunity. "Do you have children?" she asked.

"No. I don't."

"There's time," Callie said. She was pushing a little now, but it felt right. As long as she didn't push too hard. "You're a young woman. You're not that much older than me. How old are you?" She laughed. "You don't have to tell us."

Walt had gone quiet.

Emma glanced quickly at Walt, then away. "I'm thirty-three."

"You have plenty of time," Callie told her cheerfully.

Emma smiled. "Who can predict the future?" she asked rhetorically.

The private investigator's name was Artesia Garcia. A full-figured, high-cheekboned Latina in her early forties, she had been a detective in the LAPD before resigning in disgust after the Rampart scandal and setting up her own PI shop. She met Clancy and Callie at nine o'clock the next morning in her office on Wilshire Boulevard, a mile east of the Beverly Hills line.

Will had hired her; the Los Angeles branch of his firm had recommended her. Her specialty, which derived from her police background, was in tracing elusive characters like drug dealers and security scammers who used multiple false identities, moved their money around in shell bank accounts, laundered money from illegal to legitimate businesses. The feeling Will had gotten from her over the phone was good—she seemed no-nonsense, professional, but not full of herself. They agreed that she would get working on their problem immediately, and would meet with his brother and sister-in-law when they came to L.A. He wired a two-thousand-dollar deposit into her bank account as a retainer.

Ms. Garcia's office was spartan, functional, cramped. She picked up a thin folder that was lying on her desk and opened it. "So far, I have drawn a blank," she informed them. "There is no record of an Emma Rawlings anywhere in Los Angeles, Orange, Ventura, San Diego, Santa Barbara, or Riverside counties. No address for anyone with that name. Your brother told me she had an apartment in Westwood, one of the high-rises on Wilshire?"

"I told him that," Clancy said. "Or maybe it was Tom, our other brother. I distinctly remember my dad telling me that."

Garcia nodded. "I checked them all out, thoroughly. *Nada.* No resident of that name owns, leases, rents in any of them. I couldn't find a phone number, even unlisted or cellular, no driver's license, no enrollment in any college anywhere in the state of California."

"That's bizarre," Clancy muttered.

The investigator shook her head. "No, it isn't. It means that this woman's name is not Emma Rawlings. The question that has to be answered is, who is she, really? She's hiding her past, using a false name. Why?"

She looked at the meager folder and frowned. "Surveillance wasn't supposed to be included in my initial investigation, it eats up money and I didn't know how much you people want to spend on this, but I spent an afternoon following her, anyway. The woman left no trail. Shopped at Nordstrom, paid in cash. Ate lunch, cash. Did everything by herself, she didn't meet anyone or go anywhere that might have given me a lead. I ran her license plate number down with DMV. It was leased through a New York bank, and I can't get into bank records without a warrant, which is out of the question for a private investigator."

Clancy nodded somberly. "Well, it's not like this comes as a big surprise."

"I'm sorry," Garcia said apologetically. She closed the folder and placed it back on her desk. "What do you want me to do now?" she asked.

Callie shifted in her chair. Her back was stiff. She was only a little more than a month pregnant, but she could feel her body changing, becoming less flexible. "Let's put a hold on this," she suggested. "We're going to be spending plenty of time with her for the next couple of days. Maybe we'll find something out you can use."

Garcia nodded. "Good idea. You'll be on the inside." She smiled wickedly. "I thought about trying to swipe her wallet to see her driver's license, but I couldn't bring myself to do it. I'll bend the law as much as I can without jeopardizing my license, but I won't break it."

Clancy nudged Callie. "Maybe you can sneak into her purse," he suggested. "You wouldn't have any moral scruples about that."

She punched him on the arm. "That's not my style, bozo, as you well know." She stood and shook hands with Garcia. "Thanks for your help. We'll be in touch."

Walt was impatiently waiting for them when they returned. "Where were you?" he asked, his voice testy, almost whining. "I've got a million things planned for us to do today."

Clancy glanced at his watch. It was barely ten-thirty—the entire day was still ahead of them. He noticed that Emma's car wasn't in the driveway. He would love to know where she went during the day, the details of her secret life.

"We had coffee with a couple of Callie's old volleyball teammates," he lied easily. "I told you Callie wanted to see friends when I called you two weeks ago, don't you remember? You and Emma weren't up when we left, so we took off. Sorry if we miscommunicated."

Walt looked momentarily confused; then he nodded. "Slipped my mind. I better up my dosage of ginkgo biloba," he joked. "A mind is a terrible thing to waste. Anyway, no big deal," he said buoyantly. "Is there anything you two want to do? I could suggest a million things. Do you want to do the tourist shtick, Universal Studios or one of those places?"

Callie shook her head emphatically. "We came out to see you, not to gawk at dumb movie effects. Let's do something personal, the four of us. Go to the Getty, go bike-riding along the strand in Santa Monica. Or just hang out. You don't have to entertain us, Walt. We're just happy to see you, your new house, your new"—she bit her tongue at "lady"—"friend. Speaking of Emma, where is she?"

Walt went back into the kitchen and poured himself another cup of coffee. "Do either of you want a cup?" he asked. "There's plenty."

"No, dad, we had coffee out," Clancy answered. "So Emma went where?"

Walt blew on his mug. "She had an appointment. Something to do with school, or her advisor, I don't know exactly," he said with a vague air. "She'll be back soon." He thought for a moment. "You're both good athletes, want to do something fun that you won't be able to do in Chicago till next spring, now that the weather's freezing back there, or will be shortly?"

"Like what?" Clancy asked. "Surfing? Skateboarding?"

"Yeah, right," Walt laughed. "Like I want to break a leg. Sorry, Callie," he said, catching himself.

"Don't worry," she told him. "That's ancient history. And if I hadn't bunged up my leg I wouldn't have met Clancy, so all's well that ends well. So what do you have in mind, Walt?"

"Golf!"

"Golf?" Clancy repeated. "You play golf?"

Walt nodded vigorously. "Yes, and I'm pretty good for someone who never swung a club a single day in his life until he was sixty."

"This takes the cake," Clancy said in slack-jawed astonishment. That his father had taken up golf was as off-the-wall—although harmless for a change, thankfully—as any of the other radical changes he had undergone over the past year-plus.

"You play," Walt reminded his son.

"Yes, but I'm a yuppie," Clancy answered. "You're a man of culture. Have you joined a country club?" he asked, trying to make a joke out of the question.

"Hell, no. They're way too expensive. My neighbors around here are all members of clubs, the best ones, they take me." He pointed out the front window. "That house, across the street? He's a member of Bel Air, he manages James Garner and all these hotshot actors. Jim's a member, we've played a few times, hell of a nice guy. Down the street are two members of L.A. Country Club, awesome golf course. You've got to know God or one of his disciples to get in there. Plus I have friends who are at Riviera, Brentwood, Hillcrest. I play all over, public courses, too."

"How egalitarian," Clancy said dryly. His father, the renowned university scholar, the self-proclaimed champion of the common man, now a golfing partner of

Hollywood stars in Bel Air, California, one of the most exclusive communities in the world? Is this what happens when your wife is killed and four million dollars drops into your lap? Or was it nothing more than a function of age, an inevitable tilt toward conservatism? If so, he hoped it wasn't hereditary.

"And Emma?" Callie asked. "Does she play, too?"

"No."

They turned. Emma had slipped in without anyone noticing. She was dressed nicely, in a chic skirt and blouse, stockings and low heels, as if coming or going to a meeting.

"I don't play golf," she said, as she crossed into the room and flopped her purse on the kitchen counter. "I don't have the time to practice, and I don't like to do anything I'm not good at."

Telling, Clancy thought. He caught Callie's eye. They were on the same wavelength. He noticed Callie eyeballing Emma's purse.

"I have to go shopping for dinner," Emma added. "I'm cooking tonight."

"That'll be something to look forward to," Walt told Callie. "Emma's a true gourmet chef, as you well know, Clancy."

"I'm not, but thank you," she answered graciously. "But you three go. It'll be fun."

"I'd rather go shopping with you," Callie said to Emma.

Emma seemed startled at the suggestion. "Don't be silly. Shopping's a drag. It's beautiful outside, and the courses Walt mentioned really are spectacular. You don't even have to play to enjoy them, you can walk alongside. Walt always walks, he hates carts, he's too macho."

"Carts are for old men and slackers," Walt declared

disdainfully. He picked up the phone. "Let me make a few calls," he said as he began dialing. "We'll get on one of those courses." He smiled at Clancy. "Me and you, father and son. A friendly wager on the side, not enough to break you, Clancy," he joshed.

"You really don't have to go with me," Emma told Callie again. Her voice seemed to have an edge of discomfort to it.

"But I want to," Callie answered, sweetly but firmly. "The boys need their time together."

Whoever Walt had called had picked up the phone. "Ed?" Walt said, in a hearty, hail-fellow-well-met voice. "Walt Gaines. How you doing, buddy?" There was a brief pause. "Good, good. Listen, Ed, is there a chance you can get my son and me on your wonderful golf course today? He flew in all the way from Chicago because I told him I could get him on. You don't want to make a liar out of me, do you?" he said, laughing.

Clancy, listening to this end of the conversation, felt like he was eavesdropping on a couple of small business owners from a burg in Illinois, members of the local Masonic lodge. His father had always been disdainful of such mundane conventions. Now he was part of one.

"Super," Walt was saying. "Just give them your name at the pro shop? Thanks, Ed. I owe you one."

He hung up the phone. "We have a tee time in an hour. Normally you have to play with the member, but this guy's got enough clout he can phone us in. You're going to love this course, it was one of Ben Hogan's favorites. Or maybe it was Nicklaus, one of those legends." He gave Emma a quick hug. "Anything but bouillabaisse," he chided her affectionately. "Otherwise, Clancy's going to think you can only cook one dish."

* * *

Clancy wore his running shoes. He rented clubs and bought balls and a golf glove at the pro shop. His father paid for everything; he didn't even bother to put up a token protest, he knew Walt would have been (or acted as if he had been) insulted. They shared a caddie, a middle-aged Chicano named Raúl, who knew the course blindfolded.

As it was midweek, they had the course practically to themselves. Walt, having only recently taken up a sport that is frustrating even to those who have played it their entire lives, was all over the place. A sliced drive off the first tee, followed by a wormburner second shot left him muttering; but a decent long-iron third shot, a good chip, and two okay putts gave him a bogey on the par five, a respectable-enough score.

"I'm happy if I can play bogey golf," he informed Clancy as they walked to the second tee box. "As long as I don't embarrass myself, that's all I ask for. I'm happy breaking a hundred."

And beating me, Clancy thought. His father had been ultracompetitive his entire life, even with his progeny. He might not play well, but he wanted to win.

Clancy had only played a couple of times over the summer—his practice and the bar kept him too busy. He double-bogeyed the first hole, and needed a good bunker save to salvage a bogey on the second. With the strokes his father was getting from him he was already down two. But starting with his tee shot on the third hole, a long dogleg par four, he found his rhythm. He laced his drive down the fairway, long and straight. Then he stiffed a seven-iron a hundred and sixty yards to within eight feet of the pin on his second shot. Raúl read the putt for him, giving him the correct speed and break. When the ball curled into the hole for a birdie he and the caddie tapped each other's fists, the way he'd seen Tiger do it on television with his caddie.

And with that, what should have been a friendly game between a son and his father, two men who were struggling to come to terms with each other, became a contest of skills and wills. Walt had the will, but Clancy's intensity matched his father's, and his skill levels were far better. He parred five of the remaining six holes on the front nine, and carded a thirty-nine. Walt, whose frustration level mounted every time Clancy hit a good shot, which was almost every shot he hit, had a fifty-two.

They took a short lunch break, basking in the sun on the clubhouse veranda as they waited for their tuna sandwiches to be brought out. Walt totaled the scores, computed the strokes he was getting from Clancy, then reached into his wallet and pulled out a ten and two ones, placed them on the table between them.

"What's this?" Clancy asked, as his father pushed the money toward him.

"You're five up. You won ten bucks on stroke, and two on the front. That was our bet."

Clancy pushed the money back. "You're paying for everything. I don't want your money."

Walt placed the bills in front of his son. "You won it, fair and square. I pay my debts," he said stubbornly.

Fine, you want to play the injured party, be my guest, Clancy thought. He picked the money up and stuffed it in his pocket. Later, he'd give it to Raúl, with the rest of his tip.

"You'll win it back on the back nine," he told his father encouragingly. More likely, he thought, I'll crush you. He wanted to win the rest of the holes, every one.

Their sandwiches came, along with cold Snapples in iced cups. The waiter put the check in front of Walt, who signed it and handed it back. "I'll reimburse Ed later," he explained to Clancy. "This way, he can apply it toward his minimum. Even mega-millionaires watch their nickels and dimes," he said gravely, as if he was giving his son a piece of deep, important advice.

Walt took a healthy bite of his sandwich, chewed, swallowed, drank some Snapple. He looked at Clancy with a serious expression on his face. "Emma and I are thinking of trying to get pregnant," he announced.

Clancy almost spewed out his mouthful of drink. "Are you kidding?"

Walt's face clouded. "No," he said stiffly. "Why would I kid about something as important as that?"

"Because it's too *weird*, dad, come on. You're going to have a kid who'd be younger than mine but would be what, my stepbrother or sister, my kid's aunt or uncle? You want to be father to a teenager when you're eighty? Dad, get real."

"Men my age are having children all the time, more and more," Walt informed Clancy with a pedantic, high-handed air. "Look at Larry King, Jesse Jackson. Strom Thurmond had a kid when he was in his seventies."

"Strom Thurmond?" Clancy shook his head in disbelief. "He's your role model now?"

"I'm merely pointing out that it happens, all the time."

Clancy put his sandwich down. "It doesn't happen all the time," he rebutted. Anger was rising from his gut. "Those men are freaks. Are you and Emma getting married? Or are you going to pull a Jesse and just have a love child?" he asked bitingly.

Walt glared at Clancy. "That was uncalled for."

"You're right, I apologize," Clancy said. He was flustered. "Are you getting married, then? You and Emma are actually thinking of doing that?"

His mind was reeling. His father marrying any woman, but particularly one half his age? Particularly this woman, whose life, what they were finding out about it, made Mata Hari look transparent? This was like watching a bad sitcom; worse, being in one against your will. His father remarrying would be brutal for him and his brothers to swallow under normal circumstances, without also having to deal with their investigation into their father's and now Emma's hidden and frightening actions of the past two years. Did his father even know this woman wasn't who she claimed to be? He doubted it, the ramifications of which were chilling by themselves, let alone the rest of this Pandora's box.

"What about mom?" he asked.

Walt stared at him unblinkingly. "Your mother is dead," he said flatly.

"I know, dad," Clancy replied harshly. "You don't have to tell me."

"Are you saying I wasn't a good husband?" his father rasped. "Implying it? Because that would be blasphemous, Clancy. I mean that." His voice was rising. "I was a wonderful husband. I was completely devoted to your mother. "

"That's not what I'm talking about." This was turning into a grade-A screwup, the same pattern that had been played out between him, his brothers, and his father ever since his mother died. A dead-end pattern he couldn't seem to stop. His father wanted to keep them off-balance but they couldn't let him set the agenda, not anymore, not with what they knew about him now. He needed to back off, not let his dad get under his skin like this.

"Don't I deserve to be happy with a partner as I get older?" Walt asked.

"Yes, dad, you do." That wasn't what was upsetting him. It was with *who.*

"If I hadn't been a good husband, if our marriage for whatever reason hadn't worked out, if your mom and I had gotten divorced, would you feel this way?" Walt asked.

Clancy shook his head. "No."

"Then why is this different? You're saying it's like I should be penalized for having been a good husband. An exemplary husband. I worshipped the ground your mother walked on."

No, dad, Clancy thought. You might have loved her—you did love her, that I will grant you—but you did not worship her ground, or her. You left the worshipping to others, to do about you.

"She felt that way about you, too, dad," he said, swallowing, yet again, his true feelings. "She died because she was supporting you, being with you, helping you."

Walt rose up in his chair. "Are you saying I'm responsible for mom's death?" he almost shouted.

"No," Clancy said, backtracking. "Of course I'm not. That's the last thing I'd ever think."

Except that was precisely what he was thinking. The facts had been thrust to the foreground: the secret insurance policies, all the lying, his father's mysterious lover. How could he and his brothers not think of that possibility, as grotesque and horrifying as it might be?

"Good," Walt said, sitting back. "Because if I ever believed you had those thoughts, it would kill me." He leaned toward Clancy, put his hand on his son's. "If I could have taken that bullet for her, I would have." His voice quivered. "I wish I had."

* * *

They played the back nine, although neither of them had much heart for it. Clancy's game went to hell, and when the eighteen-hole score was totaled he had barely broken ninety. Walt didn't fare any better. He played as he had on the front, erratically, self-critical and impatient after every bad shot.

"Tough game, golf," Walt said as he put his clubs into the trunk of his car. "You're supposed to keep the world outside at bay, that's the secret." He slammed the trunk shut. "We didn't do a good job at that today, did we?"

Clancy shook his head sadly. "I'm sorry, dad. I get emotional, thinking of mom. You caught me off-guard, and I didn't handle the situation gracefully."

His father clapped him on the back. "It hurt, I'm not going to lie to you about that, but it means you care, too."

"Of course I care."

"I shouldn't have sprung it on you like that," Walt said. "I should've alerted you in a letter, letting you and your brothers know Emma and I were more serious than you realized, that down the road . . ."

Clancy thought about that. "It happens when it happens," he said quietly, fatalistically. "When are you two going to make a decision about getting married?"

"I don't know," Walt answered. "We've been talking. Soon. I'm not getting any younger, kiddo." He gave Clancy a tap on the biceps. "But there's still plenty of fuel in the tank," he asserted.

"You'll be young till you die," Clancy told his old man.

He meant it. Whatever faults and problems his father had, his motor only ran at one speed—full out, balls to the wall. It always had; and, Clancy knew, it always would.

* * *

While the men were golfing, Callie and Emma shopped at the Farmers' Market in Santa Monica. After they finished, which included a stop at a specialty butcher store that sold Muscovy duck, the main course Emma was going to prepare for dinner, they browsed Main Street, buying matching T-shirts and sweaters like two sisters, or at least longtime good friends. Emma had insisted on buying baby clothes for Callie and Clancy's unborn child, even though the sex was unknown. "Yellow and white goes with either sex," she'd stated. Before she was finished she had rung up a baby clothes bill of over three hundred dollars, which she paid for with cash, just as she had paid for the groceries and the cappuccinos they drank at Starbucks on the Third Street Promenade.

All the while, Callie had obliquely but persistently tried to pry open the lockbox of Emma's life, remarking about siblings (did she have any, what sex, etc.), family background ("I'm from South Dakota, of all places, where are you from?"), whatever she could think of to draw Emma out. Emma was polite and cordial, even funny at times, but it was like throwing a tennis ball against a wall, it came bouncing back. The small tidbits Callie got from Emma were that she was somehow ashamed of or repelled by her background, or both, that she had disassociated herself from her family when she was young, still a teenager, and had never looked back. It was as if she had reinvented herself at an early age, and didn't leave a trace.

After only a few such questions it became apparent to Callie that her snooping was too obvious and that Emma was on to her, so she dropped it. Later, if the moment presented itself, she'd try again.

*　　*　　*

Walt and Clancy were both subdued when they arrived home shortly after dark. Callie followed Clancy into the guest bedroom when he went in to shower and change for dinner.

"How did it go?" she asked. "Did you have fun?"

He slumped down on the bed and peeled off his shirt, shoes, and socks. "We started out okay, but as always now, it seems, we went for each other's jugulars."

"Why this time?" She sighed. "This trip hasn't been what I'd hoped it would be. We're not having any fun and we're not learning anything about him or her, especially her, except that she doesn't exist, which leaves us nowhere."

"No go with cracking her shell?" he asked, stripping off his pants and shorts.

"I struck out. She's a master of obfuscation, she's been doing it a long time, that was the one thing I got from her. So what ignited the fire between you and him today?"

He looked up at her and almost laughed, but it hurt too much. "He wants to marry her." He paused. "Have a baby with her."

Callie's hand went to her mouth. "You're shitting me."

"Swear to God. He says they're trying."

"They? Or *him?"*

"Probably more him than her," he agreed. "It felt desperate, hearing him go on about geriatric fathers. It sounded to me like he's afraid if he doesn't do it, he'll lose her."

Callie shook her head. "They do seem happy together, although God knows what the truth of any of this is. But she doesn't want children."

She told him about the shopping for baby clothes, her clear perception that Emma wanted to participate vicariously, but not for herself.

"You can't live in the shadows and have children," she said. "Because you can't hide."

Dinner was a gourmet feast, as exceptional as the restaurant meal of the night before (which had cost a cool thousand dollars with tip; Clancy had almost gagged when he'd caught a glimpse of the bill).

Clancy and Callie praised Emma to the skies. "You could go into the catering business, or open your own restaurant, you're that good," Callie told her. "The Alice Waters of Los Angeles."

"I wish I had that kind of talent," Emma laughed. "I did a stint as a chef for a short time," she mentioned casually. "Too much work, too much devotion. I wasn't serious about it, it was one of those things you do when you're young and want to try everything once, like sing backup with a rock band or go trekking in Nepal."

"Where was that?" Callie asked. Come on, lady, give us one crack in the dike. We flew two thousand miles to find out something about you, anything. Don't make us go home empty-handed.

Emma remained inscrutable. "That was a long time ago, in a country far, far away," she said with an enigmatic smile, as she began clearing the table.

Now it was late. Callie and Clancy lay in bed, side by side. They were leaving tomorrow, and they didn't know any more about Emma Rawlings, or what she was doing with Walt, than they had before they had come. Only that she was a woman of deep mystery, taking great care to hide her identity and her past.

Outside it was warm, even though it was November. A Santa Ana condition had blown in earlier in the day, bringing with it a hot, dry wind. The moon, full and low, shone on the gently moving water in the swimming pool, casting reflected, moving rhythmic shadows through the open-curtained window onto the ceiling above them. Clancy stared at the almost hypnotic movement.

"I'm going to have to confront him," he declared.

She grabbed his hand. "Don't," she said quickly.

"What other options do I have?"

"I don't know. But that's not going to solve anything. All it'll do is anger him and make him retreat." She turned over and looked at him. "At least now we're in communication. He isn't hiding from you anymore. But you can't get in his face, he'll slam the door on you. You're going to have to keep trying to come at this from the side."

"For how long?" He thought for a moment. "Do you think he's suspicious?"

"Of what?"

"Of us. Of everybody. If he isn't, he ought to be. He's been lying his ass off ever since mom died. Liars are paranoid. He's got to be wondering when the dime's going to be dropped on him."

"Not necessarily," she said in disagreement. "Maybe he thinks he's pulled it off, not telling you guys the truth."

She got up and sat cross-legged in the middle of the bed, facing him. "If he hadn't bought this expensive house, we wouldn't be here," she said. "If he had moved to some reasonable place, no one would have thought to look into all the other stuff, the stocks, the insurance, none of it. It was the only chink in his armor, because what father expects his children to investigate him? Plus he's in heavy denial, you don't need to be a shrink to see that. Your mother's death, leaving the school, I know he could have fought to stay on but let's face it, they screwed him over, a man of his achievement and reputation. Those were bitter blows to absorb. We've talked about this before, but you can't forget it, Clancy. He is not seeing the world through a clear lens. So confronting him is not the way."

He fell back. "So we do nothing?"

"No. We keep trying."

"How?"

"I don't know yet," she answered. "But I have a feeling that sooner or later we'll figure something out that'll give us a key."

Callie didn't know how long she had been awake. She was warm and uncomfortable. She wasn't sleeping well—ever since the hormonal changes that came with pregnancy she hadn't been able to sleep through the night. Clancy, lying beside her, slept heavily, his body curled up into itself. Quietly, so as not to disturb him, she slipped out of bed, took off her nightgown, donned the thick terry cloth robe that Emma, ever the gracious hostess, had laid out for her, grabbed a towel from the bathroom, and tiptoed out of the bedroom.

When she stepped out onto the back deck, she saw she wouldn't be swimming alone. Emma was already in the pool, stroking back and forth with practiced ease.

As she watched Emma swimming she thought, do I or don't I? This would be her final opportunity to try to pry open Emma's shell.

Let it go, she decided. She was too tired to engage Emma in psychological warfare. She had done what she could, and had drawn a blank. She'd have a nice swim, tire herself out so that she could fall asleep, and worry about Emma later on down the line. She stepped off the deck and walked barefoot across the lawn, which was damp with nighttime dew, toward the pool.

Emma was naked. Callie wasn't wearing a bathing suit, either; she hadn't expected anyone to be out here. As she stood at the edge of the pool, she hesitated for a moment. She was an athlete, she had been naked with scores of women in the locker room, but there was something about this situation and this woman that caused her to waver.

As Emma came to the shallow end of the pool she stopped swimming and looked up at Callie. "Couldn't sleep?" she asked with a smile.

"No," Callie answered.

"It's the moon." Emma pointed skyward. "I always have a hard time sleeping when the moon's full. Plus the Santa Ana winds. The Devil's Wind, I've heard it called."

It's an ill wind that blows no good, Callie thought. "With me it's being pregnant," she responded. "I'm having a hard time sleeping in general."

Emma stood. The water dripped off her hair and body in shimmering rivulets. "Come on in. The water's soothing. We keep it warm, I don't like swimming in cold water."

Callie dipped a toe in. It was almost bathlike. "Does Walt swim with you?" she asked, involuntarily glancing over her shoulder.

"Not very often," Emma replied. "He's not coming out here, if that's what you're concerned about. He's dead asleep."

A revealing phrase, Callie thought? Don't read too much into this, she cautioned herself. You're not out here to psychoanalyze.

She sat on the edge of the pool, dangling her legs in the water. Then she slipped in, ducked her head under, and pushed off from the wall. As she started a slow, methodical crawl toward the other end, she could see from out of the corner of her eye that Emma was swimming in tandem with her.

Back and forth they went like synchronized swimmers, stroking languidly. Callie lost herself in the rhythm, feeling her muscles expanding with the effort. It felt good, swimming. When she got back to Chicago she'd join a health club that had a pool. Emma was swimming effortlessly, an easy reach, catch, and pull, then gliding. She's good, Callie thought. I wonder if she ever swam competitively. I could ask her, that's innocuous. But not now. She was too tired to be a detective at the moment. Maybe in the morning, if the opportunity presented itself.

When she started to feel winded she stopped; she didn't have as much energy now as she'd had before she had gotten pregnant.

Emma also stopped. Callie sensed that Emma was timing her movements to hers. It made her feel uncomfortable for a moment, as if Emma was playing a subtle head game with her, trying to match their internal rhythms. It reminded Callie of a phenomenon that occurred when she played team sports with other women, and spent a lot of time with them in intimate situations. Gradually, over a period of months, they would all begin having their periods at the same time. Some kind of vestigial pack instinct. This was different, of course, but she felt a certain psychic similarity. An attempt to bond. Or perhaps, to control.

They got out and lay down on chaise lounges on the deck, towels draped modestly across their midsections, the water rapidly evaporating from their bodies from the hot, dry deserty wind.

"It's a shame you have to leave tomorrow," Emma

said. "I'd like to get to know you better." She paused. "We're like sisters now, in a way."

That was bold, Callie thought. She had decided not to probe anymore, but here was an opening that shouldn't be missed. "Are you and Walt thinking about getting married?"

Emma sat up with an involuntary jerk. Her towel dropped to the deck. "Why would you ask that?" she said, a note of perturbation in her voice.

Callie sat up, too. "Walt mentioned to Clancy that you might be thinking about having a child. If you're planning on having one, you might be getting married, too."

Emma shook her head. Her expression, rather than being one of anger or annoyance, was almost sad. "I'm not going to have a child with Walt."

"Why not?"

"This is going to sound callous, but it isn't meant to be." She hesitated for a moment. "Walt's too old."

Callie was taken aback by Emma's frankness. These were the first honest words of consequence out of the woman's mouth since we've been here, she thought. "Men his age have children. He even recited a list to Clancy."

"I know. I've heard it. I don't mean too old biologically. I mean he's too old for me." She sighed. "That sounds cruel, doesn't it?"

Callie didn't answer.

"I don't know how much longer Walt and I are going to stay together," Emma confessed.

Callie tried to keep her face from registering the shock she felt.

"I care deeply about Walt," Emma declared. "He's a wonderful man, and he's been through hell, you know that as well as I do. But when he's eighty, I'll be fifty. I don't want that. I want a man who can be my equal partner, not only in the mind, but physically." She paused. "Like you have with Clancy. A man your own age, whose life is all ahead of him. Not behind him."

Callie fidgeted. This was too personal; it was almost painful in its openness. Why are you telling me this, she thought? We are not sisters, not even remotely.

"I agree there are advantages to being with a partner who's close to you in age," she said. "I can't imagine myself being with a man—" She stopped herself—she had almost said "Walt's age." Instead, she said, "That much older than me." It didn't sound any better, but there was no way around it, no matter how you said it.

"You're lucky," Emma told her. "Clancy's a terrific guy."

"I know."

"All the Gaines men are. Tom, too," Emma said. "Can I confess something to you?"

"If you want to." This was getting closer to the bone than she could have imagined.

"I almost made a play for Tom, when he was out here."

Callie was mystified by this revelation, not that it had happened, but that Emma was confiding in her about it. Was she trying to ferret out if Tom had told her and Clancy? Or was she looking for some way out of her relationship with Walt and was setting herself up to be busted? Either way, this was getting more serious than she'd bargained for.

A confession like that had to be responded to, and she couldn't have held her tongue anyway, this was too juicy. "You're kidding me!"

Emma looked serious, almost wistful. "No, I'm not. There was a charge between us."

"That's pretty heavy, Emma."

"I know. I felt ashamed, but it was there, I couldn't deny it."

"So did anything happen?" Callie asked, almost too eagerly.

Emma started to speak, then she paused. "I wouldn't do that to Walt." She looked at Callie. "Tom would have, though. I could feel it. It was very powerful."

Callie felt the need to defend Tom's honor. "You can't say that, since it didn't happen."

Emma shook her head in disagreement. "If you had been there, you would have felt it, too. There was real anger—rage, almost—between them, first under the surface, then it broke through into the open. Walt was bullying Tom unmercifully, it was ugly, especially in front of me, a woman who Tom barely knew. Tom would have had sex with me just to get back at Walt."

Callie stared at Emma. Am I being set up, she wondered? What's with this sudden soul-revealing? It seemed so out of character.

"Why are you telling me this?" she asked. "We barely know each other."

"Because it's wrong for Walt not to be dealing with reality," Emma said firmly, almost harshly. "He's been living in a false world, ever since his wife died. When I try to think of what it was like for him, her being killed in the jungle, then having to deal with the funeral . . ."

The funeral. Callie's mind flashed back to that terrible time. "I know," she said with sadness in her voice. "I was there."

"And then all the trouble with the university afterward, and—"

Callie put up a hand to stop her. "We've all been through this way more than any of us want." Sighing heavily, as if the memories were too painful to bear, she stood up. "I'm going inside. I'm tired, and Clancy and I have a long day of traveling tomorrow."

Emma got up with her. "I didn't mean to dredge up bad memories." She took Callie's hand. "I've really unburdened myself on you, haven't I? I apologize."

"I'm glad you did," Callie said honestly.

"If you can, I'd like what I've told you to stay between us," Emma asked. "I kind of put myself out there."

Callie smiled at her. "I know you did, and I appreciate that. You can trust me. I've been wanting to get to know you better, and now I have."

Callie shook Clancy violently. "Wake up!" she whispered urgently.

"What is it?" he asked in a voice thick with sleep.

She sat on the bed on her knees. She was bouncing up and down, she was so energized. "I remembered where I've seen her! When we first got here and I asked her if we'd ever met? And she said no? Do you remember?"

"What're you talking about?"

"The funeral!"

"What?" He shook his head, trying to clear the cobwebs.

"Your mother's funeral! We were looking at a cluster of mourners grouped around your dad and I asked you about a particular woman. You didn't know who she was, so I asked him. He said he didn't know, that she was one of your mother's friends. But it was *her*! *Emma*!"

Clancy sat bolt upright. "Are you sure?"

"Yes! Her hair was layered and a darker shade of blond then, but it was her. You don't remember? Think back!"

Clancy closed his eyes for a moment, trying to recall.

"No, I don't," he answered, opening them again. "I had more important things on my mind that day. Are you sure? That was over a year ago, and nobody was thinking too clearly back then."

"I'm positive! No doubts at all." She stared at him. "You believe me, don't you?"

"If you're really sure, then yes." He leaned back against the headboard, stunned.

"This points us in a clear direction now," Callie said urgently. "Walt knew her *before* he moved to L.A., not after. That changes everything."

Clancy nodded. "It sure as hell does. The question is, how did they meet?"

"And when, and where."

He gave her a lopsided smile, shaking his head. "You called it, on the nose. Female instinct about wanting to come out here and see her in person—we laughed at you, but you were right. I will never doubt a woman's instincts again—at least not yours."

"I'm glad you're figuring me out, finally," she teased him. "But that's not important. What we have to do now is find out who Emma Rawlings really is. And what part she plays in all of this."

The wind had died down with the rising of the sun. Emma was her usual early-to-rise industrious self. She stood at the center island, squeezing oranges. The coffeepot was perking. As Callie came to pour herself a cup Emma leaned toward her. She glanced over at the table, where Walt, comfortably disheveled in a T-shirt and shorts, was busy reading the L.A. Times financial section. "Are we still secret friends?" she asked quietly.

Callie nodded. "Absolutely," she whispered back.

"I don't want to hurt Walt, regardless of what might happen in the future. He's already suffered enough."

"You can trust me."

"Thank you."

Walt looked up from the paper. "Sleep well?" he asked his son and daughter-in-law.

"Like a log," Clancy told him, grabbing the sports section.

"Two logs," Callie chimed in. She and Emma exchanged a quick, conspiratorial look. She kissed Walt on the top of his head.

"I wish you could stay longer," Walt said. "You just got here."

"We'll be back," Clancy assured him. "Now that we know you want us to."

"Anytime," Walt told him. "I needed to get my legs under me, but that period's over now."

They ate outside on the deck. To go with the fresh juice and coffee, Emma made sourdough French toast, topped with caramelized bananas and berries.

"If I stayed here a week I'd put on ten pounds," Clancy told Emma, as he forked up a mouthful of toast.

"We don't generally eat like this," she said. "We wanted to spoil you."

"You're doing a great job."

Callie rummaged around in her purse. "I'll be right back," she declared. She jumped up and ran inside.

Walt put his paper down and turned to Clancy. "How are your brothers doing? I know Will's fine, but what about Tom? For real?"

"He's okay," Clancy said, pouring milk into his coffee and stirring it. "He needed a break."

Walt looked worried. "Is he going back?"

"I don't know. I don't think he knows."

Walt shook his head sadly. "All that time and talent wasted. It's criminal."

Emma leaned toward him. "It's his life, Walt. You can't live it for him."

"Smile!"

Everyone turned instinctively toward Callie, who was looking through the viewfinder of a throwaway camera. She clicked the button, and the flash went off.

"That was a good one of the three of you," she said happily. "Walt, move closer to Emma. Let me get one of the two of you."

"No, please," Emma protested. "I don't like the way I look this morning. I don't have any makeup on, my hair's a mess . . ."

"You always look great," Callie told her, laughing. "Like you just stepped out of a magazine ad. I wish I could look as good as you, first thing in the morning or anytime."

"No, really," Emma said, trying to get away from Walt, who had draped an arm over her shoulder. "I need to refresh the coffeepot."

"And . . . good!" The flash went off again. "That was a nice one. I'll send you copies after I develop them."

Emma stood up. "Why don't you leave it here? I'll do it, and send you the pictures. Sometimes when you take a camera on an airplane the negatives get ruined, especially now that they've turned up the X-ray machines."

"I've never had any problems," Callie reassured her.

"Okay," Emma conceded. She held her hand out. "Let me take one of the three of you."

"Great." Callie reached toward Emma to hand the camera over, then pulled her arm back. "Except this one's finished," she said, as she looked at the counter. She dropped the camera into her purse, pulled out another. "This has a full roll." She handed it to Emma as she walked over to Clancy and Walt and knelt down between them. "How's this?"

"Perfect." Emma put her eye to the viewer. "Smile into the camera, everyone."

Walt helped Clancy carry their bags out to the rental car. "'Bye, dad," Clancy said. He gave his father a hug. "Sorry we couldn't stay longer."

"Next time." Walt hugged him back fiercely. "All of you. Will, Tom, Callie. Your baby. A family reunion. We're overdue."

"Way overdue," Clancy agreed. How sad this is, he thought, this deception.

Walt looked back to the house. The two women were still inside. "What we talked about yesterday," he asked. "Emma and me. Did you mention anything to Callie?"

"No, dad," Clancy answered. "I assumed you wanted that to be between you and me."

Walt nodded. "Let's keep it that way, okay? Until Emma and I are ready to go public."

"You'll tell me when."

They leaned against the side of the car. "Life," Walt said heavily. "It's too damned complicated, isn't it?"

"If you make it," Clancy replied. "Me, I try to make it simple, direct, and honest."

Walt nodded. "That's good advice, my son," he said sagely. He looked back at the house again. "It isn't always possible, unfortunately."

"Yes," Clancy replied, unable to look him in the eye. "I know."

CHICAGO

♦ ♦ ♦

Tom, wearing polypropylene long johns under his sweats and a Michigan Wolverines watch cap pulled down around his ears to ward off the below-freezing late-autumn cold, went for a long morning run along Lake Shore Drive. Then he showered, shaved, dressed, made himself a late-breakfast omelet, read the Tribune and Sun-Times cover to cover, and did a load of laundry. By then it was one, and he went to an early-bird movie, a Denzel Washington cop film. When he got out, the sun was already beginning to arc down into the west, casting an industrial-feeling pink-orange glow across the rooftops and watertowers. He browsed a bookstore for a short time, but didn't buy anything—he already had enough unread books lying about the floor of his bedroom. In the end, he grabbed a coffee near DePaul University, checked out the coeds, and walked back to the apartment. It was almost four o'clock. He had managed to get through another day.

That was the problem. Except when he was working at the bar, he had nothing to do. For a few weeks, when he'd first started there, he had fallen into his old undergraduate routine—sleep late, start the day slowly, then work (it used to be study) late and stay up later. The nights he wasn't working he'd have dinner with Will, Clancy, and Callie, but that was only a few days a week. Mostly, he was on his own. The only friends he'd made were people who worked at the bar, or came in regularly. But meeting people at the bar, in his position behind it, rather than on the customer's side, didn't promote anything deeper than surface acquaintanceship. He had resisted asking Rhonda the barmaid out, because of Clancy's no-fraternization rule, but rules were made to be broken, and he wasn't a normal employee, he was family. Tending bar wasn't going to be his life's work, he wasn't going to be there much longer. Nor was she, once she got her teaching certificate. They could have lunch together, go to a movie, have an afternoon lay. They were both adults, they could be discreet. Clancy wouldn't have to know.

Of course, she might turn him down. Or she might have a boyfriend.

He thought yet again, as he watched the late-afternoon news on CNN, about Emma Rawlings. Clancy and Callie had walked Will and him through what they had learned in Los Angeles—most important, Callie having placed Emma at their mother's funeral. That had been an incredible revelation. The overriding question that needed to be answered now, as soon as possible, was how Walt and this woman had met, and under what unsavory circumstances, which would cause her to lie about herself as thoroughly and deeply as she had. They also needed to find out if their father knew she was lying: was he complicitous with her, or was he being duped, too? Given the evidence, they had to assume the former, but they hoped it was the latter. Either way, they had to know. And then, of course, they had to find out who she really was.

The first thing they did was to check over the list of the volunteers who had accompanied Walt and Jocelyn to Central America, but they'd drawn a blank. They weren't surprised to discover that there was no Emma Rawlings on that trip. Earlier this morning Callie had developed the pictures she'd taken of Emma, and overnighted a set of prints to the L.A. detective. Hopefully something would come of that.

Tom's stomach had knotted into a fist as he had listened to Callie talk about Emma. This woman was dangerous, probably a criminal, but he had a raging emotional hard-on for her anyway. That was going to be a sonofabitch to deal with, especially if, or more likely, when, he and she got together again. Before that, though, he was going to have to come to grips with how she played him for a sucker, charming him, seducing him.

He was going stir-crazy, and the old fifth-wheel feeling was creeping back in. The TV news was depressing. He clicked it off. He needed to do something.

The accordion file containing the list of the volunteers from the trip to La Chimenea was tucked away in the bottom drawer in the desk in his room. Maybe there was a kernel of information they had overlooked, something peculiar in a résumé. It wouldn't hurt to check it over again. He still had a couple of hours to kill before he had to go to work.

He started down the list, working alphabetically. The first two names he called weren't in; he left a brief message on their services. The third picked up.

"Kurt Campbell?" Tom asked, reading from the list.

"Yes?" came the tentative reply.

"I'm not a telemarketer," Tom said quickly, before the

man could hang up on him. "My name is Tom Gaines. My father is Professor Walter Gaines."

"I see," came the slow reply.

"Do you have a second? I have a couple of quick questions."

There was a pause.

"Only a few questions," Tom reiterated. "It won't take any time at all. I know it's dinnertime, but just give me a minute or two, can you?"

"Okay," came the grudging reply.

"Great, thanks. I appreciate it." Tom plunged in. "You were present when my mother was killed, weren't you?"

"Yeah, I was there." The voice sounded younger, more college-age. "I'm really sorry, man. That was such a stupid, tragic accident," he added with the anger of memory. "She was a super woman, your mother."

"Thank you." Tom hesitated before pressing on. "Thinking back on that, and I know it might be fuzzy, it was over a year ago, and the circumstances were terrible, was there anything you noticed, or saw, or heard during that time that seemed . . . well . . . unusual to you?"

"Unusual like what?" came the muted question.

"I don't know, frankly. Anything strange involving my parents, or one of my parents and a volunteer, or someone connected with the government. Have you been on other digs?"

"Uh huh. I worked in Belize the year before that one. The summer before," the student said, more specifically.

"And this one wasn't any different?" Tom asked.

"It was better. More complete. Your dad was the best teacher in the field I've ever had. He really made ancient civilizations come to life. It was like the ancient Maya were living with us. It's a shame what happened to him, afterward," the student commiserated. "He didn't do anything wrong."

It's great that you feel that way, Tom thought. "One last question," he said.

"Shoot."

"Do you remember all the people on the trip?"

There was silence for a moment. "I don't know," the student answered.

"If I asked you a name, you'd know if they were on the trip or not."

"Yeah," the student replied. "For sure."

"Emma Rawlings," Tom said. "Does that name mean anything to you?"

"No," came the immediate reply.

"There was no one named Emma Rawlings in the group."

"Nope, there wasn't."

"Okay, then," Tom said, deflated. "Thanks for your time."

"No problem," the student replied. "How's your dad doing these days?"

Tom thought for a moment before answering. "He's doing remarkably well, under the circumstances," he decided to say.

"That's great to hear. Is he teaching anywhere?"

"Not currently."

"Well, I hope he does again," the student said with enthusiasm. "He's the best I've ever had. Almost anybody who ever had him would tell you the same thing."

"Thank you," Tom said sincerely. "I'm glad you feel that way."

He hung up. Nothing there, except that his father was a saint.

He continued calling: two nonanswers, two volunteers

who repeated what the first one had told Tom. Nothing unusual happened until the incidents of the last day, there weren't any problems they saw or knew about, it had been a great summer of work. What happened to Jocelyn Gaines had been a terrible and shocking accident, but nothing more than that. Nothing sinister.

He glanced at his watch as he hung up from his last call. He needed to get rolling, change into his working clothes and head out. A couple more calls, and that would be that. He dialed a telephone number in Vermont.

"Hello?" a woman answered.

"Is this . . ." He glanced at the volunteer list. ". . . Bridget O'Malley?"

"Yes? Who is this?" came the reply, in a strong New England accent.

"My name is Tom Gaines, Ms. O'Malley. I'm the son of Walt and Jocelyn Gaines."

There was silence from the other end.

"Ms. O'Malley?" he said into the receiver.

"I'm here. What do you want?" The voice was cold, distant.

"I'd like to ask you a few questions about the summer work you did with my dad and mom. The summer my mother was killed," he said, almost wincing as he said the word "killed."

"I can't help you," came the terse reply.

"Look, Ms. O'Malley," Tom said wearily. "I realize it was a traumatic experience for everyone. But no one suffered more than my father did, and my brothers and me. He lost his wife. We lost our mother. So please—just answer a few questions for me. I promise it won't take any time at all."

"That's not what I mean," the woman replied.

"How so?" Tom asked.

"I can't help you, because I wasn't there."

"You weren't? But . . ." He glanced down at the list. There was her name, her telephone number, her school information, passport information.

"No," she said. He could hear anger from the other end of the line. "I was dropped."

"Dropped?" he repeated, a beat behind her.

"Yes, dropped," she said emphatically. "I was all set to go. I had everything in order. I had already turned down two other summer fellowships for it, and then with a week to go, they dropped me." The woman was still livid and carrying a chip on her shoulder about it, a year and a half later.

"How did that happen?" he asked. "Did my dad call you?"

"He sent me a goddamned e-mail. He said they had overbooked, that the government down there wouldn't let as many students in as he had planned. So I was dumped."

"I'm sorry," Tom said.

"No kidding. I blew my entire summer," the woman ranted, "it was too late for me to get anything else going. I wound up waitressing in Provincetown, which was the pits, in case you've never been there. I had great credentials, it was wrong of him to do that, so close to when we were leaving."

"I'm sorry," Tom said again, taken aback at the vehemence of the woman's wrath. "I'm sure my dad explained it to you the best he could."

"He didn't explain anything. All I got was this damn e-mail, and that was it. Not even a phone call." She paused. "I heard about what happened to your mother. I'm sorry about that. But I can't help you."

The phone went dead in his hand. He placed the receiver back in the cradle.

A last-minute change of plans. That didn't sound like his parents. One of the secrets to their success was their organizational skills, particularly his mother's. When it came to his father's work, especially the out-of-country trips and excavations, she was extremely buttoned-down. If there had been problems such as the one the rejected woman described, the professors Gaines would have dealt with them long before the eleventh hour.

It was time to go. Tom went into his bedroom, opened the desk drawer, and pulled out the accordion file, which was bulging with old correspondence. As he was about to put the manifest back in, he noticed a couple of other pages, similar to the one he had been using to make the phone calls, that had been clipped to a cover letter to the authorities in the district where La Chimenea was located. The cover sheet was basically a form letter, informing them when they would be arriving, how many, and so forth. Flipping it over, he saw it was like the ones he had just replaced: the names of the volunteers, along with their vital information.

He scanned through it quickly. It contained the same names as on the other sheets, with one exception—no Bridget O'Malley. This must be a revised list, he thought, to account for her not being on the trip.

Putting the list down, he thought about the conversation he'd had with the disgruntled woman. How many others had gotten that unfortunate e-mail, he wondered. He took the original list from the file and laid it out on top of the desk, then placed the new list next to it and scanned the names.

They were all similar, with the one exception of the omission of Bridget O'Malley from the trip list. Instead, a new name had been inserted, another woman. He read the name: Diane Montrose. A new student-volunteer named Diane Montrose was replacing Bridget O'Malley. No biographical information, not even a telephone number. Just a name.

His father had notified Bridget O'Malley that she was being dumped because the list had to be pared down, but it hadn't been; one person was substituted for another, but the total had remained the same.

Bridget O'Malley had been lied to.

He picked up the telephone and dialed.

"Hello?" A man's voice.

"Kurt Campbell?"

"Yes? Is that you, Mr. Gaines?"

"Tom. Yes. Sorry to bother you again, but I have one more question I forgot to ask. Does the name Diane Montrose ring a bell?"

"Sure," came the immediate response. "Diane was on the trip."

"Could you describe her for me at all? Approximate age, height, hair coloring." His leg was starting to do a Saint Vitus' dance on the floor. He pushed down on his knee to keep it still.

"She was older than most of us," came the reply. "I guess maybe early thirties? Fairly tall, five-eight or nine." He coughed. "Sorry. I'm coming down with a cold."

"That's okay," Tom said. He was feeling feverish himself. "Hey, thanks, buddy."

"Glad to help out," Campbell said. "Do you know Diane?" he asked.

Tom licked his lips—they were dry. "I don't know anyone named Diane Montrose."

"She's a knockout," Campbell told him, with a young

man's sexually charged enthusiasm. "A lot of the guys had the hots for her."

"I see." Oh man, do I see. He was fearful of asking the next question, but he had to. "Was she friendly with my dad?"

"Yeah, they got along okay. She was kind of aloof but she got along fine with everybody."

Tom was reeling. "Thanks," he told Campbell. "Sorry I butted in on your evening again. I won't be calling you again, I promise."

"Not a problem. Glad I was able to help you."

Tom left a message for Will, telling him he'd come across more damaging data about the situation at La Chimenea and that Will should contact him at Finnegan's. Then he called Clancy and told him the same. They agreed to meet at the bar at seven-thirty when the happy hour rush would be over and they could talk without being disturbed.

It was impossible for Tom to keep his mind on his work. His brain was spinning with the ramifications of his discovery. He and his brothers and sister-in-law had been revolving in the unsettling revelations of his parents' lives since they'd started their investigation into their mother and father's—basically, their father's—dark side. Emma had been part of it, true; but as an adjunct, one element of many, not as a principal. But now, with this new knowledge, she was front and center.

Clancy, Callie, and Will all arrived together. "Pete, can you handle both ends of the bar?" Clancy called out as Callie and Will grabbed the last booth in the back.

"Ten-four," Pete called back.

Tom took off his bartender's apron and ducked under

the opening at the end of the bar, joining the others in the booth.

"It's her," Callie said emphatically, as soon as Tom finished delivering his bad news. "It has to be. She was put on the list at the last minute under false pretenses which were engineered by your dad, she was there the entire summer, she was there when your mom was killed, and she was at the funeral. Now they're living together."

Clancy was absolutely shaking. He said what they had all been thinking, but had never spoken out loud. "Were dad and her in a conspiracy against mom?" he asked.

"It looks bad," Tom said.

"Terrible," Will agreed.

"So were they having an affair?" Clancy asked, more a rhetorical statement than a question. "We know dad was less than pure in his sexual forays." He grimaced. "Jesus, that sounds so tawdry. With mom there and all."

Callie shook her head. "I don't think so," she said thoughtfully. "I mean, they might have been, but I don't think that's the reason Emma—I can't not call her Emma, that's how I know her—was brought onto this trip. I think Walt wanted her there for another reason."

"What?" Will asked.

"That's the million-dollar question." She clapped her hands together. "Okay. We have a name now. I'll call the detective out in L.A. tomorrow morning . . ." She glanced at her watch. "It's only five-thirty back there. I'll call her now. Give her the name, what else we know, let's see what she can come up with."

Clancy buried his head in his hands. Callie put a supportive arm on his shoulder. He looked up at his brothers, sitting across the table from him. "Did she have anything to do with mom being *killed?* That's what we've all been scared about, isn't it?"

Will and Tom nodded. They were too numb to talk.

"It was an accident," Clancy said in anguish. "A tragic, senseless accident. That's what we've always thought, what everyone's said, everyone who was there, starting with dad. It's what the student you talked to tonight said, right?" he asked, looking at Tom.

"Just the way dad told it," Tom confirmed.

"At least he wasn't lying about that," Callie said.

"Small consolation," Clancy told her. He slumped back.

"I need to go home." Callie slipped out of the booth and put on her parka. "The detective's phone number's there, I want to call her right now."

"I'll come with you," Clancy said. "There's nothing else we can do here now." He clapped Tom on the shoulder. "Take the rest of the night off. None of us are in any shape to be working."

Artesia Garcia, the Los Angeles private investigator, called back the following afternoon. They listened in on the speaker as the detective laid out what she'd learned.

She had struck out with the phantom Emma Rawlings, but not with Diane Montrose. The woman presently involved with Walt Gaines is, in fact, Diane Montrose, she confirmed. She had been able to match the photo that Callie had sent her with one from a New York driver's license that had been issued to Diane Montrose in 1999 (which was going to cost an additional five hundred dollars, she told them, she had to call in some heavy favors). So that part of the mystery was solved. They knew who she was, and equally important, that she had known Walt before he moved to Los Angeles.

Diane Montrose was not and had never been enrolled

in any Ph.D. program at any university in the United States. She did, however, have a master's degree in Art History from the University of North Carolina in Chapel Hill. Her last current residence of record was New York City, borough of Manhattan, but she no longer lived there and had dropped out of sight—there was no forwarding address.

"When was that?" Clancy asked, leaning forward in his chair.

"About two years ago," Garcia answered.

The detective recited the rest of what she had found out: Diane was not a fugitive, there were no outstanding warrants on her that Garcia could find. Her last known employment had been as a consultant to some private art galleries and wealthy individual collectors in New York. That was two years ago, which coincided with when she had left her apartment and dropped from sight. Garcia read out the names, addresses, and telephone numbers of the galleries and collectors. Callie wrote them down.

"What do you want me to do now?" Garcia asked.

"Nothing," Callie immediately mouthed.

"Why not . . ." Will whispered.

"Trust me on this," Callie whispered back urgently.

Clancy leaned in to the speaker box. "We'll get back to you," he told Garcia. "Thanks for your help."

Will had to go out of town on business, so Clancy, Callie, and Tom met with Laurel Johnstone in her office at the Art Institute. Laurel, a couple of years older than Callie, was an assistant curator. Both women had gone to Stanford. They hadn't known each other there but they had friends in common, so when Callie and Clancy moved to Chicago they had struck up an acquaintanceship, meeting for drinks or lunch about once a month, usually in the company of other mutual friends. Callie had phoned Laurel after the conversation with Artesia Garcia and asked if she and her husband and one of his brothers could come by and pick her brain.

Laurel, a dark-eyed woman with long, curly brown hair that billowed out from her heart-shaped face, listened attentively as they told her what they had learned about Diane Montrose.

"Did you ever find out what happened at La Chimenea that caused the government to revoke your father's privileges?" she asked, when they had finished. "Did your father ever tell you what the specific problem was?"

"He hasn't said anything about it to us at all," Tom told her. "Just the opposite—he's avoided it. He says he doesn't want to go back because of the bad memories, that he's lost his zest for it."

"We're not sure they've been officially revoked," Clancy said. "Everything we know is secondhand."

"It would be useful to find out if they were, and if so, why," Laurel counseled them. "The professor you met at UCLA who told you there was a problem. Why don't you ask him?"

"We can't do that," Clancy said. "It's too delicate."

Laurel's full eyebrows came together in a frown. "I hate to bring this up." She paused.

Tom beat her to the punch. "Looting at the site."

She nodded. "It's a huge problem at every pre-Columbian site, particularly when they're in the early stages of excavation."

"That possibility's been growing in our brains like a cancer," Tom said. "But we haven't had the guts to face it."

Clancy was almost writhing in his chair, he was so distraught. "I don't want to believe that," he proclaimed.

"This was his life. He had too much integrity to do anything that would be unethical or immoral in his work."

Laurel smiled sympathetically. "I believe you. I certainly want to," she qualified. "But this Montrose woman might have," she pointed out. "She could have been stealing priceless artifacts for some of the private museums, or more likely, collectors, on your list. If looting had happened while your father was in charge down there, the consequences would have rubbed off on him whether he was involved or not."

"Without his knowing it?" Tom asked doubtfully. "That doesn't feel right. He would have known. He was the one who put her on the list, don't forget."

Clancy buried his head in his hands. "If that were true, it would be the pits. All the other shit is terrible enough, but that? Jesus."

"I don't want to believe dad was dirty any more than you do," Tom said, "but I'm not going to close my mind to anything anymore. We've had our eyes screwed tight about this, but we're going to have to open them. First we have to find out about Diane. If we do, then the rest might fall into place."

Laurel nodded briskly in agreement. "One thing that will help will be to find out what kind of transactions took place between her and the people on your list of galleries and collectors, the one the detective gave you." She flipped open her Rolodex. "I know someone in New York who is uniquely qualified to help you with that."

The wind off Lake Michigan almost knocked them over when they stepped outside the museum. They took a cab to Finnegan's. They were calmer now, they'd had time to let the pain and anger dissipate.

Pete was manning the bar when they walked in. "Make me an Irish coffee, will you?" Clancy asked him.

"Two," Tom added.

"Nothing for me," Callie said.

They hunkered down in the last booth.

"It makes sense," Callie said.

"Part of it," Clancy agreed. "But only . . ."—he held his thumb and forefinger an inch apart— ". . . this much. Emma, Diane, whatever she wants to call herself, didn't speculate on the stocks all those years. She didn't buy the multimillion-dollar life insurance policies. That was dad and mom."

"Was it?" Tom countered. He slammed his fist into the side of the booth. "We don't know how long Emma, Diane, whoever she is, and dad knew each other before that summer. It could have been years. We don't know."

"What, it was all a setup between her and dad?" Clancy was riled up. "The stocks, the insurance? You're nuts, man."

"It's all been a pack of lies up until now, hasn't it?" Tom said in rebuttal. "Has dad told us anything that was true over these last years? Why couldn't he have known her? He's given lectures at North Carolina, he could have met her there. Who knows anything anymore?"

Clancy balled his hands into fists and knocked his knuckles against his temples. The words that he had been holding back for months gushed out of his mouth, a tidal wave breaking through the dam. "So what does that mean, the two of them conspired to kill mom? Some grandiose scheme going back years?"

Callie sucked in air. "Oh, my God!" Her head was shaking like she was a rag doll being pummeled. "You can't say that. You can't even think it. That your father and Diane would concoct such a monstrous plan? That's crazy, that's insane!" She started crying. "It can't be that. It can't. Not your father. He couldn't have. Whatever his faults or problems were, he loved your mother."

Clancy put his arm around her and pulled her to him. She was shaking.

"I don't believe that he did anything like that," he said, stroking her hair, holding her tight. "But I've thought it. We've all thought it. It's impossible not to. Not after what's happened." He turned her face to his. "Mom was killed down there, and ever since, our world's been turned upside-down. Anything's possible." He paused. "And nothing is impossible."

NEW YORK

◆ ◆ ◆

Security at O'Hare was tight as a drum. Tom stood in a line that snaked a couple of hundred yards down the corridor for over half an hour until he was able to pass through the metal detectors. Once on board the airplane, he sat in cramped discomfort with his fellow travelers for an hour past departure time, stuck behind dozens of other planes until it was their turn for takeoff. By the time his flight got to La Guardia and taxied into their landing dock (another forty-five-minute delay, waiting for the dock to clear), he had been in airports or on an airplane for almost six hours, for a flight that took less than an hour and forty-five minutes. I could have driven here almost as fast, he thought sourly, as he made his way through the jammed-up terminal and out to the taxicab stand.

A cold, sleetlike rain was falling; the sunless sky, at four-thirty in the afternoon, was a dull charcoal ceiling of thunderheads and gloomy, London-like fog. Tom, carry-on garment bag slung over his shoulder, raincoat pulled up over his head in a futile attempt to keep dry, inched his way along the taxi line. When it was finally his turn, the dispatcher yanked open the door of a dull orange Chevrolet Impala, driven by a turbaned Sikh with a full black beard.

"Where to?" the cabbie asked, in a thick New York accent.

Tom climbed in. "Thirty-first and Madison." The hotel he'd booked had recently completed a major renovation and was offering cut-rate prices to entice customers, a deal he'd found on the Internet. Clancy and Will had fronted the money for the trip—he needed to spend it frugally.

The cabbie immediately tore out into the heavy traffic, ignoring a battery of blaring horns as he cut across three lanes. Tom was jolted back against the seat.

"I'm not in a hurry," he called out, as the taxi braked suddenly, then plunged forward again.

"No problem," the driver barked, leaning on his horn and cutting in front of a UPS truck. "I'll get you there safe and sound."

Let's hope so, Tom thought, as he pulled his seat belt down and buckled it firmly. That's all I need, an accident. Like I don't have enough problems already.

As he had arrived in New York at rush hour, the drive into Manhattan was slow and tedious, but true to his word, the cabbie got him to his destination without incident. Tom paid him, left a decent tip, and went inside under the shelter of the doorman's umbrella.

The first thing he'd do after he checked in was buy an umbrella from a street vendor. The forecast was for intermittent rain for the next several days, and he hadn't brought one. After that, dinner somewhere, maybe a movie, then early to bed. He wanted to get going first thing in the morning. He had reserved a room for two nights. He hoped that would be enough.

* * *

Waking up to the sun shining through the venetian blinds, Tom got out of bed and looked out the window. Not a cloud in sight. He could feel the brittle, cold morning air on the windowpane as he touched it with the tips of his fingers. Flipping on the television, he channel-surfed until he found a local weather station. The amended forecast was for a bright, cold day, but no rain. A good sign, hopefully.

He shaved, showered, dressed. Clean white shirt, tie, a pair of black dress loafers he'd bought at a high-class men's shoe store on Michigan Avenue, and his one good suit, a dark blue pinstripe he'd picked up at a Brooks Brothers outlet store outside Santa Fe, New Mexico, a couple years before. He'd hardly ever worn it, but he'd felt, at the time, that he should own one good suit, so he could look like a grown-up, in case the occasion arose. This trip to New York was such an occasion.

The reason he had come, rather than using Garcia or a local detective, was that this was a family affair. It was up to them, personally, to find out what had happened. There had been no debate over who would go—Tom was the only one who could take off on a moment's notice. He was still the fifth wheel, but at least now his life had a genuine purpose.

The room service menu was too expensive for his budget, so Tom had coffee and a toasted bagel at a nearby luncheonette and then headed north, crossing at 42nd Street by the Public Library and then turning up Fifth Avenue. His first appointment was with a specialist in art and antiquities thefts. Laurel Johnstone had arranged the meeting. The man's office was on 58th Street, between Seventh and Eighth Avenues.

Thanksgiving was still three weeks away, but Christmas had already arrived in the shop window displays and the colorful red and green banners that hung from the streetlight posts. In his spare time, of which there was plenty, Tom had been reading Melville, *Moby-Dick.* One of the great descriptive paragraphs from the first chapter came to mind: *Circumambulate the city of a dreamy Sabbath afternoon.* Melville was writing about Ishmael, a man about to embark on a mission. Tom, walking along the streets of New York as Ishmael had, more than a hundred and fifty years ago (*circumambulating,* a fine way to describe it), was also on a mission. One, hopefully, of discovery.

This is the perfect time to be here, he thought, before it's too cold and the streets are filled with winter slush. Sometime in the future, when he could afford it, he'd come with a woman and spend a week or so, see some plays, go to museums, concerts, eat fine meals, Christmas-shop.

He thought, for the thousandth or ten thousandth time, of Emma, now Diane. Who had she worked for, who had she sold art to, what kind of art did she deal in? Dozens of questions. For himself he wanted to find out who she was as a woman. What kind of life had she lived? Who had she been involved with? Reluctantly, he had come to the painful belief that Diane, the übergoddess of his dreams, was a woman lacking in any moral center, who did whatever she felt was necessary to get what she wanted, whether that meant having an affair with a renowned archaeologist to get access to stolen artifacts, or screwing his son because she wanted a younger man at that particular time, or simply because she could, or because she thought she might need the son as an ally. Would she even—this was his biggest fear—arrange to have a woman murdered, if that woman had gotten in the way of her plans?

Over the next couple of days, if he was lucky (or unlucky, depending on how things played out), he would find the answers to these questions.

The expert Laurel Johnstone had referred Tom to was named Alvin Whiting. His office, in a nondescript building, was one of several small spaces on an upper floor that fed out into a long common hallway. Among the signs stenciled on the opaque glass doors, besides Whiting's, which listed his name but not his occupation, were those of a bail bondsman, a talent agency, a bill collection agency, and an obscure literary magazine.

Whiting appeared to be in his middle sixties, a few years past his father's age, Tom guessed, although he looked a decade older. Recently retired, he had been employed by Sotheby's for several years as their in-house specialist in art thefts and forgeries; before that, he'd been a senior director with the U.S. Customs Department.

Whiting's office was one room; there was no secretary. Most of the space was taken up by old metal filing cabinets, an ancient refrigerator, and a microwave oven.

"Diane Montrose." Whiting pronounced the name slowly, as if tasting it, tilting back in his wooden office chair and gazing at the ceiling above Tom's head. "A piece of work, that one. So you know her."

"Yes," Tom answered. The heat was turned up. He took off his raincoat and draped it on the back of his chair.

Whiting rocked forward, his hands splayed out on his thighs. "I haven't seen or heard of her in a couple of years. Where is she now?"

"I'd rather not tell you, unless you won't help me otherwise."

Whiting shook his head. "It doesn't matter to me, I'm out of that game, thankfully. So what do you want to know about her? That's why you're here, am I correct?"

Tom nodded. "I'm trying to find out what galleries and clients she worked for, what she did for them, and how I can find people who will give me information about her."

Whiting rocked back again. He had small hands and feet, no larger than a child's. "The first two parts of your question are easy. She advised her clients—galleries and private buyers—on pieces of art they were interested in acquiring. She was quite good at coming up with things that aren't usually found on the open market."

"Works of art that were stolen."

"Sometimes."

"She's an art thief?"

Whiting shook his head from side to side. "It's not that clear-cut. She's never stolen anything herself—not directly. She's too clever to nakedly expose herself. She's the classic middleman, for the modern age."

He leaned forward. "Here's how a gray-market transaction would work. A client would approach her, usually through an intermediary, so the authorities can't trace them back to the real buyer or seller. 'I'm interested in acquiring whatever.' They would agree on a price, and so forth. Then she would try to get it, if she could." He swiveled in his chair, his feet barely touching the floor. "Or more commonly, someone who had a piece of stolen art in his possession would approach her and ask her to find a buyer. She was well connected, and completely discreet."

"Would pre-Columbian artifacts be one of the areas of interest she dealt in?" Tom asked.

Whiting nodded. "Diane follows the money, wherever it leads her. I assume that's what you're trying to find out about her. If she was selling stolen items from Central American archaeological sites."

"Yes," Tom replied.

Whiting leaned forward and tapped a small, freshly manicured finger on Tom's knee. "It's a ruthless business. Millions of dollars of priceless artifacts and church icons, altarpieces, statues, are being stolen from those countries every year, even though importing and exporting them has been illegal since 1983." He shifted in his chair again. "The problem is in knowing whether or not the article in question was in this country before then. If it was, then it's not against the law to buy it. There's no enforceable legislation requiring proof of date. Immoral and unethical, but not illegal. Do you understand the distinction?"

Tom nodded. "If I buy something that I don't know was stolen, I can't be prosecuted later if it turns out that it was."

Whiting nodded. "That's correct. The art trade has to police itself, and they do a miserable job. Last year, to give you one example, Sotheby's held an auction for over a hundred and fifty pre-Columbian works of art, and they didn't provide a find-spot for one of them—*not one.*" He scowled. "Although there have been some notable exceptions to that. Last year an antiquities dealer here in the city was convicted of selling stolen artifacts from Egypt. He was caught because what he did was so blatant it was impossible to ignore. So there has been some cutting back. No one wants to go to jail. Still, it happens. More than anyone in the art community is willing to acknowledge. There are many Diane Montroses out there trafficking in stolen artifacts. Including," he added with anger, "government officials from the very countries that profess to be leading the struggle to stop it. It's a sieve, a corrupt system from top to bottom."

Tom took the list of names Detective Garcia had given them from his pocket. "What can you tell me about these people?" he asked, handing it over. "Do you know if any of them dealt in stolen art, and used Diane?"

Whiting looked at it. "I don't know all these names, but the ones I do know are important dealers or collectors. Whether or not any of them sold or bought artifacts that had been stolen, from Diane or anyone else, I can't say from firsthand experience."

He handed the list back to Tom. "What I can tell you is that these are people with buckets of money. They think their wealth gives them license to break the law when it suits their purpose." He sighed. "What are you trying to find out, specifically?"

"I'm hoping someone will talk to me about Diane. About art she might have been trying to sell that came from La Chimenea."

"Oooh." Whiting rocked in his chair. "That's certainly not going to be easy, because that's clearly post-1983."

"I know." Tom looked imploringly at the older man. "Any ideas how I might do it anyway?"

Whiting thought for a moment. "You're going to have to play your cards close to the vest, because these people don't know you, and they're going to be very cautious about talking to someone they don't know." He thought for a moment. "Coming in cold, as you're doing, a total unknown, could be the best way to broach that. It would be so out of left field that you might find what you're looking for." He paused again. "But you might not. I wouldn't get my hopes up for a positive result if I were you."

Tom got up and put on his raincoat. "Thanks for the

help," he said, shaking Whiting's hand. "I've given up hoping for anything good about this. I just want to try to find some truth—if there is any."

Leaving Whiting's office, Tom headed north, cutting through Central Park. The first dealer Whiting had recommended he try was on the Upper East Side, a few blocks from the Metropolitan Museum of Art. He ambled through the park, checking out the joggers and bike-riders, the dog-walkers and baby-carriage-pushers, the old ladies in furs, the kids on Rollerblades.

At Whiting's suggestion, he was going to using a pseudonym—Thomas Lucas. Lucas was his middle name. Walter Gaines was famous in the field of pre-Columbian archaeology and art. Antiquities dealers would know the name Walt Gaines. They would run for cover if they knew his son was trying to pry information out of them.

The gallery was on the ground floor of a converted brownstone. Tom entered and looked around. The soft-white interior walls had been knocked out to make one long, high-ceilinged space. He was the only customer in the place. Looking up, he spied a video camera in the corner of the ceiling. It was pointing at him, the red light blinking steadily. He smiled at it.

Wandering about the gallery, he looked at various pieces with what he hoped would pass for a critical eye. The house specialty seemed to be Mexican and Central American art. There were several artifacts from the region, as well as some very old church icons and frescoes. Expensive pieces, he assumed.

A middle-aged man with a balding, mottled scalp, pink-skinned as if scrubbed hard in his shower, wearing an Italian-cut business suit, emerged from the rear and approached him. "May I help you?" the man asked, in a well-modulated but brisk voice.

Tom turned toward the art on the wall. "Beautiful pieces," he said. "Are you the owner?"

The man nodded. "I am. Are you interested in anything particular?"

"I'm not buying art at the moment, but thanks."

"Well, feel free to look around," the owner told him.

Tom squinted at a statue of a woman that was displayed on a pedestal. "This is a nice piece," he said complimentarily. "It reminds me of similar ones I've seen on trips to Central America."

The owner cocked an eyebrow. "What type of art would that be?"

"Maya, primarily," Tom answered. He looked at the statue again. "This is Mayan, isn't it?"

"Yes," the owner answered. "It is."

"Pre-1983, of course."

The man took a step back. "I don't handle illegal art." His face flushed pink. "Is this some kind of sting? I have nothing to hide, believe me," he said indignantly.

"You've got me wrong," Tom said hurriedly, and hopefully, reassuringly. "A gallery like yours obviously wouldn't do anything illegal. You wouldn't need to, and you could get into too much trouble. I was simply commenting on the problems that go on down there. The incredible amount of theft. Everywhere I went, people talked about it."

The man arched an eyebrow. "Where in Central America have you been going to exactly?"

"All over," Tom answered easily. "Recently I was at a new excavation called La Chimenea. It's one of the most incredible sites that's been discovered since Tikal and Chichén Itzá. I was there a couple of years ago, too, when they were just getting started on the excavation of some of the most important areas."

The owner nodded. "I know of La Chimenea," he said cautiously. "It's supposed to be spectacular."

"It is. But they're having problems with what I just talked about. When I was there that first time, two years ago, the problem was terrible."

"Yes," the owner acknowledged. "So I've heard."

Tom glanced around. Except for the two of them, the gallery was empty. "The name of your gallery rings a bell, and now that I think about it, I remember why," he said. "That first time I was down there, I met a woman who was in the art business. I don't know what she did exactly, but she may have dealt in Mayan art. I know she was interested in it, because she took the trouble to go down there at a time when it wasn't very easy. The conditions were pretty primitive. Anyway, she was a nice woman. Very . . ." He paused. ". . . attractive. We got to be kind of friendly and . . ."

The gallery owner stared at him blankly.

"I lost track of her," Tom continued, "and since I was here in the city I thought I'd look her up, but she isn't in the phone book. Then I walked by here and saw your sign and it jogged my memory. She told me she did business with you."

The man stared at him. "Did business with me?" he asked suspiciously.

Tom nodded. "Acquiring things for you, I assume." He paused. "Her name is Diane Montrose. Ring a bell?"

The man stood perfectly still. Only the twitch on his left cheek betrayed any sign of nervousness or worry. "I'd like you to leave," he said.

Tom stared at him. Gotcha, pal, he thought. "Does that mean she didn't work for you, or that you don't want to talk about her? I really would like to get back in touch with her, or at least find out where she is and what she's doing."

The owner took another step back. "I'm not going to talk about my business with a stranger," he said. His voice was choked, as if it was hard to force the words out of his throat and mouth. "Now please . . ." He pointed to the door. "Get out of here, and don't come back."

Tom worked his way downtown, stopping in four more galleries. In each case, he got a response similar to his first encounter: they all denied knowing Diane Montrose, and they were all lying—their body language gave them away. One woman actually started shaking at the mention of Diane's name. But no one would talk to him about her.

It was almost dark. Tom had been on his feet all day, and hadn't eaten since his meager breakfast. There were three more galleries on his list, and half a dozen individual collectors. He was saving them for last, because he knew they would be harder nuts to crack—if he could get to them at all. One more gallery, then he'd bag it and start fresh tomorrow.

Addison Galleries was located in a block-long second-story loft in SoHo. The ceilings were twenty feet high, the floors were wide planks, bleached white. An entire wall of double-glazed industrial windows looked out onto the street. Most of the art on display was more contemporary than in the other galleries Tom had visited, but there were a few beautiful older sculptures. The gallery was staffed by two younger people around his age, who were at the far end of the room: a short, stocky man in khakis and a bottle-green button-down shirt, his brown hair pulled back in a ponytail, a wisp of goatee under his chin; and a woman a few years older, tall, angular, dressed in black—tight skirt, ribbed-cotton turtleneck sweater, black tights, ballet flats. Her ears were multiply-pierced, and her flaming red hair was cut spiky-short.

A couple of middle-aged female patrons in stiletto boots and designer jean outfits were conversing with each other in the center of the room, gesturing toward one of the sculpture pieces, a black, heavy, sensual, semi-abstract block that to Tom's untrained eye might have been a woman nursing a child, or something completely different, not even representational. Tom, in his conservative suit, felt dorky. I should come back here tomorrow in my jeans and leather jacket, he thought.

The man seemed to be in charge of the gallery, the woman subordinate. He conferred briefly with the two women, pointing something out about the sculpture. The spiky-haired redhead was in the back talking on the phone, writing something down while sipping a latte from a takeout container.

The man looked up and noticed Tom. He smiled briefly, then turned away. I'll wait a couple of minutes, Tom decided. If it doesn't work today I'll bail and come back tomorrow.

One of the two women said something to the ponytailed man, who scribbled on a small card and handed it to her. As they left they checked out some other works, commenting to each other about them as they descended the stairs.

The man ambled toward Tom, stopping a few feet away, poised on the balls of his gray ostrich-hide cowboy boots, hands jammed into his back pockets.

"Hello," he said, in a friendly tone.

"Hello," Tom said back.

"Jesse," the guy said.

"Tom. You're the manager?"

"I'm the owner." There was a touch of swagger in his tone, as if to say, "don't judge me by my age, my hairstyle, my thousand-dollar custom boots."

"Nice stuff," Tom said agreeably. "Nice space."

"Thank you. If you need any help, holler." Jesse turned to walk away.

"What about pre-Columbian art?" Tom said to his back.

Jesse pivoted. "What about it?"

"Do you deal in it?" Tom looked around at the work being exhibited. Pre-Columbian didn't fit here, not with the gallery, not with this man or the woman, who was casually checking him out over the lip of her coffee cup. Even from a distance he could see the blood-red lipstick impression she had left on the rim of the cup.

Jesse shook his head. "Not our thing. We show some older African stuff"—he gestured toward the sculpture Tom had observed—"but mostly we're contemporary, as you can see. If you're interested in pre-Columbian, there are places I can refer you to."

"Buying it as well as selling it?" Tom asked.

Jesse rocked on his heels, eyeballing Tom. "What's the deal, man?" he asked. "You're not just browsing on your way home, are you?"

"No, I'm not," Tom said. "I'm trying to locate a woman I met a few years ago who dealt in pre-Columbian. I was told she did business with you."

Jesse's face scrunched up. "Oh, yeah? Who's that?"

"Diane Montrose."

There was a long beat. Jesse rocked on his expensive heels. "Diane Montrose," he said in an almost hushed voice. "That's a blast from the past. I haven't done any business with Diane for a couple of years. I don't know anybody who has, or even knows where Diane is these days. It's like she went out for a pack of smokes and never came back."

"That's what I've been hearing," Tom said, "I've heard other things, too."

"Like what?"

The subtle approach hadn't worked. It was time to lob a grenade and see what the explosion uncovered. "That she sold you post-1983 pre-Columbian artifacts she had smuggled into the country."

Jesse almost levitated off the floor. "That's bogus! You could put me in serious trouble, pal, spreading lies like that," he cried out, his voice rising an octave in panic. "What are you, a cop?"

"No. And I'm not out to bust your chops. All I want is information about what Diane sold you in the past, what you bought, who you sold it to."

Jesse exhaled through his nose. "I can't help you."

"I think you can."

Jesse shook his head in denial. "Like I said—I haven't heard from or about Diane Montrose in over two years. And if I never do again, that's excellent with me."

The sidewalks were crowded with end-of-the-day workers and shoppers. Tom stepped off the curb into the street. He was going to hail a cab back to the hotel and get out of this uncomfortable suit. Then he'd find a happening bar, have some drinks, go somewhere for music. Forget his cares and woes for a few hours.

"Hey! Wait up!"

He spun around.

The woman from Addison's was jogging toward him. "I'm Celia." Her face was flushed from running. "From back . . ." She pointed behind her.

He nodded. "I recognize you."

Up close, she had more mileage on her than he would have guessed. Late thirties. Maybe forty. A tiny diamond in one nostril. An interesting face; not conventionally pretty—both her nose and chin were too long—but attractive. Good legs.

"Got time for a drink?" she asked.

All bars are the same in the end, Tom thought as he looked this one over with a practiced eye via the long mirror behind the backbar: a combination of secular church, analyst's office, clubhouse. Most of the patrons were his age or younger—NYU and the New School were in the neighborhood.

They were sitting at a tiny triangle-shaped table near the back. Celia had thrown down two fast vodka shooters, chasing them with a Panamanian beer Tom didn't know. He nursed an Anchor Steam draft. Later, maybe, he'd allow himself to get a buzz on, depending on her intentions.

She lit a Marlboro Light, inhaled deeply, and exhaled through her nostrils. "I overheard you and Jesse," she said. She took another heavy drag, blew a perfect smoke ring up toward the ceiling. "So you really know Diane Montrose, huh?"

He nodded. "Did," he corrected her. "I'm trying to get back in touch with her."

"You and her were what . . . partners?"

It sounded to him as if she wanted to say "lovers," but

was afraid he'd answer yes. She's hitting on me, he realized. Is that all this is about?

"We were involved. But not romantically." That was what she wanted to hear, he assumed.

"So like, you and she were in business?"

He shrugged. She took it for a yes. He could see that she wanted to.

"It's been a while since anybody's heard from her," she told him.

"I assume she's lying low," Tom lied.

"How did you meet her?"

"Through a close mutual friend."

Celia caught the waitress's attention and held up her glass, mouthing the word "double." The waitress nodded.

"You're throwing those down pretty fast," Tom observed. He was a bartender now, he had developed an eye for people who drank too much too fast.

Her look to him was fragile, vulnerable. "I'm nervous."

"Why?"

"Because of what I'm going to tell you."

He pushed his beer away. He wanted his head to be completely clear. But not hers. He wanted her well lubricated. Not so much that she'd fall down drunk and wouldn't be of use to him, but enough so that whatever inhibitions she had about being with him, divulging information to him, would flush through her system on a river of alcohol.

"I have to be really careful talking to you," she said gravely. She didn't seem to be unduly feeling her liquor. A seasoned drinker with a big capacity. Not a bad quality in a woman, as long as she didn't abuse it.

Easy, boy, he reminded himself. Don't let this woman

think there's more than you're giving her. "So you have moved pieces for her."

She nodded. "We have, shall we say, acted as a discreet go-between for appropriate sellers and buyers." She tossed down the rest of her drink and grabbed the loose bills from the table, leaving a few for the tip. "We can't talk here," she told him. "We'll go to my place. It isn't far."

Celia's apartment, a Lilliputian-sized one-bedroom, was in NoHo off Great Jones Street, a couple of blocks from the Angelika movie theater. There was interesting art on the walls, some of it, to his untrained eye, original. He was going to have to be very careful about how he managed this. If she figured out he didn't know his ass from third base about art and the art world, this delicate endeavor would go up in smoke.

They shared a joint, drank Dom Perignon straight from the bottle. She unzipped his fly. After a minimal amount of foreplay he entered her from behind, holding back so they could climax together.

They rested side by side, playing with each other's genitals, one of his fingers slipping in and out of her tight, lubricated pussy, she stroking him easily, gently. They finished the bottle of champagne and she took him in her mouth and sucked him until he was hard again and they fucked again, this time using the missionary position.

After Tom got out of the shower, clad in his suit pants and untucked-in shirt, he found his hostess sitting on her couch Indian-style, wearing a silk kimono. "I ordered in a pizza," Celia told him. "Peppers and mushrooms, I'm a vegetarian. That okay? Or did you have dinner plans?"

"No plans." He dropped down next to her, smiling to

himself. Some vegetarian: she'd gone for his piece of meat like it was a prime filet from Smith & Wollensky.

They toasted each other with another glass of champagne. She lit a cigarette, blew out a thick cloud of smoke. "I might have a former client of Diane's to hook you up with," she said.

"That would be helpful," he replied, trying not to sound too excited.

"When can you meet with him?"

"Any time. The sooner the better."

"Let's hope he's in town," she said, biting a nail. "He travels a lot." She got to her feet, crossed the room, and booted up a laptop that was on a small desk. "I'm going to need my glasses for this," she said self-consciously. She rummaged around in a drawer under the desk and found a pair of old-fashioned, librarian-style half-glasses.

Okay, so she was older than he'd thought, if she needed reading glasses. After the excellent sex they'd had he didn't give a damn if she was a hundred.

"I'm accessing Jesse's personal files," she explained, when the screen lit up. "He doesn't know I have his secret codes." She giggled. "He'd kill me if he knew." She squinted at some information that came up on the screen. "Here you are, you sly dog."

She picked up the phone and punched in the prospective buyer's numbers. "Keep your fingers crossed he isn't in Japan or somewhere." She waited a moment, then smiled, giving Tom a thumbs-up. "Mr. Michaelson? This is Celia Pettibone, from Addison Galleries. Do you have a minute?"

Tom got off the Number 1 subway at the Franklin Street stop in TriBeCa and walked west toward the Hudson

River. He had left his suit back at the hotel and was wearing a pair of khakis, a sweater, his well-worn leather jacket, and running shoes. He felt more comfortable in this attire, although he could have worn an evening gown and high heels, it wouldn't have made any difference. What he was hoping to find out today didn't require fancy clothing.

Checking the address Celia had given him, he stopped in front of a former industrial building that had been converted into loft apartments. A young doorman with a Gold's Gym physique guarded the entrance.

"I'm here to see John Michaelson," Tom announced.

The doorman picked up the intercom telephone and punched in a number. "Guy here to see Mr. Michaelson." He listened a moment. "What's your name?" he asked Tom.

"Tom Lucas." He hoped he wouldn't be asked for ID.

The doorman repeated the name Tom gave him into the phone. "Okay." He hung up. "Top floor," he instructed Tom.

He buzzed Tom in. Tom walked through the stark lobby to the elevator, and rode it up to Michaelson's apartment.

Diane's former client's apartment was the penthouse duplex. It covered the length of the building, front to back, a full city block long. Tom stood at a southwest-facing window in the main lower-floor room, looking out. He could see past the devastation that had been the Twin Towers to the tip of Manhattan, the Statue of Liberty, and beyond. Far below, tiny ants on a vast landscape, people walked the sidewalks, cars drove the West Side Highway, boats chugged up the Hudson River.

This is the real deal, he thought, as he watched the passing parade from this imperial aerie. Serious money.

The apartment's decor was a wild mixture of sports bar, video arcade, and fraternity house. PlayStations and Xboxes were scattered around the huge open room. Three classic pinball machines were against one wall, and two Sony plasma high definition television sets were hung side by side in a separate screening area. One television was turned to VH1, the other to ESPN. The sound on both was muted. A commercial-sized bar in another section of the room featured several beers on draft. It was the kind of over-the-top place a college kid might have if he had as much money in the world to spend as he wanted.

Celia had made the arrangements with Michaelson the night before while Tom listened in on her end of the conversation. Michaelson had agreed to meet with Tom as soon as he heard the name Diane Montrose. They could meet right now, Michaelson had said, if that's what Tom wanted, or the following day. He was up to his ass in a million projects and was on his way out of town, but he would shoehorn Tom into his schedule.

Tom had been eager to make the connection, but he wasn't going to do it after a night of smoking dope, drinking, and screwing himself jelly-legged. They had agreed to meet at Michaelson's apartment the next day, at nine in the morning. Just the two of them; Celia wasn't invited. She had nothing more to contribute, and for her own security she had to put as much distance between herself and them getting together as possible.

For the moment, Tom was alone. He had been admitted into the apartment by a beefy security employee. The security person had politely but firmly requested that Tom spread his arms and legs so he could be patted down. Not that they were concerned that Tom had a gun on him, the man explained as he was doing his frisk, but to be sure that he wasn't wired, as part of some kind of law enforcement scam. The cops had tried to entrap Michaelson before on art deals and other business transactions, so he was extra careful.

After assuring himself that Tom was clean the security man got him a Coke, told him Michaelson would be with him in a moment, and vanished into another area of the vast space.

"I bought this place for the view."

"It's a good one." Tom turned to face his host, who was standing a few feet behind him.

Michaelson was young, not much older than Tom, if that. Despite his obvious wealth, he didn't appear to be pretentious—just the opposite. His wardrobe was a Nike workout T-shirt and a baggy pair of jeans over which hung his ample gut. No belt, no socks, no shoes. His hair was straggly and he sported a couple days' growth of beard. In one hand he held a slice of cold pizza and in the other a Sprite—his version of the breakfast of champions.

"I got a good deal," Michaelson said through a mouthful of pizza. "The building, I'm talking about. I own the whole pile of bricks. Bought it off a dot.com competitor who hung on too long." He swallowed and chugged from the Sprite can. "That's the secret. You can't be greedy. Bulls make money, bears make money, but hogs get slaughtered."

Sounds familiar, Tom thought. Too damn familiar.

John Michaelson was a geeky computer entrepreneur who had hit a grand slam home run almost on the scale of Michael Dell or Mark Cuban. He and two partners had started an Internet information company in their dorm suite at Rutgers, and in less than five years they had sold it to

Yahoo! for almost three billion dollars. Michaelson's cut had been a third. Since then he had raced sports cars, bought and sold two minor league baseball teams, put together a three-thousand-bottle wine cellar, dated MTV starlets, and become an eclectic, serious art buyer.

"Lucky break you caught me," Michaelson said. "I was going to Paris this morning. Delayed my flight. An advantage of owning your own airplane. But I do have a lot on my plate, so this can't take long." He gave Tom a lupine smile. "I couldn't resist after you said the magic word—Diane Montrose."

They sat at a massive granite dining table. Tom put his empty Coke can to the side.

"Nobody's had a whiff of Diane in a coon's age," Michaelson said. "She folded her tent after that woman was killed down in the jungle in Central America."

The woman who was killed was my mother, Tom thought with a heavy heart. And I've had more than a whiff of Diane, he also thought, flashing back yet again to that insane, magical night.

But that was all he had. What he needed was information about her, and this man, he hoped, could provide it. If he struck out here, the investigation he and his brothers had undertaken would be seriously stalled, if not derailed.

"So," Michaelson said. "Why do you want to know about Diane? And what?"

Tom skirted the first part of the question. "Did you buy art from her?"

"Yes, but indirectly," Michaelson answered, swigging down some more soda. "She's not a dealer, she's more like an agent. She would buy art for me and other collectors. At auctions, through private sellers, the usual. She has a great eye and a good sense of value.

Her clientele list was excellent, particularly for someone who wasn't that old. I'd show you some of the stuff she got for me, but I keep my serious art at my place in the Hamptons." He smiled. "Here it's fun and games. Out there, I try to act like a grown-up."

Tom didn't know how much time Michaelson was going to give him. He had to cut to the chase, hopefully without scaring the man off. "Some of the stuff Diane bought from you. Was any of it pre-Columbian art?"

Michaelson leaned back in his chair. "We might talk about that, but you've got to answer my question first. What's your interest in Diane?"

Tom stared at him. "She burned me on . . . let's call it a transaction. I'm trying to find out how legitimate she really is. Or was. So I can figure out where to go with my problem with her."

Michaelson smiled. "Join the party. Like I said, she had the eye, but she was a world-class confidence man, too." He leaned forward. "We're in the same boat, I can see that from the sour look on your face." He thought for a moment. When he spoke again it was clear he'd decided that he and Tom were kinsmen to Diane Montrose's machinations. "I did buy some pre-Columbian stuff from her," he admitted. "Actually," he amended, "I was going to, but she went to ground before we could finalize the deal, so technically, I never did."

"From that place where the woman was killed?"

Michaelson put his soft drink can down. "This is a ticklish matter. I don't know if I should be talking to you about that."

"Because technically it's illegal?" Tom asked.

"More than technically," Michaelson answered. "People have gone to jail for selling it." He snorted, like a bear shaking off an aggravating swarm of flies. "Not that I personally give a shit about taking stuff out of backward-ass countries. If they're so lame down there they can't secure their own borders then the stuff ought to get out. Better in a good collection or a museum than buried in the mud where no one's ever going to see it."

Tom nodded, as if silently agreeing.

"I could tell you of an ugly incident I heard about between Diane and one of her other clients about art from that region," Michaelson said.

"Can you give me a name?" Tom asked. This might be it—a direct link between Diane and La Chimenea.

Michaelson shook his head. "Yeah, but then I'd have to kill you." He smiled. "Seriously, no names. But what I can tell you is damn interesting."

Tom didn't want to reveal how antsy this conversation was making him. "Whatever you can tell me I'm sure will be helpful," he said as calmly as possible.

Michaelson got up, walked to a huge built-in refrigerator in the open kitchen, and got himself another Sprite. He walked back to the table, lobbing Tom another can of Coke. They popped their tops and drank. Michaelson put his drink down.

"The word on the street was that Diane had a connection down at that place where the woman was killed, who was smuggling artifacts out. Awesome stuff, millions of dollars' worth of antiquities. It's also been said that her person down there was one of the archaeologists who was working on the site. I don't know about that but I could believe it, because it would have to be someone who had sterling access and wouldn't normally be suspected of stealing." He paused. "On the other hand, it easily could have been someone in the government down there, they're incredibly corrupt. One of those two options, most likely." He took a drink from his can. "Doesn't matter," he continued. "She had an ironclad setup, supposedly." He scowled. "But then that woman was killed and the shit hit the fan, because Diane didn't get the artifacts out."

"So the deal between this friend of yours and Diane was never completed?" Tom asked.

"That's correct. Or any other deals Diane had in the fire." Michaelson's tight grimace was not one of mirth. "The problem was that in this particular instance her client had given her a quarter-million dollars up-front money to pay bribes and whatever other grease she had to apply. But when Diane got back to the States, she didn't pay the client his money back. She took off into the wild blue yonder. And nobody's heard diddly about her since."

Tom managed to control the emotions he was feeling from what he had just heard. It's you, he thought, looking at his host. You're the fish she didn't pay back. Michaelson was trying to distance himself both from the attempted theft and from looking stupid by being ripped off by Diane, but his clumsy body language had given him away.

"That's tough," Tom commiserated, playing out some line. "Did this friend of yours try to find her?"

Michaelson shook his head. "Not yet. He's been too busy, and a quarter of a million isn't going to break him, he drops that in a weekend in Vegas. It was the principle of the thing," he said darkly. "The betrayal. He'll catch up with her sooner or later," he added ominously. "'Cause he's one of those guys who under his good-natured facade doesn't put up with being burned."

He finished his Sprite and crushed the can in his fist. "Diane's gone underground, but she'll turn up. They always do. Sometimes they don't turn up alive, but eventually, they turn up. Even Jimmy Hoffa's going to be accounted for someday."

Your threat isn't very veiled, Tom thought. I can understand why Diane wanted to lose herself and invent a new personality.

Michaelson glanced at his watch. "I've got to get going."

He walked Tom to the front door. They shook hands.

"Sorry I wasn't more helpful," Michaelson said.

"It helped," Tom said. "I'm sorry you didn't feel okay about telling me the name of the collector Diane screwed out of that money."

Michaelson smiled. "Like I said . . ." He put his forefinger to his temple, cocked his thumb.

"I understand that," Tom told him. "Completely."

"How are you doing?" Clancy asked, when Tom called him from his hotel room.

Tom slumped onto his bed. "Diane was in cahoots with someone down there who was helping her try to smuggle artifacts out. A person in a position of authority, who could pull it off without being challenged."

"Who told you that?"

"A collector who buys on the black market. Diane was smuggling artifacts out for him when mom was killed. With all the hue and cry that went down around mom's being killed she never got the goods out. The collector had advanced her a lot of money on the come, and she didn't pay him back."

"That explains the name change and all the other hush-hush stuff she's been doing," Clancy said.

"That's right," Tom agreed. "What really ripped it was

this rich guy heard from good sources that her partner was an archaeologist."

"He said dad's name?"

"No names were mentioned. But who else could it have been?"

"You think mom found out?" Clancy asked.

"How could she not have?" Tom answered. "Dad could never keep a secret from her. She would have busted him," he declared somberly.

Clancy was silent for a moment. "And was killed for it?" he finally said.

"Can you think of another possibility? Why else would he have constructed such a fabric of lies? All the money he lost, the huge life insurance policy? What else could it be?"

"I don't know," Clancy replied. "But there's no turning back now. We have to find out what happened down there. No matter what."

SAN DIEGO, CALIFORNIA

◆ ◆ ◆

Clearing customs had always been laboriously time-consuming at the San Diego International Airport, where thousands of non-Americans, particularly those from Mexico and Central and South America, passed through daily, but with the new security measures in force, conditions resembled a densely packed, teeming-with-humanity Calcutta train station. Outgoing passengers were thoroughly checked to make sure they weren't carrying anything, be it a nail file or a Coptic cross with a pointed shaft, that could be used in a hijacking.

Those entering the country, especially foreign men who fit one of dozens of profiles the government had instituted to weed out anyone the slightest bit suspicious, were rigorously scrutinized. They were often body-searched and their baggage was gone over with a fine-tooth comb. Even items as innocuous as foot powder were confiscated, and their carriers were questioned. If they didn't come up with the right answers they could be taken into custody by on-site INS or FBI agents, and roughly interrogated. By now, it was well known south of the border, and also in Muslim countries, that if you were coming to the U.S. as a foreign visitor you had better be squeaky clean, or you could be kept in seclusion for months, denied access to your family or even a lawyer.

A few days after Tom Gaines had learned the connection between Diane Montrose, his father, and the world of stolen art, a friendly, good-looking, well-dressed Latino in his mid-thirties, whose English was fluid and cultured (he had studied at Stanford University), was coming through this port of entry, a passage he had taken dozens of times over the past several years. His name was Mario Ernesto Rodríguez. He came from a wealthy, well-connected family. His firm, which manufactured automobile parts on contract from General Motors, Toyota, BMW, and DaimlerChrysler, had a large office in Carlsbad, in northern San Diego County. As vice president in charge of distribution, he came and went almost like a commuter.

Usually, he sailed through customs. He traveled light, because he kept spare clothes and accessories at the apartment his company maintained near the office. He came, did his business, and went home, usually within forty-eight hours.

This time, his schedule was different. The company was holding a series of meetings stretching out over a week with their automaker counterparts, first here in California but then in Detroit as well, so he'd had to bring a larger bag to hold his cold-weather clothing.

The other difference was that the customs agents manning the checkpoints were new. None of the faces were familiar. These agents had been rotated in from Texas, as part of a recent policy shift in Washington to insure tighter border security. Familiarity, such as Rodríguez had with the old agents, could breed laxity, which could lead to disaster.

Even so, this would not be a problem. His papers were all in order, and it would be obvious to anyone looking at his passport that he was a regular on this circuit. In addition, he was carrying letters from the American companies he did business with, which signified his legitimacy.

Slowly inching his way, now only a few more people from the head of the line, Rodríguez impatiently looked at his watch, which he had set for U.S. Pacific time. He had a dinner engagement with a colleague from Toyota's American design division, and with this heightened security in effect he was going to be late. He took his cell phone out of his pocket and started to speed-dial his appointment's office number.

There was a tap on his shoulder. Annoyed, he looked up. A customs agent, another new, unfamiliar face, had come up behind him.

"You'll have to turn that off, sir, until you clear customs," the agent told him, politely but firmly.

"I'm late for an appointment," Rodríguez explained, flashing a smile. "People are waiting for me. I need to let them know."

The agent shook his head. "I'm sorry, but you'll have to turn it off. Otherwise, I'll have to take it from you."

Rodríguez turned the telephone off and jammed it in his pocket. "Do I look like a raghead terrorist to you?" he muttered in Spanish, under his breath. He picked up his suitcase and pushed it forward—he was one person away from the head of the line now. Finally.

The agent's hand gripped his arm at the biceps. "Come with me, please." The voice was low, but urgent.

"What for?" Rodríguez asked, trying to twist away.

The agent pointed toward his expensive-looking leather suitcase. "Is this yours?"

Rodríguez nodded. "Yes." That was obvious—he had just moved it.

"What else belongs to you?" There was no politeness in the agent's manner now.

"My carry-on." Rodríguez held his garment bag up for the agent to see.

The agent let go of Rodríguez's arm and picked up his bag. "Come with me."

Rodríguez held his ground, rubbing his arm where the agent had been squeezing it. "This is a mistake," he said indignantly. "Is Agent Holloway in charge today? Please get him. He'll identify me. I can't be delayed, it's urgent."

"Holloway's off."

The people behind Rodríguez, watching this, started talking to each other, a low buzz. They also began backing away.

"Then Agent Shapp." Rodríguez's voice had taken on a pleading tone. "He'll clear this up. I'm an important businessman. Look at my passport. You'll see."

"Shapp's on vacation. Please come along. If you're cooperative, this won't take long."

"Get your supervisor," Rodríguez said harshly, as if talking to a civil servant in his own country.

The automatic, a huge S&W, was out of the agent's holster.

"Come with me. Now."

It was humiliating, being treated like a common criminal. At least they let him call his dinner companion and explain his tardiness, once they had checked his passport and other credentials. Still, they had to search his luggage and put him through a pro forma interrogation. Once the process started, it had to be completed.

This was all explained to him by Special Agent in Charge Wendell Tucker, who was a buddy of Shapp and Holloway.

"Sorry about this inconvenience," Tucker apologized to Rodríguez in a thick Texas twang. He spoke in English, which Rodríguez had assured him he was fluent in. "You use the word 'terrorist' these days, even kidding around, your ass is in deep grass."

"Yes, I understand," Rodríguez answered. "It was stupid of me to say that. I should have been more sensitive. God knows, I'm glad you guys are on the ball. I wish the security in my own country was half as good."

They were in a windowless holding room. Rodríguez sat on a hard plastic chair. Across the room, his suitcase was open on a table. A woman agent was carefully looking through the contents, one item at a time.

"How much longer will this take?" Rodríguez asked politely.

"Couple more minutes," Tucker drawled. He was leaning against the wall, next to Rodríguez. "She's new at this," he confided in a low, friendly voice. "She goes by the book. I don't want to discourage her, you savvy?"

Rodríguez nodded. "Of course not."

He sat back and waited, feeling better. So he'd be late. There was still plenty of time to have a fine dinner.

"Chief?" the woman called.

Tucker looked up. "Yeah?"

"See you over here a sec?"

Tucker smiled at Rodríguez. "Excuse me."

He walked over to the woman agent. They conferred for a moment; she did the talking, keeping her voice low.

Tucker listened. Rodríguez, watching them, felt a stab of nerves in his stomach.

It's the typical bureaucratic runaround, he told himself. He'd be out of here and in his limo in five minutes.

Tucker closed the suitcase and walked back to Rodríguez. "Did you do your own packing, Mr. Rodríguez?" he asked. No smile now.

Rodríguez stared at him. "My wife helped me," he acknowledged. He smiled, his teeth white, perfectly straight. "She's better at folding my shirts."

"Your wife?" Tucker stared at Rodríguez. "Nobody else?"

Rodríguez shook his head. He hesitated for the slightest moment; less than a second. "No," he answered firmly. He forced another smile. "There's no problem, is there?"

They drove Rodríguez, handcuffed, in an unmarked sedan, to FBI headquarters in San Diego. He asked—begged—that he be allowed to call the company's lawyer, but they refused, which under the post–9/11 United States security laws governing noncitizens they were permitted (and unofficially encouraged) to do. After booking him, confiscating his bags and all of his personal articles, they strip-searched him and threw him into an empty cell. The door was locked, and he was left in darkness.

He didn't know how much time passed before they came and got him. It could have been hours. He had no sense of time. He was scared out of his wits.

The door to his cell swung open and two men in plainclothes entered.

"What's going on?" Rodríguez asked them, his voice

quivering with fear. "Why are you doing this?" More shrilly: "Say something. Please."

They said nothing. One of them rehandcuffed him, then he was led down a jail corridor, into an elevator, which was empty except for his escorts and him, and after going up some flights (he didn't know how many, there weren't any indicator lights in the elevator) the door opened and he was led down another hallway and into an interrogation room. Agent Tucker was there, as well as three other men Rodríguez hadn't seen before. One of them was dark-complexioned, Latino like himself. This man's features were almost Indian-like, especially the hawk nose and flat, sloping forehead.

There was a dull-metal conference table in the center of the room, surrounded by cheap plastic chairs. Three of the walls were bare, painted institutional dirty-white. The fourth wall was a mirror, the glass tinted dark. Rodríguez, seeing it, assumed it was a one-way mirror. The circumstances felt like those of an American television show, *NYPD Blue* or *Law and Order*, except this was real, not playacting.

"Uncuff him," Tucker told his escorts.

The cuffs were removed. Rodríguez rubbed his wrists, more from nerves than from pain.

"Sit down, Mr. Rodríguez." Tucker pointed to one of the plastic chairs.

Rodríguez sat. The others remained standing. They all stared at him with stern, unsmiling expressions on their faces.

"What is going on?" Rodríguez asked again, this time of Tucker.

Tucker looked at him a moment longer. Then he grabbed one of the chairs that faced Rodríguez from across the table, turned it around, and sat down, resting his elbows on the chair-back.

"So you know," Tucker told him, "you're being recorded. Audio and video. For your protection as much as ours. You got a problem with that?"

Rodríguez knew it wouldn't matter if he did or not. "No," he answered.

"Good." Tucker leaned forward. "One more time, Mr. Rodríguez, so there's no misunderstanding: nobody packed your bags except you and your wife. Nobody asked you to bring anything with you, either here or in your own country."

Rodríguez wet his lips nervously. "No. Only my wife and I packed."

Tucker shrugged, as if to say "I gave you a chance to be straight with me, and you blew it." Without taking his eyes off Rodríguez's face, he held up a hand. One of the other agents placed a large padded envelope in it. Tucker put the envelope on the table between him and Rodríguez, opened the clasp, and reached inside. He brought out two objects—a small statuette about a foot tall and a man's wristwatch. He placed the two items in front of Rodríguez.

"Do you recognize these?" he asked. "Go ahead, you can pick them up."

Rodríguez's heart sank. "Yes, I recognize them," he answered dully, without touching them.

"They belong to you?"

Rodríguez was about to say yes, but he hesitated.

Tucker picked up the statuette, held it a few inches from Rodríguez's face. "Where did you get this?"

"A friend gave it to me," Rodríguez told him. "They are very common, they are sold everywhere."

Tucker looked at the object in his hand. "What is this, precisely?"

"A figure of the Virgin," Rodriguez said. "People like to have them for luck," he explained. "They keep them in their homes, their cars, offices."

"That's why you have it? For luck?" Tucker asked.

Rodríguez shook his head. "It isn't for me. I brought it to give to someone."

Tucker cocked his head. "Who?"

"The mother of one of my co-workers from my office," Rodriguez explained sheepishly. "She lives in Los Angeles. Legally," he added hastily, "she has a green card. She has lived in Los Angeles for many years."

Tucker nodded thoughtfully. "Your co-worker gave it to you to bring to the States to give to his mother. That's correct?"

"Yes."

"So when you told us nobody gave you anything to bring into this country you were lying, weren't you, Mr. Rodríguez?"

It was warm in the room. Rodríguez was sweating, particularly under his armpits, which he did when he was nervous. When this ordeal was over he would have to shower and change his clothes before meeting his American friends.

"Yes," Rodríguez stammered. "I had forgotten. It's such a cheap item. They're very common, they're sold everywhere."

"Did your friend tell you what he paid for it?"

Rodríguez calculated in his head. "Four or five dollars in American money."

Tucker turned the statuette over in his hand. "This looks like it's worth more than four or five dollars to me," he said. "Look at these stones here." He touched some small jewels that were inlaid in the Virgin's crown. "These look like real jewels, not fakes."

Rodríguez shook his head. "They are glass," he told his interrogator. "Believe me. They aren't real."

"Then why did you have it hidden away in your bag, buried under your socks and underwear?"

Rodríguez was sweating profusely now. He could feel the warm brine running down his arms, drenching his shirt. "I wasn't hiding it," he protested. "I didn't want it to break. That's why I had it . . . covered up like that," he finished. He knew he sounded like an imbecile.

Tucker swiveled around in his chair and leaned back, motioning to the Latino-looking agent. The other stepped forward and bent down, his face next to Tucker's. The two spoke in whispers for a moment. Then Tucker turned back to Rodríguez.

"What if I told you this was a real statue, not a knock-off? That it's made of gold, and the jewels are real rubies and garnets. That it is worth more than a quarter of a million dollars."

Rodríguez's jaw dropped. "That can't be. It's a cheap trinket," he said, his voice rising with fear.

Tucker leaned in toward Rodríguez. "And what if I also told you," he continued, his voice low and flat, "that a statue exactly like this one was stolen from a church in your country less than a month ago?"

Rodríguez closed his eyes. His heart was hammering madly in his chest, like a caged bird beating itself to death against the bars. "I am not a smuggler," he managed to say. "I was doing a friend a favor. Nothing more. You must believe me," he pleaded.

"I would if you'd tell the truth," Tucker answered. He handed the small statue to the Latino-looking agent, who put it back into the padded envelope. Then he turned again to Rodríguez, and picked up the watch.

"And this is yours, as well?" Tucker asked. "Or did your friend give this to you to give to his mother, also?"

Rodríguez shook his head. He had to stay cool, no matter what. "That is my watch."

"A TAG Heuer. Very nice. They're used for scuba diving, aren't they?"

Rodríguez nodded.

"Are you a diver, Mr. Rodríguez?"

"I have tried it," Rodriguez answered, "in Belize and off the coast of Mexico, but only a few times."

"So to you, it's a timepiece."

"Yes."

"And a nice piece of men's jewelry."

"Yes," again.

Tucker ran a finger along the crystal. "Did you buy this watch new?"

"I bought it from—" Rodríguez began. He stopped.

"From?"

"It was a gift."

"A gift?" Tucker's face registered a look of surprise. "You didn't buy it?"

Rodríguez shook his head. "No. I had forgotten. It was given to me."

"By the same pal who gave you the Virgin to deliver to his mother?"

"No." Now not only his underarms, but his entire upper body was drenched with his sweat. He could smell it coming off him. He knew his interrogators could, too. It was humiliating, to be in this position.

"By who?" Tucker asked.

"A friend," Rodríguez said. "An old friend."

"Another old friend, huh? Someone you must be awfully close to, to give you a present this nice." He turned and looked back at the Latino agent. "What do these go for down there, Felipe?" he asked the man. "In American dollars."

"Two thousand," the other replied. His accent was heavy, but not like an American chicano. Like someone from Central America, Rodríguez realized with a feeling of despair. Perhaps even his own country.

Tucker's eyes bore into Rodríguez's. "Your friend who gave you the statue to give his mother. What's his name?"

Rodríguez swallowed. "Carlos."

"Carlos what? And his telephone number, what's that? His e-mail address, his home address, whatever you have."

"I don't know," Rodríguez answered. "You have all my effects. My phone book, my cell phone."

"And his mother," Tucker pressed. "You have her name? Her address, telephone number? You were going to call her, weren't you, so you could meet up with her and give her this gift from her son?"

"I . . . it is there somewhere, in my things," Rodríguez stammered. He wet his lips. "May I have some water?"

Tucker whirled the watch around his finger. "In a minute. And this," he said. "The friend who gave this really neat present to you. What did he give it to you for? You did something special for him, or what?"

"It was . . . yes," Rodríguez admitted. "I had done him favors in the past. He gave me the watch as a token of his thanks. Because he was a friend. He also did favors for me." He sat up straight, trying to appear strong, in control. "Have you never done a favor for a friend, Agent Tucker?" he asked. "Have you never given or received a present from a friend?"

"Oh sure, I've given gifts and gotten them," Tucker said cheerfully. "Nothing this expensive, though." He held the watch up against his wrist and compared it to his own, a digital Seiko. "Me and you, we move in different financial circles, Mr. Rodríguez. You're an important businessman, and I'm just a humble civil servant." He put the watch back down on the table. "When did your friend give you this watch?" he asked. "A year ago? Two?"

Rodríguez thought for a moment. "About a year ago, that's right."

Tucker smiled. "What a coincidence." He picked the watch up again and turned it over. "You see these initials engraved on the back here? Take a good look."

He handed the watch to Rodríguez. Rodríguez looked at the back. "Yes. I see them."

"They aren't yours, are they."

"No."

"Read them to me."

Rodríguez squinted. "They're small. And they have been rubbed almost smooth."

"Give it a shot, anyway."

Rodríguez looked closely at the watch-back. *"W?"* he ventured. "And a . . . I think a *C*?"

Tucker took the watch from him. "Close enough." He looked at the initials himself. "Somebody wore this for a long time to have rubbed them that smooth, as you noticed." He looked at Rodríguez, his eyes unblinking. "So this watch, that your friend gave you. It wasn't a new watch that he bought in a store, or from a catalogue, was it? He got it used from somebody, didn't he?"

Rodríguez shrugged. "He must have. I didn't ask him where he got it."

"So it could have been stolen. Did you ask him if it was?"

Rodríguez shook his head. "No."

"You weren't at all curious where he got this fine

watch that he was presenting to you as a token of his friendship?"

"It was a gift," Rodríguez said. "You don't question where a gift comes from. You accept it, with gratitude."

Tucker leaned back. "If you had known this watch was stolen, would you have accepted it?"

Rodríguez thought for a moment. "I don't think so," he answered slowly.

"But you might have."

"I didn't think to ask."

"Somebody could have been murdered for this watch, but as long as you didn't know, you wouldn't care, is that what you're telling me?"

Rodríguez shook his head. "I wouldn't take it under those conditions, of course not."

Tucker nodded. "I'm glad to hear that, at least." Abruptly, he stood up. "That's enough for now."

Rodríguez looked up at him. "Am I free to leave now?" he asked hopefully.

Tucker laughed, a dry, humorless snort. "You're going back to your home away from home, otherwise known as the San Diego County Jail. The judge will arraign you sometime tomorrow, or maybe the next day. It'll depend on how long the U.S. attorney takes to file the charges against you."

Rodríguez, already scared out of his mind, turned to chalk. "What charges?" he asked in a choked voice.

"Bringing stolen national cultural items into the United States, for openers," Tucker told him. "That's for the statue, which in case you actually didn't know, is real, not fake. You could do five or ten years for trying to smuggle that in."

Rodríguez was shaking. He felt bile forming in his throat.

"But that's small potatoes, in the grand scheme of things," Tucker went on. He picked up the watch again. "This one's the big enchilada. This one is for participating in the killing of an American citizen, in your country. The wife of a prominent archaeologist, a little over a year ago. You may remember it, it was a big deal. Her name was Jocelyn Gaines, and her husband was named Walter Gaines."

He dangled the watch in front of Rodríguez's terrified face. "This watch belonged to Professor Gaines. It was among his personal items that were stolen, the night his wife was killed. Those initials on the back you read? W.C.? That was W. *G.*, not C. Walter Gaines."

He paused to let the impact of what he was saying sink in.

"I . . . did not . . ." Rodríguez told him, almost breaking into tears. "I had nothing to do with that."

"You have the watch," Tucker pointed out. "Prima facie evidence."

Rodríguez didn't know what prima facie meant, but he knew he was in terrible trouble now, much worse than smuggling in a single piece of native art. "I had nothing to do with that," he cried out again.

Tucker shook his head. "This piece of evidence says you were either an accessory or a perpetrator, it doesn't matter. Either way, it's murder."

"Murder?" Rodríguez choked out.

"The woman was killed for a watch. It's not an accidental killing anymore. This"—again, he held the watch under Rodríguez's nose— "makes it murder."

The bile rose up in Rodríguez's throat, into his mouth. He tried to hold it in, but by then he had lost all control.

*   *   *

They let Rodríguez call his attorney. By the time the lawyer arrived at the jail, it was well after midnight. The two men met in a small room near Rodríguez's jail cell. Rodríguez was wearing a jail-orange jumpsuit that was several sizes too large. His feet were shod in paper slippers. He had not showered, he stank like a billy-goat, and his breath was still foul from vomiting.

The two talked for over an hour. When they were finished, and Rodríguez was led back to his cell, the lawyer, who was top-notch, called Fred Levy, the head of the district U.S. Attorney's Office, and arranged two meetings, the first between himself and Levy, to try and work out a plea agreement, and if that could be done to both parties' satisfaction, to proceed with the second meeting, between Levy and his client.

"My client's a sharp businessman," Rodríguez's lawyer told U.S. Attorney Levy, "but he's a naïve asshole when it comes to trying to smuggle contraband into this country, especially after 9/11. He comes and goes in and out of the San Diego airport all the time, he's wired up with the customs agents, they never check his bags—he probably slips them a bottle of Jack Daniel's at Christmas—he figured he wouldn't have any trouble. So when it was new faces, he was screwed. We're not going to lie to you about that, you caught him red-handed.

"The watch is another story. He assumed it was hot, but so what? A watch is a watch, there's thousands exactly like the one he's wearing, all over the world. But he says he didn't know who it came off of, and I believe him. He figured it was a foreign tourist, maybe an American, but that's no big deal down there, ripping off gringos is par for the course, nobody gives it a second thought.

"But now he does know where the watch came from and he's scared out of his everlovin' mind, because he's going up on a murder charge, unless he can make a deal. So what he's prepared to do is give you the name of the guy who gave him the watch, and more importantly, who that guy's connected with. It wasn't just some random robbery, according to him, it was political, it's a heavy scene that was directly connected to the woman who was killed. It involves smuggling, political payoffs, all kinds of stuff.

"So here's my offer. You investigate his story. I know that won't be easy, because who knows who's involved, you know how corrupt things can be in these banana republics. But at the end of the day, if what he tells you leads to the real killer of that woman and the reasons behind it, you cut him loose."

Levy listened patiently. He had been down this path many times before. "If that woman was really murdered," he replied, "rather than it having been a random killing, and if we can identify her actual killers and bring them to trial based on evidence he presents us, then we'll cut him loose. But it has to be rock-solid, because we have to go after extradition, which is very difficult. So tell him not to try to get cute, because if he does, we'll bury his sorry ass so deep he'll never see the light of day again."

They quickly came to an agreement—Rodríguez was desperate to do anything to avoid going to jail in America. He would give the Americans whatever information he had. *If* his information could be substantiated in his country, and *if* warrants for the arrest of Jocelyn's killers were issued, either there or in the U.S., he would be deported from the United States. He could never return, but he wouldn't go to federal prison in this country, a prospect that terrified him.

He'd still have to face the music back home, but if he had to go to jail, better he do it at home, where he could easily bribe his way out of prison, than in the U.S., where he was absolutely dead meat.

Los Angeles

♦ ♦ ♦

Special Customs Agent Tucker and U.S. Attorney Levy drove from San Diego to Los Angeles to meet with Walt Gaines. The government men brought Walt's recovered watch with them, along with eighty pages of testimony from their witness, Rodríguez.

They had contacted Walt over the phone, telling him they wanted to discuss some new information they had uncovered about the events surrounding the death of his wife in Central America. They deliberately hadn't given him any specifics. Although they had Rodríguez's confession, they knew they had nothing to tie Walt to Jocelyn's killing. His name had never come up in their conversations with their prisoner, and even if it had, anything Rodríguez told them was hearsay, almost impossible to corroborate. And they knew Rodríguez would say anything to try to get out of doing time in an American jail, including bringing down an innocent man.

The best result they figured they could get from this meeting was to elicit a feeling, one way or the other, as to whether Professor Gaines actually was involved in his wife's killing, or if it really had been a tragic accident, as everyone had supposed until recently. They had both been in this business a long time—their noses were pretty reliable when it came to sniffing out bullshit.

Walt had agreed to meet with them, but his attitude, they could tell from his tone of voice over the phone, was going to be one of caution and suspicion, an understandable combination, under the circumstances. Whether his reaction had been from having an old, painful wound reopened or something more sinister, they didn't know. They were hoping to find that out.

"Come in," Walt greeted them, as he opened his front door. "I was afraid you might get lost. The streets meander all over in this neighborhood."

He led them into the living room. "Have a seat," he told his guests, indicating a couch that was perpendicular to the fireplace. He flopped down on the one facing it. The wooden coffee table separated him from his visitors, both physically and psychologically.

"This is a nice house, Professor," Tucker said conversationally, looking around. "Lived here long?"

"Not long, no," Walt replied.

"Do you live alone?"

Walt gave him a bemused expression. "Why do you ask?"

"It's a big house for one person," Tucker answered.

"I have three sons."

Tucker smiled. "That would explain it. I have kids of my own. They sure fill up the space, don't they?"

"Mine don't live here though, they're grown men," Walt said with a smile. "They have their own lives, this isn't like *Bonanza.* But to answer your question: I have a woman friend who stays here occasionally, but she's out of town at the moment. Do you need to talk to her?"

Tucker shook his head. "That won't be necessary." They didn't want to get sidetracked with peripheral players.

Walt leaned forward. "When you called, you said you have fresh information about my wife's killing. What is it?"

"It's complicated," Levy answered. "First, there's something we want to show you." He reached into his briefcase and took out a specimen Baggie that contained Walt's wristwatch. Removing the watch from the bag, he laid it on the coffee table.

Walt regarded the watch as if it was radioactive. He picked it up and slowly turned it over in his hands. "Where did you get this?" he asked in a whispery voice.

"From a man who told us he bought it off a guy who was one of the people who killed your wife," Tucker told him.

The look on Walt's face was one of shock and disbelief. "Are you serious?"

"Yes, sir," Tucker answered.

Walt put the watch on his wrist, examining it with a sense of awe and wonderment. Looking up at the two government men again, he asked, "Where did you find him? The man who had my watch?"

Levy jumped in. "We'll get to that in a moment," he said. Dipping into his briefcase, he pulled out the transcript of Rodríguez's testimony. Several Post-its were interspersed throughout the document, protruding from the edges. Flipping to the first marked page, he turned his look to Walt.

"Did you ever know about, or hear about, or have any awareness of thievery at the archaeological sites you worked on, Dr. Gaines?" he asked. "La Chimenea, to be specific."

Walt nodded affirmatively. "That's always a problem," he said. "A site like La Chimenea, which is spread out over thousands of acres, is impossible to control completely. I'm sure there was looting, particularly when the site was first discovered. In fact, one of my first orders of business was to take steps to prevent theft, including armed guards patrolling the site. I won't say there wasn't any theft after that, particularly during the months I wasn't there. But regarding looting in any systematic, widespread form, I would say no."

Levy and Tucker exchanged a glance. Levy flipped through a few more pages of transcript. He looked up. "Our witness contradicts you, Professor Gaines," he said. "He's told us there was widespread looting during the time you were there."

Walt stared at him. "Who is this so-called witness of yours?" he demanded.

"We're not at liberty to tell you that," Levy answered calmly. "We're in the middle of an investigation, and we can't talk about it."

Under his calm facade, Levy was nervous. If Rodríguez was lying, if this man sitting across from them had nothing to do with the theft of banned artifacts, this could blow up in the government's face. Walt Gaines was no schmo off the street.

"Look, Professor Gaines," he said deferentially, "we don't know if the witness we have is telling the truth about anything. That's what we're trying to find out, what happened. If there was looting, and by who. And if your wife's killing was connected to it. That's why we came up here to talk to you. You would like to know who killed your wife, wouldn't you?" he asked. "If it was more complicated than a random accident?"

Walt looked up. "Will that bring her back to life?" he asked forlornly.

The question brought his interrogators up short.

"Of course it won't. And you know what? Who killed her doesn't matter to me anymore. Are you going to put a gun in my hand and let me kill the bastard back? Of course not, and I wouldn't do it if you did."

Walt shook his head in sorrow. "I've spent the past year and a half with this grief. It's taken me a long time to get over it. I never will, completely, but I'm slowly getting my life back together. And what I don't need, more than anything, is to go back over the past and try to change it. Because I can't."

He got up. "I don't think you drove a hundred miles up here to tell me this. You could have done that over the phone, or with an e-mail. Somebody's accused me of a crime, and you're trying to figure out if it's true or not."

He towered over them. "This isn't the first time this damn calumny has surfaced. It goes back to shortly after Jocelyn was murdered. It was a factor in my having to leave my position at Wisconsin, and it's a big deal as to why I'm not down at La Chimenea anymore." He pointed an angry finger in their faces. "You listen to me, because what I'm going to tell you is the truth: I don't give a rat's ass about this so-called witness you have. I had nothing to do with my wife's being murdered, and I never stole anything from any site I ever worked on. And anyone who says I did is an absolute liar!"

He walked to the front door and flung it open. "I don't know who my accuser is that you're hiding from me, I don't know what he's accusing me of, and I don't give a damn about either one," he told them. "Now get out of my house, and don't come back unless you're coming to arrest me."

Levy and Tucker stood up. Levy packed the documents back in his briefcase.

"Sorry to have bothered you, Professor Gaines," Levy said. "We have a job to do. It isn't always pleasant."

They walked to the door. Levy put out his hand, palm up. "The watch, please."

Walt stared at him. "What?"

"Your watch. It's evidence. Sorry," he said blandly. He reached over, took ahold of Walt's wrist, and slid the watch off. He handed it to Tucker, who dropped it into its evidence Baggie.

"We'll mail you a receipt," Levy promised Walt.

Tucker drove around the corner and parked the car. He was annoyed, but he'd been around long enough not to take it personally. Taking it personally was for civilians. "I haven't gotten a bum's rush like that in years," he commented.

"His wife was brutally killed," Levy reminded his rougher-edged partner.

"He's hiding something," Tucker said steadfastly. "Should we put him under surveillance?"

Levy shook his head. "It would be a waste of time, and I couldn't get an order to do it anyway." He sat up. "Let's get going. The 405's going to be a bitch all the way down, and I'd like to be home by dinnertime." He glanced back toward Walt's house. "We have to look at the possibility that it could be nothing more than an accidental murder, like everyone's always assumed. Rodríguez is a weenie, he'll grasp at any straw he can grab hold of."

"If I'm a betting man," Tucker said, "I'm betting on the fink."

Levy turned on the radio, fiddling with the reception. All-news-radio KNX 1070 came on. The traffic on the southbound 405 was stop-and-go, mostly stop. Levy turned the radio off as Tucker pulled away from the curb.

"It's been over a year," Levy said. He was a realist—he knew that tomorrow was always another day. "This isn't going away."

CHICAGO

♦ ♦ ♦

It was a slow night in the bar. Tom was on his own. He'd sent Pete home earlier, and half an hour ago he'd let the barmaid take off, too. The few stragglers who were still hanging around could bus their own orders. Physically, he was half-asleep on his feet, but his mind was racing.

Since he had come back from New York he and his brothers had been going around and around on how to deal with the information he had uncovered. Tom had wanted to storm the barricades—go see the old man immediately and have it out, once and for all. Clancy and Will were still dubious about a frontal approach being the best way. Their father had been stonewalling them for well over a year. If they went at him head-to-head he might withdraw even more, cut them off from any further contact, and refuse to talk to them about anything.

"His name was never mentioned directly," Will pointed out. "We know it must have been him who was doing the smuggling with Diane, but there's no absolute, direct proof."

"What more do you need?" Tom protested vociferously. "This isn't a trial. This is about our family, our mother. I don't care what you guys think, I've got all the proof I need."

"And if we confront him, and he says he didn't do it, or that he didn't know Diane was doing it, then what?" Clancy countered.

"So what're we going to do?" Tom argued. "We can't do nothing."

"We'll figure out something," Clancy said. "Let's not go off half-cocked."

After each of these arguments Tom felt like jumping on a plane to L.A. and getting it on with Walt himself. But the three of them had agreed that whatever they did, they would do it in unison. So he held his fire. But he was getting more and more impatient by the day.

The telephone rang. He walked down to the other end of the bar and picked it up. "Finnegan's," he said lethargically.

"Mr. Gaines?"

The voice was familiar, but he couldn't place it immediately. "Yes?"

"This is Alvin Whiting. From New York."

Whiting. Right. "Hello, Mr. Whiting," he said. "How are you?" He glanced at the wall clock. It was almost eleven—midnight in New York. "You're up late."

"Old men don't sleep much," Whiting told him. "The reason I'm calling is that I got a phone call from a man named Wendell Tucker. He's a customs agent, based in San Diego."

Tom's energy level shot up. "What about?" he asked.

"Tucker and I are old friends," Whiting explained. "After you and I had our meeting I cast my nets out, checking in with former colleagues who might be able to help out with what you're looking into."

Tom listened intently as Whiting told him about the

bust in San Diego, the witness who had given incriminating, albeit hearsay, evidence against his father, and the interview between Tucker, Levy, and Walt Gaines.

"What did my father say when they talked to him?" Tom asked. "Did he cop to anything?"

"They wouldn't tell me," Whiting answered. "Federal investigations are confidential. But the fact that they interviewed him struck me as something you would want to know about."

"I certainly do," Tom said. "Thanks a lot, Mr. Whiting. I appreciate your help."

"Well, I hope it does some good."

Tom thought about the other player in this game, the woman who had been tormenting him in his dreams for months. "What about Diane Montrose?" he asked.

"Her name wasn't mentioned," Whiting replied.

"It wasn't?" Tom asked. That was a surprise. Given her background, he would have thought she would be front and center in any investigation of stolen art objects.

"From the way agent Tucker recounted the details to me," Whiting said, as if reading Tom's thoughts, "I got the impression they don't know about her."

"Shit," Tom said involuntarily. "Excuse me."

"I understand," Whiting told him. "That would be my reaction, too. But that's typical of someone like Diane—they never leave their fingerprints at the scene of a crime."

No, Tom thought. She doesn't leave anything. It's what she takes that's so brutal, so devastating.

"Thanks for passing this along," Tom said.

"I hope it helps."

He had no choice now. He wasn't going to wait on his brothers anymore—he had to confront his father. They all had reasons to do it, but his were deeper, more personal.

* * *

Will and Clancy were upset and angry that Tom was going to Los Angeles without them, but they didn't try to stop him. They knew that once Tom got fixated on something he couldn't be budged.

Tom had told Will and Clancy about his phone call from Whiting after he closed up the bar and went back to Will's apartment. They had been freaked out by the news, but not surprised. What they were opposed to was Tom's going out there on barely a moment's notice.

"You can't barge in on him and expect him to suddenly start telling the truth," Clancy argued. "This will drive him even deeper into his bunker."

"Wait a couple of days, at least," Will begged him. "I'll go out there with you, if you still feel it's the right way to go about it. But I can't go tomorrow, I have obligations at work I can't get out of. I would if I could."

"I do, too," Clancy seconded.

"No." Tom wasn't waiting anymore. Not for the moon to be in the right house, for his brothers' schedules to sync up, for anything. They had already waited too damn long. It was time to stop talking about what they might do. Now was the time to take direct action. They had already waited way too long.

"I hope you don't screw this up," Clancy warned him darkly, once he understood he and Will couldn't prevail.

"It's already screwed up," Tom answered. "What else is there?" There was no room for compromise or delay anymore, not for him.

"Be careful," Clancy cautioned, as he drove Tom to O'Hare the following afternoon. "Try to keep your emotions in check. Don't blow up because he provokes you. He'll try to. You can't let him."

Tom knew that keeping his cool was the smart approach, but whether he could when he and his father got into each other's face, that was dicey. He and his brothers had pussyfooted around for too long.

If there had to be blood on the floor, so be it.

Los Angeles

◆ ◆ ◆

Tom's plane got into L.A. after ten o'clock in the evening. He jumped into his rental car and drove to his father's house. The closer he got the more he could feel his heart climbing into his throat.

He pulled up across the street, cut the engine, doused the lights. The house was still. There weren't any cars in the driveway, nor did any lights show from inside. He sat in the dark car, trying to compose himself.

It took him a few minutes to calm down enough to feel he could handle this encounter, however it went. But it didn't matter whether he could or couldn't—he was here, he couldn't wait on this, ready or not. He got out of the car, walked up the fieldstone pathway to the front door, and knocked.

There was no reply. He waited a moment, than knocked again, louder.

Lights went on inside. He could hear someone fumbling around. The door swung open.

"Did you forget your key? This is—" Whatever else she was going to say caught in her throat. "Oh, my God," she exclaimed, as she saw who was standing there in front of her.

She was wearing a nightgown with a light robe thrown over it. Instinctively, she pulled the robe tighter around her body.

"I don't have a key," he said. "I gave it back, remember?"

She took a half-step back. "I didn't know you were coming. Walt didn't tell me."

"He doesn't know. I wanted to surprise him."

She nodded slowly. "I'm sure you will." She looked at him for a moment longer. "You'd better come inside."

He followed her in. She closed the door behind them. They walked into the living room. She had her back to him.

"Why did you come out here?" she asked.

"I needed to talk to him, about you." He paused. "Diane."

Her knees buckled. She reached out to the couch to brace herself. "I need to sit down," she said. Her voice was shaking. "You sit, too. Not too close to me. Over there." She pointed to the other couch.

They sat facing each other in the dim light. She buried her head in her hands for a moment, then looked up.

"When did you find out?"

"A little while ago."

"Is that why you're here?"

"Partly." He wasn't nervous anymore—he had the upper hand. "I was in New York. I met your art collector friend Michaelson. He told me about the stealing of antiquities you and dad were into."

Her mouth opened in an almost-perfect *O*. "How in the world did you . . . oh, well, it doesn't matter how you found him. All that matters is you did." She gave him a rueful smile. "Good work, Tom. You're a first-class detective. Better than the ones who have been looking for me."

He stared at her. I know who you are now, he thought, but I don't know you at all. He could feel the longing—it was still there. But it wasn't as strong as it had been, not nearly as strong. She wasn't going to be able to seduce him again.

"That's why you're living here with dad," he said. "You're on the run from Michaelson because you stiffed him on a quarter of a million dollars he fronted you and dad to steal those artifacts from La Chimenea for him. Which is why you and dad are together. Because you were in it together."

She shook her head. "That's not how it is, Tom." She sat up straighter. "I took Michaelson's money, that's true. And I am on the run from him, that's true, too. But your father wasn't part of it. I'm with him because—"

He cut her off. "Because you're madly in love with him? We both know that's a crock. You love him so much you took me to bed the first night you ever met me. That's how you define love, Diane?"

He had to give her credit—she didn't turn away.

"That's not what I was going to say. Yes, it's true. I don't love him. But I respect him, and I needed him. And he was there for me when he didn't have to be. When he shouldn't have been," she added. "I don't know any other man who would have done what he did for me." She sighed. "I can understand your being angry with me. I used you, and I deceived you. But you have to separate me from your father."

"I can't. You two are Siamese twins in this, from the beginning."

She stood up. "We're not," she said. "But I can't expect you to think otherwise." She started to walk toward the bedroom she shared with Walt.

He stood up, too. "Where are you going? We're not finished here."

She turned back to him. "Maybe you aren't finished, Tom. But I am."

She was dressed casually, but as usual, elegantly. Her purse was slung over her shoulder. Two small bags were on the floor at her feet.

"A couple of days ago some government lackeys came here to see Walt, to talk to him about what went on down there," she told him. "I don't know what they talked about—he wouldn't tell me—but it shook him up pretty badly. Your coming here unexpectedly isn't going to make things better."

"He'll have to deal with it," Tom told her. "I'm staying here until he comes back."

"That's up to you. I don't know when that will be," she told him. "Lately he's been out all hours of the night. I don't know what he does. Drives around, probably. He never comes home drunk." There was nothing but sadness in her smile. "But he always comes home."

She opened the front door. "I can't be here when he sees you. It's too dangerous, for all of us."

They stared at each other. "I'd like to kiss you goodbye," she said.

The visions of the two of them making love that had been tormenting him for months started to flood back. He shut them off. "No," he told her. "I can't do that."

"Yes," she replied quietly. "You're right. I'm sorry, Tom." She picked up her bags. "What I said to you that night, about being a beautiful man. I wasn't playing a game with you. I meant it."

He heard the garage door open, heard the car engine starting. Then he heard her drive out, and the garage door closing.

The sound of a car pulling into the driveway jolted Tom awake: he had fallen asleep on the couch. He rubbed his eyes, stood up, looked at his watch. A quarter to three.

The front door opened. Walt came in. He looked tired. Quietly, he shut the door behind him, and started toward his bedroom.

"Hello, dad."

Walt spun around so fast he almost lost his balance. "What in the world are you doing here?"

"I came to see you." Tom was surprised with how calm and easy he felt. "We have to talk."

"What about?"

"A lot of things. You, mom . . ."

"For Christsakes!" Walt exploded. "At three in the morning? We've talked that all out, Tom, a million times. There's nothing more to talk about."

Tom didn't budge. "Yes, dad. There is."

Walt glanced toward the dark hallway that led to his bedroom. "How did you get in here?" he asked.

"Diane let me in."

Walt jerked involuntarily, but he recovered nicely. "Diane?" he parried.

Tom stared at him. Damn it, he thought, are you ever going to be honest with me? "Cut the crap, dad. You know who I'm talking about. Let's stop playing these stupid games. It's gone on way too long. Clancy and Will and I know too much now."

Walt stared at his son for a long, uncomfortable moment. "So you've found out about her." He started toward his bedroom. "If you're going to bring her into this, I'd better go get her."

"She isn't here."

Walt turned back.

"She took off," Tom said. "She didn't want to be here when you got home." He took a step toward his father. "We know all about Diane," he told Walt. "That she's an art smuggler. That you were working with her. That you kicked some student off the trip down there so Diane could come with you and help you smuggle out artifacts."

"No," Walt protested. "You don't know what you're talking about."

"Bullshit! You're lying, dad!"

"I'm not lying," Walt answered insistently. "Diane and your mother were good friends."

"Yeah, right," Tom said bitingly. "That's why she moved in with you and shared your bed, is that it? Because she and mom were such good friends? Why she changed her name and went underground? Jesus, dad, this is your *wife* we're talking about, our *mother*. Don't you have any shame, dad?" he pleaded. "Where's your soul?"

His father looked at him with dead eyes. "I lost my soul in the jungle, the night your mother was killed."

Tom felt the earth breaking open under his feet. "Is that why you're living in this house with the money you got from her insurance? Because you lost your soul? Why you took up with Emma . . . I mean Diane, damn it . . . when mom was still warm in the ground?" He could feel tears welling in his eyes, but he fought them off. This was no time for weakness. "Clancy and Will and I know all about the remortgages, dad. About the stocks you bought that went in the toilet. About the artifacts that were stolen from down there. Which the government down there also knows about, don't they? And our government, too."

"No!" Walt shot back with unexpected vigor, jumping to his feet. "That is totally untrue!"

"It's why they kicked you out! They cut your legs out from under you, they cut off the most important thing in the world to you. More important than mom, even. Or us. You were always our idol, dad, but you fell off your pedestal a long time ago."

The two stood nose-to-nose. "You don't know jack-shit!" Walt yelled. "You *think* you know the truth, but you don't know *anything*!"

Tom pushed him back down onto the couch. "Stop it! You can't lie to us anymore, dad. It's too late for that."

Walt shook his head in stubborn rebuttal "You've got it all wrong. You don't know what happened down there. Not a clue." He slumped back. "My life's been a living hell for over a year, it's going to be a living hell for the rest of my life, and frankly, I'm all tired out." He waved a hand in dismissal. "Go home, Tommy. I'm sorry you wasted your time and money coming all the way out here to get me to confess my sins, but I ain't gonna, 'cause I've already paid for them, a million times over."

He looked up at his son. "I'm no angel, but you always knew that. I shouldn't have taken up with Diane, but I was lost, and she rescued me. I mean that literally, I couldn't have survived without her. I knew it wasn't going to last. She's not the type to settle down with any man, let alone one twice her age, with a broken career to boot. But we needed each other. And I'm not going to apologize for that, not one tiny bit." He stared at Tom. "You think I killed your mother? That's what you and your brothers think?"

Tom didn't answer.

"You going to try to prove it?"

Tom took a deep breath. "Yes," he said. "We don't have a choice."

Walt waved his hands in disgust. "You're going to have your hearts broken. For Godsakes!" he cried out in anguish, "hasn't this family suffered enough? Isn't one terrible tragedy enough for a family to bear?"

"Dad. . . ." Tom said, his voice breaking. "You can't . . ."

"You're right, Tom," Walt said curtly, cutting him off. "I can't stop you. I can only warn you: don't open this Pandora's box. You don't know what you're going to find. I do, and that's why I don't want you to." He buried his face in his hands. "Damn it. You're still my sons. I still want to protect you, if I can. Don't do this."

"We have to, dad. We have to know the truth."

"So it will set you free?" Walt's laugh was painful. "If you do find out the truth, the real truth, you are going to be more shocked, hurt, and disillusioned than you already are."

Tom shook his head. "We've already been hit with a ton of shit. We won't feel another shovelful."

His father nodded in bitter acknowledgment. "Yes, you have. And I dropped most of it on you, by not being honest earlier. But I'm telling you the truth now." He buried his face in his hands. "Let it go."

What truth? Tom thought sadly. He hasn't told me anything. Nothing ever changes. "We can't, dad."

"You're going to keep pursuing this. Even if it kills you. In your heart."

"Yes, dad," Tom told him. "Even if it does."

PART FOUR

Central America

◆ ◆ ◆

Winter came early and hard to the upper Midwest, the cold snap dropping down low into central Iowa and Illinois; Chicago had been hit with almost zero-degree weather and six inches of snow. But at ten in the morning, when Tom and Clancy's plane landed in Santa Margarita, the capital, they stepped out into a virtual steambath: temperature in the high eighties, a humidity reading over ninety. They had anticipated warm weather, but not this hot—they had left one extreme only to arrive at another. They didn't know if that was an omen.

If they had come here under more pleasant circumstances, as they had done in the past with their parents, they could enjoy the benefits of this tropical climate—hit the beaches for snorkeling and scuba-diving, take nature hikes into the mountains, visit archaeological sites, particularly La Chimenea. But they weren't here on vacation. They were on a grim mission, and they didn't anticipate that even an hour of their time would bring them anything remotely resembling pleasure.

Will hadn't been able to come. He was overwhelmed

with work. Not being able to accompany his brothers had been anguishing for him. Clancy and Tom promised to keep him abreast of events with e-mails and phone calls, and would fill him completely in when they returned.

"There he is," Tom said, as the brothers emerged from customs and walked outside. He raised his arm and waved to the small man with strong Indian features who was standing next to a mud-encrusted Isuzu minivan parked at the curb.

Manuel raised his own arm and waved back. He came forward with quick, small steps, his face creased into a broad smile. "Ah, *Señores* Gaines," he said in his heavily accented English. "It is good to see you again."

They had hired Manuel to escort them around the country while they were here. He had been thrilled to help; they'd had to force him to take payment for his services.

"You, too, Manuel," Clancy told him, reaching out and engulfing his father's former right-hand man in a hug. The top of Manuel's head barely came up to his chin. "Thanks for helping us out like this."

"It is nothing," Manuel protested. "It is my privilege to be able to assist you." The smile left his face, replaced by a solemn resolve. "In any way I can."

They threw their bags into the minivan and piled in. Manuel pulled away from the curb. There wasn't much traffic, mainly taxicabs and motor scooters.

"So, Manuel," Tom said, "how're things by you these days? Still working at the dig?"

Manuel shook his head sorrowfully. "I'm working for the National Museum now."

"You aren't working at the site anymore?" Clancy asked, surprised.

"Not anymore," Manuel confirmed. "It's different, now that your father is no longer running things."

"I'm sorry to hear that," Tom said sympathetically. "That's a waste of talent."

Manuel ducked the compliment. "There have been many changes." He hesitated. "We will talk about them at the appropriate time."

It was obvious to the boys that their father's old friend didn't want to talk about La Chimenea, their parents, or the present situation. Maybe he was afraid he was under surveillance for associating with the sons of Walt Gaines. If he was, they didn't blame him.

After the meeting with their father had blown up in his face, Tom had called Whiting in New York again and explained his dilemma—they desperately needed to find out, once and for all, who had killed their mother, and whether their father and Diane Montrose were conclusively tied to it. Could Whiting go back to his friend in the customs department and see if he could pry any more information out of him?

Whiting had called back a couple of days later. Yes, he had some fresh intelligence, but it was hearsay—whether or not it was truthful was highly debatable. Supposedly there had been an archaeologist involved in smuggling artifacts, and the killing was somehow connected to him. But exactly how, and who the players were, his friend wouldn't tell him. Whiting suspected the customs people were still trying to figure out whether or not the man in custody was holding back vital information that he could use as a bargaining chip. They also told him there was a woman involved, but again, they wouldn't (or couldn't) say who she was.

Tom and his brothers were going to have to investigate this themselves. Whiting suggested they start with the government minister who was in charge of archaeology for the country. He would have information that could help them. Whether he was willing to cooperate or not, they wouldn't know until they met with him face-to-face.

The following day, Tom and Clancy had gotten their passports and visas in order, been in touch with the minister's office, and booked their flight. And now, here they were.

In less than fifteen minutes they had left the city behind, and were in open countryside. The terrain was flat and green. Scattered fields were under random cultivation on either side of the potholed two-lane asphalt highway. The houses were small and primitive—paint peeling, leaky tin roofs, pigs and goats foraging in the front yards. Atop some of the dwellings, television antennas and small satellite dishes stood out against the clear morning sky. In between the small plots of farmland, native vegetation grew wild: hibiscus, frangipani, marsh grasses. Beyond that was the jungle, often as close as a hundred yards from the road.

After a few miles, the paved road became a dirt-gravel surface. The minivan bumped its way along. Manuel was skillful as he steered around the deepest potholes. Barefoot women bearing large clay vessels on their heads walked along the edge of the road, carrying water, food, myriad goods. To the right, a slow-moving river at the bottom of the steep embankment meandered a course parallel to the road. Women squatted at the river's edge, washing clothes against rocks, and entire families bathed, the children frolicking in the muddy water. Tom, who had been to India, thought of the Ganges, of the dense crowds of people who bathed amidst turds and garbage. The conditions weren't that unsanitary here, but that was because there wasn't as much population, not from any superior understanding of hygiene.

Along with the human flow there were horses, cattle, sheep, pigs, dogs, wandering along the road. Rickety wooden fences had been built in front of some of the houses to try to keep the stock in, but they were ineffective. The animals were everywhere. Manuel was constantly standing on the brakes to avoid collisions. Kids, too, blithely walked on the road, sometimes right down the center line.

Besides the livestock crissrossing their path, there were dead animals in the road as well. Mostly horses, goats, and dogs. Some of the carrion was on the side in the matted-down grass, others smack-dab in the middle. Vultures squatted next to the rotting carcasses, plucking the meager meat from the bones. As the minivan passed by, the large ugly birds scattered, then flew back to resume their meal.

After a dozen more miles they rounded a corner and the road was paved again with a fresh coat of tar. "Why are some parts of the highway paved and others not?" Clancy asked Manuel.

"Because someone who is in the government or is rich lives nearby," their guide answered. "Like there."

He pointed to a low hill off to the side. A long, winding macadam driveway snaked up the hill to a high, cement wall. A gated entrance was cut into the wall, next to which stood a guardhouse that further protected access to the property.

"That wall has broken glass embedded into the top of it," Manuel informed them. "If you were foolish enough to try to scale it to get to the mansion it protects, the broken shards of glass would cut you to ribbons."

"Not very hospitable," Tom commented dryly.

"The owner has the concession for Coca-Cola for the entire country," Manuel continued. "So the road in front of his house is paved. He has his own helicopter as well, behind the house." He glanced back at the forbidding wall through his sideview mirror. "He is only here two or three weeks a year. The rest of the time he lives in Miami Beach."

They crested a low rise and dropped into a shallow valley. Ahead of them, two young boys on horseback were herding three dozen slow-moving animals—cows, bulls, horses—down the road. The livestock were spread out all across the road, from one edge to the other. The boys were bare to the waist, jeans and boots on their legs and feet, straw cowboy hats on their heads. They rode bareback, with rope halters to guide their horses, moving in and out of their herd with easy confidence.

The minivan came up behind them. Manuel braked to a slow crawl. Slowly, carefully, he pushed the minivan through the herd. The boys helped, herding the animals to either side. As the minivan passed, the boys smiled gap-toothed grins and raised their hats in greeting.

The road became bumpy and potholed again. "Check that out," Tom called. He pointed out the window to the skeletal remains of a Ferris wheel in the middle of a weed-infested field. Nearby, there were rotting frames of buildings that had fallen apart.

"That was an amusement park," Manuel informed them. "Parents brought their children here. It was very pleasant."

"It's like out of a Fellini movie," Tom said. "What happened to it?"

"The owner was killed in an ambush, for his payroll. After that, the families stopped coming. So now, it is a wreck. In five years there will be no trace of it left."

"Unlike La Chimenea, which was built for the ages," Clancy commented. "That's why sites like La Chimenea are so important." He looked back at the hulk of the old carnival as it receded from view out the back window. "Why people like dad spend their lives trying to preserve them."

An hour passed. After driving through a town composed of a few houses and a store, they came upon an army barracks set back behind a high barbed wire fence. As they drove by the entrance, a convoy of guardia, riding tandem on black Kawasaki motorcycles, wearing black uniforms, knee-high polished boots, and Darth Vader helmets, was coming out of the gate. They were all armed, some with machine guns strapped across their backs. As the motorcycles cruised by the minivan, proceeding in the opposite direction, the troops, all of them young, glanced in the windows, checking them out. Some of the guardia were women.

"This reminds me of Paris during their riots," Tom remarked. "Cops doing whatever they wanted."

"To me, this is scarier," Clancy said. "It feels like there's no moral authority here at all."

Manuel was careful not to make eye contact with any of the soldiers. His vision was fixed on the road ahead, knuckles tightened on the steering wheel, not relaxing until they had passed the barracks and the motorcyclists were no longer in sight. Then he checked again in the rearview mirror, to make certain the guardia were gone and hadn't doubled back to follow them.

"They are everywhere," he said. "Except when they are needed," he added in a flash of anger. "We're lucky they did not stop us and shake us down for money. If you were on your own, they would have, no question. They always hassle gringos." He sighed heavily. "For them, this is the only way to have a better life. They are fed, clothed, they go to school. Being in the military, the guardia, is one of the few ways the poor people, especially the young ones, can ever get anywhere in this wretched, godforsaken country."

As they approached the district capital, the highway improved and there were more houses and small businesses. Clusters of people were on the streets, walking and driving motor scooters and old cars.

"You are staying at the Excelsior for tonight?" Manuel asked, as he deftly maneuvered his vehicle onto the main highway that led into the center of the city.

"Yes," Tom confirmed. "How is it these days?"

The Excelsior was an old hotel in the center of the city. They had stayed there with their parents on previous forays. It had been faded around the edges for years now, but it still had a funky colonial style and a good bar. Journalists in the country, regardless of where they were staying, could often be found at the Excelsior bar after dark, drinking and swapping war stories. CNN had done a brief profile on it a few years back, describing it as a throwback to a bygone era, a place where you would expect to see Humphrey Bogart and Lauren Bacall having drinks and trading bon mots with Errol Flynn and Ingrid Bergman.

"It is comfortable enough," Manuel said. "Most Americans stay at the newer hotels now, the ones that have swimming pools and cable television. But the Excelsior is plenty fine," he added quickly, not wanting the boys to think they weren't staying at a decent establishment.

They would settle in here tonight, relax, recharge

their batteries after their long, sleepless trip. Tomorrow they were scheduled to meet with the Minister of Archaeology and Culture, the official who had withdrawn his troops' support for the ill-fated journey away from La Chimenea, and had then, after Jocelyn's killing, rubbed salt in the wound by denying Walt further access to it. The meeting had been confirmed, with reluctance, before they left the States—they weren't going to fly five thousand miles to chase a wild goose. Although the Smithsonian Museum no longer sponsored Walt, they had cooperated to the extent of putting pressure on the minister to meet with his sons.

Manuel dropped them at their hotel, promising to pick them up early the following morning to drive them across town to the capital building.

"Thanks for all your help, Manuel," Tom said, leaning in the driver's-side window and shaking Manuel's hand. He reached into his wallet and pulled out some money. He knew that American money was good here, preferable to the native currency, which could fluctuate in value, overnight sometimes, from barely acceptable to close to worthless. He tried to press the money into Manuel's hand, but Manuel wouldn't take it.

"No," he said firmly. "You don't have to pay me, *Señor* Tom."

"Come on, Manuel, take it, please," Tom cajoled their guide. "You're working for us. We want to pay you for that."

Again, Manuel politely but firmly refused to take the money. "Perhaps later, if you find out what you are looking for," he told Tom. "But not now."

"Okay," Tom said, backing off. "But we're settling accounts before we leave. Agreed?"

"All right. Yes. *Hasta mañana.*" The minivan pulled

away into the narrow street, a plume of dark smoke coming from the tailpipe. The brothers stood on the sidewalk and watched him disappear into traffic.

"Let's get settled in and grab some beers," Tom said, pushing the front door open. "I've got a thirst that needs attending to."

This place hasn't been renovated in forty or fifty years, Clancy thought, as they walked across the black-and-white-tiled floor to the registration desk. Ceiling fans spun listlessly in the afternoon heat. Battered wicker tables and chairs were haphazardly arranged in the lobby, and a low bookcase along one wall featured old novels and back issues of National Geographic. Through a large double door at the far end of the room they saw the bar, now empty, the lights off.

The registration clerk, who leisurely emerged from a room in the back after Tom rang the front-desk bell, was a stout, middle-aged woman who looked part black, part Indian, part Spanish—a common mixture, particularly near the coast, which had been the center of the country's slave trade two centuries ago. Clancy dug into his bag and handed her the fax printout of their confirmation. She handed them their registration cards.

"We have you a fine room," she told them in thick Spanish-flavored English. "*Dos camas.*"

"Air-conditioned?" Tom asked hopefully. "*¿Aire aconedicionado?*" He had four years of college Spanish—he would do the talking when Spanish was required.

"No," she answered, favoring him with a sad smile that revealed more teeth missing than intact.

"*No problema,*" he assured her. "*¿Ventiladores?*" He pointed to the ceiling fans.

"*Sí,*" she answered, smiling more broadly.

"Then we're in business," he told her. *"Muy bien."*

They rode the creaking copper-paneled elevator to the third floor and walked halfway down the narrow hallway to their room. "I'll bet we're about the only guests they've got here," Tom said. He ran his hand along one wall of faded wallpaper that featured flamingos, macaws, and other wild birds in a bright green forest.

"Probably," Clancy agreed. "These old places aren't popular anymore, without air-conditioning and video rooms and pools."

"That's too bad," Tom said. "There's something to be said for genteel decay."

The mattresses on the two narrow beds were thin and swaybacked, but the sheets looked clean. Threadbare towels were laid out on the beds, along with sealed bottles of water for drinking, and cellophane-wrapped glasses. At the end of the hallway, the bathroom door was open. They could see a sink, a toilet, a bathtub. It looked clean.

They tossed their bags on the beds and left, locking the door behind them. They kept their passports, wallets, and necessary documents with them—if their clothing and toilet articles were stolen they could be replaced, but not their identification, cash, and credit cards. Bypassing the elevator, they walked down the stairs, through the empty lobby, and out into the street.

The streets in the center of the city were narrow. Some were cobblestoned, as they had been for over a century. Many of the side streets had never been paved at all; they were no more than dirt cart paths that had been worn smooth over the years.

This part of the city was the original settlement. It had been established by the early Spanish invaders, who, after subjugating the native population by killing most of them off, had erected houses and other buildings in the style of their own country. These structures were built to seventeenth- and eighteenth-century scale, so the streets and sidewalks, meant to accommodate people, horses, and carriages, were cramped, a tight squeeze for modern cars and trucks, which cruised up and down them without regard for stop signs or traffic lights, creating mini–traffic jams at every intersection.

It was almost five in the afternoon. Siesta was over, the streets were full of life. The brothers edged their way along the main avenue's congested sidewalk, rubbing elbows with locals and a few other *turistas*, passing street vendors selling a mishmash of goods—knockoffs of Gucci and Prada handbags, Polo golf shirts, Rolex watches, Hermès scarves, as well as crude hand-carved wooden Maya artifacts, old music cassettes, sandals, blankets, shawls. Hundreds of items—anything a tourist, which to any native's eye they certainly were, might want to take back home.

A group of American kids, clothes filthy, hair long, some of them in Rastafarian dreadlocks, sat on the sidewalk, panhandling.

"Spare change?"

They ignored the kids. One of the girls, her blond hair matted, her bare feet dirty from road dust, jumped up and lightly grabbed on to Tom's shirtsleeve.

"Got any dope, man?" she asked in a breathless whisper.

"No." He looked her over. She couldn't be older than eighteen.

"Wanna buy some? Good shit, Jamaican. Good price."

He shook his head. "No, thanks."

"Blow job for five dollars?"

He shook his head. "Not today." He pulled away from her.

"Faggot," she called after him, halfheartedly.

They ate dinner at an Indian restaurant—tandoori chicken, vegetable curries, shrimp, riata, rice, washed down with decent local beer. Afterward, the Sri Lankan proprietor, who was also the chef, served them thick Turkish coffee and tiny snifters of Rémy Martin. The bill, including a generous tip, came to twenty-five dollars American, which Clancy put on his Visa card.

"You could live like a king for almost nothing down here," Tom observed as they walked along the busy sidewalk again.

"Except you'd be living here," Clancy said.

"There's worse places," Tom replied. "You could have a little motel or shop, live on the beach, what's wrong with that? Open up a branch of Finnegan's, I'll bet it would do well."

"When I retire," Clancy said. "Let's head back. We'll have a couple of beers at the hotel and take it mellow."

The half-dozen drinkers gathered in the Excelsior bar, four men and two women, looked like refugees from a Graham Greene novel. Europeans, Clancy thought, as he and Tom walked in. Europeans don't look like Americans. He didn't know why that was, they came from the same root stock, but he'd seen enough Europeans in his bar and in his work to know that most of the time that was true. A couple of them, one man and one woman, were in their thirties; the rest looked a decade or more older. They all had the faces of seasoned drinkers. They sat in two groups at two adjoining tables. No one was sitting at the bar. The bartender was washing glasses.

The other patrons looked up as the brothers sat down

at an empty table. One of them, a pale-complexioned man with sparse reddish hair and rimless glasses, saluted them with his highball glass. "It's serve yourselves here, gents," he informed them in an oatmeal-thick Irish brogue. "The barmaid left early."

"By about ten years," laughed the younger of the two women in a husky, also Irish or English, voice. She, too, had red hair, a deep luxurious auburn pulled back from her face in a long, thick braid halfway down her back. She was pretty, with an Irish-English woman's fair, freckled complexion. She shook a Marlboro from a pack on the table, lit up.

"What do you want?" Clancy asked Tom.

"A shot of tequila and a beer."

Clancy walked to the bar and ordered their drinks—he knew bar Spanish, which was good enough for in here.

The woman smiled at Tom. "Smoke?" she offered. She pushed her pack toward him.

He smiled back. "No, thanks." An attractive woman, he thought. I wonder if she's with any of these guys. A quick size-up was that she was a friend to all, a lover to none.

He thought, yet again—it was like a song stuck in his head he couldn't shake—of Diane. This was an attractive woman sitting here, but not in Diane's league. Which was becoming a problem—he mentally compared every woman he met with Diane, and they all came up short. He had to get rid of that song and replace it with a better one.

"Americans," the Irishman said.

"Yep," Tom answered.

"From whereabouts?"

"The Midwest. Chicago."

"Good town, Chicago," the man said approvingly. "Good drinking town."

"You know it?"

"I've been through."

Tom grinned. "Ever been to a bar called Finnegan's?"

The man scrunched up his face in thought. "Don't think so. Is it in the center of the city?"

"North side."

The man shook his head. "I only know Michigan Avenue. You stay at a hotel, you do your job, eat and drink locally, go to the next assignment. Nice pub, Finnegan's?"

Tom resisted the natural inclination to brag on his brother's place. "They pour an honest shot," he said.

"I like that," the man said. "Have to try it the next time I pass through."

"You won't be disappointed," Tom promised him. "What sort of work do you do?" he asked. "You sound like you travel in your job."

The man nodded. "Journalist. Freelance video. Right now I'm with CNBC. Me and Anton here." He nudged the man seated next to him. "The mad Hungarian. He's my soundman. We're a team. Anton and Patrick."

"All Hungarians are mad," the man called Anton said gaily, in a middle-European accent. "Except not me, tonight." He held up his glass. "I have my faithful companion to keep me in good company," he added with a laugh.

"You're all journalists?" Tom asked. "Broadcasters? Thanks," he told Clancy, who had returned to the table with two shot glasses of tequila entwined in the fingers of one large hand, two bottles of beer with a local label in the other.

The man called Patrick nodded. "Burt and Dickie"—

he pointed to the other two men—"are stringers for Reuters and the BBC. Lorna's a reporter."

Lorna was the redhead with the pretty face and the long braid. Burt and Dickie raised their glasses in acknowledgment.

"All except Vera," Patrick went on, nodding to the other woman.

Tom looked over at Vera, who was sitting at the table with the two Brit stringers. She was the oldest one here. Fifty, maybe a few years over that. If faces are a road map of life, Tom thought as he looked at her, she had been in many places and seen many things. She's as old as mom was when she was killed, he realized with a shudder of sadness.

"And you?" he asked her. "What's your game?"

She smiled politely. "I own an art gallery. In Amsterdam." Another smile. "And your game, as you Americans put it? What's yours?"

"I'm a physical therapist," Clancy answered. "He's a mathematician," he said, pointing his thumb at Tom.

"On holiday?"

"Yep. Always wanted to check this part of the world out."

Tom leaned a bit closer to Vera. "Is that why you're here?" he asked her, glancing at Clancy. "Buying art?"

She nodded. "Yes."

"What kind?" he asked.

"Native work," she told him. "There is a big market in Europe now for indigenous Central and South American art."

"Contemporary art?" He traced a finger around the rim of his beer bottle.

"Yes," she replied. "And older pieces, too. From the

the 1930s and 1940s. Whatever appeals to me, that I can afford."

Tom knocked back a hit of tequila. It was mediocre in quality, hot and rough going down. "What about real old stuff?" He paused. "Maya."

She frowned. "Do you mean from the ruins?"

He nodded.

She shook her head vehemently. "No," she said firmly. "That is forbidden."

"I've heard it happens anyway," he said.

"It is an abomination," she replied fiercely. "It is like stealing a child from its parents."

"So it isn't done?"

She shook her head. "It *is* done. But not by scrupulous dealers. Not by me," she added emphatically.

"Good for you," he told her. "I have heard about it, though. The thievery."

She made a face. "Some people will do anything for money."

Clancy drank some tequila, chased it with a swallow of beer. "Do you ever go out to the sites?" he asked her. "Are you interested in that?"

"Of course," she answered. "Who wouldn't be? They're spectacular."

He toyed with his bottle for a moment. "I've heard of this really incredible place, in the south. It's called . . ." He stopped for a moment, as if trying to recall it. "La Chimenea. Have you ever been there?"

She shook her head. "No."

"It's not worth seeing?"

"Oh, no. It is beautiful, from everything I've heard," she said. "But it's not a good place for foreigners to visit now."

"Why not?"

"There were problems. With what you were talking about."

"Looting?"

She nodded.

He knew he was pushing, but he couldn't help it. "By who?"

"Some of the Americans who were working there," she told them. "A famous archaeologist, who was in charge, and an art broker, a woman named Diane Montrose." She shuddered. "An unscrupulous woman. There were stories of thefts they were involved in." She sipped from her glass. "And there was a terrible incident at the same time, that stopped everything in its tracks."

"What kind of incident?" Tom asked, trying to sound uninformed.

"A woman who was one of the team there was killed. Shot to death." She paused. "Why do you want to know?" she asked with a curiosity that bordered on suspicion. "Are you in the art trade, too?"

"No," Tom said quickly. "We're just tourists. We want to visit some of the sites, like that one."

"Why in the world did you choose this hotel?" Patrick interjected.

Because we stayed here one time with our parents, went through Tom's mind. The woman who was killed, and her archaeologist husband who you say was stealing the country's treasures.

"Tourists never come to the Excelsior," Patrick explained. "Only drones like us, on limited expense accounts. And Vera, who has a weird romantic streak."

"I abhor tourist hotels," Vera said, smiling and patting Patrick's hand. "La Chimenea would be a good site to see," she told them. "But I don't think you should attempt to go to that one. They don't want foreigners there anymore. Particularly Americans, like you lovely gentlemen."

Tom drank down the rest of his tequila. What a downer. They'd been in the country less than twelve hours, and already they were being hit with these accusations. Where there's smoke there's fire, he thought. And the smoke was awfully damn dense.

"I'm bushed," he said, standing and stretching. "I'm turning in."

Clancy stood also. "Nice meeting you all," he told the correspondents and Vera. "Thanks for the company and the conversation."

"Good luck on your travels," Patrick said cheerfully. "Be careful as you move about the country," he advised them. "It can be dangerous here."

We know, Tom thought. We've lived through it.

The following morning, Manuel drove them across the city for their meeting. The capital building, a large neocolonial structure of impressive ugliness, was situated on a high knoll overlooking the main business district.

Manuel pulled up in front. "I will be in there," he told them, pointing to a cantina across the square. "Leave everything with me except your necessary documents. Things do not move quickly around here," he warned them. "Be patient."

They went inside and gave their names to a military aide who was seated at the reception desk. Behind him, a security gate barred further entrance into the building. The aide located the brothers on the appointment list, and placed a telephone call.

"Sit over there," he ordered them brusquely in Spanish, pointing to a bench against the far wall.

They sat on the hard bench for close to half an hour without being paid any attention. Finally, Tom got up and walked to the front desk. "What's the holdup?"

The aide answered with a bureaucrat's automatic response: "The minister is in a meeting. I will inform you when he's free."

"Still in his so-called meeting," Tom told Clancy as he plopped down again. "It's petty game-playing."

Clancy looked at his watch. "There's nothing we can do about it," he replied pragmatically. "We're at their mercy."

"He'll see us if we have to camp out here overnight," Tom said with determination. "'Cause we ain't leaving till he does."

As if their impatience had been psychically transmitted, the telephone rang on the military aide's desk. He picked it up and listened. Standing, he beckoned Clancy and Tom.

"Follow me." He unlocked the security gate and led them down a high-ceilinged, marble-floored hallway to a set of elaborately carved mahogany double doors. Opening one of the doors, he ushered them inside.

The office of the Minister of Archaeology and Culture was large, almost the size of a small courtroom. Faded oriental carpets covered the polished wooden floor. Behind the ornate desk, a bank of floor-to-ceiling windows opened onto a narrow balcony that overlooked the city. The windows were closed, covered with thin gauzy curtains through which the afternoon sun filtered, bathing the room with a golden light.

The minister was next to his desk. He was thin, middle-aged, his balding hair shaved almost to his skull. He wore a well-cut dark business suit, a crisp white shirt with doubloon cuff links, a light blue tie. Like the boots worn by the guardia, his black wingtips were shined to a high gloss.

"Please," he said in English, "sit down." His English, although accented, was clear and assured.

They sat in wing chairs facing his desk. The sun was in their eyes, an obvious ploy, Tom thought—he had delayed this meeting until the sun was in the right position.

"I'm sorry to have kept you waiting." The minister gave them an insincere smile of apology. "We had an emergency. There is always an emergency, and it always winds up on my desk. Can I offer you a refreshment? Something to drink?"

"No, thank you," Tom replied.

The minister sat down, facing them. As the sun was over his shoulder, his face was in shadow while theirs were in bright sunlight. *"¿Hablan español?"* he asked them.

"No mucho," Tom replied. "Decently enough," he said in English. "But my brother doesn't," he added.

"We can converse in English, then," the minister said. "I was in college in your country. Southern Methodist University, in Dallas, Texas. I got my master's degree in business administration," he told them with a proud smile. "They have an excellent archaeology department there," he added, "as I assume you know."

"Yes, we know," Tom replied. Walt had guest-lectured at SMU, and had also written a chapter of a book about Maya life that had been compiled by a prominent archaeologist who taught there.

The minister leaned forward on his elbows. "You are here to talk about your father."

"Yes," Tom said. They were speaking in English, but as he had been prepared to handle the conversation in Spanish, he took the lead.

"How can I help you?" the minister asked, looking from one of them to the other. "What do you want to know?"

"Why isn't our father in charge of the excavation at La Chimenea anymore?" Tom asked bluntly.

The minister sat back, steepling his fingers at the tips and looking up at the ceiling. "That is a complex question. As are the reasons." He brought his gaze down to them. "There was a mutuality of agreement."

"Was there a problem with the quality of his work?"

"No, no," the minister responded quickly. "His work was excellent. He has always done fine work. He is highly respected here for . . ." He paused. "The work."

"Then what was the problem?" Clancy interjected. "Did he step on somebody's toes? Rub somebody important the wrong way?" He leaned forward. "Like you?"

"No," the minister said. "He did not rub me the wrong way."

"Someone else then?" Clancy continued. "Higher up than you?"

The minister showed them a blank face. "There is no one higher up than me. Not even the President. I make the decisions about our archaeological heritage."

"So you made the decision," Tom said. "Personally."

"Yes," the minister confirmed. "I made it."

"Why? If there was nothing wrong with the work he was doing?" His voice was rising in anger.

"Tom," Clancy admonished him. "Take it easy."

Tom took a deep breath. "Our father raised millions of dollars for La Chimenea. He brought together the National Geographic Society, the Smithsonian Museum, his university, all the other donors. Why in the world wouldn't you have wanted that man to stay here and keep working? No one else can do it as well."

The minister stood up. Turning his back on them, he looked out the window. "There were other reasons." He paused. "There were accusations made. Serious accusations."

"What were they?" Clancy asked.

The minister turned to face them. "We discovered that artifacts had been stolen from the site. We investigated, and traced it to the archaeological team that was led by your father."

"You know that for a fact?" Tom asked. They had to know: absolutely, completely, irrevocably.

The minister furrowed his eyebrows. "Professor Gaines was in charge," he said. "No one else had free rein of the site like he did. He was the logical suspect."

"Suspected, but without proof," Tom pressed.

The minister flushed. "There was no one else who could have done it," he insisted.

"So you kicked him off the project, even though by your own admission you didn't have proof."

"This is *our* country, *Señor* Gaines," the minister responded strongly, clearly angered and offended. "Not your father's, not the National Geographic Society's, not the Smithsonian Museum's, not the University of Wisconsin's. *Ours.* We had the absolute right to terminate his contract, and we did." He took a moment to compose himself. "And it was the right decision, that we know."

"How do you know?" Clancy demanded.

"Because since he left, there have been no more thefts." The minister's smile was triumphant. "That is more than enough proof for me. And for the President and the cabinet as well." He paused. "I am sorry you came all this way to hear this, but it is the truth."

"What about our mother?" Clancy asked bluntly.

The minister's face took on a look of grave piety. "That was a terrible misfortune."

"A *misfortune*? The wife of a prominent American is shot to death and you call that a misfortune?"

The minister shrugged. "People die in this country every day. From malnutrition, from earthquakes, at the hands of Marxist rebels. Yes, it was a misfortune. Any time someone is killed it is a misfortune."

"Do you know who killed her?"

The minister rubbed his hand up and down his chin. "There are suspects we are aware of."

"Have you made any arrests?" Clancy asked.

The minister shook his head. "No."

"Why not, if you know who the suspects are?"

"They are hard to find," came the unconcerned reply. "They live in the jungles and the mountains, where it would be difficult for our soldiers to reach them without inflicting unacceptable casualties." He shrugged apathetically. "There have been insurrections in this country for many years. Our resources to combat them are limited. We cannot go after all the forces that are opposed to us, like your country does."

"Her killing was not important to you, is what you're saying," Tom said heatedly.

"I am sorry for your loss," the minister replied flatly. "But it is not my hands that are stained with her blood."

In a foul and depressed mood, they walked across the busy square, dodging ancient taxis and buses belching diesel fumes from their exhaust pipes, and entered the cantina where Manuel was waiting. The light inside was dim and thick with cigarette smoke. They saw Manuel sitting at a table in a corner, at the back of the room. He spotted Clancy and Tom through the gray-blue haze and waved them over.

"Beers?" Manuel asked.

"Absolutely," Clancy said. "I could use a real drink, too."

Manuel called to the woman who was serving. *"Dos cervezas, y nos trae una botella de tequila.* How did your meeting go?" he asked.

"Lousy," Clancy said. "He didn't give a damn."

Manuel shrugged, as if to say, "of course not." "Did he give a reason for why your father can no longer come here?"

Clancy hesitated—Manuel had been their father's closest aide and most loyal supporter. "Yes," he said.

The woman put their beers in front of them and set the bottle of tequila, along with glasses, in the center of the table. Manuel poured three shots of tequila. He raised his glass.

"To happier times." He tossed his drink down.

"Amen to that," Tom seconded. "Whew!" he exclaimed, as the drink hit home. "That packs a punch!"

"It is not distilled for very long," Manuel said with a smile, pouring some more into his glass and Tom's. Turning serious again, he asked, "Did the minister say anything about your mother?"

"They think they know who killed her," Clancy said, "but they're not going to do anything about it. It's not important enough to them," he said bitterly.

"They do not want to awaken the sleeping bear," Manuel said, sagely.

"He told us it was because dad was involved in smuggling," Clancy said. "Some kind of retaliation."

Manuel nodded slowly, but didn't speak.

"Look, Manuel," Tom said. This was crunch time—

their best and maybe their last chance to learn the truth. "We know you loved our dad and you don't want to say anything bad about him. But if you know about thefts that went on, we want you to tell us." He looked over at Clancy, who seconded him. "We had heard about that before we came down here. That was one of the reasons we came, to find out if it's true. And to find out more about why our mother was killed. Most importantly, if her death was connected to it."

Manuel looked at them intently. "You are sure you really want to know?" he asked finally. "No matter what you find out?"

"Yes," Clancy said. "We really want to know. We have to."

Manuel nodded. "I can understand that you must." He waited another moment before speaking again. "There is a man who can tell you the truth of what happened. I can arrange for you to meet with him." Another pause. "I knew the government would dismiss your concerns, so I have already been in contact with this man."

"That's great!" Tom exclaimed. "That's really wonderful of you to do this, Manuel."

Manuel raised a finger of caution. "He and his people are in opposition to the government, so you will have to go where the government soldiers are not willing to go—deep into the jungle. It will be a difficult journey."

"That's okay," Tom assured him eagerly. "We can handle it."

"Absolutely," Clancy seconded. "How long will it take?" he asked.

"Almost a week," Manuel replied, "because you will go on foot. You will have to walk two, maybe three days into the jungle with the guide I am going to provide you, meet with this man, and then walk out."

"A week?" Clancy repeated, surprised. "We weren't counting on being away that long."

"If you truly want to know the truth, that is what you must do."

"It's okay, we'll do it," Tom said quickly. "This man we're meeting," he continued. "Was he the one who shot mom?"

Manuel shook his head slowly. "He will tell you everything. It is not for me to do it." He helped himself to another drink. "What I can assure you of, and this is important, is that these men will not harm you. They have given me their word of your safe passage, and I know they will honor it."

It took over an hour to get a phone connection to Will and Callie. Tom and Clancy explained what they had done thus far, then told of their impending journey.

"You're going to hike into the jungle for a *week*?" Callie exclaimed. "Where are you guys going? Who are you meeting with?" she demanded.

"We don't know," Clancy answered. "We don't know anything, other than Manuel told us this is the only way we can find out what we came down here for."

"It sounds dicey," Will said cautiously.

"Manuel assured us that we won't be harmed," Tom told them. "He's the last person to do anything to put us in harm's way. He was totally devoted to dad. Mom, too."

"I'm still nervous," Callie said. "Are you guys sure you want to go through with this? What if something happens out there, even if it's an accident? If you're walking three days into the middle of some jungle, who knows if—"

"It's going to be okay," Clancy said firmly. "Trust me on this."

"I'm carrying our baby, Clancy," she replied. "This family's already suffered one tragedy. We can't handle any more."

"I know that, Callie. But we don't have a choice. We can't back out of this now. You know that."

"We're going to be okay. Really," Tom said, trying to sound reassuring. "Manuel knows these people well. He vouches for them a hundred percent."

"Well . . ." Callie hesitated. "There's nothing I can do to stop you. Just be careful. Please."

"We will be," Clancy promised her.

They rang off. Clancy turned to Tom. "I hope to God Manuel's being straight with us about all of this."

"Manuel would never set us up," Tom said. "We've got to believe that." He clapped his hands together. "The only way we're going to find out is to go out there and do it."

Dawn broke with the promise of heat and high humidity. Clancy and Tom met Manuel outside the entrance to the hotel. Accompanying him was a rough-edged-looking man in his twenties. The second man was short and squat with pronounced Indian features, even more so than Manuel's.

"This is Oscar," Manuel told them. "*Estos son mis amigos de los Estados Unidos que le hablé,*" he said to Oscar.

"*Buenos días,*" Tom said, extending his hand.

"*Buenos días,*" Oscar replied, smiling self-consciously. Several of his teeth were missing.

"Oscar will be your guide," Manuel explained. "You can trust him as completely as you trust me. He is armed, but don't worry about that. In our country, all men like Oscar carry a weapon. It is like you carrying a comb in yours."

They piled into Manuel's minivan and drove out of the city in the opposite direction from which they had come. In a few minutes, they were in open countryside again. The jungle was even closer to the road than it had been on the ride to the airport, almost right on top of them.

Soon the asphalt topping was gone and the road was dirt again. It felt like they were riding on a washboard. As they dropped down into a low valley, the forest, which had been cut back from the road, came up to the very edge.

"There," Manuel proclaimed, pointing out the windshield.

An eight-foot gash, barely wide enough for a vehicle to drive through, had been hacked into the forest. Manuel turned onto it.

"This is as far as I can take you," he told them. He pointed to a barely perceptible trail that led into the jungle. "This will take you to where you need to go."

The brothers and Oscar got out of the van. Tom and Clancy rubbed on mosquito repellent and sunscreen, shouldered their backpacks, and stretched their legs.

The pack that Oscar pulled on, in contrast to theirs, was almost comically enormous. It sat on his shoulders and back like a huge boulder. The weight of it didn't seem to faze him.

"Oscar is carrying the supplies you will need," Manuel told them. "I will be back here in five days, in case you complete your journey faster than I expect. It will be an extremely formidable journey," he cautioned them. "But I know you will succeed. You are your father's sons."

* * *

They climbed into the mountains, following the narrow trail. The grade was gentle. Oscar led the way, stoically putting one foot after the other. Clancy and Tom followed single-file, taking care not to stray from the path. The low buzz of insects was a constant presence, along with the sounds of their feet trudging along the trail, and their rhythmic breathing.

After half an hour they reached a bend in the trail, and as they came around it they knew that the easy part was over. Ahead of them the dirt scar headed straight up the mountain at a breathtakingly steep slope, the switchbacks climbing the mountain in tightly woven lattices.

Oscar pointed in the direction they were heading. "Very difficult," he said in Spanish. "Very slow."

Tom turned to Clancy, who shook his head. "You don't need to translate that for me," Clancy said. "It's going to be a bitch of a climb."

Oscar pulled a water bottle from his pack and passed it to Tom. "Drink," he said.

Tom uncapped the bottle, then hesitated. "How much water did you bring?" he asked, concerned that they not drink too much too early and run out.

"There is plenty," Oscar assured him. "And higher up, there are streams to drink from. It is important you drink water now, or you will be sick later."

Tom and Clancy drank their fill. Tom extended the bottle to Oscar. Their guide shook his head. "I do not need it as much as you, because I am used to this," he explained.

Within a few minutes, they were sweating freely and breathing heavily. Oscar, in contrast, didn't seem to be having a hard time, in spite of carrying what Tom estimated to be at least sixty pounds of equipment on his back. This guy's a human burro, he marveled, watching the small man move along, one solid step after the other.

Their breathing came harder as they climbed. Rivers of sweat ran down their arms, bodies, legs. Their hearts were pounding like steam pistons in their chests. They could feel the muscles in their thighs turning to cement.

They continued up the mountain for over an hour before the trail leveled out again. Then they collapsed onto their backs, gasping, fighting the impulse to puke.

Oscar squatted nearby, breathing deeply but comfortably. "From here, not so difficult," he told Tom.

"That's a blessing," Tom answered. He translated for Clancy, who acknowledged with a groan. Tom prided himself on being in great shape, but this was beyond any physical undertaking he'd ever attempted. Running a marathon was a piece of cake compared to this.

After a few minutes of rest, Oscar strapped his pack on and motioned for Clancy and Tom to do the same. Tom pulled his pack back on. It felt like he was lugging anvils. He pulled Clancy to his feet and helped him get into his pack straps. After another drink of water, they started off again.

They were in the fullness of the rain forest now, the tree canopy so dense they couldn't see the sun. They were soaked with sweat from head to foot, their clothes black from their own salty water. Gradually, without initially realizing it, they started adapting to their forced march—it became easier. It was still grueling, but they no longer were in the throes of imminent collapse. They started noticing their surroundings, particularly the abundant and varied bird life: they were in an ornithological wonderworld. Oscar knew every bird in the rain forest, calling out each species by name as they came into sight. He identified scarlet macaws and bluewater herons, graceful

Collared aracaris, yellow-chest parrots. They saw extraordinary clusters of toucans, Tocos and Keel Bills and Rainbows as big as crows, their songs ugly, loud, grating, as they flew overhead from tree to tree.

Tom took out his camera. "If I had known we were going to be doing this, I'd have brought a longer lens," he said to Clancy, as he finished shooting a roll of film and started on another. "This is priceless."

"You can always come back."

Tom shook his head. "When this trip is over I don't think I'll ever come back here again. It's beautiful, but there are too many bad memories."

Darkness was falling. They couldn't see the sun but they could tell it was setting from the diminishing strength of the shafts of light that filtered through the thick rain forest canopy.

Tom looked at his watch. It was a few minutes past five o'clock. They had been walking for almost eight hours. He calculated that with the exception of the initial steep climb up the switchbacks, they had been walking at about a twenty-minute-a-mile pace: three miles an hour. By this reckoning, they had already traversed more than twenty miles. And according to what Manuel had told them, they had covered less than half of their journey.

Off to the right, an even smaller path had been hacked into the jungle. Oscar turned off the trail, onto the narrow path.

"Through here," he said over his shoulder. "Not far."

They followed him, pushing aside the dense foliage that whipped across their faces, until they reached a small clearing in which stood a single thatched hut, similar to the ones they had slept in at La Chimenea and other sites, but not as sturdily constructed.

"We will stay here tonight," Oscar informed them.

"Who made this?" Tom asked, looking around. "And why out here?"

"It was built by people who travel through this region," Oscar explained, somewhat cryptically. "Whoever comes by, uses it."

"Whoever comes by?" Tom asked, incredulous. "How many people come by here?"

"Not many. Those that need to. Like us."

There was a low open doorway. No windows. The floor was dirt. Outside, a fire-pit had been dug, ringed with blackened stones. Tom and Clancy ducked down, went into the small, dark hut, and dropped their packs onto the floor.

"All the comforts of home," Clancy observed.

"Beats sleeping outside."

"I'm not complaining. I'm happy to be stopping."

Outside, Oscar gathered some firewood and started a fire in the pit. Tom and Clancy watched him fan the flames until the tinder caught and ignited the dry tree branches and other scraps of wood. When he was satisfied the fire was going, he opened his huge pack and took out an old shotgun. "I will be back shortly," he told them. Within seconds he had disappeared into the jungle.

"What do you think he's doing?" Clancy asked.

"Hell if I know." Tom sat down on a rotting tree trunk. "It doesn't matter. We're at his mercy."

"This is a damn strange situation."

"Strange it is," Tom agreed. "But here we are. Manuel told us we can trust him, and we have to. We're going on blind faith here, Clance."

In the near distance the evening sky exploded with the

sound of a shotgun blast. A moment later, another blast rent the air.

They sprang to their feet as they heard the sound of someone approaching. Oscar, smiling broadly, emerged into the clearing. Over one shoulder he carried his shotgun. On his other he hefted two large birds. The diminutive guide held the birds up.

"Turkey," he proclaimed. "For dinner."

Oscar plucked and cleaned the birds, cut them into pieces, and cooked them over the fire. He had brought potatoes with him, which he also threw into the flames. In a little more than an hour, they were feasting off the fat of the land.

Oscar shook them awake. "We have to go now."

They rolled out of the hammocks Oscar had provided for them, stumbled to their feet, and went out. They had slept soundly, exhausted from the day's heavy hiking and sated with the gamy, tasty birds they had gorged themselves on.

Oscar had bivouacked outside. They had invited him to join them inside the hut, but he had declined. Now he handed them slices of mango. They ate greedily, the juice running down their chins.

They rolled their sleeping bags up and secured their packs. "How much longer before we get to where you're taking us?" Tom asked Oscar, who was stomping out the last embers of the fire.

Oscar held up a forefinger. "Maybe one more day."

"Another day of this?" Clancy asked, sign-reading.

Tom nodded. "Or more."

*   *   *

After four hours of dogged slogging, through humidity so thick they could almost drink it, they came to a dark, muddy-looking river. This was no small stream they could easily ford. It was deep and wide and fast-flowing. Eyeballing it, Tom figured it to be close to fifty yards across. They stood on the bank above the water, looking at the whitecapped torrent as it cascaded by.

"Jesus," Clancy exclaimed. "We're not gonna . . ."

Tom shook his head in agreement with his brother's apprehensive concern. He turned to Oscar. "Are we supposed to *swim* across?" he asked in disbelief.

Oscar looked at him as if he was crazy. "No!" he answered incredulously. "You would drown."

"Then what . . . ?"

Oscar put up a hand that meant "take it easy." He looked across the river, to the other side. Then he formed a megaphone with his hands around his mouth and called out in a Mayan dialect. His voice resounded loud and clear above the cacophonous jungle noises.

A voice called back to them, in the same language. Oscar turned to Clancy and Tom. "They will be here in a few minutes," he announced with a relieved smile.

"Who is *they*?" Tom asked apprehensively.

"My friends who will take you to the man you have come to see."

A small flatbed boat, powered by a noisy outboard motor belching gasoline exhaust fumes in its wake, came toward them from the other side of the river. Two young men were in it—one navigating it, the other standing in the bow, staring at them with a fierce demeanor. Both men were armed to the teeth, full bandoliers draped across their chests and automatic rifles in their hands.

The brothers stared at the oncoming boat with trepidation as it approached. "This does not look good," Clancy murmured.

Tom, although as unnerved as his brother, was determined not to let anything impede them, even the possibility (remote, he hoped, since Manuel, who loved his father like a brother, had set this up) of being kidnapped or killed. "Too late to turn back," he answered, as he kept his eyes locked on their approaching escorts. "We're in the hands of the gods now."

The boat glided to a stop at the edge of the riverbank. The bowman threw Oscar a line. Oscar pulled it tight, securing the boat against the bank. "Get in," he instructed Clancy and Tom.

Tom stepped onto the gunwale and jumped into the center of the boat. Clancy followed. The bowman and the navigator watched them, their black eyes unblinking. Oscar lithely jumped in. He gave the bowman a brief, brotherly hug, nodded to the navigator, who waved to him and smiled. Oscar and the bowman spoke to each other in their Mayan dialect, Oscar gesticulating toward the brothers, the other answering.

Oscar turned to Clancy and Tom. "Sit down," he ordered them.

They sat on a narrow bench in the center of the boat. The navigator turned the boat around, opened the throttle, and steered them toward the far shore.

The bowman jumped onto a dock on the other side of the river that was hidden under a protective canopy of low-hanging branches and tied up the small vessel. Oscar, Clancy, and Tom followed him. The navigator got out last. He took the spark plug out of the engine and slipped it into a shirt pocket. He spoke again to Oscar, pointing to the brothers. Oscar smiled and answered in return, shaking his head as if in bemusement.

"They want to know you aren't going to try to jump them and take their weapons," he explained. "I promised them you would not."

"Tell him not to worry," Tom answered. "That's the last thing we'd do."

Oscar relayed the message to their two bandoliered escorts. The bowman spat a thick stream of dark tobacco juice on the ground in response. He said something in Mayan.

"They don't trust you, even though I have vouched for you," Oscar explained. "They are going to keep a close watch on you."

As if to emphasize what Oscar had just said, both men jacked a round into the chambers of their rifles.

Tom put up a quick cautionary hand. "Tell them not to freak out on us, okay? We're not going to do anything stupid. We just want to find out whatever it is we're supposed to find out, that's all."

"I told them that already," Oscar said. "But still, they don't trust you. They have had too many bad encounters with people like you—people from outside their world who come to plunder and destroy and then leave."

He turned to the armed man again and spoke some more. The two men nodded.

"It will be all right," Oscar said, trying to reassure the brothers. "Follow me and do what I tell you, and you will be safe."

They marched single-file along the trail which meandered farther up the side of the mountain at an easy grade.

One of the armed guards led the parade, then Tom, Oscar, Clancy, with the other guard bringing up the rear. It was mid-morning now, hot again, and steamy. The sweat coming off Tom's and Clancy's bodies turned their shirts black, their hair fell in wet clumps about their faces. Oscar handed them water bottles and they drank greedily. Oscar and the guards did not drink, and they did not sweat.

They could barely see sky or sun through the dense tree canopy, but they could hear the ongoing sounds of the rain forest, the screaming of monkeys, the calls of birds, once in a while a cry that sounded like it came from something big and dangerous. The trail slowly, inexorably led them higher. Finally, after several hours of hard, nonstop hiking, they reached a crest, and the forest suddenly and dramatically gave way to a crystalline-brilliant, almost blinding sky. The lead guard, who had moved up ten yards ahead of Tom, stopped at the top for a moment and looked into the unseen distance. Then he disappeared down the trail. Tom, Oscar, Clancy, and the trail guard scrambled to keep up with him.

The clearing they emerged into was similar to locations they had visited with their parents over the years. About a dozen small huts, the walls made of thin tree limbs interwoven with vines, the roofs tightly thatched, were laid out in a haphazard grid. A couple of larger buildings were bunched in the center. Off to one side there was a corral that held several rawboned horses. Beyond the corral, a large garden was under cultivation, and next to that, a pen that held goats, sheep, and chickens. Various muddy vehicles were scattered about the area.

Surrounding this cleared-out area were dozens of tall mounds, some close to a hundred feet in height. They were covered in shrubbery and scraggly trees, but in a few places there were faint signs of the hand of man: a set of limestone steps in the side of a hill leading from nowhere to nowhere; a plaster floor cut into the side of a mound; what looked like columns reaching tentatively toward the sun.

Several men came into the center of the clearing. Like the boatmen, they were all young, and heavily armed. Some had automatics in holsters in their belts, others brandished rifles, a few bore machine guns. As they came closer they jabbered to one another, mostly in Mayan, some in Spanish, although in a regional dialect too thick for Tom to understand.

"Oscar!" a voice boomed out in Spanish.

A tall, bearded man with strong Indian features strode toward them. A matching pair of black Glock .44 automatics hung loosely from his waist. The man embraced Oscar in a bear hug, lifting his smaller friend off his feet.

"Was it an easy trip?" he asked Oscar.

"Yes, *jefe,*" Oscar said respectfully. "We saw no one. And no one saw us."

The man smiled. "Good work, Oscar." He stared at Tom and Clancy. "These are the men that Manuel sent to me?"

"Yes."

The man turned to the brothers. *"¿Hablan Español?"* he asked brusquely.

Tom nodded. *"Sí."*

"Good," the man replied in Spanish, "because my English is not good." He laughed, a dry ironic cackle. "So it is good you speak *my* language, since you are in *my* country." He smiled, revealing a mouthful of gold teeth. "You can call me Che. I cannot divulge my real name because the government would use my family to get to me, if they knew who I really am. You would not think it from these surroundings, but I am well educated, and my family is one of the most prominent in our country. I've had to leave all that behind, to fight for our freedom."

He gave them a piercing look. "There is a substantial bounty on my head. There are many men—jackals—who would betray me for it, so I have to be careful. Do you understand?"

Tom nodded. "You don't have to worry about us," he told their host. "We're not interested in that." He turned to Clancy. "He's political," he explained. "Calls himself Che, like in Guevara. The government has a bounty on his head. So he's skittish."

Having declared his colors, the man gave Clancy and Tom a squinty-eyed look. "You are the sons of the woman who was killed."

"Yes," Tom answered tightly.

"And you want to know why."

"Yes," Tom said. "And by whom."

Che nodded gravely. "I will tell you those things," he declared. "Every son deserves to know how his mother died. And why."

Before getting down to business, Che took Tom and Clancy on a tour of the area. Several of his men followed closely, their hands at the ready on the stocks and barrels of their rifles and shotguns.

"We are self-sufficient," Che boasted, showing off the garden and the animals. Pointing to the livestock in the corral and the vehicles, he said, "There are roads we use that connect us to neighboring countries that are more friendly to our cause. Only we know where they lead—they are heavily camouflaged. We cannot allow anyone outside of our cadre to know where they are, which is why you had to walk in and why you will have to walk out."

Clancy pointed to one of the nearby mounds that had been cleared away just enough to reveal that there had once been a structure underneath the dirt and trees. "Ask him what that is," he told Tom. "This must've been a city. All these mounds are covering up structures, from the looks of them."

Tom relayed the request to Che, who nodded. "Your brother is right," he said. "This was a prominent city. Not as grand as Tikal or El Mirador, but significant."

"Was it ever excavated more than this?" Tom asked.

Che shook his head. "No. This is all that was done, several years ago. We are a poor nation. We have to spend our money in feeding our people and building schools and factories. We do not have time to dwell in the past, because the present is too harsh."

He scooped up a handful of dry dirt, let it sift back to the ground between his fingers.

"Those few sites that are restored, it is only because foreign teams come in to do it, like your father's." He waved an arm, taking in the vista. "Most are deep in the jungles, like this one. It is impossible to guard them, so there is looting and plundering. If a site cannot be guarded, and the artifacts from them kept from looters, it is better not to open them at all." His face flushed in anger. "When the tomb raiders come, they steal the heart and they leave the skeleton. Which is what happened at La Chimenea." He paused. "Except there, the tomb raiders were the government. And the archaeologists themselves."

* * *

They sat at a battered wooden table in the structure which was the headquarters for Che's operation—Che on one side of the table, Clancy and Tom on the other, opposite him. The other men, including Oscar, stood outside, looking in through the small screenless windows.

The air inside the hut was still, fetid. These guys bathe once a week at best, Tom thought, as Che's rancid B.O. drifted across the table into his nostrils. Clancy, too, could smell their host's funkiness—he kept running his hand across his nose and mouth, as if using it for a filter.

Che cleaned his fingernails with the tip of a large Bowie knife, then ran a pinkie finger around the inside of his mouth as a toothbrush. Finished with his casual toilet, he laid the knife on the table and leaned forward toward Clancy and Tom, his large, rough hands splayed out in front of him.

"We are at war in our country between those who stand shoulder to shoulder with the people and the corrupt regimes that suppress them. This is no secret. All the world knows it. It is a conflict that has been fought for many, many years. But no one wants to put a halt to it, except the people who are suffering because of this unjust war: the original people, the children of the great Maya empire."

He spread his arm in an expansive gesture, taking in his men and the ancient ruin. "We are of Maya descent. Most of us, like me, are not pure. We are mongrels, bastards created from centuries of cross-breeding by subjugation. But in our hearts we are Indian, not Spanish."

He stared at them sharply, to make sure they were listening carefully. "The current regime is particularly harsh. They are determined to crush our revolution. They will go to any means they think is necessary—murder, false imprisonment, torture. They do this with the knowledge of the rich nations like yours, who look the other way. You know this, I'm sure."

He paused for Tom to translate his remarks to Clancy. When Tom was finished, Che spoke again.

"But our subjugation is not enough for these jackals. They also turn a blind eye to the stealing of our priceless heritage, our monuments and the symbols of our former greatness. Not only because they are venal, or corrupt, or weak. But also, too often, because they are accomplices."

He slammed his open palm down hard on the table. "In this small area, like so many others, all of the important artifacts have been spirited away. You want to see the remains of our great civilization? You won't find them here. You will have to go to the British Museum, the Metropolitan Museum, so many places in your country and Europe, even in Japan." He shook his head sadly. "There you will see the monuments to our greatness."

After pausing to wait for Tom to translate this diatribe to Clancy, Che continued. "These thefts are terrible. But it is not only the *guaqueros*, or the *chicleros*. They, at least, are our countrymen, as poor and desperate as we are. It is the *outsiders* who steal who are the most offensive to me and to my people—*because they have no right!* They come like pirates. They plunder, and then they leave."

He banged his fist on the table again. "With the cooperation of our government they do this. Who turn a blind eye to this plundering." He grimaced. "You met with the Minister of Archaeology and Culture?"

Tom nodded.

"He told you there had been looting at La Chimenea?"

Tom nodded again. "Yes."

"And from the time your father stopped being there it stopped?"

Another yes. This one difficult to acknowledge.

"This minister," Che continued. "Did he also tell you it was he who removed the military escort that was to guard your father's party on their perilous way from La Chimenea to the airport? So that they had to travel without armed support?"

"We knew about that," Tom answered carefully. "But how did you?"

"We have informers everywhere," Che responded. "We have to, for our survival." He picked his knife up from the table and twirled it between his fingers, a bit of bravado to indicate to them that he considered the sharp weapon no more dangerous to his health than a letter opener.

"This minister is a scurvy dog," he proclaimed disdainfully. "He works both sides of the street, and shits on both sides of the street as well. For years he had been taking bribes to permit our precious heritage to be stolen and taken out of the country. But then, shortly before your mother was killed, he realized the noose was closing around his neck, because one of the workers at La Chimenea discovered what was going on. He was going to report the thievery to one of the handful of men in our government who has not been corrupted. The Minister of Archaeology and Culture was afraid his involvement would be uncovered. He had to put distance between the looters and himself, for his self-preservation, even if it meant betraying his accomplices."

He twirled the knife between his fingers again, like a magician playing with a coin. "Through an emissary, he sent his informant to me. He knew that I would do what he could not: stop the thefts, by whatever means were necessary. This is why the troops were removed. So that my men and I would not encounter resistance." He spat a stream of tobacco juice onto the floor. "Protecting their own hides is all our government officials care about, because they are vermin. And they are cowards. They come to men like me when there is dirty work to be done, because they want to keep their own hands clean."

He waited for Tom to relay this burst of information to Clancy, then continued.

"I spoke for a long time with the informant, to be certain he was telling the truth. And I insisted that he accompany us when we set out to stop your father's party from leaving the country with the stolen artifacts, to make sure we weren't being set up. Because once I knew, beyond a shadow of doubt . . ." He paused. "*Beyond a shadow of a doubt*," he repeated, his voice rising, "that there had been looting at La Chimenea, I had no choice. I am Maya—I had to take a stand."

With a sudden, violent motion, he stabbed the knife into the table. "We had to show these thieves that we are men!" he shouted impassionedly. "That we are not scurvy dogs who run away with our tails between our legs! That we will not allow our culture and our heritage to be stolen, to be bought and sold like pigs or cattle!"

His voice dropped back to a matter-of-fact conversational level. "I shot your mother," he said.

Both brothers gasped.

"It was not me directly," Che told them quickly. "It was the man who had come to me with the information." He scowled. "He was a coward. But I take responsibility, because I was in charge."

In meticulous detail, Che told them everything that had transpired up to the moment of their mother being killed. Then, he continued, after they had ridden away with the trunk of stolen artifacts and other personal valuables in tow, he and the turncoat archaeologist had gotten into a terrible fight. He knew the man had fired at Walt deliberately and he was enraged, because he hadn't wanted a killing unless it was necessary, which hadn't been the case. Now it was going to be much harder to rally sentiment to his side, because both his government and the American government, the power that held all the cards, would condemn them as one more group of bloodthirsty bandits, rather than men with a true political and revolutionary cause.

They had returned the artifacts to the tomb from which they had been stolen, and sealed it back up. It had been almost a year and a half now, and he was sure that no one had gone back to steal them again. There were no archaeologists working there anymore, he informed them. Without Walt's involvement the money had dried up, and the government had been forced to abandon it. The site was rapidly returning to its natural state. In a few years, no one, except the handful of people who had been there, would know it had ever existed.

After the artifacts had been replaced, he had confronted Jocelyn's killer. The argument had ended badly—the man had gone against his orders, which he couldn't permit. If his people thought, even for a moment, that he was soft, he would lose control.

He had been forced to kill the man. It was that or lose face with his own people. He had shot him in cold blood, in the same manner that the man had shot Jocelyn. So there had been some rough justice for her murder, even though it was hollow.

The final irony was that until several days later, Che hadn't known that the archaeologist's wife, rather than the archaeologist himself, had been the one to take the fatal bullet.

When the rebel leader was finished telling his story, the sun had fallen low in the sky to the west. Clancy and Tom were exhausted, less from the rigors of their journey into the jungle than from the emotional battering they had just undergone.

"Sometimes it is better not to learn certain things," Che said somberly, observing their distress. "But you had to find out the truth for yourselves. I can understand that." He extended a hand to them, not to be shaken, but as a gesture of conciliation. "I am sorry your mother was killed. But if the rape of our national heritage had not happened, she would still be alive."

Los Angeles

♦ ♦ ♦

Will met his brothers at the Los Angeles airport. They had flown all night, with two plane changes and hours of tedium between connections. Although they were exhausted, both physically and emotionally, having hiked out of the jungle nonstop without pausing to rest, driven across the country to the airport, and been in the air or in airports breathing stale, artificial air for another fourteen hours, the two of them immediately piled into Will's rental car and drove to Walt's house.

Clancy and Tom had filled Will in briefly the night before over the phone from Atlanta, their port of reentry into the U.S. Now, as they crawled up the gridlocked I-405 freeway and then turned off onto the surface streets, they related to Will, in detail, what Che, the rebel leader, had told them. And for Will, as it had been for them, hearing what had happened, and why, was a sobering and heartbreaking recitation.

Walt's street was lifeless. No cars moving, no pedestrians walking on the sidewalks: a quiet, upscale street where people mind their own business and keep their dirty secrets to themselves. Will, who was driving, slowed to a stop and parked across the street from their father's house.

The driveway was empty, the garage door closed. There was no sign of life outside the house: no newspapers on the front walk, no sprinklers watering the lawn. They got out of the car and crossed the street.

"What if he isn't home?" Will asked nervously.

"We'll wait," Tom said flatly. "We're not going home until we confront him."

They stood in front of the door, looking at each other in nervous anticipation. Almost as if girding to mount a commando raid, Clancy squared his shoulders and rang the doorbell.

A few moments passed. It seemed to them like time was running in slow motion. Then they heard a lock being turned, and the door swung open. Their father blinked against the onslaught of sunlight in his eyes.

"Hello, boys," he greeted them in a weary voice. "I was expecting you, but not this soon."

"Why were you expecting us at all?" Clancy asked.

"Manuel called. He told me you'd been down there nosing around. He knew you'd be coming to see me. He wanted to prepare me." He stood aside. "Come on in."

The house was dark. The shades were drawn, no lights on. Walt led them into the living room. "You want something to drink, or eat?" he asked. His voice was hoarse, soft, as if rusty from disuse. "There isn't much to offer, I haven't been to the store for a while."

Clancy shook his head. "Is Diane here?" he asked, looking around.

Walt shook his head. "She's gone," he said flatly. "Flown the coop."

"For good?" Clancy asked.

Walt nodded. "It wasn't a question of if with her, but when. She's a survivor, Diane. More than I can say about myself." He ran a hand through his hair. "Sit down, boys," he said, slumping onto one of the sofas. "I don't know how much you found out down there. But since you know some of it, you have to know all of it." He shook his head regretfully. "It would've been a hell of a lot better if you had never opened this Pandora's box. But you have, and none of us can keep burying our heads in the sand about what happened down there anymore."

He paused. His three sons were sitting opposite him in the dark living room. They were motionless, waiting.

"This is going to take a lot of time, because I don't want to leave anything out," Walt told them. "Do you want a break before I start?"

"Just tell it, dad," Clancy said, speaking for all of them. "As long as it takes. That's why we're here."

"Okay," Walt said. He paused for a moment. "It was all a ruse, boys, what happened that night. Stealing our valuables, threatening to take hostages. I'm not saying those men wouldn't have done those things, maybe even killed more of us—but those actions were a fake-out to disguise their real purpose, which was to get into my trunk, which their informant had told them contained priceless artifacts that had been stolen from the site, supposedly by me. And they got what they came for. They found the trunk, and the artifacts that were inside.

"But I wasn't the one who stole them. I've done some bad things and some dumb things in my time. I've said it before and I'll say it again—I'm no saint, boys. Which you know. But the one thing I would never do is what they've accused me of: stealing artifacts, in this case from La Chimenea, or from any site. I couldn't—it would violate every core belief I stand for."

* * *

From the moment he first set foot on the newly discovered site, he knew it was an unbelievable find. The government, so friendly and welcoming then, didn't have the resources to develop it themselves, not the way it would have to be done if it were to be recognized as a world-class monument on the level of Copán, Tikal, Chichén Itzá, Palenque. They needed an important archaeologist with access to foundation funds to spearhead the excavation. Walt Gaines was one of a handful of such luminaries who had both the reputation and the connections, and he was the most important one who wasn't currently involved with a project of this magnitude.

He came, he saw, he fell in love. The potential for greatness! And for glory.

He struck a deal with the government: he would raise the money for the beginning phases of the restoration of La Chimenea, and in return he'd be given the exclusive franchise to develop it. He would provide the expertise, select the groups of volunteers, and train them to do the work. And most important, he would make the critical decisions. Except for the regulations of official government and international policy, he would have final say.

It was the score of a lifetime, the one he had been waiting and hoping for his entire career.

The initial funding package didn't take long to put together. This was an extraordinary opportunity for his university, as well as for major institutional nonprofits with deep pockets. In less than a year he had raised enough money to get started.

The first obstacle to be overcome was providing decent access to the site for the substantial amounts of people, equipment, and supplies that would be needed to do the work. The only way in was an arduous three-day trek through the jungle, which is how he had gotten there that first time. He was opposed to putting in an airstrip, as had been done in other remote locations. Too much of the surrounding jungle would have to be clear-cut to make room for even a basic runway. He also was afraid that poachers would use a strip to fly their own planes in and out. And large numbers of volunteers and equipment couldn't be flown in; that would be prohibitively expensive.

A road was the most feasible—really the only—solution. It would be virtually impassable at certain times during the rainy season, but it would do the job, and it would be relatively easy to guard—a few men could throw up a roadblock and deny access in or out.

It took over a year of backbreaking labor to cut the road through the jungle. As soon as it was completed, Walt led the first team of workers into the site. The university had granted him a leave of absence for the spring semester, so he was able to be there for five uninterrupted months.

The work had gone better and faster than he could have hoped for. By the end of the summer they had begun excavating a section of the main temple, as well as parts of other buildings in the Central Plaza. Jocelyn had joined him in June, after she finished her own teaching workload, and had jumped right in. She had assumed the critical responsibility of cataloguing the large quantities of artifacts they discovered—the place was a treasure trove of antiquities.

Shortly before it was time to leave the site and return to the States, they discovered that a small number of artifacts were missing. It was almost certain that looting had occurred, rather than the objects having been misplaced—Jocelyn had been extremely careful in her cataloguing. Only a handful were unaccounted for; but to have lost even a few was upsetting.

Walt was faced with a dilemma: whether or not to inform the government. After discussing the problem with Jocelyn, who was the only person besides him who knew about the thefts, they decided to keep quiet about it.

As he assumed the looting had been the work of *guaqueros*—tomb raiders—Walt rationalized keeping the looting a secret by taking steps to insure it wouldn't happen again. He strengthened the guards at the site to keep the tomb raiders out, leaving Manuel in charge while he was gone. He felt guilty about not telling the authorities about the looting, but he knew that thefts of antiquities are an unfortunate fact of life at the beginning of a newly discovered site's development. And he was resolute that the thievery would be a one-time occurrence. Starting with the next trip to the site, he would sternly warn everyone who was going to work there, before they were permitted to enter the area, that anyone caught stealing anything, even the smallest fragments of a pot, would be turned over to the government for prosecution, without exception.

This was no idle threat. It was common knowledge how the government treated tomb raiders: brutally. With these stringent measures in place, Walt convinced himself he had resolved the issue.

The first unsettling shift in the government's attitude started with a small, ugly incident. His in-country archaeologist (a requirement on all modern excavations), a man he had worked comfortably with before, got sick and had to be replaced. The new native archaeologist (that was a generous description; the man had no academic credentials and barely more experience than most of Walt's students) who was assigned to the site as a representative of the Minister of Archaeology and Culture's office almost immediately got a hair up his scrawny ass, claiming that too many outside volunteers and not enough native ones were working on the excavation. He insisted that Walt bring in more native "volunteers," who would be paid, of course, from Walt's budget.

Walt resisted; with restraint at first, then with impatient anger. He was already using all the local volunteers who were qualified. He was happy to use native workers, but they had to meet his standards—that was his agreement, he was in charge of selecting who worked on the site. What he didn't tell the local guy was his fear of more tomb-robbing. As he hadn't divulged the prior incident, he couldn't very well come out with that now. And if he brought in more native workers, he'd have to release some of his American volunteers.

He tried to reason with the man, promising he'd look into it the next time, etc., but the other was steadfast. This was his country, he stated with the out-thrust chest of a bantam cock, Walt was a guest, he had to bring in more local workers.

Walt blew. He couldn't help himself, the guy was an asshole, pure and simple. He pulled rank, kicked the local archaeologist off the site, and harshly warned him not to set foot on it again.

A week later he was in the minister's office, being dressed down royally. Of course they were very grateful for what he was doing, but it still was their country, the minister reminded Walt. Professor Gaines had to respect the citizens of the country, particularly the professionals (Walt almost gagged when he heard that title applied to the little prick he'd had the fight with) who the government assigned. Even though he was in charge, he didn't have absolute carte blanche. If Professor

Gaines remained obdurate, the minister warned Walt, the government might have to make some basic changes in the management of the dig.

That threat was as subtle as a two-by-four right between the eyes. Walt was being warned that he could be kicked out, or at least have the control taken away from him.

He wanted to tell the minister to shove it up his ass, but he held his tongue. He agreed to employ a few more native workers, and to allow the dismissed local archaeologist to return to work at the site. He and the minister parted company under amicable (on the surface) terms. This was a problem for both of them, and they would solve it jointly, and cooperatively, as they did with everything else. La Chimenea was bigger than either of them, they both agreed on that.

He expressed his anger over a few drinks with Jocelyn, who had accompanied him to the capital. They had used him, he groused. Now that they had his money and expertise, they were threatening to pull the rug out from under him.

With the aid of a few beers and shots of tequila, Jocelyn calmed him down. This was all about machismo. The government needed him as much or more than he needed them. Keep your eye on the big picture, she reminded him.

The new workers started the following week. They weren't as good as his own people, but they were diligent and eager to learn.

A week before he and Jocelyn were ready to go home, something incredible happened that took his mind off that petty problem. One afternoon, when lunch was over and the others were taking a midday siesta, they went off together, ostensibly to check on one of the unexplored mounds at the far edge of the site, in an area far removed from where any work was being done. What they really wanted was a few hours to themselves, because they had no privacy in the camp.

After they made love they casually looked about the mound, which was covered with a thousand years of growth. Their poking around was nothing more than idle curiosity—this area would not be developed for years. But as they looked more closely, Walt's practiced eye noticed what looked like an entrance to a hidden vault. Pushing aside the dirt and boulders, they started in.

After several minutes of slow crawling on their hands and knees, Walt shining his flashlight to illuminate their way, they emerged into a large chamber. Once Walt got his bearings, he realized they were in the burial tomb of a king or a high-ranking member of a royal family. The skeleton was mummified but amazingly intact, and surrounding it was the most extraordinary assortment of jewelry, pottery, and other important artifacts he had ever seen outside of a museum. There were several intricately carved jade statues, many embossed with gold and other precious metals and stones. Along with them was pottery and stela that would explain who these people were and what they had done.

My God, Jocelyn had exclaimed.

My God, indeed. The artifacts in this tomb were priceless, because there was no way to put a true value on them. If there was one—if this was pre-1983, and artifacts could be removed and sold to collectors or museums—he would estimate the value of what was in here to be in the millions. But that was beside the point, because they weren't going anywhere. They would be preserved, studied here at the site, and then eventually removed to a proper museum, here in their country of origin.

He knew he should declare the find immediately and safeguard it with armed guards, around the clock. But they had to leave in a few days. The rainy season was upon them, he simply didn't have time to put all that together. And he was worried about leaving these treasures here, even under heavy native guard. There had already been the other thefts. If tomb raiders wanted these treasures badly enough, they would find a way to steal them.

He and Jocelyn covered up the entrance, and told no one. Walt vowed to himself that he would do everything by the book the next time he came down, when he would have time to move the priceless antiquities to a safe repository.

A week before Walt and Jocelyn were about to embark on their next trip another element was tossed into the equation that caused him to rethink his plan.

National Geographic, one of his principal sponsors, informed him that they wanted to do a major article about La Chimenea and combine it with a TV special. Showing this treasure trove on film, as if it were a spontaneous discovery, would be an incredible event. But there was a logistical problem. National Geographic couldn't get their end of the project together until later in the year. The filming would have to be done over Christmas break, and the article and television special would come out the following spring.

After agonizing over what to do, he decided to keep his discovery a secret. This was too important, both to his career personally and to the project, not to maximize the opportunities for publicity. What difference would it make, he rationalized, if the hidden treasures came to light now or in a few more months? The site was fifteen hundred years old. Four months is an eye-blink in the continuum of such time.

As soon as he arrived back at La Chimenea, Walt snuck away to the secret location. From the outside, it was as he had left it. He cleared away the entrance and crawled deep into the tomb, his heart pounding like a hummingbird's. Finally, he reached the burial chamber, and shone his flashlight into the center of the enclosure.

The burial tomb was intact.

He collapsed onto the cold floor in relief; he realized that he had been fighting off an ulcer for months, worried that the site might have been discovered and looted. He had committed one of the most fundamental sins of his profession, even before the National Geographic situation further clouded his ethics. Not having had time to properly secure the treasures before leaving, he had rationalized that they might have been stolen had he reported their existence prematurely. But that was solipsistic buck-passing and he knew it. He had fallen into a pernicious trap—that he alone knew what was best for the preservation of the site.

It was all about his ego, the worst part of him. But he had pulled it off, and knowing he could, he was less anxious about doing it for a few more months.

One more time. He had to see the treasures in the buried tomb one last time before they left. He hadn't been inside the hidden space for the past couple of weeks; he didn't want to chance anyone seeing him. But he felt it was safe to go there now. He had a couple of hours yet—at the latest, it was three in the morning. No one, not even

Manuel, would be up until five; there was no need to be. Everything was already packed up and ready to go.

Why had Diane come on to him? He flattered himself that it was simple attraction—he was almost twice her age, but he was still more of a man than anyone else here. And he was the leader, the biggest star in this constellation. Was that it, or did she have another motive? He hadn't thrown off any vibes that he was looking for outside action. Or had he, subconsciously?

Whether he had or not, it didn't matter. He had betrayed his wife with another woman, and he'd have to live with the guilt. He was human, and she had caught him unawares. A lame rationalization, he knew.

He hadn't cheated on Jocelyn in a long time. He didn't plan on doing it again. He was too old to have the kind of occasional affairs he'd had when he was younger.

The entrance to the tomb was open.

This can't be, he screamed silently. Then he was scrambling inside on all fours, eating dirt in his frantic haste to get to the inner sanctum.

The tomb had been stripped bare. Only the mummified remains were left. All the artifacts—the precious jewelry, pottery, statues, and figurines—all gone. Someone had found this tomb, and had robbed it.

He crawled back out and sat at the mouth of the entrance, rocking like a crazed parent who has just found out his child had died in some horrible, completely unexpected accident. Which was how he felt. He had lost something of immeasurable value, a piece of his soul.

Greed, ego, hubris. He had succumbed to them, and they had risen up and slain him. He had deluded himself into believing he was a god, above the rules of men. He didn't have to play by their rules, he made his own.

Well, he was a man, as mortal as any. This proved it.

Who had done this? he thought. Who would have found it? It was far removed from any area they had been working on. He couldn't fathom, in the furthest stretch of his imagination, that the looter came from his people. If someone from his team of volunteers had stumbled on this they would have come to him immediately. But security had been so tight. How had a thief from the outside come in and taken all that stuff without being noticed?

With a heavy, fearful heart, he covered the entrance up and returned to camp, where the others lay in blissful, ignorant sleep.

"That's why I was so upset that morning we were to leave, when the alternator didn't work," Walt told his sons, taking a break from his merciless narrative. "Not only because of the physical danger to us, which was very real, as it too horribly turned out, but because I had betrayed a sacred trust and had it blown up in my face. What I should have realized, but I was too screwed up to think clearly at that point, was that the events were directly linked: the looting of that hidden burial ground, and the delay. I didn't make the connection. Going back to the troops being pulled, too. I didn't connect that to the theft of the artifacts, either. Because I was sure no one else except your mother and I knew of their existence, until the moment before she was killed.

"I had been wrong all along. And my misconception cost your mother her life. I found all that out, and why, when I got home."

After Jocelyn's funeral was over and the boys had left Madison, Walt began the painful process of tying up Jocelyn's affairs. She had been the keeper of their finances—he didn't even know how much money they had

or how it was invested, except in a vague, general way. He knew they owned their house free and clear, that they were well vested in their pension plans, and that they owned a few conservative stocks. Now he was going to have to get into the specifics, and figure out what changes would transpire because he was suddenly a widower. Among other things, he needed to know if she had left a will. She had a small amount of money of her own, which had been left to her by her parents. He knew that he was in good shape financially, but perhaps there was money that was earmarked to go to their sons, or to charitable causes.

He was still in incredible pain over what had happened down there. His wife had been murdered by the disgruntled local archaeologist who had raided the tomb. The man had then planted the artifacts in Walt's case, to make it appear as if Walt had done it. Walt knew those things with certainty—in hindsight, it all fit. When he returned—and he was going to return as soon as he could—he would go to the highest level of the government, the President if necessary, and demand that they take action. But first he had to take care of his wife's affairs.

The deed to the house, as well as other important financial documents, were in a safe-deposit box Jocelyn kept at their bank. Two days after he buried his wife of thirty years he mustered the courage to go down to the bank and open the box. He took everything home and read through it all, over and over, because he couldn't believe what he was seeing. When, late at night and several fortfying bourbons later, he finally figured out what had happened, it was an emotional blow that was almost as devastating as her killing had been.

They didn't own their house anymore—the bank did. Their pension plans were almost empty. All they owned were a bunch of virtually worthless stocks. Except for their salaries, they were broke. They had worked hard all their lives, and had nothing to show for it.

Walt was able to piece together how this catastrophe had happened by the order in which the various incriminating documents were dated, from the oldest to the most recent. Many of the documents detailed investments Jocelyn had been making over the past few years, most of them in tech stocks. In almost every instance, the value of the investments had gone up at first, some of them dramatically, but then, after the market crashed in 2000, they had plummeted. The figures on the pages informed him, in chilling black and white, that their net worth was less than a quarter of what it had been five years before. Even worse, the remortgages they had been taking on the house, which he had thought were going into their 401(k)s and other conservative investments, had been used to buy more exotic stocks, and then, when the prices fell, to cover the losses. And it wasn't only the remortgage money; she had also been borrowing against their pension plans, the rock of their retirement.

After he read the documents over more carefully, he almost threw up. They had gone from owning their house outright to having assumed a huge mortgage, their pension plans had been shrunk dramatically, and most of these stocks they held, which he'd never known about, had either tanked or in some cases were completely worthless.

He had never paid attention to their financial affairs. Jocelyn gave him papers to sign and he signed them, often without even bothering to ask her what they were for. She was the practical partner, making sure their health insurance was accurate and up-to-date, that the university was making the proper contributions to their pension plans, that the money from his speaking engagements and book contracts didn't lag.

Now he learned that she had been playing the market like all those other suckers who thought it would never go down. She had been doing a lot of day-trading, small purchases of hot stocks she read about on the Internet, a few hundred dollars at a time. It must have been exciting, like going to Las Vegas. Except she was beating the house, every roll of the dice, every hand of blackjack. Everything she bought doubled, tripled, in some cases went up ten, twenty, fifty times in value in a month or two. It was so easy—she couldn't lose, she had the touch.

She started plunging more heavily. She opened an account with the brokerage house in Milwaukee and hooked up with a young broker who was killing the market for those of his clients who had the guts and foresight not to be mired in the old clichés about whether a company was making a profit or showed the right value ratios, like Amazon, which had been in the red every month of its existence but kept going up, whose CEO had been named Time magazine's Man of the Year. Amazon was actually one of her more conservative buys. She had invested in all kinds of wild offerings.

And for two years, she had ridden an endless wave. Up, up, and up. Until the bubble burst.

The losses began accumulating slowly at first, then faster, then it was a tsunami. She couldn't keep up with the downward spiral. And she couldn't get out, because she had already lost too much. So she stayed in the game, trying to get back to where she had been. But she didn't. They had made a lot of money, but when the market went south, she, like millions of other holy fools, lost it. That's why she had been remortgaging the house, borrowing against their pension plans, insanely throwing good money after bad.

As bad as all that was, it wasn't the worst of their calamities. A year before she was killed she had taken out a short-term loan of a quarter-million dollars, to buy time until the market went up again. She had falsified the loan papers, putting up assets they no longer owned, as collateral. She knew it was crazy but she couldn't help herself, she had to try anything she could think of. But the market didn't go up, and the balloon payment on the loan was due at the end of the year. If she didn't pay it, the bank would find out about the fraud and go to the authorities.

At this point, Diane Montrose came into the picture. Diane had a reputation in the art world as someone who was willing to bend the rules if the payoff was high enough and the risks were acceptable. Jocelyn had found out about her, explained her desperate situation, and they made a deal, a real pact with the devil. Diane would help Jocelyn smuggle artifacts from La Chimenea out of the country and find a buyer for them. Jocelyn's share of their profits would cover the pressing shortfalls of her disastrous financial forays. She and Walt would still be in lousy shape compared to where they had been before she had decided she could beat the house, but at least in their old age they wouldn't be living in a room over one of their sons' garages.

There were numerous components to Jocelyn and Diane's plan, and they all had to come off with clockwork precision. Diane had insisted that she come on the trip, both to verify the artifacts to her satisfaction and, more importantly, because Jocelyn would need her expertise in getting the pieces out of the country and into the U.S.—she had done this before, she knew how to get around customs agents. The problem, of course, was that the trip was already filled. Jocelyn had solved that by e-mailing the O'Malley girl with the lie that the trip was oversubscribed, then sending the fake e-mail under the girl's name so Walt would think the girl was pulling out. On the heels of that came Diane's prearranged e-mail, and giving her the suddenly vacant slot seemed perfectly natural.

The tomb-raiding was the easiest part, although it was certainly nerve-wracking. Jocelyn was able to pull it off because it was so brazen no one would ever expect it. And she thought she was vigilant about not being followed. She had worked slowly and carefully, taking a few pieces at a time, always thoroughly covering the entrance to the tomb back up, making sure no one knew it was there.

Jocelyn believed she had finessed the problem—badly, but successfully. But there was one piece of grit in the machinery of this audacious scam that she didn't know about: someone had been spying on her. Despite her precautions, someone had seen her take the artifacts out of the tomb.

Her secret spy was the local archaeologist Walt had tried to kick off the site the year before. Walt had been forced to take the man back, and with great reluctance, he had—but theirs had been an uneasy truce. Walt had frozen his adversary out whenever he could, which made a bad relationship turn even more sour.

The stringent security measures that Walt had instituted against looting had brought about Jocelyn's downfall. Like Walt, she would go off by herself in the evening, after the day's work was done and everyone else was relaxing. No one questioned where she was going—she was Walt Gaines's wife. No one, that is, except Walt's disgruntled foe, who had started tailing both of them almost from the day they arrived. He had seen Jocelyn go in and come out of the hidden, secret tomb, and he had seen her emerge with the artifacts that she had stolen and carried back to the camp. She had kept them with her own stuff until the last night after everything was packed up and she could hide them deep within Walt's equipment, the last place anyone would ever look for stolen contraband.

But he had made one critical miscalculation. He had assumed that Jocelyn was stealing the artifacts on Walt's behalf and on his orders—that Walt, not she, was the mastermind behind the thefts. The man was the product of a macho culture, where the woman did the man's bidding without questioning why. And more importantly, he hated Walt. He was eager to pin this on Walt, the man who had humiliated him, rather than on his wife, a nice lady who treated him decently.

He had notified the minister of the thefts of the antiquities, laying the blame on Walt rather than Jocelyn, and the two had concocted their devious plot. The minister was afraid to confront Walt directly. Walt was too powerful, he had too many important friends all over the archaeological spectrum, and he was well thought of in the country, for the potential of La Chimenea, which he had supported with outside money. Besides, until Walt took the artifacts from the site and out of the country, he technically hadn't stolen them. He could claim he had removed them to examine them more closely, or for one of several other legitimate reasons. But if the informer was wrong (this was the minister's private fear, which he didn't share with his co-conspirator)—if Walt didn't have the artifacts in his possession, if this local archaeologist was trying to set him up to settle that old grudge—they would all look ridiculous.

The minister acted through omission rather than commission. He pulled the troops who were intended to guard Walt and his party through the dangerous jungle back to the airport. And then, through the contacts by which he accomplished many of his illegitimate affairs, he got word to the rebel force that the party of Americans would be traveling without military protection. He knew that for years, Che's and other rebel organizations had been thirsting for an opportunity to make a political statement against the outside forces from the United States who were doing what their own country should have been doing but couldn't, because they were too poor and too weak. Here was a chance—small in the actual nature of it but huge psychologically and emotionally—to kick sand in their faces.

So a plan was hastily formed and put to work. The local archaeologist sabotaged the alternator on the van, and Che's people blocked the road, which guaranteed there was no chance of Walt's party getting out of the jungle before dark. The rainstorm helped, too, one of those unlucky strokes that inevitably happen when the only luck to be had is bad.

Regardless of all those setbacks, Jocelyn and Diane knew that they had to get out of the country that night, because the customs fix, both in-country and in the States, had already been arranged. If they delayed, they might not have cleared customs. That was why both she and Diane were so insistent that they not turn back.

The minister had hoped there wouldn't be bloodshed. A murder was not in his country's best interests. The negative publicity and scrutiny from outside the country would be intense and counterproductive, particularly with a conservative administration in Washington. What he wanted was to be able to show the world how they were being ripped off, so they could shine a strong light on a concern that all fair-minded people would hearken to, and in the bargain, make himself look good.

When you make a deal with forces you don't control, though, you can't tell them how to act, or what not to do. The killing had not been accidental. But the victim had been. The shooter had wanted to kill someone, but Jocelyn Gaines was not the intended target. Except it was dark, and she was next to her husband, and the shot missed. The bullet that killed her was meant for Walt, who had never known the artifacts had been stolen and hidden in his equipment, until the very moment they were revealed on a dark, rainy night in the middle of the jungle.

This incredible barrage of information hit Walt like a bombshell. The turncoat archaeologist hadn't been the outlaw, after all. The culture thief had been his wife.

The night after the funeral, before she was scheduled to go back to New York, he sat Diane down and forced her to tell him what she knew. They had already started to grow close—Diane had been instrumental in cutting through the red tape to get Jocelyn's body out of the country, and she had been steadfastly at his side during the ordeal of planning for the funeral, and getting through it.

Diane's recitation of her part in the attempted thefts was sad and painful. She explained how Jocelyn had gotten in touch with her and had pleaded with her to help pull this off. She had been reluctant to get involved because of the risks they would be taking, but Jocelyn had refused to take no for an answer.

Jocelyn's compelling argument, which finally tilted the scales for Diane, was one of love and redemption. She had financially ruined the proud man who was the father of her children, and she had to make things straight with him. For him. She knew her scheme was horribly wrong, that it violated Walt's core beliefs, but given the horrible circumstances and time constraints, she believed she had

no other options. She didn't want Walt to have to live an impoverished life as an old man, particularly since the mess she'd made had been solely her creation. And she was afraid that he'd be so angry, hurt, and distrustful of her that he would leave her. That was the one thing she couldn't bear.

Besides her fervent emotional pleading, what had made Jocelyn's plan acceptable for Diane was that if they pulled it off, no one would ever know. Walt would discover that the tomb had been robbed, but he would assume it was local thieves. He would carry the guilt of having hidden it with him, but he would survive that. He would still make La Chimenea into one of the greatest archaeological sites in Central America. She would reimburse their pension plans, pay off the mortgage to their house, and in a few years they'd begin the long, happy journey into their old age.

She had sent Diane out that last night as a diversion. She had to make sure she had time to hide the artifacts in his trunk.

"Your mother needed to keep me occupied and away from the camp long enough for her to conceal what they had stolen in my equipment. She couldn't put the artifacts in my case before that night, because I was still packing away the legal stuff and the rest of my equipment until that afternoon. And she knew I'd go back to the Central Plaza one last time before we left—I always did, it was a ritual with me. She knew that Diane, who was as invested in this as she was, would make sure I didn't return to camp until she'd safely—so she thought—hidden the stuff."

He paused. There was no reason to tell his sons about his infidelity with Diane that night; it didn't matter anymore. They needed to have as many positive memories of their mother as possible, given the tragic particulars he had been laying out in front of them.

"Diane did what she had to do," he said without elaboration. "I didn't get back until mom was finished."

In the end, of course, they didn't pull it off. Everything went downhill fast. Jocelyn was dead, and Walt's career, his marriage, his life, was finished. The artifacts stayed in the country, but the government couldn't go public with the story because of the firestorm that came up over the mindless, brutal, anarchistic killing of an American civilian.

Walt made the decision to keep silent about the whole scheme, to protect Jocelyn's memory. Until the insurance broker sent him the check for four million dollars, he hadn't known she had changed their death benefits and bought the double-indemnity life insurance policies as a hedge against the dangers of working and traveling in Third World countries, a fear that too horribly had been confirmed.

He could have renounced the insurance money, but what would that have proved? Jocelyn was dead. She had paid for it with her life. He used some of the money to pay off her debts, moved to L.A., and tried to pick up the pieces of his life. He didn't expect there would ever be any happiness in it.

Diane joined him there. She had left New York and was on the run. Before going on the trip she had approached one of her wealthy clients, a collector who had no scruples about buying black- and gray-market art.

"Michaelson," Tom interjected. "His name is Michaelson. I met him. That's how I knew about Diane."

Walt stared at him soberly. Then he nodded once, and continued.

Michaelson had advanced Diane a quarter of a million dollars. She had given most of the money to Jocelyn, to cover her worst debts. Now Michaelson was pressing Diane for the money, and she didn't have it. She knew he was going to come after her for it, and she was scared for her personal safety. So she went on the run. She took on a new identity, and tried to stay out of the limelight. Walt was a safe harbor. No one knew where he was—he had cut himself off from his friends, his colleagues, even his children.

Despite themselves, and for all the wrong reasons, they started living together, more out of need than love—he knew she didn't really love him, but they had a terrible bond, which they hoped no one else would ever discover.

For a while, it worked. Everyone had bought into it, including his sons. That was why he had shunned them—he didn't want them to get too close, because the truth might come out. He was cutting his children off from him, to protect them.

But once he and Diane found out the brothers were on their trail, first when Tom came to see him and then when he learned they had gone down to Central America, they knew it was only a matter of time before their cover was blown. He had come home one day, shortly after Tom's last visit, and she was gone. He didn't know where she was now, and he didn't think he ever would. That was over, another buried part of his tormented past.

Walt leaned back against the couch. "That's it, boys," he told them. "Now you know everything. And I can't tell you how awful I feel that you do."

EPILOGUE

Madison

◆ ◆ ◆

They all drove up to Madison together in a limo Will rented for the occasion. It was the second anniversary of Jocelyn's death. They were going to have a small memorial in honor of her memory, and to introduce her to the newest member of the family.

Their lives had changed considerably in the eight months since that soul-baring meeting they'd had with their father. Clancy was a father himself now—Jocelyn Jorgensen Gaines was four months old. She was going to be a big girl, like her mother, and beautiful like her mother, too; she had the same Paul Newmanesque blue eyes, the same long legs (she was almost twenty-five inches long at birth), even at this tender age the same aggressive sweetness.

Clancy's businesses were booming. He and his partners had opened a second fitness center in Winnetka and Finnegan's was doing better than ever, in large part due to the Bears and Cubs finally becoming bona fide contenders instead of mere institutions.

Will was the rising star of his office. He had been written up in Forbes as a newcomer on the move and he was about to be transferred, with a huge raise and major responsibilities, to the New York office, the mother ship. As usual, he was beating the women off with a stick, but he hadn't yet found anyone he wanted to be serious with. His mother and his sister-in-law had set a high standard for him to strive for.

Tom had found peace with himself, which was the most dramatic story in the clan. Late one night, when he came back to Will's apartment from working his shift at Finnegan's, he picked up part of his dissertation and looked at it for the first time in a long while. And it hit him—he still loved math: the beauty of the abstractions, the challenge of solving problems, the muscularity demanded of his brain. He completed his work, and in a few weeks he was going to be defending his thesis. His advisor had assured him he would be approved, and that he'd be published. When that was done, he'd be Dr. Gaines. Another Ph.D. in the family, like his parents before him.

And he had a girlfriend: Laurel Johnstone, Callie's friend from the Museum of Art who had helped him with the New York art connections. He had called to thank her for helping him find out about Diane Montrose, and wound up asking her out for coffee. Afterward they had gone back to her apartment and talked until late in the evening. The following night they went out again, and started going steady a week later.

She shared many of his interests, like listening to jazz and taking long hikes. She even hung around Finnegan's on Sunday afternoons, although she didn't care about football. The sex was good, too, easy and stressless. For the first time in over a decade he believed he was going to have a good life, and as important, that he deserved one.

He rarely thought about Diane anymore.

Even their father was beginning a rehabilitation, although by his former lofty standards it was a small one. He had gone back to working on his book about Central America, and his editor liked the chapters he had sent her. Tom had spoken to Dr. Janowitz at UCLA and persuaded him (with a bit of gentle arm-twisting) to bring Walt in as a guest lecturer. That had gone well, and they'd had him back a few more times. There was the possibility (a slim one, but slim is better than none) that UCLA would hire him for a few years until he was ready to retire—they wouldn't need to give him tenure, so they could get him on the cheap. He was still one of the brightest and most knowledgeable minds in his field.

The rest of Walt's life was humdrum, which worked for him. He had come to Chicago to see his granddaughter a few weeks after she was born, but hadn't been back since. Other than that, the boys didn't hear much from him, but enough so that they knew he hadn't gone off the deep end again. He was going to have to live with the tragedies of his life and there was nothing they could do about that except be there for him when he wanted them to be.

He hadn't heard from Diane Montrose again. He assumed he never would. He missed her, but he knew it would be better if he didn't.

The limo driver dropped them near the gravesite shortly before eleven. He'd come back in an hour to pick them up. Clancy removed a portable stroller from the trunk and snapped it open. Callie carefully laid baby Jocelyn, who had fallen asleep during the ride up from Chicago, into the little carriage and pulled the sunshade over her.

Will carried a bouquet of flowers, roses and lilies. Their mother's garden had always had roses and lilies. They walked across the manicured lawn to Jocelyn's small stone. Although the weather was warm and humid, as it had been when they came the year before, they were dressed up this time, the men in suits and ties, Callie in a dress and low heels.

They stood in front of the grave. Will knelt down and placed the flowers next to the stone. "Hey, mom," he said. "We're here."

Tom glanced at his watch. Clancy put a hand on his brother's arm. "Relax," Clancy said. "He'll make it."

Tom, looking fretful, nodded.

Carefully, Clancy took the sleeping infant from the stroller, and, cradling her in his arms, knelt by the grave. It was the first time they'd been here since the baby was born.

"This is your granddaughter, mom," he said, placing a hand on the stone. "We named her Jocelyn, after you."

The baby squirmed and gurgled in her sleep. Clancy handed her over to Callie.

A taxi approached along one of the narrow lanes that meandered from the cemetery entrance to the gravesite. Will, shading his eyes against the sun, pointed to it.

"There he is."

The cab stopped. Walt got out of the back. He, too, was dressed appropriately, in a nice sports coat and slacks. He was carrying a wicker basket under one arm and a bouquet similar to the one the boys had brought in the other. He paid the driver. The cab took off, and he walked toward his sons.

There was an awkward moment; then the brothers enveloped him, and they all embraced. When they separated, Walt walked closer to the stone. He hadn't visited his wife's gravesite since he buried her.

"Hello, Jocelyn," he said in a soft voice. "I've missed you." He knelt down and placed his bouquet next to the one his sons had brought. "I've really missed you. More and more, as time goes by."

In the distance, some birds sang out to each other, but otherwise it was very quiet. The brothers stood tall and still. Clancy, standing in the middle, put an arm around each of his brothers' shoulders, and they draped their arms over him. Callie, the baby pressed against her chest, cried quietly into a tissue.

Walt stood up. He walked over to Callie and looked tenderly at his sleeping granddaughter. "Maybe part of mom is with us, in this little one," he said. "I'd like to hope that."

"I'm sure she is, Walt," Callie told him, wiping her eyes again. "There's no way she couldn't be."

"I've been reading the Bible lately, believe it or not," Walt said, almost cheerfully. "There's a passage; we've all heard it, it was even a big pop song back when I was your age, that there's a time to weep—we've done our share of that—and a time to laugh. A time to mourn—we've done that, too. So let's laugh a little, okay? Or at least, smile."

He took a sweating bottle of Veuve Clicquot out of the wicker basket and passed it to Clancy. "It should be cold, I picked it up on the drive here."

Clancy twisted the wire on the cork. Walt reached into the basket and brought out five champagne flutes. He handed one to Tom, Will, and Callie, holding the remaining two for Clancy and himself. Clancy uncorked the bottle carefully, so it wouldn't splatter. He poured into each of the glasses.

Walt held his glass aloft. "To Jocelyn," he toasted.

They clinked glasses, and drank. Walt stood over the gravestone. "Your mother loved champagne," he said. He poured a few drops onto the stone. "Here's to you, darling. You'll always be with us."

The limousine showed up precisely at noon. The brothers and Callie knelt by the grave one last time to say goodbye. Only Walt was left to bid farewell.

"You go ahead," he told them. "I want to spend a few moments here by myself. After you get to the restaurant you can send the driver back for me."

They each gave him a fierce hug, then walked across the lawn to the limo. Clancy handed baby Jocelyn to Callie, who buckled her into her car seat. They piled in and drove away, toward the exit.

As they were leaving, the boys looked back through the car windows. Walt was standing next to the grave. He was staring at the stone; he seemed to be talking to it. They weren't sure, because he was getting smaller and smaller in the distance, but he looked as if he was at peace.

ACKNOWLEDGMENTS

In the course of researching this novel, which included a field trip to Guatemala and Belize during the spring of 2001, I was assisted in my efforts by several wonderfully helpful people.

Dr. Anabel Ford, Director of the MesoAmerican Research Center, Institute for Social, Behavioral, and Economic Research Center (ISBER) at the University of California at Santa Barbara, and Director of the El Pilar Archaeological Reserve for Maya flora and fauna in the Cayo District, Belize, was very gracious in guiding me through all aspects of my research having to do with Maya archaeology. She read and gave me copious notes on the sections of this book pertaining to Central American archaeology and current archaeological life, and also invited me to her site, El Pilar, in Belize, where she and her staff gave me firsthand instruction and tutoring. Any mistakes of fact relating to any aspects of archaeology, Maya or otherwise, are completely mine.

Jennifer Purcell, Assistant Dean of Development for the Donald Bren School of Environmental Science and Management at UCSB, directed me to all the people at UCSB who assisted me with the various aspects of university procedures relating to tenure, pension plans, and other technical and academic matters.

Roger B. Perry, of Perry Insurance Service in Santa Barbara, worked with me on the insurance portions. Julie Miller, of the Los Angeles accounting firm of Kaufman, Bernstein, Oberman, Tivoli, and Miller, and Jon Ratner, of CIBC Oppenheimer in Los Angeles, helped with the investment sections. Michael Haskell, of Haskell Antiques in Montecito, California, gave me valuable information on the art gallery parts, including those having to do with illegal art transfers.

My wife, Carol, was supportive of this effort, as she is of all my work. She read every sentence I wrote, from first draft to last, gave me notes and insights, and kept my spirits up during those inevitable times when the writing isn't going the way you want it to.

This novel evolved from a series of "what-if" conversations that my brother, David A. Freedman, of Albuquerque, New Mexico, and I had over the course of several get-togethers, phone conversations, and e-mails. He also accompanied me on my research trip to Central America, and was, as always, excellent company.

I also wish to thank my friend Markus Wilhelm of The Literary Guild/Book-of-the-Month Club, for his ongoing support.

This is the first book I've worked on with Rick Horgan, my editor. It was a terrific experience. He labored tirelessly (and almost endlessly) to help me shape this into a far better piece of work than it was when he got it. I also want to thank his assistant, Katharine Rapkin, for her help in the numerous tedious but necessary details that I asked her to assist me with.